See page 4

"I SUPPOSE YOU'VE GIVEN HIM NO REALLY SERIOUS CAUSE
FOR COMPLAINT"

MRS. MAXON
PROTESTS

BY
ANTHONY HOPE

AUTHOR OF
"THE DOLLY DIALOGUES"
"THE PRISONER OF ZENDA" ETC.

ILLUSTRATED BY
R. F. SCHABELITZ

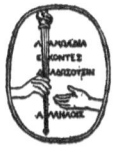

HARPER & BROTHERS PUBLISHERS
NEW YORK AND LONDON
MCMXI

ILLUSTRATIONS

MRS. MAXON PROTESTS

MRS. MAXON PROTESTS

I

"INKPAT!" She shot out the word in a bitter playful-
ness, making it serve for the climax of her complaints.

Hobart Gaynor repeated the word—if it could be called
a word—after his companion in an interrogative tone.

"Yes, just hopeless inkpat, and there's an end of it!"

Mrs. Maxon leaned back as far as the unaccommodating
angles of the office-chair allowed, looking at her friend and
counsellor with a faint yet rather mischievous smile on her
pretty face. In the solicitor's big, high, bare room she
seemed both small and very dainty. Her voice had trembled a little, but she made a brave effort at gayety as she
explained her cryptic word.

"When a thing s running in your head day and night,
week after week and month after month, you can't use that
great, long word you lawyers use. Besides, it's so horribly
impartial." She pouted over this undesirable quality.

A light broke on Gaynor, and he smiled.

"Oh, you mean incompatibility?"

"That's it, Hobart. But you must see it's far too long,
besides being, as I say, horribly impartial. So I took to

calling it by a pet name of my own. That makes it come over to my side. Do you see?"

"Not quite." He smiled still. He had once been in love with Winnie Maxon, and, though that state of feeling as regards her was long past, she still had the power to fascinate and amuse him, even when she was saying things which he suspected of being unreasonable. Lawyers have that suspicion very ready for women.

"Oh yes! The big word just means that we can't get on with one another, and hints that it's probably just as much my fault as his. But inkpat means all the one thousand and one unendurable things he does and says to me. Whenever he does or says one, I say invariably, 'Inkpat!' The next moment there's another—'Inkpat!' I really shouldn't have time for the long word even if I wanted to use it."

"You were very fond of him once, weren't you?"

She shrugged her thin shoulders impatiently. "Supposing I was?" Evidently she did not care to be reminded of the fact, if it were a fact. She treated it rather as an accusation. "Does one really know anything about a man before one marries him? And then it's too late."

"Are you pleading for trial trips?"

"Oh, that's impossible, of course."

"Is anything impossible nowadays?" He looked up at the ceiling, his brows raised in protest against the vagaries of the age.

"Anyhow, it's not what we're told. I only meant that having cared once made very little difference really—it comes to count for next to nothing, you know."

"Not a gospel very acceptable to an engaged man, Winnie!"

She reached out her arm and touched his coat-sleeve

lightly. "I know—I'm sorry. I'm longing to know your Cicely and be great friends with her. And it's too bad to bother you with the seamy side of it just now. But you're such a friend, and so sensible, and a lawyer too, you see. You forgive me?"

"I'm awfully glad to help, if I can. Could you give me a few—I don't want a thousand and one, but a few—instances of 'inkpat'?"

"That wouldn't be much use. Broadly speaking, inkpat's a demand that a woman should be not what she is, but a sort of stunted and inferior reproduction of the man —what he thinks he would be if he were a woman. Anything that's not like that gets inkpatted at once. Oh, Hobart, it is horrible! Because it's so utterly hopeless, you know. How can I be somebody else? Above all, somebody like Cyril—only a woman? It's absurd! A Cyrilesque woman! Oh!"

"I don't know him very well, but it certainly does sound absurd. Are you sure you haven't misunderstood? Can't you have an explanation?"

"Inkpat never explains; it never sees that there is anything to explain. It preaches or lectures or is sarcastic or grumbles or sulks—and I suppose it would swear, if Cyril didn't happen to be so religious. But explain or listen to an explanation—never!"

She rose and walked to one of the tall windows that looked on to Lincoln's Inn Fields. "I declare, I envy the raggedest, hungriest child playing there in the garden," she said. "At least, it may be itself. Didn't God make me just as much as He made Cyril?"

It was high summer, and the grate held nothing more comforting than a dingy paper ornament; yet Hobart Gaynor got up and stood with his back to it, as men are wont to do in moments of perplexity. He perceived that there was not much use in pressing for his concrete cases. If they came, they would individually be, or seem, trifles, no doubt. The accumulation of them was the mischief; that was embraced and expressed in the broad sweep of incompatibility; the two human beings could not keep step together. But he put one question.

"I suppose you've given him no really serious cause for complaint ?"

She turned quickly round from the window. "You mean— ?"

"Well, I mean, anybody else—er—making friction ?"

"Hobart, you know that's not my way! I haven't a man - friend except you and my cousin, Stephen Aikenhead—and I very seldom see either of you. And Stephen's married, and you're engaged. That's a ridiculous idea, Hobart."

She was evidently indignant, but Gaynor was not disturbed.

"We lawyers have to suspect everybody," he reminded her with a smile, "and to expect anything, however improbable. So I'll ask now if your husband has any great woman-friend!"

"That's just as ridiculous. I could be wicked enough to wish he had. Let somebody else have a try at it!"

"Can't you—somehow—get back to what made you like him at first ? Do you understand what I mean ?"

"Yes, I do — and I've tried." Her eyes looked bewildered, even frightened. "But, Hobart, I can't realize what it was. Unless it was just his looks—he is very handsome, you know."

"He stands well at the bar. He's getting on fast, he's very straight, and I don't think he's unpopular, from what I hear."

She caught his hint quickly. "A lot of people will say it's my fault?—that I'm unreasonable, and all in the wrong?"

"You'd have to reckon with a good deal of that."

"I don't care what people say."

"Are you sure of that?" he asked, quietly. "It's a pretty big claim to make for one's self, either for good or for evil."

"It's only his friends, after all. Because I've got none. Well, I've got you." She came and stood by him. "You're against me, though, aren't you?"

"I admit I think a wife—or a husband—ought to stand a lot."

"It's not as if my baby had lived. I might have gone on trying then. It wouldn't have been just undiluted Cyril."

"That makes some difference, I agree. Still, in the general interest of things—"

"I must be tortured all my life?" Her challenge of the obligation rang out sharply.

With a restless toss of his head, he sat down at his table again. She stood where she was, staring at the dingy ornament in the grate.

"Life the other way mayn't turn out particularly easy. You'll have troubles, annoyances—temptations, perhaps."

"I can face those. I can trust myself, Hobart. Can he prevent my going if I want to?"

"No."

"Can he make me come back?"

"No. He can, if he chooses, get a formal order for you to go back, but it won't be enforced. It will only give him

5

a right to a legal separation—not to a divorce, of course—
just a separation."

"You're sure they can't make me go back?"

"Oh, quite. That's settled."

"That's what I wanted to be quite clear about." She
stepped up to his chair and laid her hand on his shoulder.
"You're still against me?"

"Oh, how can I tell? The heart knows its own bitterness—nobody else can."

She pressed his shoulder in a friendly fashion; she was
comforted by his half-approval. At least, it was not a condemnation, even though it refused the responsibility of
sanction.

"Of course, he needn't give you any money."

"I've got my own. You got it settled on me and paid
to myself."

"It's very little—about a hundred and fifty a year. I
want you to look at all sides of the business."

"Of course, you're right. But there's only one to me—
to get away, away, away!"

"It's just about five years since you came here with your
mother—about the marriage-settlement. I thought it rather
rough you should come to me, I remember."

"Mother didn't know about the—the sentimental reason
against it, Hobart—and it doesn't matter now, does it?
And poor mother's beyond being troubled over me."

"Where will you go—if you do go?"

"I am going. I shall stay with the Aikenheads for a bit
—till I'm settled on my own."

"Have you hinted anything about it to—him?"

"To Cyril? No. I must tell him. Of course, he
knows that I'm silly enough to think that I'm unhappy."

"It 'll be an awful facer for him, won't it?"

She walked round the table and stood looking at him squarely, yet with a deprecatory droop of her mouth.

"Yes, it will," she said. "Awful! But, Hobart, I not only have no love left, I've no pity left. He has crushed a great deal in me, and he has crushed that with the rest."

Gaynor's hands played feebly with his big pad of blotting-paper.

"That it should happen to you of all people!" he mumbled. His air expressed more than a lament for unhappiness; as well as regretting sorrow, he deplored something distasteful. But Winnie Maxon was deaf to this note; she saw only sympathy.

"That's your old dear kindness for me," she smiled, with tears in her eyes. "You won't turn against me, anyhow, will you, Hobart?"

He stretched out his hand to meet hers. "No, my dear. Didn't I love you once?"

"And I do love your dear round face and your honest eyes. Yes, and the nose you used to be unhappy about—because it was a pug—in those very old days; and if my ship gets wrecked, I know you'll come out with the lifeboat. Good-bye now; I'll write to you about it."

The tender note struck at the end of their talk, old-time memories, the echo of her soft, pleading voice, availed for some minutes after his visitor's departure to blind Hobart Gaynor's shrewd eyes to the fact that she had really put before him no case that could seem at all substantial in the eyes of the world. To her, no doubt, everything might be as bad, as intolerable and hopeless, as she declared; he did not question her sincerity. But as the personal impression of her faded, his hard common-sense asserted forcibly that

7

it all amounted to no more than that she had come not to
like her husband; that was the sum of what the world would
see in it. May women leave their husbands merely because
they have come not to like them? Some people said yes, as
he was aware. They were not people whom he respected,
nor their theory one which he approved. He was of conservative make in all things, especially in questions of sex.
He was now uneasily conscious that but for her personal
fascination, but for his old tenderness, her plea would not
have extorted even a reluctant semi-assent. The next moment he was denying that he had given even so much. Certainly the world in general—the big, respectable, steady-
going world—would not accord her even so much. Talk
about being "crushed" or having things crushed in you
needs, in the eyes of this world, a very solid backing of facts
—things that can be sworn to in the box, that can be put in
the "particulars" of your petition, that can be located,
dated, and, if possible, attested by an independent witness.
Now Mrs. Maxon did not appear to possess one single fact
of this order—or surely she would have been eager to produce it?

Comedians and cynics are fond of exhibiting the spec-
tacle of women hounding down a woman on the one hand,
and, on the other, of men betraying their brethren for a
woman's favor. No exception can be taken to such pre-
sentments; the things happen. But when they are not happening—when jealousy and passion are not in the field—
there is another force, another instinct, which acts with
powerful effect. The professed students of human nature
call it sex-solidarity; it is the instinct of each sex to stand
together against the other. This is not a matter of individual liking or disliking; it is sex politics, a conflict be-

tween rival hosts, eternally divided. With personal prepossessions and special relations out of the way, the man
is for the man, the woman for the woman. As minute followed minute after Mrs. Maxon's departure, it became more
and more probable to Hobart Gaynor that Cyril Maxon
had something to say for himself. And was not Hobart
himself a prospective husband? Too much in love to
dream of a like fate befalling his own marriage, he yet felt
a natural sympathy for the noble army in which he was so
soon to enlist.

"Well, right or wrong, I promised to stand by her, and I
will," was his final thought, as he drove himself back to
the current business of his office day. Sympathy for Mrs.
Maxon mingled in it with a certain vexation at her for
having in some sense involved him in so obscure and troublesome a matter. He felt, without actually foreseeing, difficulties that might make his promise hard to keep.

The tendency of personal impressions to lose their power
when personal presence is withdrawn did not occur to Mrs.
Maxon. As she drove home to Devonshire Street, she comforted herself with the assurance that she had not only
kept a friend—as she had—but also secured a partisan.
She thought that Hobart Gaynor quite understood her
case.

"Rather wonderful of him!" she reflected. "Considering
that I refused him, and that he's at this moment in love with
Cicely Marshfield."

Her heart grew very warm toward her old friend, so loyal
and so forgiving. If she had not refused him? But the
temper of her present mood forbade the soft, if sad, conclusion that she had made a mistake. Who really knows anything about a man until she is married to him? And then

9

it is too late. "Don't marry a friend—keep him," was her bitter conclusion. It did not cross her mind that friendship, too—a friendship that is to be more than a distant and passive kindliness—must make reckoning with incompatibility.

II

M RS. MAXON'S memory of the evening on which she administered to her husband his "awful facer" was capricious. It preserved as much of the preliminary and the accidental as of the real gist of the matter. They dined out at the house of a learned judge. The party was exclusively legal, but the conversation of the young barrister who fell to her lot did not partake of that complexion. Fortune used him in the cause of irony. Much struck by his companion's charms—she was strung up, looked well, and talked with an unusual animation—and, by no means imputing to himself any deficiency in the same direction, he made play with a pair of fine, dark eyes, descanted jocularly on the loneliness of a bachelor's life, and ventured sly allusions to Mr. Cyril Maxon's blessed lot.

"I hope he knows his luck!" said the young barrister. Well, he would know it soon, at all events, Winnie reflected.

In the drawing-room afterward, a fat, gushing woman gave the other side of it. "We must be better friends, my dear," said she. "And you mustn't be jealous if we all adore your clever, handsome, rising husband."

Such things are the common trivialities of talk. Both the fat woman and the young barrister had happened often before. But their appearance to-night struck on Winnie

Maxon's sense of humor—a bitter, twisted humor at this moment. She would have liked to cry, "Oh, you fools!" and hurl her decision in her husband's face across the drawing-room. Compliments on our neighbor's private felicity are of necessity attended with some risk. Why are we not allowed to abide on safe ground and say, "I beg leave to congratulate you on the amount of your income and to hope that it may soon be doubled "? Only the ruined could object to that, and treading on their corns is no serious matter.

On the drive home—the judge lived in a remote part of Kensington—Cyril Maxon was perversely and (as it seemed to his wife) incredibly fertile in plans for the days to come. He not only forecast his professional career—there he was within his rights—but he mapped out their joint movements for at least three years ahead—their houses for the summer, their trips abroad, their visits to the various and numerous members of the Maxon clan. He left the future without a stitch of its dark mantle of uncertainty. Luckily he was not a man who needed much applause or even assent; he did not consult; he settled. His long, thoroughly lawyer-like, indisputably handsome and capable profile—he had a habit of talking to his wife without looking at her—chained the attention of her eyes. Was she really equal to a fight with that ? A shadowy, full-bottomed wig seemed even now to frame the face and to invest it with the power of life and death.

"Then the year after I really do mean to take you to Palestine and Damascus."

Not an idea that even of Cyril Maxon the rude gods might make sport!

"Who knows what 'll happen three years hence ?" she asked in gay tones, sharply cut off by a gasp in the throat.

A CASE OF NECESSITY

"You've a cold?" he asked, solicitously. He was not lacking in kindly protective instincts. Yet even his solicitude was peremptory. "I can't have you taking any risks."

"It's nothing," she gasped, now almost sure that she could never go through with her task. Even in kindness he assumed a property so absolute.

The brougham drew up at their house. "Nine-fifteen sharp to-morrow," Cyril told the coachman. That was no less, and no more, certain than Palestine and Damascus. He went through the hall (enlivened with prints of lord chancellors surviving and defunct) into his study. She followed, breathing quickly.

"I asked the Chippinstalls to dine next Wednesday. Will you send her a reminder to-morrow morning?" He began to fill his pipe. She shut the door and sat down in a chair in front of the fireplace.

There had always seemed to her something crushing in this workshop of learning, logic, and ambition. To-night the atmosphere was overwhelming; she felt flattened, ground down; she caught for her breath. He had lit his pipe and now glanced at her, puzzled by her silence. "There's nothing else on on Wednesday, is there?"

"Cyril, we're not happy, are we?"

He appeared neither aggrieved nor surprised at her sudden plunge; to her he seemed aggressively patient of the irrational.

"We have our difficulties, like other married couples, I suppose. I hope they will grow less as time goes on."

"That means that I sha'n't oppose you any more?"

"Our tastes and views will grow into harmony, I hope."

"That mine will grow into harmony with yours?"

He smiled, though grimly. Few men really mind being

13

accused of despotism, since it savors of power. "Is that such a terrible thing to happen to my wife?"

"We're not happy, Cyril."

"Marriage wasn't instituted for the sole purpose of enabling people to enjoy themselves."

"Oh, I don't know what it was instituted for!"

"You can look in your prayer-book."

Her chin rested on her hands, her white, sharp elbows on her knee. The tall, strong, self-reliant man looked at her frail beauty. He was not without love, not without pity, but entirely without comprehension—nor would comprehension have meant pardon. Her implied claim clashed both with his instinct and with his convictions. The love and pity were not of a quality to sustain the shock.

"I wish you'd go and see Attlebury," he went on. Attlebury was, as it were, the keeper of his conscience, an eminent clergyman of extreme High Church views.

"Mr. Attlebury can't prevent me from being miserable. Whenever I complain of anything, you want to send me to Mr. Attlebury!"

"I'm not ashamed of suggesting that you could find help in what he represents on earth."

She gave a faint, plaintive moan. Was heaven as well as this great world to be marshalled against her, a poor little creature asking only to be free? So it seemed.

"Or am I to gather that you have become a sceptic?" The sarcasm was heavily marked. "Has a mind like yours the impudence to think for itself?" So she translated his words—and thereby did him no substantial injustice. If his intellect could bend the knee, was hers to be defiant?

"I had hoped," he went on, "that our great sorrow would have made a change in you."

14

A CASE OF NECESSITY

The suggestion seemed to her to be hitting below the belt. She had seen no signs of overwhelming sorrow in him.

"Why?" she asked, sharply. "It made none in you, did it?"

"There's no need to be pert."

"When you say it to me, it's wisdom. When I say it to you, it's pertness! Yes, that's always the way. You're perfect already—I must change!"

"This is becoming a wrangle. Haven't we had enough of it?"

"Yes, Cyril, enough for a lifetime, I think." At last she raised her head and let her hands fall on her lap. "At least, I have," she added, looking at him steadily.

He returned her glance for a moment, then turned away and sat down at his writing-table. Several letters had come by the late post, and he began to open them.

He had made her angry; her anger mastered her fears.

"I was brought up to think as you do," she said. "To think that once married was married forever. I suppose I think so still; and you know I've respected my—my vows. But there are limits. A woman can't be asked to give up everything. She herself—what she owes to herself—must come first—her own life, her own thoughts, her freedom, her rights as a human being."

He was reading a letter and did not raise his eyes from it.

"Those are modern views, I suppose? Old-fashioned folk would call them suggestions of the devil. But we've had this sort of discussion several times before. Why go over it again? We must agree to differ."

"If you would! But you don't, you can't, you never will. You say that to-night. You'll begin drilling me to your

15

march and cutting me to your pattern again to-morrow morning."

He made no reply at all. He went on reading letters. He had signified that the discussion was at an end. That ended it. It was his way; if he thought enough had been said, she was to say no more. It had happened thus a hundred times—and she had inwardly cried "Inkpat!"

Well, this time—at last—she would show him that the topic was not exhausted. She would speak again, and make him speak. Malice possessed her; she smiled at the grave-faced man methodically dealing with his correspondence. For the first time there came upon her a certain satisfaction in the actual doing of the thing; before, she had dreaded that to her heart, however much she desired the freedom it would bring. To hit back once—once after five long years!

"Oh, about the Chippinstalls," she said. "You can have them, of course, but I sha'n't be here."

He turned his head quickly round toward her. "Why not?"

"I'm going to the Stephen Aikenheads' to-morrow."

"It's not been your habit to pay visits alone, nor to arrange visits without consulting me. And I don't much care about the atmosphere that reigns at Aikenhead's." He laid down his letters and smiled at her in a constrained fashion. "But I don't want to give you a fresh grievance. I'll stretch a point. How long do you want to be away?"

He was trying to be kind; he actually was stretching a point, for he had often decried the practice of married women —young and pretty married women—going a-visiting without their husbands; and he had just as often expressed grave disapproval of her cousin, Stephen Aikenhead. For him a considerable stretch! Her malice was disarmed. Even a

16

pang of that pity which she had declared crushed to death reached her heart. She stretched out her slim arms to him, rather as one who begs a great boon than as the deliverer of a mortal defiance.

"Cyril, I'm never coming back."

For a full minute he sat silent, looking steadily at her. Incapable as he was of appreciating how she had arrived at, or been driven to, this monstrous decision, yet he had perception enough and experience enough to see that she was sincere in it and set on it; and he knew that she could give effect to it if she chose. In that minute's silence he fought hard with himself; he had a mighty temptation to scold, a still mightier to flout and jeer, to bring his heavy artillery of sarcasm to bear. He resisted and triumphed.

He looked at the clock. It was a quarter-past twelve.

"You'll hardly expect me to deal with such a very important matter at this hour of the night, and without full consideration," he said. "You must know that such separations are contrary to my views, and I hope you know that, in spite of the friction which has arisen, I have still a strong affection for you."

"I sha'n't change my mind, Cyril. I sha'n't come back."

He kept the curb on himself. "I really would rather not discuss it without more consideration, Winnie—and I think I have a right to ask you to give it a little more, and to hear what I have to say after reflection. Is that unfair? At least you'll admit it's a serious step?"

"I suppose it's fair," she murmured, impatiently. She would have given the world to be able to call it grossly unfair. "But it's no use," she added, almost fierce in her rejection of the idea that her determination might weaken.

"Let us both think and pray," he said, gravely. "This

17

visit of yours to the Aikenheads' may be a good thing. It'll give you time to reflect, and there'll be no passing causes of irritation to affect your calmer judgment. Let us treat it as settled that you stay with them for a fortnight—but treat nothing else as settled to-night. One thing more—have you told anybody about this idea?"

"Only Hobart Gaynor. I went and asked him whether I could do it if I wanted to. I told him I meant to do it."

"He'll hold his tongue. Mention it to nobody else, please."

"I won't till—till it's settled." She smiled. "We've actually agreed on one or two things! That's very unusual in our wrangles, Cyril."

He came up to her and kissed her on the forehead. "For God's sake, think! You don't in the least know what it means to you—or to me either."

She drew her head quickly back; a bitter retort was on the tip of her tongue. "Yes—but I know what life with you means!" She did not utter it; there was a pinched weariness in his face which for the moment disarmed her. She sighed disconsolately, turned away from him, and drifted out of the room, her shoulders bent as though by great fatigue.

She had suffered one or two transient pangs of pity; having feared a storm, she had experienced relief at his moderation, but gave him no credit for it. She did not understand how hard it was to him. She was almost inclined to hold it a device—an exhibition (once again exhibited) of how much wiser, more reasonable, and more thoughtful he was than the happy-go-lucky being to whom he was mated. She carried her grievances out of the room on her bowed shoulders—just as heavy as ever, just as insupportable.

The handsome, clever, rising man was left face to face

with what he feared and hated most in this world—a failure. He had fallen in love with the pretty body; he had never doubted that he could shape and model the malleable mind. Why not? It was in no way a great or remarkable mind. She was not very talented, nor exceptionally strong willed, nor even very obstinate. Nor ungoverned, nor ultra-emotional, nor unmoral. She was a woman more than ordinarily attractive, but hardly more than ordinary in other respects. And, looking back on five years, he realized the enormous and constant pains he had taken with her. It had been matter of conscience as well as matter of pride; when the two join forces, what is left to fight them? And they constantly form an alliance. Defeat threatened even this potent confederation—defeat at the hands of one whom he counted little more than a charming, wilful child.

Charming? Softer emotions, offspring of memory, suffered a resurrection not in the end charged with much real import. He was of the men who satisfy emotion in order to quiet it; marriage was in his view—and in the view of authorities in which he believed—better than being in love as well as different from it. In the sense appropriate to voluptuaries, he had never been in love at all. What remained, then, to combat his profound distaste and disapproval for all she now advanced, her claims, pretensions, and grievances? In the end two disparate, yet closely allied, forces—loyalty to a great cause and hatred of personal defeat. Let him make himself champion of the cause: the two became one. Could Heaven and he conjoined succumb to any onslaught?

He faced his theory logically and boldly. "She is my wife. I'm as responsible for her as I am for myself. She may deny that—I can't."

For good or evil, for joy or pain, one flesh, one mind, one spirit, *usque in æternum.* There was the high, uncompromising doctrine.

His wife did not consciously or explicitly dissent from it. As she had told him, she was bred to it. Her plea was simply that, be it right or be it wrong, she could not live up to it. She could observe the prohibitions it implied—she had kept and would keep her restraining vows—but she could no longer fulfil the positive injunctions. If she sought at all for an intellectual or speculative justification, it was as an afterthought, as a plea to conciliate such a friend as Hobart Gaynor, or as a weapon of defence against her husband. To herself her excuse was necessity. If she had given that night the truest account in her power of what she felt, she would have said that she was doing wrong, but that she could not help it. There were limits to human endurance—a fact of which Divine Law, in other matters besides that of marriage, has not been considered by the practice (as apart from the doctrine) of Christendom at large to take adequate account.

III

"WELL, you see, things are rather in solution just now."
Most people have a formula or two by which they
try to introduce some order into the lumber-room of the
mind. Such a lot of things are dumped down there, and
without a formula or two they get so mixed. The above
was Stephen Aikenhead's favorite. Many of his friends
preferred to say "in transition." That phrase, he maintained, begged the question. Perhaps, after all the talk and
all the agitation, nothing would be changed; the innovators
might be beaten; they often had been; the mass of mankind
was very conservative. Look at the ebb and flow of human
thought, as history recorded it—the freedom of Athens and
the license of Rome followed by the Dark Ages—the Renais-
sance tamed, if not mutilated, by the Counter-Reformation
on the one hand and the rigors of Puritanism on the other.
Certainly the foundations of all things were being, or were
going to be, examined. But it is one thing to examine
foundations, a different one to declare and prove them un-
sound. And even when the latter process has come about,
there is the question—will you shore the building up or will
you pull it down? The friends who favored "transition"
often grew impatient with this incurable doubter; they were
as convinced that the future was going to be all right and

going to come very soon as they were certain that the present
was all wrong and could not possibly resist the assault of
reason for many years more. They were sanguine people,
apt to forget that, right as they undoubtedly were (in their
own opinion), yet the Englishman at least accords his support to progress only on the definite understanding that it
shall be slow. "Put the brake on!" he urges, envisaging
innovation as a galloping downhill. Stephen's friends
pathetically pictured it as a toilsome assent—toilsome, yet
speedily to be achieved by gallantly straining horses. No
need of brakes, though! Argument by metaphor is perilous
either way.

In this case the formula was administered to Winnie
Maxon within the space of two hours after her arrival at
Shaylor's Patch. Stephen's pretty house in Buckingham-
shire—it lay Beaconsfield way—took its unassuming title
presumably from a defunct Shaylor and certainly from a
small plot of grass which lay between two diverging roads
about a hundred yards on the way down to the station. The
house was old, rambling, and low—a thoroughly comfortable dwelling. The garden was fair to see, with its roses,
its yews, and its one great copper-beech, with its spread of
smooth lawn and its outlook over a wide-stretching valley.

"A home of peace!" thought Winnie, relaxing weary body
(she had packed that morning for more than a fortnight's
absence) and storm-tossed mind, as she lay on a long chair
under the shade of the copper-beech.

Stephen sat opposite to her, a tall man of three-and-thirty,
fair, inclining to stoutness, with a crop of coarse, disorderly,
mouse-colored hair; always and everywhere he wore large,
horn-rimmed spectacles. He had inherited a competence
more than merely sufficient; he had no profession, but wrote

articles when the spirit moved him and had them published more rarely. At twenty-two he had married. It was before the days when he began to doubt whether people ought to—or anyhow need—marry, and his union had been so happy that the doubt could not be attributed to personal experience. His wife was not pretty, but pleasant-faced and delightfully serene. She had very strong opinions of her own, and held them so strongly that she rarely argued and was never ruffled in argument. If anybody grew hot over a discussion, she would smile at him and hand him a flower, or at appropriate moments something nice to eat. They had one child, a girl now ten years old, whom they had just sent to a boarding-school.

It was in connection with little Alice's being sent to the boarding-school that the formula made its appearance. Winnie had expressed the proper wonder that her parents "could bear to part with her." Stephen explained that they had been actuated by a desire to act fairly toward the child.

"If I was sure I was right, and sure the ancients were wrong, I would teach her myself—teach her to believe what I believe and to disbelieve what they believe. But am I sure? What do I believe? And suppose I'm right, or at all events that they're wrong, most people mayn't think so for many years to come. I should be putting her against the world, and the world against her. Is that fair, unless I'm bang sure? Not everybody can be happy when the world's against them. I can't teach her what I can't believe, but why shouldn't she learn it from people who can? She must settle it in the end for herself, but it seems fair to give her her chance of orthodoxy. While things are, as I said, in solution—in a sort of flux, don't you know?"

"What do you mean by things being in solution—or in a flux?"

The daughter of a clergyman, wife of Cyril Maxon since she was nineteen, a devout member of Attlebury's flock, she came quite fresh to the idea. In her life and her world things had seemed tremendously solid, proof against an earthquake!

"I suppose it's really been the same in every age with thinking people, but it's more wide-spread now, isn't it? It gets into the newspapers even! 'Do we Believe?' 'Is Marriage a Failure?' It's not the answers that are most significant, you know, but the questions."

"Yes, I think I see what you mean—partly." The words came in slow, ruminating tones. "Do you go very far?" she went on, in accents drolly apprehensive.

He laughed jovially. "There are no bombs. I'm married to Tora. Is it terrible that I don't go to church very often? Never, I'm bound to add in candor, if I can help it."

"I shall go while I'm here. Do you think it funny that I should suddenly propose myself for a visit?"

"To tell the truth, I didn't think Maxon would come."

"Or that I should come without him?"

"We pictured you pretty extensively married, I confess."

"So I was—so I am, I mean." She remembered her promise; she was not to mention her great resolve. But it struck her that the pledge would be hard to keep. Already the atmosphere of Shaylor's Patch suggested that her position was eminently one to talk over, to discuss with an open-minded, sympathetic friend, to speculate about in all its bearings.

"But you mustn't think I'm absolutely hidebound," she

24

went on. "I can think—and act—for myself." She was skirting the forbidden ground.

"I'm glad of it. Is Maxon?" There was a humorous twinkle behind his spectacles.

"Why are we to talk of Cyril when I've just begun my holiday?" Yet there was nothing else that she really wanted to talk about. Oh, that stupid promise! Of course, she ought to have reserved the right to lay the case before her friends. But a promise is a promise, however stupid. That certainly would be Cyril's view; and it was hers. Was it, she wondered, the Shaylor's Patch view? Or might a question of ethics like that be to some extent "in solution"?

"He thinks me an awful reprobate?" Stephen asked.

She nodded, smiling.

"So they do down here, but my friends in London call me a very mild specimen. I expect some of them will turn up while you're here, and you'll be able to see for yourself."

"You don't mind being thought a reprobate down here?"

"Why should I? I don't want their society, any more than they want mine. I'm quite well off, and I've no ambitions." He laughed. "I'm ideally placed for defying the world, if I want to. It really needs no courage at all, and would bring me no martyr's crown."

"You mean it would be different if you had to work for your living?"

"Might be—or if I wanted to go in for public life, or anything of that kind."

"Or if you were a woman?"

"Well, if I were a woman who was sensitive about what society at large thought of her. That's one of the reasons why I don't preach my views much. It's all very well for me, but my converts, if any, might end by thinking they were paying too dear, while the prophet got off for nothing."

He had a book, she a newspaper. With an easy absence of ceremony he began to read; but she left her paper lying on the ground beside her, and let her thoughts play as they would on the great change which had come over her life, and on what it would mean to her if it persisted, as she was resolute that it should.

"I can think—and act—for myself," she had said. Perhaps, but both would be new and strange exercises. She had walked on lines very straightly ruled; she had moved to orders peremptorily conveyed. A fear mingled with the relief of emancipation. They say that men who have been long in prison are bewildered by the great, free, bustling world. It may be as true of prisons of the mind as of the Bastille itself.

Stephen interrupted his reading to give another statement of his attitude. "It's like the two horses—the one in the stable-yard and the wild one. The one gets oats and no freedom, the other freedom and no oats. Now different people put very various values on freedom and on oats. And, at any rate, the wild horse must have fodder of some kind."

His face vanished behind the book again, and she heard him chuckling merrily over something in it. If he did not get oats, he certainly seemed to thrive excellently on such other fodder as he found. But, then, it was undeniable that Cyril Maxon throve equally well—successful, rising, with no doubts as to his own opinions or his own conduct. Or had her resolve shaken him into any questionings? He had shown no signs of any when she parted from him that morning. "I shall be glad to see you back at the end of your fortnight," he had said. The words were an order.

Tora Aikenhead, on her way to the rose-beds, with a basket and scissors in her hand, came up to them.

"Resting?" she asked Winnie in her low, pleasant voice.

In the telegram in which she had proposed her visit, Winnie had said that she was a little "knocked up" with the gayeties of town, but she fancied that her hostess's question referred, though distantly, to more than these, that she had discerned traces of distress, the havoc wrought by the passing of a storm.

"Beautifully!" Winnie answered, with a grateful smile.

"Dick Dennehy is week-ending with Godfrey Ledstone, and they're coming to lunch and tennis to-morrow; and Mrs. Lenoir is motoring down to lunch, too," Tora went on to her husband.

"Mrs. Lenoir?" He looked up from his book with that droll twinkle behind his big spectacles again.

"Yes. Quite soon again, isn't it? She must like us, Stephen."

Stephen laughed. His wife had not in the least understood the cause of the twinkle. She would not, he reflected. It never occurred to her that any human being could object to meeting any other, unless, indeed, actual assault and battery were to be feared. But Stephen was awake to the fact that it might be startling to Winnie Maxon to meet Mrs. Lenoir—if she knew all about her. Naturally he attributed rigid standards to Mrs. Cyril Maxon, in spite of her proud avowal of open-mindedness, which, indeed, had seemed to him rather amusing than convincing.

"Ledstone's our neighbor," he told Winnie, "the only neighbor who really approves of us. He's taken a cottage here for the summer. You'll like him; he's a jolly fellow. Dennehy's an Irish London correspondent to some paper or other in the States, and a Fenian, and all that sort of thing, you know. Very good chap."

"Well, I asked no questions about your guests, but since you've started posting me up—who's Mrs. Lenoir ?"

"Tora, who is Mrs. Lenoir ?"

"Who is she ? Who should she be ? She's just Mrs. Lenoir."

Tora was obviously rather surprised at the question, and unprovided with an illuminating answer. But then there are many people in whose case it is difficult to say who they are, unless a repetition of their names be accepted as sufficient.

"I must out with it. Mrs. Lenoir was once mixed up in a very famous case—she intervened, as they call it—and the case went against her. Some people thought she was unjustly blamed in that case, but—well, it couldn't be denied that she was a plausible person to choose for blame. It's all years ago—she must be well over fifty by now. I hope you—er—won't feel it necessary to have too long a memory, Winnie ?"

"I don't exactly see why it's necessary to tell at all," remarked Tora. "Why is it our business ?"

"But Winnie does ?" The question was to Winnie herself.

"I know why you told me, of course," she answered. She hesitated, blushed, smiled, and came out with, "But it doesn't matter."

"Of course not, dear," remarked Tora, as she went off to her roses.

All very well to say "Of course not," but to Mrs. Cyril

Maxon it was not a case of "of course" at all. Quite the contrary. The concession she had made was to her a notable one. She had resolved to fall in with the ways of Shaylor's Patch in all possible and lawful matters—and it was not for her, a guest, to make difficulties about other guests, if such a thing could possibly be avoided. None the less, she was much surprised that Mrs. Lenoir should be coming to lunch—she had, in fact, betrayed that. In making no difficulties she seemed to herself to take a long step on the road to emancipation. It was her first act of liberty; for certainly Cyril Maxon would never have permitted it. She felt that she had behaved graciously; she felt also that she had been rather audacious.

Stephen understood her feelings better than his wife did. He had introduced himself to the atmosphere he now breathed, Tora had been bred in it by a free-thinking father, who had not Stephen's own scruples about his child. In early days he had breathed the air which up to yesterday had filled Winnie's lungs—the Maxon air.

"I suppose these things are all wrong on almost any conceivable theory that could apply to a civilized community," he remarked, "but so many people do them and go scot-free that I'm never inclined to be hard on the unfortunates who get found out. Not—I'm bound to say—that Mrs. Lenoir ever took much trouble not to be found out. Well, if people are going to do them, it's possible to admit a sneaking admiration for people who do them openly, and say 'You be hanged!' to society. You'll find her a very intelligent woman. She's still very handsome, and has really—yes, really—grand manners."

"I begin to understand why you let her down so easy," said Winnie, smiling.

29

He laughed. "Oh, well, perhaps you're right there. I'm human, and I dare say I did do a bit of special pleading. I like her. She's interesting."

"And nothing much matters, does it?" she put in, acutely enough.

"Oh, you accuse me of that attitude? I suppose you plausibly might. But I don't admit it. I only say that it's very difficult to tell what matters. Not the same thing—surely?"

"It might work out much the same in—well, in conduct, mightn't it? If you wanted to do a thing very much, couldn't you always contrive to think that it was one of the things that didn't matter?"

"Why not go the whole hog, and think it the only proper thing to do?" he laughed.

She echoed his laugh. "You must let me down easy, as well as Mrs. Lenoir!"

"I will, fair cousin—and, on my honor, for just as good reasons."

Stephen had enjoyed his talk. It amused and interested him to see her coming, little by little, timidly, out of her —should he call it sanctuary or prison-house?—to see her delicately and fearfully toying with ideas that to him were familiar and commonplace. He marked an alertness of mind in her, especially admiring the one or two little thrusts which she had given him with a pretty shrewdness. As he had said, he had no itch to make converts; it was not his concern to unsettle her mind. But it was contrary to all his way of thinking to conceal his own views or to refuse to exchange intelligent opinions because his interlocutor stood at a different point of view. Everybody stood at different points of view at Shaylor's Patch. Was conversation to be banned and censored?

IN SOLUTION

Winnie herself would have cried "No" with all her heart. Revelling in the peace about her, in the strange freedom from the ever-present horror of friction and wrangles, in the feeling that at last she could look out on the world with her own eyes, no man saying her nay, she reached out eagerly to the new things, not indeed conceiving that they could become her gospel, her faith, but with a half-guilty appreciation, a sense of courage and of defiance, and a genuine pleasure in the exercise of such wits as she modestly claimed to possess. She had been so terribly cramped for so long. Surely she might play about a little? What harm in that? It committed her to nothing.

As she got into her bed, she said, as a child might, "Oh, I am going to enjoy myself here—I'm sure I am!"

So it is good to fall asleep with thanks for to-day and a smile of welcome ready for to-morrow.

IV

KEEPING A PROMISE

MODERN young women are athletic, no doubt with a heavy balance of advantage to themselves, to the race, and to the general joyousness of things. Yet not all of them; there are still some whose strength is to sit still, or at least whose attraction is not to move fast, but rather to exhibit a languid grace, to hint latent forces which it is not the first-comer's lot to wake. There is mystery in latent forces; there is a challenge in composed inactivity. Not every woman who refuses to get hot is painted; not every woman who declines to scamper about is tight-laced. The matter goes deeper. This kind is not idle and lazy; it is about its woman's business; it is looking tranquil, reserved, hard to rouse or to move—with what degree of consciousness or of unconsciousness, how far by calculation, how far by instinct, Heaven knows! Of this kind was Winnie Maxon. Though she was guiltless of paint or powder, though her meagre figure could afford to laugh at stays (although arrayed in them), yet it never occurred to her to scamper about a lawn-tennis court and get very hot and very red in the face, as Tora Aikenhead was doing, at half-past eleven on a Sunday morning. (Be it observed, for what it is worth, that in spite of her declaration of the day before Winnie had not gone to church.)

KEEPING A PROMISE

Tora's partner was her husband; she was very agile, he was a trifle slow, but a good placer. Against them Dennehy rather raged than played—a shortish, thick-built man of five-and-thirty, with bristling, sandy hair and a mustache of like hue, whose martial upward twist was at the moment subdued by perspiration. He could not play anywhere — and he would play at the net. Yet the match was a tight one, for his partner, Godfrey Ledstone, was really a player, though he was obviously not taking this game seriously. A brilliant shot at critical moments, with a laughing apology for such a fluke, betrayed that he was in a different class from his companions.

The game ended in the defeat of the Aikenheads, and the players gathered round Winnie. Dennehy was grossly triumphant, and raged again when his late opponents plainly told him that his share in the victory was less than nothing. He declared that the "moral effect" of his presence at the net was incalculable.

"That quality is certainly possessed by your strokes," Stephen admitted.

Under cover of the friendly wrangle, Winnie turned to Ledstone, who had sat down beside her. She found him already regarding her; a consciousness that she desired his attention made her flush a little.

"How easily you play! I mean, you make the game look so easy."

"Well, if I want to impress the gallery, old Dennehy's rather a useful partner to have, isn't he? But I did use to play a good bit once, before I went into business."

"No time now? I'm told you go to London as much as three days a week!"

"I see Mrs. Aikenhead's been giving me away. Did she tell you anything else ?"

"Well, she told me what you looked like, but I know that for myself now."

"Did she do me justice, Mrs. Maxon ?" He had pleasant blue eyes, and used them to enhance the value of his words.

"I don't want to put you and her at loggerheads," smiled Winnie.

"Ah, you mean she didn't ?"

Winnie's smile remained mysterious. Here was a game that she could play, though she had perforce abstained from it for many, many days. It is undeniable that she came back to it with the greater zest.

"I shall ask Mrs. Aikenhead what she said."

"That won't tell you what I think about it."

"Then how am I to find out ?"

"Is it so important to you to know ?"

"I feel just a sort of—well, mild interest, I must admit." There seemed ground for supposing that lawn-tennis was not the only game that he had played, either.

"Mere good looks don't go for very much in a man, do they ?" said Winnie.

"There now, if you've given me anything with one hand, you've taken it away with the other!"

"What is your business, Mr. Ledstone ?"

"I draw designs—decorative designs for china and bro-cades, and sometimes fans. I can do a lot of my work down here—as Mrs. Aikenhead might have told you, instead of representing me as a lazy dog, doing nothing four days in the week."

"I've been led into doing you an injustice," Winnie admitted with much gravity. "Is it a good business ?"

"Grossly underpaid," he laughed.

"And I may have eaten off one of your plates ?"

"Yes, or sat on one of my cushions, or fanned yourself with one of my fans."

"It seems to serve as an introduction, doesn't it ?"

"Oh, more than that, please! I think it ought to be considered as establishing a friendship."

The other three had strolled off toward the house. Winnie rose to follow them. As Ledstone took his place by her side she turned her eyes on him.

"I haven't so many friends as to be very difficult about that," she said, with a note of melancholy in her voice.

The hint of sadness came on the heels of her raillery with sure artistic effect. Yet it was genuine enough. The few minutes of forgetfulness—of engrossed satisfaction in her woman's wit and wiles—were at an end. Few friends had she indeed! She could reckon scarcely one intimate outside Shaylor's Patch itself. Being Mrs. Cyril Maxon was an exacting life; it limited, trammelled, almost absorbed. Husbands are sometimes jealous of woman-friends hardly less than of men. Cyril was one of these.

Ledstone's vanity was flattered, his curiosity piqued. The hint of melancholy added a spice of compassion. His susceptible temperament had material enough and to spare for a very memorable first impression of Mrs. Maxon. Though still a young man—he was no more than seven-and-twenty—he was no novice either in the lighter or in the more serious side of love-making; he could appreciate the impression he received and recognize the impression he made.

It is to the credit of Mrs. Maxon's instinctively cunning reserve that as they walked back to the house he still felt more certain that he wanted to please her than that he had already done it to any considerable extent. The reserve was not so much in words—she had let her frank chaff show plainly enough that she liked her companion; it lay rather in manner and carriage. Only on the hint of melancholy— only that once—had she put her eyes to any significant use. He was conscious of having made greater calls on his. That was right enough; he was the man, and he was a bachelor. Ledstone could not be charged with an exaggerated reverence for marriage, but he did know that he paid a married woman a poor compliment if he assumed beforehand that she would underrate the obligation of her status.

When they entered the long, low, panelled parlor that gave on to the garden, Mrs. Lenoir had already arrived and was sitting enthroned in the middle of the room; she had a knack of investing with almost regal dignity any seat she chanced to occupy. She was a tall woman of striking appearance, not stout, but large of frame, with a quantity of white hair (disposed under an enormous black hat), a pale face, dark eyes, and very straight, dark eyebrows. She had long, slim hands which she used constantly in dramatic gesture. Stephen Aikenhead had credited her with a "really grand" manner. It was possible to think it just a trifle too grand, to find in it too strong a flavor of condescension and of self-consciousness. It might be due to the fact that she had been in her own way almost an historical figure—and had certainly mingled with people who were historical. Or it was possible to see in it an instinct of self-protection, exaggerated into haughtiness, a making haste to exact homage, lest she should fail even of respect. Whatever its origin, there it was, though not in a measure so strong as fatally to mar the effect of her beauty or the attraction of her personality. Save for the hat, she was dressed very simply; nay,

even the hat achieved simplicity when the spectator had enjoyed time to master it. On one hand she wore only her
wedding-ring—she had married Mr. Lenoir rather late in
life and had now been a widow for several years; on the
other, a single fine diamond, generally considered to be ante-
Lenoirian in date. Lord Hurston was a probable attri-
bution.

Winnie was at sea, but found the breeze exhilarating and
was not upset by the motion. She was a responsive being,
taking color from her surroundings. A little less exaction
on the part of her husband might have left her forever an
obedient wife; what a more extended liberty of thought, of
action, of the exploitation of herself might do—and end in—
suggested itself in a vague, dim question on this her first
complete day of freedom.

At lunch Dick Dennehy could not get away from his victory at lawn-tennis. He started on an exposition of the
theory of the game. He was heard in silence, till Tora
Aikenhead observed in her dispassionate tones, "But you
don't play at all well, Dick."

"What!" he shouted, indignantly, trying to twist up a
still humid mustache.

"Theory against practice—that's the way of it always,"
said Stephen.

"Well, in a sense ye're right there," Dennehy conceded.
"It needs a priest to tell you what to do, and a man to
do it."

"Let's put a 'not' in the first half of the proposition," said
Ledstone.

"And a woman in the second half?" Mrs. Lenoir added.

"That must be why they like one another so much,"
Dennehy suggested. "Each makes such a fine justification

37

for the existence of the other. They keep one another in work!" He rubbed his hands with a pleasantly boyish laugh.

"I always try to be serious, though it's very difficult with the people who come to my house." Stephen was hypocritically grave.

"Ye're serious because ye're an atheist," observed Dennehy.

"I'm not an atheist, Dick."

"The Pope 'd call you one, and that's enough for a good Catholic like me. How shouldn't you behave yourself properly when you don't believe that penitence can do you any good?"

"The weak spot about penitence," remarked Tora, "is that it doesn't do the other party any good."

Winnie ventured a meek question: "The other party?"

"There always is one," said Mrs. Lenoir.

Stephen smiled. "I always like to search for a contradictory instance. Now, if a man drinks himself to death, he benefits the revenue, he accelerates the wealth of his heirs, promotes the success of his rivals, gratifies the enmity of his foes, and enriches the conversation of his friends. As for his work—if he has any—il n'y a pas d'homme nécessaire."

"It seems to me it would be all right if nobody wasted time and trouble over stopping him," said Dennehy—a teetotaller, and the next instant quaffing ginger-beer immoderately.

"He would be sure to be hurting somebody," said Mrs. Lenoir.

"And why not hurt somebody? I'm sure somebody's always hurting me," Dennehy objected, hotly. "How

"YOU CAN'T EXPECT WOMEN TO STAND BEING SAT UPON AND SQUASHED ALL
THEIR LIVES"

would the world get on else? Don't I hold my billet only till a better man can turn me out?"

"Yes," said Stephen. "'The priest who slew the slayer, and shall himself be slain'—that system's by no means obsolete in modern civilization."

"Obsolete! It's the soul of it, its essence, its gospel." It was Mrs. Lenoir who spoke.

"A definition of competition?" asked Stephen.

"Yes, and of progress—as they call it."

Tora Aikenhead was consolatory, benign, undismayed. "To be slain when you're old and weak—what of that?"

"But ye don't think ye're old and weak. That's the shock of it," cried Dennehy.

"It is rather a shock," Mrs. Lenoir agreed. "The truth about yourself is always a shock—or even another person's genuine opinion."

Winnie Maxon remembered how she had administered to her husband his "awful facer"; she recollected also, rather ruefully, that he had taken it well. You always have to hurt somebody, even when you want so obvious a right as freedom! A definite declaration of incompatibility must be wounding—at any rate, when it is not mutual.

It is an irksome thing to have—nay, to constitute in your own person—an apposite and interesting case and to be forbidden to produce it. If only Winnie Maxon might lay her case before the company while they were so finely in the mood to deal with it! She felt not merely that she would receive valuable advice (which she could not bring herself to doubt would be favorable to her side), but also that she herself would take new rank; to provide these speculative minds with a case must be a passport to their esteem. Bitterly regretting her unfortunate promise, she began to arraign the justice of holding herself bound by it, and to accuse her husband's motives in extorting it. He must have wished to deprive her of what she would naturally and properly seek—the counsel of her friends. He must have wanted to isolate her, to leave her to fight her bitter battle all alone. To chatter in public was one thing, to consult two or three good friends surely another. Promises should be kept; but should they not also be reasonably interpreted, especially when they have been exacted from such doubtful motives ?

Thus straying, probably for the first time in her life, in the mazes of casuistry, the adventurous novice was rewarded by a really brilliant idea. Why should she not put her case in general terms, as an imaginary instance, hypothetically? The promise would be kept, yet the counsel and comfort (for, of course, the counsel would be comfortable) would be forthcoming. No sooner conceived than executed! Only, unfortunately the execution was attended with a good deal of confusion and no small display of blushes—a display not indeed unbecoming, but sadly compromising. It was just as well that they had got to the stage of coffee and the parlor-maid had left the room.

Dennehy did not find her out. He was not an observant man, and he was more interested in general questions than in individual persons. Hence Winnie had the benefit of listening to a thoroughgoing denunciation of the course she had adopted and was resolved to maintain. Kingdoms might—and in most cases ought to—fall; that was matter of politics. But marriage and the family—that was matter of faith and morals. He bade Winnie's hypothetical lady endure her sufferings and look for her reward elsewhere. At the close of his remarks Tora Aikenhead smiled and offered

him a candied apricot. He had certainly spoken rather
hotly.

Stephen guessed the truth, and it explained what had
puzzled him from the first—the sudden visit of his cousin,
unaccompanied by her husband. He had suspected a tiff;
but he had not divined a rupture. He was surprised at
Winnie's pluck; it must be confessed that he was also rather
staggered at being asked to consider Cyril Maxon as quite
so impossible to live with. However, Winnie ought to know
best about that.

"Oh, come, Dick, there are limits—there must be. You
may be bound to take the high line, but the rest of us are
free to judge cases on the merits. At this time of day you
can't expect women to stand being sat upon and squashed
all their lives."

Godfrey Ledstone had not talked much. Now he came
forward on Winnie's side.

"A man must appreciate a woman, or how can he ask her
to stay with him?"

"I don't see why she shouldn't do as she likes," said Tora.
"Especially as you put a case where there are no children,
Winnie."

Mrs. Lenoir was more reserved. "Let her either make
up her mind to stand everything or not to stand it at all any
more. Because she'll never change a man like that."

Only one to the contrary—and he a necessarily prejudiced
witness! She claimed Mrs. Lenoir for her side, in spite of
the reserve. The other three were obviously for her. Winnie was glad that she had put her case. Not only was she
comforted; somehow she felt more important. No longer
a mere listener, she had contributed to the debate. She
would have felt still more important had she been free to

declare that it was she herself who embodied the matter at issue.

For such added consequence she had not long to wait. After the guests had gone, Stephen Aikenhead came to her in the garden.

"I don't want to pry into what's not my business, but I think some of us had an idea that—well, that you were talking about yourself, really, at lunch. Don't say anything if you don't want to. Only, of course, Tora and I would like to help."

She looked up at him, blushing again. "I promised not to tell. But since you've guessed—"

"I'm awfully sorry about it."

"At least, I promised not to tell till it was settled. Well—it is settled. So I've not broken the promise, really."

Stephen did not think it necessary—or perhaps easy—to pass judgment on this point.

"At any rate, it's much better we should know, I think. I'm sure you'll find Tora able to help you now."

She was not thinking of Tora—nor of Dennehy's tirade, nor even of Mrs. Lenoir's reserve.

"Do you think Mr. Ledstone—guessed?"

Stephen smiled. "He took a very definite stand on the woman's side when you put your parable. I should say it's probable that he guessed."

Thus it befell that the secret leaked out, though the promise was kept; and Winnie found herself an object of sympathy and her destinies a matter of importance at Shaylor's Patch. It is perhaps enough to say that she would have been behaving distinctly well if, for the sake of a scrupulous interpretation of her promise, she had foregone these consolations. They were very real and precious.

They negatived the doleful finality which she had set to her life as a woman. They transformed her case; instead of a failure, it became a problem. A little boldness of vision, a breath of the free air of Shaylor's Patch, a draught of the new wine of speculation—and behold the victim turned experimentalist!

4

V

ALTHOUGH the Reverend Francis Attlebury was
vowed in his soul to celibacy and had never so much
as flirted since he took his degree at Oxford twenty-three
years ago, he had more knowledge of the mind of woman
than most married men pleasurably or painfully achieve.
Women came to him with their troubles, their grievances,
even sometimes their sins; it was no more his business to
pooh-pooh the grievances than to extenuate the sins; one
does not carry a cross the more cheerfully or, as a rule, any
farther because a bystander assures one that it is in reality
very light.

He was a tall, stout man—a grievance of his own was that
he looked abominably well-fed in spite of constant self-denial
—and possessed a face of native and invincible joviality.
He was looking quite jovial now as he listened to Cyril
Maxon, agreed that he had been shamefully used, and concluded in his own mind that if the negotiations were to be
carried on in that spirit they might just as well not be initiated at all. The thing was not to prove how wrong she
had been in going, but to get her back. She was more likely
to come back if it were conceded to her that she had at least
a fair excuse for going. Would Cyril Maxon ever make
such a concession—or let somebody make it for him?

44

"ON MY HONOR, I DON'T UNDERSTAND"

THE GREAT ALLIES

The two men were old and intimate friends; moreover, Maxon was even eager to acknowledge an authority in Attlebury's office, as well as a confidence in his personal judgment.

"You won't make her think she was always wrong by proving that you were always right, Cyril."

"Am I to say I was wrong where I know I was right?"

"You've probably said you were right already. Need you repeat it?"

"I'm ready to forgive her—absolutely and unreservedly."

"Would you go a little further—do something rather harder? Accept forgiveness?" The diplomatist smiled. "Conditional forgiveness we might call it, perhaps. Forgiveness in case there might be anything for her to forgive?"

Maxon broke out in natural impatience at the incomprehensible. "On my honor, I don't understand what she's got to complain of. I took her from a poor home, I've given her every luxury, she shares my career—I needn't use mock modesty with you, Frank—I've given her absolute fidelity—" He ended with a despairing wave of his hands.

Attlebury neither argued nor rebuked. "Is there anybody who has influence with her—whom she likes and relies on?"

"I should hate anybody else being dragged into it—except you, of course. I asked her to come to you."

"Oh, I know I'm suspect. I should be no good." He smiled contentedly. "Nobody you can think of?"

"Well, the man she consulted about it was Hobart Gaynor." His tone was full of grudging dislike of such a consultation.

"Hobart Gaynor? Yes, I know him. Not a bad choice

45

of hers, Cyril, if she felt she had to go to some one. Not quite our way of thinking, but a very good fellow."

"Why is he to poke his nose into my affairs?"

"Come, come, she poked her pretty nose into his office, no doubt, and probably he'd much rather she hadn't. I've experience of ladies in distress, Cyril. I am, in fact, as the Great Duke said of authors—when he was Chancellor of Oxford, you know—much exposed to them."

"I didn't come here to discuss Hobart Gaynor."

"I hope we sometimes do wiser things than we come to do—or what's the good of a talk? Let's discuss Hobart Gaynor in the light of, say, an ambassador or a go-between. You're looking very formidable, Cyril. Did you often look at Mrs. Maxon like that? If so, I hope she'd done something really wicked. Because, if she hadn't, you did."

For just that moment the note of rebuke and authority rang clear in his voice. The next, he was the friend, the counsellor, the diplomatist again.

"Let Gaynor go to her with a message of peace—bygones to be bygones, faults on both sides, a fresh start, and so on."

Cyril Maxon had felt the rebuke; he bowed his head to it. But he fretted terribly.

"I can't bring myself to speak to him about it."

"Let me. She's your wife, you know. If she went wrong, mightn't you feel that some effort of yours would—well, have made the difference?"

"What am I to tell him to say?"

"Let me tell him what to say—you try to honor my draft when it's presented. Perhaps—God knows—we're fighting for her soul, Cyril, and we shall be asked how we've borne ourselves in the fight, sha'n't we?"

THE GREAT ALLIES

Cyril Maxon was always ready to own that he might have
been wrong—to own it to God or to God's representative;
he hated owning it to a fellow-creature uninvested with pre-
rogatives. Attlebury had skilfully shifted the venue and
changed the tribunal. A man may be sure he is right as
against his wife—or *vice versa*. Who dares enter an un-
qualified 'Not Guilty' before High Heaven's Court ? There
some count in the indictment is sure to be well laid and well
proven.

"I think I know my faults," he said, in a complacent
humility.

Attlebury's smile became more jovial still. "O learned
gentleman!"

The disciple still held the natural man under control.
Maxon smiled, if sourly.

"I may have been exacting."

"You may have been an ass," sprang to the clergyman's
lips, but stayed unuttered. "Allowances, Cyril, allowances!" he murmured, gently. "We all have to work
through allowances."

"Do as you like, Frank. I want the thing put straight.
You know I do. I think I ought to have from her an expression of—well, of regret."

"Won't coming back convey it ?" Attlebury smiled.
"In fact, rather forcibly ?"

Left alone, the priest indulged himself in a bout of one of
his diversions—the contemplation of the folly of his disciples.
Not folly in believing in him and his authority—on that he
was unimpeachably sincere. What moved his satiric vein
was that they all had to be gulled—and were all gullible.
Before they could be made better, they all had to be persuaded that they were better than they were already. Mis-

erable offenders? Certainly. But with "potentialities"? Even more certainly—and to an unusual degree. No question of breaking the bruised reed—it must be put in splinters. And the smoking flax would be revived with a dash of kerosene. That Pope had been entirely wrong about Tannhäuser; he should have told him that his recent doings did not represent his true self. There is joy over a sinner that repenteth. To Attlebury there was excitement in one that might. He knew it, he chided himself for it; the glory was not in him or to him. But the sporting instinct was deep— a cause of sore penitence and of unregenerate perpetual amusement at himself.

"I'd like to beat these free-thinking beggars!" A.M.D.G.? He prayed on his knees that it might be so—and so exclusively—that the Reverend Francis Attlebury might look for and gain no advancement, no praise, not even the praise of God, but might still say "I am an unprofitable servant," and still believe it.

Besides all this—right down in the depths of his being— came the primitive rivalry of man to man—obstinate in the heart of the celibate priest. "Dear old Cyril is a fool about women. He doesn't know a thing about them." This phase of thought was sternly repressed. It is not a branch of knowledge on which it behooves a man—not even a clergyman—to flatter himself. In the first place, it is wrong; in the second—or same—place, dangerous.

Thus great forces began to deploy into line against little Winnie Maxon, holding her assertion of freedom to be grave scandal and offence. There was the Family, embodied in her lawfully wedded husband; there was nothing less than the Church Catholic, speaking inexorably in Mr. Attlebury's diplomatic phrases; the Wisdom of the World, its logic, its common-sense, were to find expression—and where better expression ?—in the sober friend, the shrewd lawyer, the moderate man Hobart Gaynor. Could she hurl defiance at these great allies ? If she did, could she look for anything save utter and immediate defeat ? Just one little woman, not very strong, not very wise, with really no case save a very nebulous, hazy notion that, whatever they all said, it was too bad that she should be miserable all her life! The allies would tell her that many people were miserable all their lives, but (they would add) nobody need be. Between them they had a complete remedy. Hers was the blame, not theirs, if she would not swallow it.

At Shaylor's Patch, as the summer days passed by in sunshine and warm, flower-scented breezes, where she was comforted, petted, made much of, where an infinite indulgence reigned, she was swallowing something quite different from the medicine that the allies proposed for her treatment. She was drinking a heady new wine. She was seeing with new eyes, travelling through new lands of thought and of feeling. Her spirit rejoiced as in a great emancipation—in being allowed, at last, to move, to live, to find itself, to meet its fellows, to give thanks to a world no longer its taskmaster but the furnisher of its joys and the abetter in its pleasures. Of what should she be afraid in such a mood, of what ashamed ? At Shaylor's Patch it seemed that rebellion might not only be admirable, as it often is, but that it would be easy—which it is very seldom.

For the real Great World—that amalgam of all the forces of the three allies, that mighty thing which so envelops most people from the cradle to the grave that their speculations stray beyond it no more, and often much less, than their actions—this great thing had hardly a representative

among all who came and went. These folks belonged to
various little worlds which had got, as it were, chipped off
from the big one and had acquired little atmospheres and
little orbits of their own; from time to time they collided
with one another, but nobody minded that—neither planet
seemed a pin better or worse for the encounter. Each was
inhabited by a few teachers and a body of disciples sometimes not much more numerous; teachers and disciples alike
seemed very busy, very happy, and (to be frank) in many
cases agreeably self-satisfied. Afraid of the big world—lest
they should come into collision with that and be shattered to
miserable atoms? Not a bit of it! For, you see, the big
world was, for all its imposing and threatening appearance,
really moribund, whereas they were young, vigorous, growing. Paralysis had set in in the Giant's legs. He could not
catch them. Presently the disease would reach his heart.
He would die, and they would parcel out all his possessions.
Would they quarrel among themselves, these children of
progress? Probably they would, as they cheerfully admitted. What matter? Such quarrels are stimulating,
good for brain and heart, illuminating. Nay, in the end,
not quarrels at all. The only real deadly quarrel was with
the Giant. Would there be no danger of a new Giant coming into being, born of a union of all of them, just as despotic,
just as lethargic, as the old? Into this distant speculation
they did not enter, and their discreet forbearance may par-
donably be imitated here.

On the whole they were probably too hard on the Giant;
they did not allow enough for the difficulties involved in being so big, so lumbering, so complex. They girded at him
for not trying every conceivable experiment; he grumbled
back that he did not want to risk explosion on a large scale.

THE GREAT ALLIES

They laughed at him for not running; a creature of his bulk was safer at a walk. They offered him all manner of new concoctions; he feared indigestion on a mighty scale. Some of them he dreaded and hated; at some he was much amused; for others he had a slow-moving admiration—they might be right, he would take a generation or two to think about it, and let them know in due course through his accredited channels.

Of some of Stephen Aikenhead's friends it was a little difficult to think as human beings; they seemed just embodied opinions. Doctor Johnson once observed—and few will differ from him—that it would be tiresome to be married to a woman who would be forever talking of the Arian heresy. Mrs. Danford, a bright-eyed, brisk-moving woman, was forever denouncing boys' schools. Dennis Carriston wanted the human race to come to an end and, consistently enough, bored existing members of it almost to their extinction or his murder. These were of the faddists; but the majority did not fairly deserve that description. They were workers, reformers, questioners, all of them earnest, many clever, some even humorous (not such a very common thing in reformers), one or two eminent in achievement; but questioners and speculators all of them—with two notable exceptions, Mrs. Lenoir and Godfrey Ledstone. These two had no quarrel with orthodox opinion, but a very great respect for it; they would never have thought of justifying their deviations from orthodox practice. They were prepared to pay their fines—if they were caught—and did not cavil at the jurisdiction of the magistrate.

Godfrey Ledstone would have made a fine "man about town," that unquestioning, untroubled, heathenish master of the arts and luxuries of life. Chill penury—narrow means and the necessity of working—limited his opportunities. Within them he was faithful to the type and obedient to the code, availing himself of its elasticities, careful to observe it where it was rigid; up to the present, anyhow, he could find no breach of it with which to reproach himself.

He was committing no breach of it now. Not to do what he was doing would in his own eyes have stamped him a booby, a fellow of ungracious manners and defective sensibilities, a prude, and a dolt.

The breeze stirred the trees; in leisurely fashion, unelbowed by rude clouds, there sank the sun; a languorous tranquillity masked the fierce struggle of beasts and men— men were ceasing from their labor, the lion not yet seeking his meat from God.

"I shall go to my grave puzzled whether the profile or the full face is better."

She stirred lazily on her long chair, and gave him the profile to consider again.

"Beautiful, but cold, distant, really disheartening!"

"You talk just as much nonsense as Mrs. Danford or Mr. Carriston."

"Now let me make the comparison! Full face, please!"

"You might be going to paint my picture. Now are you content?"

"I'm more or less pacified—for the moment."

Stephen Aikenhead lounged across the lawn, pipe in mouth. He noticed the two and shook his shaggy head— marking, questioning, finding it all very natural, seeing the trouble it might bring, without a formula to try it by—unless, here too, things were in solution.

She laughed lightly. "You must be careful with me, Mr. Ledstone. Remember, I'm not used to flattery!"

"The things you have been used to! Good heavens!"

"I dare say I exaggerate." Delicately she asked for more pity, more approval.

"I don't believe you do. I believe there are worse things —things you can't speak of." It will be seen that by now —ten days since Winnie's arrival—the famous promise had been pitched most completely overboard.

"Oh, I don't think so, really I don't. Isn't it a pretty sky, Mr. Ledstone ?"

"Indeed it is, and a pretty world too, Mrs. Maxon. Haven't you found it so ?"

"Why will you go on talking about me ?"

"Mayn't I talk about the thing I'm thinking about ? How can I help it ?"

Her smile, indulgent to him, pleaded for herself also.

"It is horribly hard not to, isn't it ? That's why I've told all about it, I suppose."

Stephen Aikenhead, after the shake of his head, had drifted into the house, seeking a fresh fill for his pipe. He found the evening post in, and, having nothing in the world else to do, brought out a letter to Mrs. Maxon.

"For you," he said, making a sudden and somewhat disconcerting appearance at her elbow. He puffed steadily, holding the letter out to Winnie, while he looked at his friend Godfrey with a kindly if quizzical regard.

"Good gracious, Stephen!"

"Well, I always like letters worth a 'Good gracious,' Winnie."

"Hobart Gaynor's coming here to-morrow."

"Don't know the gentleman. Friend of yours ? Very glad to see him."

"Coming from—from Cyril!"

"Oh!" The little word was significantly drawn out. "That's another pair of shoes!" it seemed to say.

She sat up straight and let her feet down to the ground.

"To make me go back, I suppose!"

"You could hardly expect him not to have a shot at it— Cyril, I mean."

Her eyes had been turned up to Stephen. In lowering them to her letter again she caught in transit Godfrey Ledstone's regard. For a second or two the encounter lasted. She swished her skirt round—over an ankle heedlessly exposed by her quick movement. Her glance fell to the letter. Godfrey's remained on her face—as well she knew.

"I must see Hobart, but I won't go back. I won't, Stephen."

"All right, my dear. Stay here—the longer, the better for us. Shall I wire Gaynor to come?"

"Will you?"

Stephen's last glance—considerably blurred by tobacco-smoke—was rather recognizant of fact than charged with judgment. "I suppose all that will count," he reflected as he went back once again to the house. It certainly counted. Godfrey Ledstone was doing nothing against the code. All the same, he was introducing a complication into Winnie Maxon's problem. At the start freedom for her had a negative content—it was freedom from things—friction, wrangles, crushing. Was that all that freedom meant? Was not that making it an empty, sterile thing?

"You'll be firm, Mrs. Maxon?"

Godfrey leaned forward in his chair; the change of attitude brought him startlingly near to her. She sprang quickly to her feet, in instinctive retreat.

54

"I must hear what Hobart has to say." She met his eyes once more, and smiled pleadingly. He shrugged his shoulders, looking sulky. Her lips curved in a broader smile. "That's only fair to Cyril. You're not coming to dinner? Then—good-night."

VI

HOBART GAYNOR undertook his embassy with reluctance. He was busily occupied over his own affairs —he was to be married in a fortnight—and he was only unwillingly convinced by Mr. Attlebury's suave demonstration of where his duty lay, and by the fine-sounding promises which that zealous diplomatist made in Cyril Maxon's name. Waiving the question whether things had been all wrong in the past, Attlebury gave a pledge that they should be all right in the future—all that a reasonable woman could ask, with an ample allowance for whims into the bargain. That was the offer, put briefly. Gaynor doubted, and, much as he wished well to Winnie Maxon, he did not desire to become in any sense responsible for her; he did not want to persuade or to dissuade. Indeed, at first, he would undertake no more than a fair presentment of Maxon's invitation. Attlebury persisted; the woman was young, pretty, not of a very stable character; her only safety was to be with her husband. Her old friend could not resist the appeal; he came into line. But when he asked Cicely Marshfield's applause for his action, he could not help feeling that she was, to use his own colloquial expression, rather "sniffy" about it; she did not appear fully to appreciate his obligation to save Winnie Maxon.

56

FRUIT OF THE TREE

He arrived at Shaylor's Patch before lunch. Stephen Aikenhead received him with cordiality, faintly tinged, as it seemed to the visitor, with compassion. Tora's manner enforced the impression; she treated him as a good man foredoomed to failure. "Of course, you must have your talk with her," Stephen said. "You shall have it after lunch." He spoke of the talk rather as a ceremony to be performed than as a conference likely to produce practical results.

"I hope you'll back me up—and Mrs. Aikenhead, too?" said the ambassador.

The Aikenheads looked at each other. Tora smiled. Stephen rubbed his forehead. At the moment lunch was announced, and, the next, Winnie came into the room, closely followed by Godfrey Ledstone.

When Hobart saw her, a new doubt smote him—a doubt not of the success (he was doubtful enough about that already), but of the merits of his mission. She looked a different woman from the despairing rebel who had come to him in Lincoln's Inn Fields. Her eyes were bright, there was color in her cheeks; her manner, without losing its attractive quietude and demureness, was gay and joyous. There might be something in what she had said about being "crushed" at her husband's house! It might not be merely a flourish of feminine rhetoric.

"The country has done wonders for you, Winnie," he said as he shook hands.

"I'm having a lovely rest." To Hobart she seemed to add, "Why need you come and disturb it?"

Another omen unfavorable in the envoy's eyes was the obvious pleasure she took in Ledstone's presence and conversation; and yet another was the young man's unobtrusive

57

but evident certainty that all he said and did would be well received. On Ledstone's fascinating attentions, no less than on the Aikenheads' affectionate and indulgent friendship, he had to ask her to turn her back. For what? A parcel of promises made by Attlebury in Maxon's name! Were they of much more practical value than what godfathers and godmothers promise and vow at a baby's christening? Could they change the natural man in Maxon and avail against his original sin? But, on the other hand, were not indulgent friendships and, still more, charming attentions exactly the dangers against which he had come to warn her? She was young, pretty, and not of a very stable character—Attlebury's words came back. The indulgent friendship would mine her defences; then the charming attentions would deliver their assault. No—Attlebury was right, his own mission was right; but it bore hard on poor Winnie Maxon. A reluctant messenger, a prophet too sensible of the other side of the argument (which prophets should never be), he found himself no match for the forces which now moved and dominated Winnie Maxon. She had been resolved when she was only crying for and dreaming of liberty. Would she be less resolved now that she had tasted it and was enjoying it, not amid frowns or reproofs, but with the countenance of her friends and the generally, though not universally, implied approval of all the people she met? Attlebury could make the disapproval of the great world outside sound a terrible thing; sheltered at Shaylor's Patch, Winnie did not hear its voice. Attlebury might hint at terrible dangers; such men thought it "dangerous" for a woman to have any pleasure in her life!

She listened to Hobart kindly and patiently enough, but always with reiterated shakes of her pretty head. At some of the promises she fairly laughed—they were so entirely different from the Cyril Maxon she knew.

"It's no use," she declared. "Whatever may be right, whatever may be wrong, I'm not going back. The law ought to set me free (this was an outcome of Shaylor's Patch!). Since it doesn't, I set myself free—that's all."

"But what are you going to do?"

"Either take a cottage down here or a tiny flat in London."

"I didn't ask where you were going to live, but what you were going to do." Hobart was a patient man, but few people's tempers are quite unaffected by blank failure, by a serene disregard of their arguments.

"Do? Oh, I dare say I shall take up some movement. I hear a lot about that sort of thing down here, and I'm rather interested."

"Oh, you're not the sort of woman who buries herself in a movement, as you call it."

"I can make friends, like other people, I suppose. I needn't bury myself."

"Yes, you can make friends fast enough! Winnie, you're avoiding the crux of the matter."

"Oh, you're back to your dangers! Well, I think I can trust myself to behave properly."

"You ought to be sure of it."

"Are you being polite?"

"Oh, hang politeness! This is a vital question for you."

The color mounted in her cheeks; for the first time she showed some sign of embarrassment. But the embarrassment and the feelings from which it sprang—those new feelings of the last fortnight—could not make her waver. They reinforced her resolution with all the power of emotion. They made "going back" still more terrible, a re-

5   59

nunciation now as well as a slavery. Her eyes, though not her words, had promised Godfrey Ledstone that she would not go back. What then, as Hobart Gaynor asked, was she going to do? The time for putting that question had not come. There was the pleasure now—not yet the perplexity.

She gave a vexed laugh. "Whether it's vital or not, at any rate it's a question for me, as you say yourself, and for me only. And I must risk it, Hobart. After all, there are different—well, ideas—on that sort of subject, aren't there?" Here Shaylor's Patch showed its influence again.

"I rather wish you hadn't come to this house," he said, slowly.

"I've been happier here than anywhere in the world. What have you against it?"

"Well, I can't claim to know much about it, but don't some queer people come?"

"Plenty!" she laughed. "It's very amusing."

He smiled, frowned, looked, and indeed felt, a little foolish—as the average man does when he finds himself called upon to take the moral line.

"Rather—er—unsettling?" he hazarded, lamely.

"Very stimulating."

"Well, I can say no more. I've done my job. Take care of yourself, Winnie."

"Oh yes, I will; you may be sure of that. Hobart, will you tell Cyril that I'm very, very sorry, and that I hope he'll be happy, and wish him splendid success and prosperity?"

"I'll tell him—if you won't write yourself."

"I couldn't. That would open it all again. I'll write to you, if there's any business to be settled."

Hobart Gaynor, thinking over the conversation on his way back to town, decided that Winnie had got on apace. Well, if she chose to take her life into her own hands, she herself must make the best of it. He did not pretend to feel quite easy—he could not get Godfrey Ledstone out of his head—but he said nothing about such apprehensions when he reported the failure of his mission. He also delivered Winnie's message to her husband. Cyril Maxon's lips set hard, almost savagely, over it. "We shall see," he said. He could not prevent her from doing what she had done, but he would not acknowledge it as setting up a permanent or recognized state of affairs. For the time disobedient, Winnie was still his wife. He would not accept her valediction. His house was still open to her and, after a decent period of penance, his heart.

A plain case of Stephen Aikenhead's "In solution"! What to Cyril was an indissoluble relationship (and more than that), not even temporarily suspended, but rather defied and violated, was to his wife a thing now at last—by her final decision—over and done with so far as it affected her position toward Cyril himself. He was out of her life—at last. She had her life—at last. Not quite entirely free, this life she had won by her bold defiance. She still acknowledged limitations, even while she nibbled at the fruit of the Tree of Knowledge that grew at Shaylor's Patch. Yet how incomparably more free than the old life! She was amazed to find with how little difficulty, with how slight a pang, and with how immense a satisfaction she had broken the bond—or had broken bounds, for she felt remarkably like a school-boy on a forbidden spree. What great things a little courage will effect! How the difficulties vanish when they are faced! Why, for five whole years, had she not seen that the door was open and walked out of it? Here she was—out! And nothing terrible seemed to happen.

61

"Well, I've done it now for good and all," she said to Stephen Aikenhead.

"Oh yes, you've done it. And what are you going to do next?"

"Just what Hobart asked me! Why should he—or why should you? If a woman doesn't marry, or becomes a widow, you don't ask her what she's going to do next! Consider me unmarried, or, if you like, a widow."

"That's all very well—excellently put. I am rebuked!" Stephen smiled comfortably and broadly. "You women do put things well. But may I observe that, if you were the sort of woman you're asking me to think about, you'd probably be living pretty contentedly with Cyril Maxon?"

The point was presented plainly enough for her. She smiled reflectively. "I think I see. Yes!"

"People differ as well as cases."

She sat down by him, much interested. They were, it seemed, to talk about herself.

"Hobart Gaynor's rather uneasy about me, I think."

"And you about yourself?"

"No, I'm just rather excited, Stephen."

"You're a small boat—and it's a big sea."

"That's the excitement of it. I've been—landlocked—for years. Oh, beached—whatever's your best metaphor for somebody wasting all this fine life!"

"Do you suppose you made your husband happy?"

The question was unexpected. But there was no side of a situation too forlorn for Stephen's notice.

"I really don't know," said Winnie. "I always seemed to be rather—well, rather a minor interest."

"I expect not—I really expect not, you know."

"Supposing I was, or supposing I wasn't—what does it amount to ?"

"I was only just looking at it from his point of view for a minute."

"Did he make me happy ?"

"Oh, certainly the thing wasn't successful all round," Stephen hastily conceded.

"He said marriage wasn't invented solely to make people happy."

"Well, I suppose he's got an argument there. But you probably thought that the institution might chuck in a little more of that ingredient incidentally ?"

"Rather my feeling—yes. You put things well, too, now and then, Stephen."

"You suffer under the disadvantage of being a very attractive woman."

"We must bear our infirmities with patience, mustn't we ?"

She was this evening in a rare vein of excited pleasure, gay, challenging, admirably provoking, exulting in her freedom, dangling before her own dazzled eyes all its possibilities. Stephen gave a deep chuckle.

"I think I'll go in and tell Tora that I'm infernally in love with you," he remarked, rising from his chair.

"It would be awfully amusing to hear what she says. But—are you ?"

A rolling laugh, full of applause, not empty of pity, rumbled over the lawn as Stephen walked back to the house.

No, Stephen was not in love with her; that was certain. He admitted every conceivable doubt as to his duty, but harbored none as to his inclination. That trait of his might, to Winnie's present mood, have been vexatious had he

chanced to be the only man in the world, or even the only
one in or near Shaylor's Patch. Winnie sat in the twilight,
smiling roguishly. She had no fears for herself; far less
had she formed any designs. She was simply in joyful rebound from long suppression. Her spirit demanded plenty
of fun, with perhaps a spice of mischief—mischief really
harmless. So much seemed to her a debt long overdue from
life and the world. Yet peril was there, unseen by herself.
For there is peril when longings for fun and mischief centre
persistently round one figure, finding in it, and in it only,
their imagined realization.

But was peril the right word—was it the word proper to
use at Shaylor's Patch? Being no fool, Stephen Aikenhead
saw clearly enough the chance that a certain thing would
happen—or was happening. But how should this chance
be regarded? The law—formed by this and that influence,
historical, social, and religious—had laid upon this young
woman a burden heavier than she was able to bear. So
Stephen started his consideration of the case. Retort—she
ought to have been stronger! It did not seem a very helpful
retort; it might be true, but it led nowhere. The law then
had failed with the young woman. Now it said, "Well, if
you won't do that, at least you sha'n't do anything else with
my sanction—and my sanction is highly necessary to your
comfort, certainly here, and, as a great many people believe,
hereafter." That might be right, because it was difficult
to deny the general proposition that laws ought to be kept,
under pain of penalties. Yet in this particular instance
there seemed something rather vindictive about it. It was
not as if the young woman wanted to rob churches or pick
pockets — things obviously offensive and hurtful to her
neighbors. All she would want (supposing the thing did

happen) would be to behave in a perfectly natural and normal fashion. All she would be objecting to would be a law-enjoined sterilization of a great side of her nature. She would be wronging her husband? If wrong there were, surely the substantial wrong lay in deserting him, not in making the best of her own life afterward? She might have children—would they suffer? Living in the social world he did, Stephen could not see that they need suffer appreciably; and they were, after all, hypothetical—inserted into the argument for the sake of logical completeness. She would wound other people's convictions and feelings? No doubt, but that argument went too far. Every innovator, every reformer, nay, every fighting politician, does as much. The day for putting ring-fences round opinions, and threatening trespassers with prosecution, was surely over.

Well, then, would she hurt herself? The argument descended abruptly from the general to the particular. It left principle and came to prudence, asking no longer what she had a right to do, but what she would be wise to do in her own interests. A man may hold a thing not wrong, and yet be a fool if he does it in a place where the neighbors are so sure of its iniquity that they will duck him in the horse-pond. But suppose him to be a mighty man of valor, whom nobody cares to tackle! He can snap his fingers at the neighbors and follow his own conscience or inclination, free from fear and heedless of disapprobation.

"That's as far as I can get," Stephen concluded, rubbing his forehead, as his habit was in moments of meditation. The conclusion did not seem wholly moral, or wholly logical, but it might work out fairly well in practice; government by the law—that is, the opinion of the majority—for the weak (themselves the majority), government by their own consciences and inclinations for the strong. Probably it was a rough statement of what generally happened, if the terms weak and strong might be taken to sum up the complex whole of a man's circumstances and character; both must by all means be considered.

But who are the strong? How can they judge of their prowess until they are in the thick of the fray? If it fails them then, it's too late—and away to the horse-pond! You do poor service to a friend if you flatter him in this matter. When he finds himself in the pond, he will not be so grateful for your good opinion.

Winnie came in, bright-eyed, softly singing, making for up-stairs at a hasty pace.

"I shall be late for dinner!" she cried. "I met Mr. Ledstone, and he made me go for a little walk."

"Did you enjoy it?" asked Stephen, politely.

"Yes, thank you, Stephen, very much."

She was gone. Stephen sighed. She had only one life—that was the unspoken plea of her youth, her beauty, and her new-born zest in living. Say what you like, the plea was cogent.

VII

TO probe Godfrey Ledstone's mind would be to come up against the odd bundle of ideas which constitutes the average young man's workaday morality — the code before mentioned. This congeries of rules, exceptions, compromises, strictnesses, and elasticities may be condemned; it cannot be sneered at or lightly dismissed. It has, on the whole, satisfied centuries; only at rare intervals has it been seriously interfered with by the powers that be, by Church or State or Church-ruled State.

To interfere seriously with it is to rouse a hive of questions, large, difficult, so profoundly awkward as to appal statesmen, lay or ecclesiastical—questions not only moral and religious, but social and economic. Formal condemnation and practical tolerance leave these questions sleeping. The code goes on, exercising its semi-secret, underground jurisdiction—a law never promulgated but widely obeyed, a religion with millions of adherents and not a single preacher. Rather a queer way for the world to live? Rather a desperate attempt at striking a balance between nature and civilization? No doubt. But then, of course, it is only temporary. We are all going to be good some day. To make us all good, to make it possible for us all to be good immediately—well, there is no telling but what that

67

might involve a radical reconstitution of society. And would even that serve the turn?

The code never had a more unquestioning, a more contented adherent than Godfrey. Without theorizing — he disliked theories and had a good-natured distrust of them— he hit just that balance of conduct whereof the code approves; if he had talked about the matter at all (the code does not favor too much talking), he might have said that he was "not a saint," but that he "played the game." His fellow-adherents would understand perfectly what he meant. And the last thing in the world that he contemplated or desired was to attack, or openly to flout, accepted standards. The code never encourages a man to do that. Besides, he had a father, a mother, and a sister, orthodox-thinking people, very fond and proud of him; he would not willingly do or say anything to shock them. Even from a professional point of view—but when the higher motives are sufficient to decide the issue, why need they invoke the somewhat compromising alliance of others purely prudential?

By now he was very much in love with Winnie Maxon, but he was also desperately vexed with her, and with all the amiable theorizers at Shaylor's Patch. The opportunity had seemed perfect for what he wanted, and what he wanted seemed exactly one of the allowed compromises—an ideal elasticity! Whom would it wrong? Not Cyril Maxon, surely? He was out of court. Whom would it offend? There was nobody to offend, if the affair were managed quietly—as it could be here in the country. And she liked him; though he had made no declaration yet, he could not doubt that she liked him very much.

But the theorizers had been at her. When he delicately felt his way, discussing her position, or, professedly, the position of women in general whose marriages had proved a failure, she leaned back, looking adorably pretty, and calmly came out with a remark of a profoundly disconcerting nature.

"If I ever decided to—to link my life with a man's again, I should do it quite openly. I should tell my husband and my friends. I should consider myself as doing just the same thing as if I were marrying again. I talked it all over with Tora the other night, and she quite agreed with me."

Agreed with her! Tora had put it into her head, of course, Godfrey thought, angrily. The idea had Tora's hall-mark stamped large in its serene, straightforward irrationality.

"But that 'd mean an awful row, and the—a case, and all that!"

"I hope it would. But Cyril doesn't approve of divorce."

"Then you'd never be able to—to get regular, as long as he lived."

"I think I should be regular, without getting regular," she answered, smiling.

"What's the good of defying the world?"

"Isn't that the only way bad things get altered?"

"It needs a good deal of courage to do things like that —right or wrong."

"I should rely on the man I loved to give me the courage."

Godfrey did not wish to admit that the man whom (as he hoped) she loved lacked courage. The answer irritated him; he sat frowning sulkily, his usual gayety sadly overcast. Winnie's eyes scanned his face for a moment; then, with a sigh, she looked over the lawn to the valley below. She was disappointed with the reception of her great idea. "Of course, the two people would have to be very much in love with each other," she added, with a little falter in her voice.

He found a way out of his difficulty. "The more a man loved a woman, the less likely he'd be to consent to put her in such a position," he argued. His face cleared; he was pleased with his point; it was good, according to the code.

"It would be the only honorable position for her," Winnie retorted.

He rose to his feet in a temper; it was all so unreasonable. "I must go."

"Are you coming to anything to-morrow?"

"No, I shall be in town to-morrow. I dare say I shall stay a night or two." This was by way of revenge—or punishment. Let her see how she liked Shaylor's Patch without him!

She turned to him, holding out her hand; in her eyes was raillery, half-reproachful, half-merry. "Come back in a better temper!" she said.

"I'm a fool to come back at all." He kissed her hand and looked steadily into her eyes before he went away.

Himself at once a poor and a pleasure-loving man, Godfrey had the good-luck to own a well-to-do and devoted friend, always delighted to "put him up" and to give him the best of hospitality. Bob Purnett and he were old school-fellows and had never lost sight of each other. Bob had four thousand a year of his own (though not of his own making), and in the summer he had no work to do; in the winter he hunted. He was a jovial being, and very popular, except with the House Committee and the cook of his club; to these unfortunate officials he was in the nature of a perpetual Assize Court presided over by a "Hanging Judge."

70

A CODE AND A THEORY

He gave Godfrey a beautiful dinner and a magnum of fine claret; let it be set down to his credit that he drank— and gave—fine claret at small dinners. He knew better than to be intemperate. Did he not want to go on hunting as long as possible ? Nor was Godfrey given to excess in wine-drinking. Still, the dinner, the claret, the old friendship, the liqueur, the good cigar, did their work. Godfrey found himself putting the case. It appeared to Bob Purnett a curious one.

"But it's rot," he observed. "You're married or you're not—eh ?" He himself was not—quite distinctly. "Must be very pretty, or she wouldn't expect you to stand it ?"

Godfrey laughed. There was a primitive truthfulness about Purnett's conversation. He was not sophisticated by thought or entangled in theory—quite different from the people at Shaylor's Patch.

"She is very pretty; and absolutely a lady—and straight, and all that."

"Then let it alone," counselled Bob Purnett.

"I can't help it, old chap." Again the primitive note— the cry that there are limits to human endurance. Godfrey had not meant to utter it. The saying of it was an illumination to himself. Up to now he had thought that he could help it—and would, if he were faced with theories and irrationality.

"Let's go to a Hall ?" Bob suggested.

"I'd like a quiet evening and just a jaw."

Bob looked gravely sympathetic. "Oh, you've got it in the neck!" he said, with a touch of reverent wonder in his voice—something like the awe that madmen inspired in our forebears. Godfrey was possessed!

"Yes, I have—and I don't know what the deuce to do."

"Well, what the deuce are you to do?" asked Purnett. His healthy, ruddy, unwrinkled face expressed an honest perplexity. "Must be a rum little card—isn't she?"

"I can't help it, Bob."

"Dashed awkward!"

In fact, these two adherents of the code—may it be written, honest adherents, for they neither invented nor defended, but merely inherited it?—were frankly puzzled. There is a term in logic—dichotomy—a sharp division, a cutting in two, an opposing of contradictories. You are honest or not honest, sober or not sober. Rough reasoning, but the police-courts have to work on it. So you are regular or irregular. But people who want to make the irregular regular—that is as great a shock to the adherents of the code as their tenets are to the upholders of a different law. The denial of one's presuppositions is always a shock—because one must start from somewhere. It is a "shock to credit"—credit of some kind—and how are any of us to get on without credit?

"Bring two more old brandies, Walter," Mr. Purnett commanded. It was the only immediate and practical step.

"Not for me, old chap."

Bob nodded accordingly to Walter. His face was inconceivably solemn.

"I sometimes feel like cutting the whole thing," said Godfrey, fretfully.

"Well, there are other women in the world, aren't there?"

"No, no. I mean the whole thing. What's the good of it?" The young man's fresh face looked for the moment weary and old; he flung his good cigar, scarcely half smoked, into the fireplace.

Bob Purnett knew better than to argue against a mood like that; one might just as well argue against a toothache.

A CODE AND A THEORY

"Let's go home and have an early bed," he suggested. He yawned, and tried to hide the action. He was devoted to his friend, but his friend had raised a puzzle, and puzzles soon fatigued him—except little ones made of wood, for which he had a partiality.

For three whole days Godfrey Ledstone fought, really trying to "cut the whole thing," to master again the feelings which had mastered him, not to go back to Shaylor's Patch. On one day he went to see his people, the father, mother, and sister who were orthodox-thinking and so fond and proud of him. They lived in Woburn Square. The old gentleman had been an accountant in a moderately good way of business, and had retired on a moderately good competence; at least, he was not old really, but, like some men, he took readily, even prematurely, to old age. Everything in the house seemed to Godfrey preternaturally settled; it even seemed settled somehow that Amy would not marry. And it was odd to think that Mr. and Mrs. Ledstone had once married, had (as it must be presumed) suffered from these terrible feelings, had perhaps doubted, feared, struggled, enjoyed. To-day all was so placid in Woburn Square; the only really acute question was the Income Tax—that certainly was a grievance to Mr. Ledstone. Godfrey appreciated the few hours of repose, the fondness, and the pride. It seemed then quite possible to "cut the whole thing"—yes, the whole of it.

Bob Purnett went off on a short visit, leaving his comfortable flat at his friend's disposal. Why not stay in London, do a good turn at work, and see some more of his people in Woburn Square? A good and wise programme. But on the fourth day came a gust that blew the good and wise programme clean out of the window—a gust of feeling like

73

a draught of strong wine, heady and overpowering. He flung down his pencil, crying aloud, "It's no use!"

He was tried beyond that he was able. He laid an indictment, vague and formless, yet charged with poignant indignation, against the general order of things, against what forced a man into folly, and then branded him "Fool" with irons hissing-hot. The old protest, the creature's cry against the injustice of creation! An hour later he was on his way to the country—back to Shaylor's Patch. So far as he was concerned, the thing was settled. He might not realize it; he went, not led by purpose, but driven by craving. But "On my terms if I can, on hers if I must," interprets the confused and restless humming of his brain.

To a man in such case the people he meets as he fares along seem strangely restful, impossibly at peace. The old man with his pipe, the young clerk with his sporting paper, the laborer in the field, the toddler with its toy, all present an illusion of untroubled existence, at which the man with the gadfly looks in envy and in scorn. They possess their souls—he is possessed. Well might Bob Purnett wear that expression of awe! For some day the normal man must resume possession, and he may find that the strangest pranks have been played by the temporary tenant—furniture smashed, debts incurred, and what not, for all of which dilapidations and liabilities he, unfortunate soul, is held responsible! Happily it chances, after all not so seldom, that the temporary tenant has made beauty, not havoc, and left behind him generous gifts, to the enrichment of life till life itself shall pass away.

Stephen Aikenhead sat on the lawn with his little girl Alice, newly come home for the holidays. She was reading aloud to him; he smoked his pipe, and now and again his big hand would pass caressingly over the little, bowed head with its soft, brown hair. The story was about a certain Princess, to whom a Fairy had given the Gift of Eternal Youth on the condition that she never fainted either from fear or from joy. All went well for a very great many years. Generations were born and died, and the Princess was still sweet seventeen. She outlived seventy-seven prime-ministers. But at last a very handsome groom, who had appeared at the castle gates rather mysteriously and been taken into the Princess's service without (as it seemed) any "character," was thrown from his horse while he was in attendance on his royal mistress, and, lo and behold, the Princess fainted for fear that he might be dead, and fainted again for joy when she found he wasn't! So he revealed himself as the King of the neighboring kingdom, and they married each other and lived happily ever afterward. Only, of course, the Princess lost the Gift of Eternal Youth.

"I love these stories about Princesses, Alice," said Stephen. "Read me another. I wish there were lots more Princesses. There aren't half enough of them nowadays. They're so picturesque, and such jolly things happen to them. Halloo, Godfrey, you back?"

Godfrey had sent the cab on with his luggage, and let himself in by the garden gate. He arrived just in time to hear the end of the story. Reader and listener were close to the parlor door. As his name was spoken, Godfrey heard a little movement from within—the sound of the movement of a woman's skirts. His impressionable nature responded to a new appeal, his readily receptive eyes beheld a new vision. As he looked at the big man and his little girl, so happy in each other, so at peace yet never in tedium, he wished that it—his affair—could be neither on his terms

6 75

nor on hers—could be neither a deceit nor a defiance, but could be the straight, regular thing, the good, old-fashioned thing that, after all, served most people's turn well enough. There were failures, but it was in the broad way of nature and broadly successful. Who really objected to it, or questioned it? To whom was the Institution obnoxious? Rips and cranks, he answered in his concise vernacular; really it did well enough for everybody else—with, no doubt, allowances made here and there.

The soft rustle sounded again from within the parlor. Then Winnie Maxon stood in the doorway with shining, welcoming eyes.

"Well, would you like the story of the Princess with the Broken Heart?" asked Alice.

"Anything about a Princess!" said Stephen, with handsome liberality.

"It sounds sad, Alice. If it's sad, don't let's have it," Winnie pleaded.

"Oh, after all the old doctors had tried to mend it, one came, looking much older and much more wrinkled than all the rest—"

"I shall keep my eye on that practitioner, all the same," Stephen interposed. "I'm beginning to know the ropes!"

"And he mended it with an enormous gold ring that he'd cut off the little finger of a giant he had once killed on a walk he took."

"What a fellow!" said Stephen. "Prince in disguise, Alice?"

"Why, father, of course he was!"

Stephen shook his big head and turned his big spectacles up to heaven. "And that fellow Dennehy dares to call himself a republican! Now who—who, I ask you—would give a fig for a President in disguise ? Read me some more Princesses, Alice."

They all enjoyed the Princesses. So sometimes, for an hour, a little child shall lead us into peace.

VIII

EMBEDDED in his own conceptions as in a rock, Cyril Maxon refused to believe that his wife would not soon "have had enough of it." He refused to accept the failure of the envoy through whose mouth he had been induced to make such great concessions and such generous promises. Could they, in the end, fail to move her?

His duty toward her—that inexorable duty from which no act of hers could free him—called upon him for another effort. Attlebury was with him in this view, though now with less hope of a favorable issue; he detected the fact that his disciple's desire for self-vindication was no less strong than his hope of saving Mrs. Maxon, and feared for the result of this admixture of objects. He ventured on a reminder.

"Of course, you want to be able to feel you've done all you could, but the great thing is to do it successfully. As we regard it, she has more at stake than you."

"I believe I can persuade her, if I go and see her."

Did he really mean persuade—or did he mean frighten? Attlebury doubted, and, because he doubted that, doubted yet more of the issue. The disciple did not give the cause fair play; a teacher has often to complain of that.

In whatever shape Cyril Maxon may have forecast in

78

his own mind the interview that he proposed, there was no question as to how Winnie received the notice of his intention to seek her out in her asylum at Shaylor's Patch. It filled her with sheer panic; it drove her to what seemed now her only refuge. Her terror must surely make an appeal irresistible alike to the ardor and to the chivalry of her lover? Or he was no lover. Tora and she were at one on the point, though it was not put too bluntly between them.

"I can't see him; I won't," she declared to Stephen Aikenhead, running to the man of the house at last, rebel against male domination as she was.

"Rather difficult to refuse, if he comes here."

"Then I won't be here when he comes—that's all." Her fright made her unjust. "If you won't protect me—or can't—I must act for myself." She flung out of the room, leaving Stephen no chance of protesting that the bolts and bars of Shaylor's Patch were at her service, and a siege by an angry lawyer all in the day's work.

She was afraid of herself; she distrusted her courage. She wanted to have a motive compulsory in its force; her instinct was to do something which should make a return home irrevocably impossible. Her husband's insistence hastened the crisis, though his patience could hardly have averted it.

Godfrey Ledstone had the news first from Tora Aikenhead. Her calm eyes asked him plainly enough what part it was his to play. Tora had taken her line, and at once conceived hesitation to be impossible. His native idea would have been to comfort her before Maxon came, and again after he had gone, and to lie by in snug hiding when he was there. So ran the code, discreet and elastic. By now he knew—only too well—that this was not what these uncompromising people expected of him. In their odd view he had already gone too far for that convenient expedient. Social liberty might, it seemed, be more exacting than social bondage. For if you were always free to do as you liked, it was obviously necessary to be very careful about intimating too unreservedly what it was that you would like to do, since there could be no such thing as pleading impossibility in defence of a pledge unfulfilled.

"She's terribly unhappy. She declares that she must be gone before he comes. She daren't meet him."

"Why not?" he asked, sharply. Another feeling was stirred in him.

"Well, he's always dominated her. He might break down her will again."

"You mean she might go back? Cave in, and go back?"

"That seems to be what she's afraid of, herself."

Tora entertained no more doubt of the soundness of her ideas than Cyril Maxon of his. Why should she, she would have asked, merely because hers were new, while his were old? To her mind newness was a presumption of merit in a view, since the old views had produced a world manifestly so imperfect all round. Holding her opinion strongly, she did not hesitate to use the weapons best suited to secure its triumph. If Godfrey's jealousy helped to that end, why was it illegitimate to let it play its part? Never was a woman less afraid of what men call responsibility.

"It's just awful to think of the poor little lady going back to that brute of a fellow," he said.

"Oh, don't abuse him. I dare say he's as unhappy as she is. And he thinks he's right. I'm not sure you don't think he's right, really." Tora smiled over her shrewd thrust. "So you're the last person who ought to abuse him."

"Oh, what does it matter what I think?" he cried, impatiently.

There was still enough of his old mood and his old ideas in him to stir a resentment against Tora, to make him feel that she was forcing his hand and constraining him to accept a bigger liability than he had bargained for. Theorists must always be up to that! They seem to take a positive pleasure in proving that you are bound to go to lengths—to all lengths—that the comfortable half-way will never serve! Perhaps they do not enough reflect that the average man is not thereby encouraged to start at all.

But Winnie herself had genuine power to stir his heart— and now, indeed, as never before, since she seemed helpless save for him, and hopeless save in him, yet in and through him both brave and confident—the most profound, the most powerful flattery from sex to sex. Mere friends could not help now; mere convictions, a naked sense of being in the right, would not avail. These she had, but she must have love, too. To this mood all the man in him responded.

"It only needed this final trouble to—to make me speak."

"I don't think I need speak," she whispered, with her delicately quavering smile. "You know it all—all the great thing it is. I'm not ashamed of it, Godfrey. And you won't be ashamed of me, will you?"

The question did not disconcert him now. For the time he had lost that vision of the future which had once disquieted and alarmed him. His phrases might be well-worn, but they were heartily sincere when he told her he would face the world, if only she were by his side.

"It shall all be just as you said you wished it to be if

6   81

ever you joined your life to a man's again. He quoted almost verbally, just missing her poetic "link."

Winnie kissed him in warm and pretty gratitude. "That takes away my last doubt," she told him. "I shall be proud now, as proud as any woman! And to-day—just for a few hours—let's forget everything except that we're plighted lovers." She put her arm through his. "You'll kill the giant, take his ring, and mend the Princess's Broken Heart!"

"I say, are you making me a Prince in disguise, Winnie?"

"Well, don't you feel like a Prince now?" she asked, with the sweet audacity of a woman who knows that she is loved, and for her lover boldly takes herself at her lover's valuation.

Obedient to her wish, the outside world effected one of its disappearances—very obliging, if not of long duration. Even Woburn Square made tactful exit, without posing the question as to what its opinion of the proceedings might likely be. Of course, that point could be held immaterial, for the present at least.

For the second time, then, in Winnie Maxon's recent experience, with a little courage things proved easy; difficulties vanished when faced; you did what you held you had a right to do, and nothing terrible happened. Certainly nothing terrible happened that evening at Shaylor's Patch. There was a romantic, an idyllic bit of courting, with the man ardent and gallant, the woman gay but shy; it was all along orthodox lines, really conventional. He had undertaken that the affair should be carried through on Winnie's lines; this was his great and fine concession—or conversion. He observed it most honorably; she grew more and more gratefully tender.

SUBVERSIVE

"Another man than you—yes, even another man I loved—
might have wounded me to-night," she murmured as they
parted at the door after dinner.

"I could never wound you—even with my love."

She took his hand and kissed it. "I'm trusting you
against all the world, Godfrey."

"You may trust me."

Her heart sang, even while her lover left her.

For what followed in the two or three days during which
she still abode at Shaylor's Patch people shall find what
names they please, since her history is, of necessity, somewhat concerned with contentious matters. Some may
speak of unseemly travesty, some of idle farce; others may
find a protest not without its pathos—a protest that she
broke with the old order only because she must, that she
would fain carry over into her new venture what was good
in the old spirit, that her enterprise was to her a solemn
and high thing. They were to be man and wife together; he
must buy her the ring that symbolized union; they must
have good and true witnesses—nothing was to be secret, all
aboveboard and unashamed. There must even be a little
ceremonial, a giving and taking before sympathetic friends,
a declaration that she held herself his, and he hers, in all
love and trust, and to the exclusion of all other people in the
world. Forever? Till death did them part? No—the
premises peremptorily forbade that time-honored conclusion. But so long as the love that now bound them together
still sanctified the bond which it had fastened. Satisfied in
her heart that the love could never die, she defined without
dismay the consequences of its death. At all events, she
would have answered to an objector, could they be worse
than what had befallen her when her love for Cyril Maxon

83

died a violent death by crushing—died and yet was, in the name of all that is holy, denied decent burial?

And yet there were qualms. "Will people understand?" was her great question.

Tora — uncompromising, level - headed — answered that most of them would not even try to, and added, "What matter?" Stephen asked, "Well, so long as your friends do?" Her lover vowed that, whether her action were approved or not, no tongue could wag against her honor or her motives.

The last day came—the day when the pair were to set out together, Godfrey from his summer cottage in the village of Nether End, near Shaylor's Patch, Winnie from her haven under the Aikenheads' friendly roof. A home had been taken in London, but they were to have a week's jaunt— a honeymoon—in North Wales first. Winnie was now putting the finishing touch to her preparations by writing her luggage labels. The name she wrote seemed happily to harmonize personal independence with a union of hearts and destinies—Mrs. Winifred Ledstone.

The sound of a man's footstep made her look up. She saw Dick Dennehy before her. He had come in from the garden, and was just clutching off his hat at the sight of her.

"Mr. Dennehy! I didn't know you were coming here to-day."

"No more did I, Mrs. Maxon, till a couple of hours ago. I found I had nothing to do, so I ran down to see how you were all getting on."

"Some of us are just getting off," smiled Winnie. "You're in time to say good-bye."

"Why, where are you off to? I'm sorry you're going."

With a saucy glance Winnie pushed a luggage label across

the table toward him.   He took it up, studied it, and laid it down again without a word.

"Well ?" said Winnie.

He spread out a pair of pudgy, splay-fingered hands and shook his shock - haired head in sincere, if humorous, despair.

"You're all heathens here, and it's no good talking to you as if you were anything else."

"I'm not a heathen, but if the Church backs up the State in unjust laws—"

He wagged a broad forefinger.   "Even a heathen tribe has its customs.   Any custom's better than none!   Ye can't go against the custom of the tribe for nothing.   I speak as heathen to heathen."

"Can't customs ever be changed ?"   Winnie was back at her old point.

"You're not strong enough for the job, Mrs. Maxon." His voice was full of pity.

But Winnie was in no mood to accept pity.   "You call me a heathen.   Suppose it was A.D. 50 or 100, and not A.D. 1909.   I think you'd be a heathen, and I—well, at any rate, I should be trying to screw up my courage to be a Christian martyr."

He acknowledged a hit.   "Oh, you're all very clever!" he grumbled.   "I'll bet Stephen taught you that.   That's from his mint, if I know the stamp!   Take it as you say, then—are you looking forward to your martyrdom ?"

Perhaps she was, and in what must be admitted to be the proper spirit—thinking more of the crown than of the stake. "I don't look very unhappy, do I ?" she asked, radiantly.

"Going off with him to-day, are you ?"   She nodded gayly.   The natural man suddenly asserted itself in Den-

nehy. He smiled. "It's more than the young dog de-
serves, sure it is!"

"Oh, well, you're being a heathen now!" laughed Winnie,
distinctly well pleased.

"I'm wondering what Mrs. Lenoir will say about it."
Winnie's pleasure suffered a slight jar.

"Why should Mrs. Lenoir be any judge of a case like
mine?" she asked, rather coldly.

"Oh, I'm not making comparisons," he murmured,
vaguely. Still there was a point of comparison in his mind.
Mrs. Lenoir, too, had been a rebel against the custom of
the tribe, and, though the motives of rebellion differ, the
results may be the same. "Well, I'll wish you luck, anyhow," he continued, holding out his hand. "I hope he'll
make you happy, for you're giving him a lot, by the powers,
you are!'

"I hope I'm giving anything like as much as I'm getting."

He grumbled something inarticulate as he passed by her
and out of the door into the garden. Winnie looked after
him with a smile still on her lips. If this were the worst she
had to expect, it was nothing very dreadful. It was even
rather amusing; she did not conceive that she had come
off in any way second-best in the encounter.

Stephen came in a moment later and, on her report of
Dennehy's arrival, went to look for his friend in the garden.
But Dennehy was nowhere to be found; he was seen no
more that day. He went straight back to London; he
could not stop the deed, but he would not be an accomplice.

"Well, if he doesn't agree with what we're doing, I think
he's right not to stay," said Tora. Yet Winnie felt a little
hurt.

Then came the travesty, or the farce, or the protest, or

whatever it may be decided to call it, in which Winnie formally—to a hostile eye perhaps rather theatrically—in the presence of her witnesses, did for herself what the powers that be would not do for her—declared her union with Cyril Maxon at an end and plighted her troth to Godfrey Ledstone. Godfrey would rather have had this little ceremony (if it had to be performed at all) take place privately, but he played his part in it with a good grace. It would be over soon—and soon he and she would set out together.

What of little Alice during all this ? She had been sent to play with the gardener's daughter. It would be a portentous theory, indeed, that forced a child to consider the law of marriage and divorce before she attained the age of eleven. Even Tora Aikenhead did not go so far, and, as has been seen, Stephen's theorizing tendencies were held in check in his child's case.

Then off they went, and on their arrival in London they were met by Bob Purnett, who gave them a hearty welcome and a champagne luncheon, where all was very merry and gay. There was, indeed, a roguish twinkle in Bob Purnett's eye, but perhaps it was no more than custom allows even in the case of the most orthodox of marriages—and in any event Bob Purnett's was not that class of opinion to which Winnie's views could most naturally be expected to appeal. He treated Winnie most politely, and called her Mrs. Ledstone. She did not realize that he would have done just the same if—well, in the case of any lady for whom a friend claimed the treatment and the title.

The next morning two letters duly and punctually reached their respective destinations. All was to be open, all aboveboard! Winnie had not found hers hard to write, and

Godfrey had said nothing to her about how extraordinarily difficult he had found his. One was addressed to Cyril Maxon, Esquire, K.C., at the Temple; the other to William J. Ledstone, Esquire, at Woburn Square. Now in neither of these places were the views of Shaylor's Patch likely to find acceptance or, even, toleration. No, nor Bob Purnett's, either. Though, indeed, if a choice had to be made, the latter might have seemed, not more moral, but at least less subversive in their tendency. A thing that is subversively immoral must be worse, surely, than a thing that is merely immoral? Granting the immorality in both cases, the subversive people have not a leg to stand on. They are driven to argue that they are not immoral at all—which only makes them more subversive still.

And the dictionary defines "subversion" in these terms: "The act of overturning, or the state of being overturned; entire overthrow; an overthrow from the foundation; utter ruin; destruction"—anyhow, clearly a serious matter, and at that we may leave it for the moment.

IX

AT Cyril Maxon's chambers in the Temple—very pleasant chambers they were, with a view over a broad sweep of the river—the day began in the usual fashion. At half-past nine Mr. Gibbons, the clerk, arrived; at a quarter to ten the diligent junior, who occupied the small room and devilled for the King's Counsel, made his punctual appearance. At ten, to the stroke of the clock, Maxon himself came in. His movements were leisurely; he had a case in the paper—an important question of demurrage—but it was not likely to be reached before lunch. He bade Mr. Gibbons good-morning, directed that the boy should keep a watch on the progress of the court to which his case was assigned, passed into his own room, and sat down to open his letters. These disposed of, he had a couple of opinions to write, with time left for a final run through his brief, aided by the diligent junior's note.

Half an hour later Mr. Gibbons opened the door. Maxon waved him back impatiently.

"I'm busy, Gibbons. Don't disturb me. We can't be on in court yet ?"

"No, sir. It's a gentleman to see you. Very urgent business, he says."

"No, no, I tell you, I'm busy."

89

"He made it a particular favor. In fact, he seems very much upset—he says it's private business." He glanced at a card he carried. "It's a Mr. Ledstone, sir."

"Oh," said Maxon. His lips shut a little tighter as he took up a letter which lay beside the legal papers in front of him. "Ledstone?" The letter was signed "Winifred Ledstone."

"Yes, sir."

"What aged man?"

"Oh, quite elderly, sir. Stout, and gray 'air."

The answer dispelled an eccentric idea which had entered Maxon's head. If this couple so politely informed him of their doings, they might even be capable of paying him a call!

"Well, show him in." He shrugged his shoulders with an air of disgust.

Stout and gray-haired (as Mr. Gibbons had observed), yet bearing a noticeable likeness to his handsome son, Mr. Ledstone made a very apologetic and a very flustered entrance. Maxon bowed without rising; Gibbons set a chair and retired.

"I must beg a thousand pardons, Mr. Maxon, but this morning I—I received a letter—as I sat at breakfast, Mr. Maxon, with Mrs. Ledstone and my daughter. It's terrible!"

"Are you the father of Mr. Godfrey Ledstone?"

"Yes, sir. My boy Godfrey—I've had a letter from him. Here it is."

"Thank you, but I'm already in possession of what your son has done. I've heard from Mrs. Maxon. I have her letter here."

"They're mad, Mr. Maxon! Mean to make it all public!

90

What are we to do? What am I to say to Mrs. Ledstone and my daughter?"

"You must really take your own course about that."

"And my poor boy! He's been a good son, and his mother's devoted to him, and—"

Cyril Maxon's wrath found vent in one of those speeches for which his wife had a pet name. "I don't see how the fact that your son has run away with my wife obliges, or even entitles, me to interfere in your family affairs, Mr. Ledstone."

Acute distress is somewhat impervious to satire. "Of course not, sir," said Mr. Ledstone, mopping his face forlornly. "But what's to be done? There's no real harm in the boy. He's young—"

"If you wish to imply that my wife is mainly in fault, you're entirely welcome to any comfort you and your family can extract from that assumption."

Ledstone set his hands on the table between them and looked plaintively at Maxon. He was disconcerted and puzzled; he fancied that he had not made himself, or the situation, fully understood. He brought up his strongest artillery—the most extraordinary feature in the case.

"The boy actually suggests that he should bring your—that he should bring Mrs.—that he should bring the lady to see Mrs. Ledstone and my daughter!" He puffed out this crowning atrocity with quick breaths, and mopped his face again.

"You're master in your own house, I suppose? You can decide whom to receive, Mr. Ledstone." He pushed his chair back a little; the movement was unmistakably a suggestion that his visitor should end his visit. Mr. Ledstone did not take the hint.

"I suppose you'll — you'll institute proceedings, Mr. Maxon?"

"I'm not a believer in divorce."

"You won't?"

"I said I was not a believer in divorce." Growing exasperation, hard held, rang in his voice.

A visible relief brightened Mr. Ledstone's face. "You won't?" he repeated. "Oh, well, that's something. That gives us time, at all events."

Maxon smiled—not genially. "I don't think you must assume that your son and the lady who now calls herself Mrs. Ledstone will be as much pleased as you appear to be."

"Oh, but if there are no proceedings!" murmured Ledstone. Then he ventured a suggestion. "Private influence could be brought to bear?"

"Not mine," said Cyril Maxon, grimly.

"Still, you don't propose to take proceedings!" He munched the crumb of comfort almost affectionately.

Cyril Maxon sought refuge in silence; not to answer the man was probably the best way to get rid of him—and he had defined his attitude twice already. Silence reigned supreme for a minute or two.

"I suppose my wife and daughter must know. But as for the rest of the family—" Mr. Ledstone was discussing his personal difficulties. Maxon sat still and silent as a statue. "It may all be patched up. He'll see reason." He glanced across at Maxon. "But I mustn't keep you, Mr. Maxon." He rose to his feet. "If there are no proceedings—" Maxon sharply struck the handbell on his table; Gibbons opened the door. "Thank you. Good-morning, Mr. Maxon." Maxon's silence was unbroken as his visitor shuffled out.

"THANK YOU. GOOD-MORNING, MR. MAXON"

NO PROCEEDINGS!

Maxon's nature, hard and proud, not tender in affection, very tenacious of dignity, found now no room for any feeling save of disgust—a double disgust at the wickedness and at the absurdity—at the thing itself and at the despicable pretence in which the pair sought to cloak it. Ledstone's intrusion—so he regarded the visit of Godfrey's father—intensified his indignant distaste for the whole affair. To have to talk about it to a man like that! To be asked to use his influence! He smiled grimly as he tried to picture himself doing that. Pleading with his wife, it must be supposed; giving wise counsel to the young man perhaps? He asked nothing now but to be allowed to wash his hands of them both—and of the Ledstone family. Really, above all, of the Ledstone family! How the thought of them got on his nerves! Mr. Attlebury's teaching about the duty of saving a soul passed out of sight. Was not he, in his turn, entitled to avail himself of the doctrine of the limits of human endurance? Is it made only for sinners—or only for wives? Maxon felt that it applied with overwhelming force to any further intercourse with the Ledstone family—and he instructed Mr. Gibbons to act accordingly, if need should arise. Mr. Gibbons had noticed Winnie's handwriting, with which naturally he was acquainted, on her letter, and wondered whether there could be any connection between it and the odd visit and the peremptory order. He had known for some two or three weeks that Mrs. Maxon was no longer in Devonshire Street; he was on very friendly terms with the coachman who drove Cyril Maxon's brougham.

Mr. Ledstone, mercifully ignorant of the aspect he assumed in Maxon's thoughts, walked home to Woburn Square, careful and troubled about many things. Though he was a good man and of orthodox views, it cannot be said

93

that he either was occupied primarily with the duty of saving souls; saving a scandal was, though doubtless not so important, considerably more pressing. He was, in fact, running over the names of all those of his kindred and friends whom he did not wish to know of the affair and who need know nothing about it if things were properly managed and if Godfrey would be reasonable. He wished to have this list ready to produce for the consolation of his immediate family circle. They—Mrs. Ledstone and his daughter— must be told. It would be sure to "get to" them somehow, and Mrs. Ledstone enjoyed the prestige of having a weak heart; it would never do for a thing like this to get to her without due precautions. Angry as he was with his son, he did not wish the boy to run the risk of having that on his conscience! As a fact, the way things get to people is often extremely disconcerting. It is a point that Shaylor's Patch ought to have considered.

In view of the weak heart—Mrs. Ledstone never exposed it to the sceptical inspection of a medical man—he told Amy first, Amy concerning whom it seemed to be settled that she would never be married, although she was but just turned twenty-five. He showed Amy the letter from Godfrey, his son; he indicated the crowning atrocity with an accusing forefinger.

"Oh, she made him put that in," said Amy, with contemptuous indifference and an absolute discernment of the truth.

Mr. Ledstone boiled over. "The impudence of it!"

Amy looked down at her feet—shod in good, stout shoes, sensible, yet not ugly; she was a great walker and no mean hockey-player. "I wonder what she's like," said Amy. "I've seen Mr. Maxon's name in the *Mail* quite often.

NO PROCEEDINGS!

What did you think of him, daddy ?" She had always kept the old name for her father.

Mr. Ledstone searched for a description of his impressions. "He didn't strike me as very sympathetic. He didn't seem to feel with us much, Amy."

"Hates the very idea of us, I suppose," remarked Amy. She turned to Godfrey's letter again; a faint smile came to her lips. "He does seem to be in love!"

"The question is—how will mother take it ?"

"Yes, of course, dear," Amy agreed, just a trifle absently. Yet, generally considered, it is a large question; it has played a big part, for good and evil, in human history.

Mrs. Ledstone—a woman of fifty-five, but still pretty and with prettily surviving airs of prettiness (it is pleasant to see their faded grace, like the petals of a flower flattened in a heavy book)—took it hardly, yet not altogether with the blank grief and dismay, or with the spasm of the heart, which her husband had feared for her. She did indeed say, "The idea!" when the crowning atrocity—the suggestion that Winnie should be brought to see her—was mentioned; and she cordially endorsed the list of kindred and friends who need know nothing about it. Also she paid a proper and a perfectly sincere tribute to outraged proprieties. But behind all this was the same sort of interest as had appeared in her daughter's comments—and had existed more explicitly in her daughter's thoughts. These Maxons—this Mrs. Maxon, for the husband was a subordinate figure, although with his own interest—had abruptly made incursion into the orderly life of Woburn Square, not merely challenging its convictions, but exciting its curiosity, bringing it suddenly into contact with things and thoughts that it had seen only in the newspapers or (in Amy's case) now and then at the theatre, where dramas "of ideas" were presented. Of course, they knew such things happened; one may know that about a thing, and yet find it very strange when it happens to one's self.

"There was always something about that boy," said Mrs. Ledstone. The vagueness was extreme, but pride lurked in the remark, like onion in the salad.

And she, like her husband, was immeasurably comforted by the news that there would be no proceedings. "His career won't suffer, father." She seemed to draw herself up, as though on the brink of moral laxity. "But, of course, it must be put a stop to at once." She read a passage in Godfrey's letter again. "Oh, what a goose the boy is! His head's turned; you can see that. I suppose she's pretty—or what they call smart, perhaps."

"The whole thing is deplorable, but the grossest feature is the woman's effrontery." The effrontery was all the woman's—an unkind view, but perhaps in this case more unkind than unjust. "How could she look you in the face, mother?" Mr. Ledstone squeezed his wife's hand sympathetically.

"Well, we must get him away from her as soon as possible."

A pessimist—one of those easily discouraged mortals who repine at nothing being effected within the brief span of their own generation—might liken the world to a ponderous ball, whereunto are attached five thousand strings. At the end of each somebody is tugging hard; but all of them are tugging in different directions. Universal effort, universal fatigue—and the big ball remains exactly where it was! Here was Winnie, heart and soul in her crusade, holding it great, almost holy. But the only idea in Woburn Square was to put an end to it as soon as possible! And meanwhile to cover it up, to keep it quiet, to preserve the possibility of being able to say no more about it as soon as it was happily over. No proceedings! What a comfort!

"Of course, we can have nothing to do with her. But what about him—while it lasts, I mean?" Mr. Ledstone propounded the question. "We ought to mark our—our horror."

"Yes, father, but we can't abandon the poor boy because he's been deluded. What do you think, Amy? After all, you're a grown-up woman now." (Mrs. Ledstone was defending herself against an inward sense of indelicacy in referring to the matter before her unmarried daughter.)

"Oh, the more we can get him here, the better," was Amy's view. "He'll realize how we feel about it then."

"Amy's right," the father declared, emphatically. "And so are you, mother. We mustn't abandon him. We must bring our influence to bear."

"I want to hear the poor boy's own story—not a letter written with the woman at his elbow," said Mrs. Ledstone.

"Will he come without her?" Amy asked.

"Without her—or not at all! It's my duty to shield you and your mother, Amy. And now, really, I must read my paper." In the excitement of the morning, in his haste to find Cyril Maxon, in his terror of proceedings, he had omitted the rite.

"I haven't been through the wash yet," said Mrs. Ledstone.

"It's time for Snip's walk," added Amy.

Life had to go on, in spite of Winnie Maxon—just as we read that some people lived their ordinary routine throughout the French Revolution.

MRS. MAXON PROTESTS

Snip was Amy Ledstone's Aberdeen terrier—and, let it be said at once, an extremely attractive and accomplished dog; he "died" for the King and whined if one mentioned the Chancellor of the Exchequer. Amy lavished on him her surplus of affection—what was left after her love for mother, father, and brother, her affection for uncles, aunts, and cousins, and a stray friendship or two which survived from school-girl days. Dogs sometimes come in for these wind-falls. But to-day her thoughts—as she made her way along the Euston Road and into Regent's Park—were less occupied with Snip than was usually the case. Obstinately they fastened themselves on Winnie Maxon; on more than Winnie Maxon—on ill-regulated affections in general. She had read about them in novels (which are so largely occupied with them), seen them exhibited in plays, pursed her lips over them in newspapers. All that was not the same thing—any more than an earthquake in China is the same thing as a burglary in one's own house. Here they were—actually in the family circle! Not mere "dissipation," but a settled determination to set the rules at naught. What manner of woman was this Mrs. Maxon? What had driven her to it? She had "borne more than any human being could"—so said Godfrey's letter. She now "claimed a little happiness," which "wronged nobody." She only "took what the law ought to give her—freedom from un-endurable bondage." The phrases of the letter were vivid in Amy's recollection. A woman who rebelled against the law—ought not her case against it to be heard? Hadn't she at least a right to a hearing? After all, as things stood, she had nothing to do with making it—nothing direct, at any rate. That sounded a plausible plea for Mrs. Maxon. But, on the other hand, because she had been wronged, or

98

suffered ill-treatment, or had bad luck, to go on and do what was, by Amy's training and prepossession, the one absolutely unpardonable thing, the thing hardly to be named—"I don't see how she could, whatever she thinks!" exclaimed Amy as she entered the Broad Walk.

People will, when they are allowed, go to see other people hanged, or to see murderers in their cells, or to watch a woman battling in open court for her fame as for her life. It was something of this sort of interest that fastened Amy's thoughts on Winnie Maxon. There is some admiration, some pity, in the feeling—and certainly a high curiosity about such people in the average mind, the law-keeping, the non-speculative mind, the mind trained to regard conventions as eternities and national customs as laws divine.

Suddenly a smile came on her lips. Would it be very wrong? She and Godfrey had always been "awfully good friends." She would like to be that still. What an awfully good friend he would think her if—if she did not treat Mrs. Maxon as dirt! If she—Amy trembled intellectually as the speculation developed itself—without saying anything about it at home, went to see her, made friends, tried to understand her point of view—called her "Winnie"! Calling her "Winnie" seemed the supreme point, the pivot on which her attitude turned.

Then came a cold doubt. "Will she care to be called Winnie?" "Will she care about seeing me?" "She's pretty, she's smart, she has been in society." Falling in love with a man may not involve a concern about the opinion of his maiden sister. How pretty was Mrs. Maxon, how smart?

Interest in Winnie Maxon accumulated from source after source. Yes, and on Amy Ledstone's part, interest in her-

99

self accrued also, mingled with a little uneasiness. She seemed to have travelled far in her meditations—and she had almost forgotten Snip. Yet it was hardly likely that these speculations would in the end issue in much. Amy herself recognized that. They would probably produce nothing save a touch of sympathy, treacherous to her home, in regard to Winnie barren and unexpressed. They could not prevent her from being against Winnie; they could only make her sorry that she had to be. Even so much was a victory— hard won against the prepossessions of her mind and the canons of her life.

X

MAUVE ENVELOPES

THE first condition of being able to please yourself is to have enough to live upon. Stephen Aikenhead was entirely right about that. Thrift, exercised by yourself or by some beneficent forerunner, confers independence; you can live upon the world, and yet flout it. (Within the limits of the criminal law, of course, but why be a criminal if you have enough to live upon? You lack the one really good excuse.) Imagine the state of affairs if it were not so—if banks, railways, docks, and breweries could refuse you your dividends on the ground of irregularity in your private life! What a sudden and profound quarter-day reformation of manners among the well-to-do classes opens before our fantastic vision! Really enough to turn the clergy and ministers of all denominations green with envy!

This economic condition was fulfilled for Godfrey Ledstone's establishment—just fulfilled according to Winnie's ideas, and no more. She had a hundred and fifty pounds a year; Godfrey's earnings averaged about two hundred, or a trifle more. His father had been in the habit of giving him a check for fifty at Christmas—but that addition could scarcely be relied on now. It was not riches; to one accustomed to Devonshire Street and a rising King's Counsel's income it was by no means riches. But it was enough; with care it would support the small quarters they had taken near Baron's Court Station in West Kensington—a studio, a small dining-room, two bedrooms, a bathroom, and "the usual offices" (unusually cramped "the usual offices"). No room for expansion! But they did not mean to expand at present.

Here Winnie sat down to defy or to convert the world. She had to begin the process with her cook-housemaid. Defiance, not conversion, was here certainly the word, and Godfrey was distinctly vexed at Winnie's opening of the matter to the cook-housemaid. Since there were to be no proceedings, need the good woman have been told at all?

The occasion of this—their first—tiff was small, but by no means insignificant. Winnie was holding Godfrey to his promise that he would not be ashamed of her.

"Among our friends, I meant, of course," Godfrey explained. "Among educated, thinking people, who can appreciate your position and our point of view. But this woman will simply think that you're—well, that you're what you're not, you know."

"How can she, when I told her all about it?"

He shrugged his shoulders. "Wait till you blow her up about something; you'll see what I mean," said he.

"Then I shall dismiss her." Winnie's proud little face was very flushed.

There were sides of life which Godfrey had observed. They had three cook-housemaids in quick succession, and were approaching despair when Dick Dennehy found them an old Irishwoman, who could not cook at all, but was entirely charitable. She had been told about the situation beforehand by Dick; there was no occasion for Winnie to refer to it. Winnie did not, and tried not to feel relieved.

MAUVE ENVELOPES

Also she ceased to tell the occasional charwomen who came in "by the day." Godfrey was perhaps right in thinking that superfluous. Dennehy came often, and they had other visitors, some bachelor friends of Godfrey's, others belonging to the Shaylor's Patch frequenters—Mrs. Danford and Mr. Carriston, for example. Mrs. Lenoir also came—not of her own accord (she never did that), but in response to an invitation from Winnie. Godfrey did not seem very enthusiastic about this invitation.

"But you seemed to like her so much at Shaylor's Patch," said Winnie, in surprise.

"Oh, yes! Ask her then, if you like." He formulated no objection; but in his mind there was the idea that Winnie did not quite realize how very careful she ought to be—in her position.

Such were the little passing clouds, obscuring for a moment the happiness of one or other of them.

Yet they were very happy. Godfrey was genuinely in love; so was Winnie, and to her there was the added joy—the new wonder—of being free. Free, and yet not lonely. She had a companion and yet not a master. Hers was the better mind of the two. She did not explicitly realize it, but unconsciously and instinctively she took the lead in most of their pursuits and amusements. Her tastes guided their interests and recreation—the books they read, the concerts and theatres which they "squeezed" out of their none too large margin of spare cash. This initiative was unspeakably delightful to the former Mrs. Maxon, an absolutely fresh thing in her life, and absolutely satisfying. This freedom, this liberty to expand, to grow, to develop, was what her nature had craved. Even if she set her love altogether on one side—and how should she?—this in itself seemed to

103

justify her refusal to be any longer Mrs. Maxon and her becoming Mrs. Winifred Ledstone. In fact, it was bound up with her love, for half the joy of these new travels and adventures of the mind lay in sharing them with Godfrey.

It still seemed as if everything were possible with a little courage, as if all the difficulties disappeared when boldly faced. Could there have been a difficulty more tremendous than Cyril Maxon? He had vanished into space!

After some six weeks of this pleasant existence—during which the difficulties at least tactfully effaced themselves, save in such trifles as have been lightly indicated—a phenomenon began to thrust itself on Winnie's notice. Godfrey was not a man of much correspondence; he did most of his business in person and conducted other necessary communications by telephone (that was a luxury which they had agreed that they must "run to" at the cost of some other, and unspecified, luxury to be foregone). Now he began to receive a certain type of envelope quite often—three times a week perhaps. It was a mauve envelope, rather larger than the ordinary. Winnie was careful not to scrutinize these envelopes—she did not even inspect the postmarks—but she could not help observing that, though the envelopes were always alike, the handwriting of the address varied. In fact, she noted three varieties. Being a woman of some perspicacity, she did not really need to inspect the postmarks. Godfrey had a father, a mother, a sister. They were writing to him, writing rather bulky letters, which he did not read in company, but stowed away in his pocket; they never reappeared, and presumably were disposed of secretly, on or off the premises. Nor did she ever detect him in the act of answering one; but in the course of his work he spent many hours away from home, and he belonged to a modest little club in the neighborhood of Covent Garden; no doubt it had writing-paper.

These mauve envelopes began to afflict the peace, or at least the happiness, of the little household. The mornings on which they came were less cheerful than other mornings; a constraint showed itself in greetings and farewells. They were reminders—ominous reminders—of the big world outside, the world which was being defied. His family was at* Godfrey Ledstone—three of his family, and one of them with a weak heart.

Three weeks of the mauve envelopes did their work. One had come on the Saturday; on the Sunday morning Godfrey made an apology to Winnie. He would not be able to join her in their usual afternoon excursion—for a walk, or to a picture-gallery, and so forth.

"My mother's not very well—she's not strong, you know. I must go to my people's."

"Of course you must, Godfrey. But—without me?"

"Yes." Passing her on his way to the mantelpiece, he pressed her hand for a moment. Then he stood with his back to her as he filled his pipe with fingers unusually clumsy. "Oh, I've tried! They've been at me for weeks—you probably guessed—and I've been back at them—letter after letter. It's no use! And yesterday father wrote that mother was really seriously upset." He turned round and spoke almost fiercely. "Don't you see I must go, Winnie?"

"Of course you must," she said again. "And I can't come if they—if they won't let me in!" She managed a smile. "It's all right. I'll have a walk by myself."

He tried to find a bright side to the situation. "I may have a better chance of convincing them, if I go. I'm no good at letters. And mother is very fond of me."

"Of course you must go," Winnie repeated yet again. What else was there for Winnie to say—with Mrs. Ledstone not strong and really seriously upset?

"I haven't seen any of them for—oh, it must be three months—and I used to go every Sunday when I was in town."

"Well, you're going to-day, dear. That's all settled!" She went up to him and kissed him daintily. "And we won't despair of them, will we? When do you go?"

"I—I generally used to go to lunch. They want me to. And come away after tea."

"Well, do just what you used to. I hope I shall be doing it with you in a few weeks."

"Oh, I hope so, dearest."

He had not the glimmer of such a hope. To ask him if he had even the wish would have been to put an awkward question. The code wherein he was Bob Purnett's pupil recognizes quite a strict division of life into compartments. He was Winnie's lover of a certainty; quite doubtfully was he her convert. Being her lover was to break the law; being her convert was to deny it. Before he met her he had been of the people who always contemplate conforming to the law—some day; at the proper time of life, or at the proper time before death—whichever may be the more accurate way of putting it. He was ready to say to the Tribunal, "I have done wrong"—but not to say, "You—or your interpreters—have been wrong." A very ordinary man was Godfrey Ledstone.

So, after a solitary lunch (a sausage left cold from breakfast and a pot of tea), Winnie started on a solitary expedition. She took the train from Baron's Court to Hyde Park Corner, with the idea of enjoying the "autumn tints" along by Rotten Row and the Serpentine. But, as she walked, her thoughts were not so much on autumn tints as on Woburn Square—on that family so nearly related to her life, yet so unspeakably remote, to whom she was worse than a menace—she was a present and active curse—who to her were something wrong-headed, almost ridiculous, yet intensely formidable—really the concrete embodiment of all she had to struggle against, the thing through which the great world would most probably hit at her, wound her, and kill her if it could. And both the family and Winnie thought themselves so absolutely, so demonstrably, right! Right or wrong, she knew very well, as she walked on toward the Serpentine, that now—this instant—in Woburn Square they were trying to get her man away from her; to make him ashamed of her (he had sworn never to be), to make him throw her over, to leave her stranded, to the ridicule and ruin of her experiment. With a sudden catch in the breath she added, "And the breaking of my heart!"

Just as she came near to the lake she saw—among the walkers who had till now seemed insubstantial shades to her preoccupied mind—a familiar figure, Hobart Gaynor! Her heart leaped in sudden joy; here was an old, a sympathetic friend, the man who understood why she had done what she had. But Hobart Gaynor was not alone. His radiant and self-satisfied demeanor was justified by the fair comeliness of the girl who walked beside him—his bride, wedded to him a month ago, Cicely Marshfield. Winnie had sent him congratulations, good wishes, and a present; all of which had been cordially acknowledged in a letter written three days before the wedding. The ceremony had taken place in the country, and quietly (because of an aunt's death); no question had arisen as to who was or was not to be asked to attend it.

Her heart went out to Hobart. He had loved her; she had always been very fond of him. In her drab, uneventful girlhood he had provided patches of enjoyment; in that awful married life he had now and then been a refuge. She did not know Cicely, but Hobart would surely have chosen a nice girl, one who would be a friend, who would understand it all, who could be talked to about it all? With a happy smile and a pretty blush she met Hobart and his bride Cicely. She saw him speak to her, a quick, hurried word. Cicely replied—Winnie saw the rapid turn of her head and the movement of her lips. He spoke once more—just as Winnie nodded and smiled at him and he was raising his hand to his hat. Then came the encounter. But, before it was fairly begun, Winnie's heart was turned to lead. Hobart's face was flushed; his hand came out to hers in a stiff reluctance. The tall, fair girl stood so tall, so erect, looking down, bowing, not putting out a hand at all, ignoring a pathetically comic appeal in her embarrassed husband's eyes.

Winnie's eager words of congratulation, of cordiality and friendship, met with a chilly "Thank you," uttered under an obvious protest, under *force majeure*. Winnie set her eyes on Hobart's, but his were turned away; a rigid smile on his lips paid a ghastly tribute to courtesy.

Winnie carried the thing through as briefly as possible. She was not slow to take a cue.

"Well, I'm glad to have run across you," she said, "and when you're settled in, I must come and see you. You won't want to be bothered just yet."

Again Hobart's glance appealed desperately to his wife. But his wife left the answer to him.

"We are a bit chaotic still," he stumbled. "But soon, I hope, Winnie—"

"I'll give you notice. Don't be afraid! Now I must hurry on—good-bye."

"Good-bye," said Cicely, with another inclination of her head—it seemed so high above Winnie's, looking down from such an altitude.

"Good-bye, Winnie." A kindliness, queerly ashamed of itself, struggled to expression in Hobart's voice.

When the pair had passed by—after a safe interval—Winnie turned and looked at their retreating figures, the haughty, erect girl, dear old Hobart's broad, solid back, somewhat bowed by much office-work. Winnie was smiling; it is sometimes the only thing to do.

"This isn't my lucky day." So she phrased her thoughts to herself, coupling together the encounter in Hyde Park with what was now—at this moment—going on in Woburn Square; for it was not yet tea-time, and Godfrey's visit would last, according to custom, till after tea.

She got home and waited for him in the dusk of the autumn evening. An apprehension possessed her; she did not know how much effect Woburn Square might have had upon him. But he came in about six, cheerful, affectionate, unchanged. On the subject of his home-visit, however, he was rather reticent.

"They were all very kind — and I really don't think mother's any worse than usual. About her frail ordinary." He seemed inclined to dismiss the matter with this brief summary. "And what did you do with yourself?"

"I took the Tube up to the Park and had a walk." She paused. "I met Hobart and Cicely Gaynor."

"Oh, the happy pair! How were they flourishing?"

"They—well, they warned me off, Godfrey. At least, she did—and he had to follow suit, of course."

Godfrey had been helping himself to whiskey and soda-water; tumbler in hand, he walked across the studio and back again.

"Hobart's one of the very few people in the world I'm really fond of."

"Well, you know, Winnie, you wanted it this way. I assure you I don't find it altogether comfortable either." He emptied the tumbler in a long draught and set it down on the table.

She jumped up quickly, came to him, and clasped her arms round his neck; she could but just reach, for he was tall.

"And they've all been at me—and at you about me—in Woburn Square, too, I suppose?"

"On my honor, you weren't once mentioned the whole time, Winnie. They were all three just awfully kind, and glad to see me."

Winnie's face wore much the same smile as when she had regarded Cicely Gaynor's erect back in retreat from her.

"That was rather clever of them," she remarked. "Never to have mentioned me!"

"Are you being quite just?" He spoke gently and kissed her.

"No, dear," she said, and burst into tears. "How can I be just when they're trying to take you from me?"

"Neither they nor anybody else can do that."

And then—for a space again—she believed her lover and forgot the rest.

But on the Monday morning there came two mauve envelopes. Winnie was down first as it chanced, and this time she looked at the postmarks. Both bore the imprint "W. C.," clearly indicative of Bloomsbury. Winnie smiled, and proffered to herself an excuse for her detective investigation.

"You see, I thought one of them might be from Cicely Gaynor. I'm quite sure she uses mauve envelopes, too."

The world of propriety seemed to be draping itself in mauve—not, after all, a very cheerful color.

Godfrey came in, glanced at the two mauve envelopes, glanced across at Winnie, and put the envelopes in his pocket. After a silence, he remarked that the bacon was very good.

XI

AS autumn turned to winter, Godfrey's Sundays at Woburn Square firmly re-established themselves as a weekly custom. Winnie could hardly deny that in the circumstances of the case they constituted a fair compromise. Woburn Square had a right to its convictions, no less than had Shaylor's Patch; it was not for her to deny that, however narrow she thought the convictions; and it would be neither just nor kind in her, even if it proved possible, to separate Godfrey from his family. At all events, as the visits became regular, the mauve envelopes arrived less frequently; some consolation lay in that, as one sound buffet may be preferred to a hundred pinches. She tried to reconcile herself to finding her own amusements for Sunday, and Godfrey, in loyalty, perhaps in penitence, dedicated Saturday's half-holiday to her instead. Yet a weight was on her spirit; she feared the steady, unrelenting pressure of Woburn Square, of the family tie, the family atmosphere, Mrs. Ledstone's weak heart. In truth she had greater cause for fear than she knew, more enemies than she realized. There was her lover's native and deeply rooted way of looking at things, very different from the way into which she had forced or cajoled him. There was the fact that it was not always only the members of the family whom he met in Woburn Square.

AN UNMENTIONED NAME

In spite of Godfrey's absence and Hobart Gaynor's defection, Winnie was not without friends and distractions on
her Sundays. Sometimes Dick Dennehy would come, quite
unshaken in his disapproval, but firm also in his affection,
and openly scornful of Woburn Square. "You'd be bored
to death there," he told her. "And as for the principle of
the thing, if you can turn up your nose at the Church
Catholic, I should think you could turn it up at the Ledstone
family."

A reasonable proposition, perhaps, but not convincing to
Winnie. The Church Catholic did not take her lover away
from her every Sunday or fill her with fears about him.

Mrs. Lenoir would come sometimes, or bid Winnie to tea
with her. With the stateliness of her manner there was now
mingled a restrained pity. Winnie was to her a very
ignorant little woman, essaying a task meet only for much
stronger hands and needing a much higher courage—nay,
an audacity of which Winnie made no display. When her
first passion had worn off, what she had got and what she
had lost would come home to her. She was only too likely
to find that she had got nothing; and she had certainly lost
a great deal—for Mrs. Lenoir was inclined to make light of
Cyril Maxon's "crushing." She was quite clear that she
would not have been crushed, and thought the less of Winnie's powers of resistance. But, being a sensible woman,
she said nothing of all this—it was either too late or too soon.
Her view showed only in that hint of compassion in her
manner—the pity of the wayworn traveller for the youth
who starts so blithely on his journey.

Winnie found consolation and pleasure in discussing her
affairs with both of these friends. Another visitor afforded
her a healthy relief from the subject. Godfrey had brought

113

Bob Purnett to the studio one day. His first visit was by no means his last. His working season had set in; he hunted five days a week; but it was his custom to get back to town on Saturday evening and to spend Sunday there. So it fell out, naturally and of no malice aforethought, that his calls generally happened on Sunday afternoons, when Godfrey was away; sometimes he would stay on and share their simple supper, often he would take the pair out to dinner at a restaurant, and perhaps come back again with them—to talk and smoke, and so go home, sober, orderly, and in good time—ready for the morrow's work.

Winnie and he were wholesome for each other. She forgot her theories; he kept better company than was his wont. They became good comrades and great friends. Godfrey was delighted; his absences on Sunday seemed in a way condoned; he was not haunted by the picture of a lonely Winnie. He ceased to accuse himself because he enjoyed being in Woburn Square, and therefore enjoyed it the more and the more freely. To be glad your lover can be happy in your absence is a good and generous emotion—whether characteristic of the zenith of passion is another question.

Accustomed rather to lavishness than to a thrifty refinement, Bob marvelled at the daintiness of Winnie's humble establishment. He admired—and in his turn pitied. His friend's circumstances were no secret to him.

"I wonder how you do it!" he would exclaim. "Do you have to work awfully hard ?"

"Well, it sometimes seems hard, because I didn't used to have to do it. In fact, I used to be scolded if I did do it." She laughed. "I'm not pretending to like being poor."

"But you took it on fast enough, Mrs. Ledstone. You knew, I mean ?"

"Oh yes, I knew, and I took it on, as you call it. So I don't complain."

"I tell you what—some day you and Godfrey must come for a spree with me. Go to Monte Carlo or somewhere, and have a high old time!"

"I don't believe I should like Monte Carlo a bit."

"Not like it ? Oh, I say, I bet you would."

"I suppose it's prejudice to condemn even Monte Carlo without seeing it. Perhaps we shall manage to go some day. I think Godfrey would like it."

"Oh, I took him once, all right, with—with some other friends."

"And all you men gambled like anything, I suppose ?"

"Yes, we did a bit." Bob was inwardly amused at her assumption of the nature of the party—amused, yet arrested by a sudden interest, a respect, and a touch of Mrs. Lenoir's pity. If there had been only himself to confess about, he would have confessed.

"You want keeping in order, Mr. Purnett," she said, smiling. "You ought to marry, and be obliged to spend your money on your wife."

She puzzled Bob. Because here she was, not married herself! He could not get away from that rigid and logical division of his—and of many other people's, such as Dennehy and the like.

"I'm not a marrying man. Heaven help the woman who married me!" he said, in whimsical sincerity.

She saw the sincerity and met it with a plump "Why ?"

Bob was not good at analysis—of himself or other people

(though he was making a rudimentary effort over Winnie).
"The way a chap's built, I suppose."

"What a very conclusive sort of argument!" she laughed.
"How's Godfrey built, Mr. Purnett?"

"Godfrey's all right. He'd settle down if he ever got
married."

The theories came tumbling in through the open door.
Cowardly theories, had they refused an opening like that!

"Well, isn't he?" asked Winnie, with dangerously rising
color.

Bob Purnett was a picture of shame and confusion.

"I could bite my tongue out, Mrs. Ledstone—hang it!
you don't think I'm—er—what you'd call an interfering
chap? It's nothing to me how my friends choose to—to
settle matters between themselves. Fact is, I just wasn't
thinking. Of course you're right. He—well, he feels himself married all right. And so he is married all right—don't
you know? It's what a chap feels in the end, isn't it? Yes,
that's right, of course."

The poor man was terribly flustered. Yet behind all his
aghastness at his blunder, at the back of his overpowering
penitence, lay the obstinate question—could she really think
it made no difference? No difference to a man like Godfrey Ledstone, whom he knew so well? Submerged by his
remorse for having hurt her, yet the question lay there in the
bottom of his mind. People neither regular nor irregular,
people shifting the boundaries (really so well settled!)—
how puzzling they were! What traps they laid for the
heedless conversationalist, for the traditional moralist—or
immoralist!

"Oh, I don't expect you to understand!" Winnie exclaimed, petulantly. "I wonder you come here!"

"Wonder I come here! Good Lord!" He reflected on some other places he had been to—and meant to go to again, perhaps.

"You're a hopeless person, but you're very kind and nice." The color faded gradually and Winnie smiled again, rather tremulously. "We won't talk about that any more. Tell me how the chestnut mare shapes?"

Yet when she heard about the mare, she seemed no more than passably interested, and for once Bob was tongue-tied on the only subject about which he was wont to be eloquent. He could not forgive himself for his hideous, inexplicable slip; because he had sworn to himself always to remember that Mrs. Ledstone thought herself as good as married. But so from time to time do our habits of thought trip up our fair resolutions; a man cannot always remember to say what he does not think, essential as the accomplishment is in society.

Winnie regained her own serenity, but could not restore his. She saw it, and in pity offered no opposition when he rose to go. But she was gracious, accompanying him to the door, and opening it for him herself. He had just shaken hands and put on his hat, when he exclaimed in a surprised tone, "Hullo, who's that?"

The studio stood a little back from the street; a small flagged forecourt gave access to it; the entrance was narrow, and a house projected on either side. To a stranger the place was not immediately easy to identify. Just opposite to it now there stood a woman, looking about her, as though in doubt. When the door opened and the light of the hall gas-jet streamed out, she came quickly through the gate of the forecourt and up to the house.

Bob Purnett emitted only the ghost of a whistle, but

Winnie heard it and looked quickly at him. There was no time to speak before the visitor came up.

"Is this Mrs. Godfrey Ledstone's?" she began. Then, with a touch of surprise, she broke off, exclaiming, "Oh, you, Mr. Purnett!" It was not surprise that he should be there at all, but merely that she should chance to come when he was there.

"Yes, er—how are you?" said Bob. "I—I'm just going."

"If you know this lady, you can introduce me," Winnie suggested, smiling. "Though I'm afraid I'm receiving you rather informally," she added to the visitor. "I'm Mrs. Ledstone."

"Yes," said the visitor. She turned quickly on Bob. "Mr. Purnett, please say nothing about this to—to Godfrey."

"It's his sister." Bob effected the introduction as briefly as possible, and also as awkwardly.

"They don't know I've come, you see." Amy Ledstone spoke jerkily.

"Oh, that's all right, Miss Ledstone. Of course, I'm safe." He looked desperately at Winnie. "I—I'd better be off."

"Yes, I think so. Good-bye. Do come in, Miss Ledstone." She laughed gently. "You've surprised us both, but I'm very glad to see you, even though they don't know you've come. Good-bye again, Mr. Purnett."

She stood aside while Amy Ledstone entered the house, then slowly shut the door, smiling the while at Bob Purnett. After the door was shut, he stood where he was for several seconds, then moved off with a portentous shake of his head. He was amazed almost out of his senses. Godfrey's sister! Coming secretly! What for? More confusion of boundaries! He thought that he really had known Woburn Square better than this. The memory of his terrible slip, five minutes before so mercilessly acute, was engulfed in a flood of astonishment. He shook his head at intervals all the evening, till his companion at dinner inquired, with mock solicitude, where he had contracted St. Vitus's dance, and was it catching.

Amy Ledstone was in high excitement. She breathed quickly as she sat down in the chair Winnie wheeled forward. Winnie herself stood opposite her visitor, very still, smiling faintly.

"I came here to-day because I knew Godfrey wouldn't be here. Please don't tell him I came. He won't be back yet, will he ?"

"Not for an hour later than this, as a rule."

"I left him in Woburn Square, you know."

Winnie nodded.

"And made my way here."

"From what you say, I don't suppose you've come just to call on me, Miss Ledstone ?"

"No." She paused, then with a sort of effort brought out, "But I have been wanting to know you. Well, I'd heard about you, and—but it's not that."

"Please don't be agitated or distressed. And there's no hurry."

"I wonder if you know anything of what daddy—my father—and mother are doing—of what's going on at home—in Woburn Square ?"

"I suppose I can make a guess at it." She smiled. "First the letters, then the visits! Didn't you write any of the letters ?"

"Yes—some." She stirred restlessly. "Why shouldn't I ?"

119

"I haven't blamed you. No doubt it's natural you should. But then—why come here, Miss Ledstone ?"

"How pretty you are!" Her eyes were fixed intently on Winnie's face. "Oh, it's not fair, not fair! It's not fair to — to anybody, I think. Do you know, your name's never mentioned at home — never — not even when we're alone ?"

"That part of it is done in the letters, I suppose ? What am I called ? The entanglement, or the lamentable state of affairs—or what ? I don't know, you see. If you don't talk about me, we don't talk much about you here, either."

"Oh, well, it is—bad. But that's not what I meant—not all I meant, at least." She suddenly leaned forward in her chair. "Does Godfrey ever talk of the people he meets besides ourselves ?"

"No, never. I shouldn't know anything about them, should I ?"

"Has he ever mentioned Mabel Thurseley ?"

"Mabel Thurseley ? No. Who is she ?"

"They live near us—in Torrington Square. Her mother's a widow, an old friend of ours."

"No, Godfrey has never said anything about Miss Thurseley."

"She's rather pretty—not very, I think. They're comfortably off. I mean, as we think it. Not what you'd call rich, I suppose." She was remembering Mrs. Maxon.

"My idea of riches nowadays isn't extravagant. But please tell me why you're talking to me about Miss Thurseley. Did you come here to do that ?"

"Yes, I did. You're never mentioned to her, either. That's it."

Winnie had never moved through the talk. Her slim
figure, clad in close-clinging black, was outlined against the
gray wall of the studio.

"Oh, that's it! I see."

"So I had to come. Because how is it right? How is it
decent, Mrs. Maxon?"

Winnie let the name pass—indeed, hardly noticed it.
"Wouldn't your ideas be considered rather eccentric?" she
asked, with a smile.

"Oh, I feel—I don't have ideas," murmured Amy Ledstone.

"In your home I'm considered the thing that exists but
isn't talked about—that's done and got over."

Again Amy's fixed gaze was on her companion. "Yes,"
she said, more than half assenting to Winnie's description
of herself, yet with a doubt whether "thing" were wholly
the word, whether, if "thing" were not the word, the home
doctrine could be altogether right.

"What about her, then?" she went on.

"What about—"

"Why, Mabel—Mabel Thurseley."

"Oh yes! Well, I suppose she—she knows what everybody knows—she knows what often happens."

"Oh, but while it's absolutely going on here! They
might have waited a little, at all events."

"You mean that—it's happening?"

Amy's figure rose erect in her chair again.

"Try and see if you can get him to utter Mabel's name to
you!"

Winnie was struck with the suggestion. Her interest in
her visitor suddenly became less derivative, more personal.
She looked at Amy's passably well-favored features and

robust physique. There was really nothing about her to suggest eccentric ideas.

"Oh, do please sit down! Don't stand there as if you were turned to stone!" Amy's appeal was almost a wail. The slim figure was so motionless; it seemed arrested in its very life.

"I like you. It's very kind of you. I—I'm trying to think. . . . I can't take your word for it, you know. I love him—I trust him."

Amy fidgeted again uncomfortably. "Daddy and mother are always at him. They think it—it will be redemption for him, you see."

"Yes, I suppose they do—redemption!" Suddenly she moved, taking two steps nearer to Amy, so that she stood almost over her. "And you think—?"

Amy looked up at her, with tears in her eyes. "Oh, I don't know! What am I to think? Why did you do it? Why did you make everything impossible either way? Somebody must be miserable now!"

"Somebody was miserable before—I was. And I've been happy for a bit. That's something. It seems to me only one person need be miserable even now. Why is that worse?"

The clock struck six. Amy started to her feet in alarm.

"He might come back a little sooner than usual—we finish tea about half-past five. By the Tube—" She was nervously buttoning her jacket. "If he caught me!" she murmured.

"Caught you here?"

"Oh, how can I go against them? I'm not married—I have to live there."

Winnie stretched out her thin arms. "Would you be

with me if you could ? Would you, Amy ? I had such a bad time of it! And he was mine first, you know."

Amy drew back ever so little. "Don't!" she gasped. "I really must go, Mrs.—oh, I really must go!"

"Yes, you must go. He might come back soon now. Shall we ever meet again, I wonder ?"

. "Oh, why did you ?"

"It's not what I did. It's what you think about it."

"Because you seem to me wonderful. You're—you're so much above him, you know."

"That doesn't help, even if it's true. I should hate to believe it."

"Good-bye. You won't let anybody know I came ? Oh, not Godfrey ?"

"You may trust me—and Mr. Purnett, too, I think."

"Oh yes; I can trust him. Good-bye!"

Without offering her hand, far less with any suggestion of a more emotional farewell, Amy Ledstone drifted toward the door. This time Winnie did not escort or follow her guest. She stood still, watching her departure. She really did not know what to say to her; Amy's attitude was so balanced— or, rather, not balanced, but confused. Yet just before the guest disappeared she found herself calling out: "I am grateful, you know. Because thinking as you do about me—"

Amy turned her head for a moment. "Yes, but I don't know that you'll come worst out of it, after all," she said.

Then Winnie was left alone, to wait for Godfrey—and to see whether he would make mention of Mabel Thurseley's name, that entirely new and formidably significant phenomenon.

XII

CHRISTMAS IN WOBURN SQUARE

WHEN holiday seasons approach, people of ample means ask, "Where shall we go?"; people of narrow, "Can we go anywhere?" The imminence of Christmas made Winnie realize this difference (no question now, as in days gone by, of Palestine and Damascus); but the edge of it was turned by a cordial invitation to spend Friday till Tuesday (Saturday was Christmas Day) at Shaylor's Patch. Her eyes brightened; her old refuge again looked peaceful and comforting. She joyfully laid the proposal before God-frey. He was less delighted; he looked rather vexed, even a little sheepish.

"They do jaw so," he objected. "Arguing about everything night and day! It bores a chap."

"You weren't bored when you were there in the summer."

"Oh, well, that was different. And I'm afraid mother will be disappointed."

"About the Sunday, you mean? Mightn't you run up for the day?"

He laid his hand on her shoulder. "I say, I leave it to you, Winnie. I leave it absolutely to you—but mother's set her heart on my spending Christmas with them. I've never missed a Christmas all my life, and—well, she's not very well, and has a fancy about it, you see."

CHRISTMAS IN WOBURN SQUARE

"Do it, of course, Godfrey. And come down to me on Sunday." Winnie was now determined that Woburn Square should have no grievances except the great, inevitable, insuperable one.

"You are a good sort, Winnie." He kissed her cheek.

"But I don't know how you'll shift for yourself here!"

"Oh, I'll put up in Woburn Square for a couple of nights, and do a theatre on Friday perhaps."

So it was settled, with some embarrassment on Godfrey's part, with a faint smile on Winnie's. He would have two nights and a whole day at Woburn Square; and he had never mentioned Mabel Thurseley's name, not even though Winnie had made openings for him, had tried some delicate "pumping." And with whom did he think of "doing a theatre" on Friday night?

Godfrey Ledstone—with whom everything was to have been straightforward, all aboveboard—found himself burdened with a double secret. He couldn't bring himself to tell Winnie of Mabel Thurseley. In the early days of his renewed intercourse with Mabel, he had half-heartedly proposed to his mother that the girl should be informed of his position; he had been tearfully prayed not to advertise the shame of his family. He had lost any sort of desire to advertise it now. He could not now imagine himself speaking of the matter to Mabel—telling her, right out, that he was living and meant to live with a woman who was not his wife in law; wives of any other sort were so entirely outside Mabel's purview. That he had been a bit of a rake—she would understand that, and perhaps in her heart not dislike it; but she would not understand and would thoroughly dislike Winnie Maxon. Anyhow, by now it was too late; he had played the bachelor too long—and, as a flattering, if

125

remorseful, inner voice whispered, too successfully—on those Sundays in Woburn Square, whither Mabel often came, whence it was easy to slip across to Torrington Square. Mr. and Mrs. Ledstone never grudged him an hour's leave of absence if it was spent in calling on Mrs. Thurseley, their esteemed friend and neighbor.

It was not that he had conceived any passionate love for Mabel. An amiable, steady, rather colorless girl, and (as Amy Ledstone said) not very pretty, she was hardly likely to engender that. He had not for her—and probably never could have—the torrent of feeling which carried him off his feet at Shaylor's Patch, and made him dare everything because of Winnie's bidding. And he was still very fond of Winnie herself. But the pull of the world—of his old world —was strong upon him; Mabel embodied it. Bob Purnett had been right about him; in his scheme of life, after the gayeties of youth, came "settling down." And when it came to seeing things as they were, when the blurring mists of passion lifted, he found it impossible to feel that life with Winnie was settling down at all. Life with Winnie—was that being settled, tranquil, serene, ready to look anybody in the face? No, it was still to be irregular, to have secrets, to be unable to tell people with whom you spent your time. It was neither one thing nor the other; it was the bond, without the guerdon, of service; it was defiance without the pleasures of lawlessness.

Covertly, persistently, let it in justice be added lovingly, his mother and father worked upon him. The old pair showed diplomacy; they made no direct attack on Winnie nor upon his present mode of life; they only tried to let him see what a much pleasanter mode of life was open to him, and what joy he would give those who loved him best in the world if only he would adopt it. Bringing gray hairs with sorrow to the grave—not a pleasant thing for a son to feel that he is doing! Without scruple they used Mabel Thurseley in their game; without scruple they risked the girl's happiness; their duty, as they saw it, was to their son, and they thought of him only. Mabel had no throng of suitors and none of the arts of a coquette. The good-looking young man soon made his impression, and soon perceived that he had made it. All looked easy, and this time really straightforward. It was a powerful assault to which he exposed himself when he once again began to frequent Woburn Square.

Amy Ledstone looked on, irritable, fretful, in scorn of herself, calling herself a traitor for having told Winnie of Mabel, and a coward for not daring to tell Mabel about Winnie. But she dared not. A lifelong habit of obedience, a lifelong custom of accepting parental wisdom even when she chafed under it, the tyranny of that weak heart, were too much for her. She lacked the courage to break away, to upset the family scheme. And to work actively for Winnie was surely a fearful responsibility, however strongly she might pity her. To work for Winnie was, in the end, to range herself on the side of immorality. Let Winnie work for herself! She was warned now—that was enough and more than enough. Yet Amy's sympathy made her cold and irritable to her brother. He misconstrued the cause of her attitude, setting it down to a violent disapproval of Winnie and a championship of Mabel Thurseley. The old people petted, Amy kept him at arm's-length, but to Godfrey their end and purpose seemed to be the same.

"Winnie doesn't realize what I go through for her," he often thought to himself, when his sister was cross, when his

mother said good-bye to him with tears in her eyes, when his
father wrung his hand in expressive silence, when he man-
fully made himself less agreeable than he knew how to be to
Mabel Thurseley.

Yet—and the fact was significant—in spite of all, it was
with a holiday feeling that, after seeing Winnie off to Shaylor's Patch, he packed his bag and repaired home—he
thought of Woburn Square as home. He was greeted with
great joy.

"Fancy having you with us for two whole days!" said his
mother.

"Like old times!" exclaimed his father, beaming with
smiles on the hearth-rug.

The theatre had been arranged for. Mrs. Ledstone's
health forbade her being a member of the party, but Mr.
Ledstone was ready for an outing. Amy would go; and
Mabel Thurseley had been invited to complete the quartette. Amy looked after her father, to Godfrey fell the duty
of squiring Miss Thurseley. They had good seats in the
dress-circle; Mr. Ledstone, Amy, Mabel, Godfrey—that
was the order of sitting. The play was a capital farce.
They all got into high spirits, even Amy forgetting to chide
herself and content to be happy. Mabel's life was not rich in
gayety; she responded to its stimulus readily. Her cheeks
glowed, her eyes grew bright and challenging. She made
a new appeal to Godfrey.

"I can't let her think me a fool." So he excused his attentions and his pleasure in them.

"I suppose you go a lot to the theatre, don't you ?" she
asked. "I expect you're *blasé !*"

"No, I don't go much."

"Why not ? Don't you care about going alone ?"

"Now why do you assume I need go alone?"

"No, of course you needn't! How silly of me! Do you ever take—ladies?" She was roguish over this question.

"Yes, now and then."

"Mamma wouldn't let me go alone with a man."

"Oh, we don't ask mamma. We just go."

"Do you go out somewhere every evening?"

"Oh no. I often stay at home, and read—or work."

He had said nothing untrue, but it was all one big lie, what he was saying—a colossal misrepresentation of his present life. The picture his last answer raised in her mind —the man alone in his lonely room, reading or working! Poor man, all alone!

"We girls get into the way of thinking that bachelors are always gay, but I suppose they're not?"

"Indeed they're not." Godfrey's answer was decisive and rather grim.

"Or else," she laughed, "they'd never want to marry, would they?"

"Anyhow, one gets tired of gayety and wants something better." His eyes rested on hers for a moment. She blushed a little; and the curtain rose on the second act.

"How your mother adores you!" she began at the next interval. "She'd die for you, I think. She says you're the best son in the world, and have never given her any trouble."

Godfrey's conscience suffered a twinge—no less for his mother than for himself.

"I'm afraid mothers don't know all about their sons, always."

"No, I suppose not. But there are some people you know you can trust."

129

"Come, I say, you're making me out too perfect by half!"
She laughed. "Oh, I don't accuse you of being a milk-
sop. I don't like milksops, Mr. Godfrey."

So she went on, innocently showing her interest and her
preference, and in the process making Godfrey feel that his
family and himself were accomplices in a great and heinous
conspiracy. But there was still time to get out of it, to put
an end to it. There were two ways out of it, just two and
no more, thought Godfrey. Either she must be told, or
there must cease to be anything to tell her.

But the sternest moralist would hardly demand that
momentous decisions and heartrending avowals should be
made on Christmas Day. That surely is a close time? So
thought Godfrey Ledstone, and, the religious observances
of the day having been honored by all the family, the rest
of it passed merrily in Woburn Square. The Thurseleys,
mother and daughter, came to spend the afternoon, and
came again to dinner.

"So good of you to take pity on us," said Mrs. Thurseley,
a soft-voiced, pleasant woman, who was placid and restful
and said the right thing. She would make an excellent
mother-in-law—for some man.

Like the old-fashioned folk they were, they had a snap-
dragon and plenty of mistletoe and plenty of the usual jokes
about both. As there was nobody else on whom the jokes
could plausibly be fastened (Mr. Ledstone's reminiscences
of his own courting tended toward the sentimental, while
the subject was, of course, too tender in widowed Mrs.
Thurseley's case), they were naturally pointed at Mabel
and Godfrey. Mabel laughed and blushed. Really, Godfrey had to play his part; he could not look a fool, who did
not know how to flirt. He ended by flirting pretty hard.

He had his reward in the beams of the whole circle—except Amy. She seemed rather out of humor that Christmas; she pleaded a headache for excuse. When Mrs. Ledstone said good-night to her son she embraced him with agitated affection and whispered, "I feel happier than I've done for a long while, Godfrey, darling."

This was the pressure, the assault, of love—love urgent and now grown hopeful. But his Christmas was not to end on that note. There was also the pressure of disapproval and of scorn. Neither was easy to bear to a disposition at once affectionate and pliable.

The old people went to bed. Amy stayed, watching her brother light his pipe.

"Not going to bed, Amy? One pipe, and I'm off!"

"What do you think you're doing?"

He turned from the fire, smiling in his disarming way. "I've known all the evening I was going to catch it from you, Amy. I saw it in your eye. But what can a fellow do? He must play up a bit. I haven't actually said anything."

"What does Mabel think?" There was a formidable directness about her. But he had his answer, his defence to what he supposed to be the whole indictment.

"Come now, be fair. I wanted to tell her—well, I wanted her to have a hint given her. I told the mater so, but the mater wouldn't hear of it. The bare idea sent her all—well, absolutely upset her."

The events of the day and the two evenings had affected Amy Ledstone.

"You wanted to tell her? Her? Which?"

"Good Lord, Amy!" He was knocked out. What a question to be asked in Woburn Square! "Which?" Had they both rights? Strange doctrine, indeed, for Woburn Square.

"I was speaking of Miss Thurseley, and I think you knew it."

"Oh, I knew it."

"Anything else isn't your business at all. I never understood why the pater told you."

"There are just two decent things for you to do, Godfrey—let Mabel alone or drop Mrs. Maxon."

His own feelings, most concisely put, most trenchantly interpreted! His vague consciousness that the thing came to that was crystallized into an ultimatum. Against this he could not maintain his peevish resentment at his sister's interference or his assumed prudishness over her talking about Winnie. The pretext of shame would not serve, and his weak nature turned for help to a stronger. She was sitting by the table, rigid, looking straight before her. He sat down by her, laying his pipe on the table.

"By Jove, you're right! I'm in an awful mess. Which is it to be, Amy?"

"Oh, that's not my business. But you needn't be a sneak to both of them, need you?"

He laid his hand on hers, but she drew hers away sharply. "You don't understand how I was led into it. I say, you're not going to—to give me away to Mabel, are you?"

"No. I'm afraid of father and mother. I believe I ought to, but I daren't."

"I say, above all things, for Heaven's sake, don't think of that!"

"But you say you proposed it yourself, Godfrey."

He jumped up from his chair in an agony of restlessness. He had proposed it, but only as a thing to be rejected. He had proposed it, but that was weeks ago—when he had not been coming to Woburn Square for very long, and had not seen so much of Mabel Thurseley. The idea seemed quite different now. He stared ruefully at Amy. His entreaty, her reply, threw a cold, cruel light on the recent workings of his mind. He saw now where he was going, where he was being led and driven, by love, by scorn, by the world he had been persuaded to think himself strong enough to defy—his world, which had only one name for Winnie Maxon.

He was exasperated. Why did the two things rend him asunder, like wild horses?

"Well, what is it to be, Amy?" he asked again.

The maiden sister sat unmoved in her chair, her eyes set on the ugly brown paper on the wall opposite. Her voice came level, unimpassioned, with a suggestion of dull despair.

"What's the good of asking me, Godfrey? What do I know about it? Nobody has ever loved me. I've never even been in love myself. I don't know what people do when they're in love. I don't know how they feel. I suppose I've been awfully unkind to you?"

"Well, of course, a fellow isn't himself." He turned sharp round on her. "It was only to last as long as we both wanted—as long as we both wanted each other. Oh, Lord, how can I talk about it, even to you?"

"You needn't mind that. I've seen her. I went to see her. I asked her if she knew anything about Mabel. She didn't. Does she now? I think her wonderful. Miles above you or me, really. Oh, I know she's—she's whatever daddy and mother would choose to call her. But you made her that—and you might as well play fair, Godfrey."

"I don't understand you, Amy. I thought you—of all people— How in the world did you come to go and see her? When?"

"One Sunday, when I knew you were here."

"She never said a word to me about—about Mabel Thurseley."

"She never would. I'm not taking her part. But I should like my brother to be a man."

"She's never told me that you came. I can't understand your going."

He was opposite to her now. She raised her eyes to his, smiling bitterly.

"Don't try. Still, she's a woman, and my brother's— friend."

"Oh, you don't know a thing about it!"

"I said so. I know it. That's how it is with girls like me. Girls! Oh, well! If I did know, I might be able to help. I'm not your enemy, really, Godfrey."

"Everybody makes it fearfully hard for me. I—I want to keep faith, Amy."

"You're not doing it."

He threw himself into the big arm-chair that flanked the grate and its dying fire. He broke out against Winnie in a feeble peevishness: "Why did she make me do it? Any fool could have seen it would never work!"

"You needn't have done it," she retorted, mercilessly.

"Needn't have done it? Oh, you don't know anything about it, as you say. What could you know? If you did know, you'd understand how men—yes, and by George, women too—do things. Things they can't stand by, and yet want to, things that are impossible, and yet have been done and have to be reckoned with. That's the way it happens."

Full of despair, his voice had a new note of sincerity. Amy looked across the table at him with a long, scrutinizing gaze.

"I expect I haven't allowed for all of it," she said at last. "I expect I don't know how difficult it is." She rose, moved round the table, and sat on the arm of the big chair beside him. "I'm sorry if I've been unkind, dear. But"— she caressed his hair—"don't be unkind to her—not more than you can help."

"To Mabel?" He was looking up to her now, and whispering.

"Oh no," she smiled. "You're going to marry Mabel. You aren't married to Mrs. Maxon, you see." She kissed his brow. "Make it as easy as you can for Winnie."

"By God, I love Winnie!"

Again her hand smoothed and caressed his hair. "Yes, but you can't do it," she said. "I don't think I could. But mightn't you tell her you can't? She's got more courage than you think, Godfrey." She rose to her feet, rather abruptly. "You see, when she knows the truth about you, she won't care so much, perhaps."

Her brother made her no answer; he lay back in the big chair, staring at the dead fire. Nor did she seem to have any more to say to him. She had said a good deal in the whole conversation, and had summed up a large part of it in her last sentence. When Winnie knew all about him she might not care so much! Was that true—or was it the judgment of the maiden sister, who thought that love was dependent on esteem?

"I'm going to bed. I've been a wet blanket this Christmas, Godfrey."

"My Lord, what a Christmas!"

MRS. MAXON PROTESTS

For the capital farce and the merry dinner, the snap-dragon, mistletoe, and jokes were all forgotten. The woman who knew nothing about the matter had set the matter in its true light. With another kiss, a half-articulate "My dear!" and a sudden sob, she left him to the contemplation of it.

XIII

CHRISTMAS AT SHAYLOR'S PATCH

ON Christmas Eve Winnie had regained her old haven at Shaylor's Patch. It seemed as restful and peaceful as ever, nay, even to an unusual degree, for the only other guest was Dennehy, and Dennehy and Alice (again home for holidays) exercised some restraining force on sceptical argument. Both father and mother were intent on giving the child " a good time," and Stephen at least could throw himself into a game with just as much zest as into a dispute or a speculation. Here, too, were holly and mistletoe, and, if not a snapdragon, yet a Christmas-tree and a fine array of presents, carefully hidden till the morrow. As they had preceded the faith, so the old observances survived all doubts about it.

But though the haven was the same, the mariner was in a different case. When she had come before, Shaylor's Patch had seemed the final end of a storm-tossed voyage; now it was but a harbor into which her bark put for a few hours in the course of a journey yet more arduous, a journey which had little more than begun; the most she could look for was a few hours of repose, a brief opportunity to rest and refit. Her relation toward her friends and hosts was changed, as it seemed to her, profoundly; she looked at Stephen and Tora Aikenhead with new eyes. The position between them

137

and her was to her feelings almost reversed. They were no longer the intrepid voyagers to whose stories her ignorance hearkened so admiringly. In ultimate truth, now newly apparent, they had made no voyages; from the safe recesses of the haven they did but talk about the perils of the uncharted sea. She was now the explorer; she was making the discoveries about which they only gossiped and speculated. She remembered Mrs. Lenoir's kindly yet half-contemptuous smile over Stephen's facile theories and easy assurance of his theories' easy triumph. She was not as Mrs. Lenoir by the difference of many years and much knowledge; for Mrs. Lenoir still had that same smile for her. None the less, something of the spirit of it was in her when she came the second time to Shaylor's Patch.

But she resolved to take her brief rest and be thankful for her respite. Tora's benignant calm, Stephen's boyish gayety, the simplicity of the child, Dennehy's loyal friendship—here were anodynes. For the moment nothing could be done; why, then, fret and worry about what to do? And if she spoke of or hinted at trouble, might it not seem to be in some sense like imputing a responsibility to her hosts? Yet she was asking much of herself in this resolve. She could hold her tongue, but she could not bind her thoughts.

In the morning Dennehy was off early on a five-mile walk to the nearest town to hear mass. The question of attending church Stephen referred to Alice's arbitrament; she decided in the affirmative.

"Whose turn?" asked Stephen of his wife.

"Mine," said Tora, with the nearest approach to an expression of discontent that Winnie had ever seen on her face.

Winnie stepped into the breach. "Oh, you look rather

138

tired, and we've a busy day before us! Let me take Alice."
So it was agreed, and Alice ran off to get ready.

"Do you always leave the question to her?"

"What else could we do? We say nothing against it,
but how could we force her?"

"She's forced at school, I suppose?"

"I don't think any doubts suggest themselves. It's just
part of the discipline. As a fact, I think the child's naturally religious. If so—" He waved his hands tolerantly.

Winnie laughed. "If so, she'll soon be rather shocked at
her parents."

"It's quite arguable, Winnie, that it's a good thing for
children to see their parents doing some things which they
would naturally think—or, at any rate, be taught to think—
wrong. They know by experience that the parents are, on
the whole, a decent sort—kind and so on—and they learn
not to condemn other people wholesale on the strength of
one or two doubtful or eccentric practices. Do you see what
I mean? It promotes breadth of view."

"I dare say it's arguable—most things are here—but I
won't argue it, or we shall be late for church."

When Godfrey Ledstone attended church with his family
on the same day, he went without any questioning, not conscious of any peculiarity in his attitude toward the Church,
though well aware of what the Church's attitude would be
toward him if its notice happened to be called to the facts.
What of that? One compromised with the Church just as
one compromised with the world; the code had provisions as
applicable to the one negotiation as to the other. He did
not go to church regularly, but, when he did, he took part
in the service with an untroubled gratification, if not with
any particular spiritual benefit. On this occasion he

achieved what was, considering the worries which oppressed him, a very creditable degree of attention.

Neither was Winnie—in the little church at Nether End—convicted of sin; after all, that is not the particular note sought to be struck by a Christmas service—the Church has its seasons. But she was overcome by an unnerving sense of insignificance. The sermon dwelt on the familiar, yet ever-striking, theme that all over the world, in well-nigh every tongue, this service was being held in honor of, and in gratitude for, the great Event of this day. That seemed a tremendous thing to stand up against. There is majesty in great organizations, be they spiritual or secular. Are insignificant atoms to flout them? Or can the argument from insignificance be turned, and the rebel plead that he is so small that it does not matter what he does? The organizations will not allow the plea. Insignificant as you are, they answer, little as your puny dissent affects us, yet it is of bad example, and if you persist in it we will, in our way, make you unhappy and uncomfortable. Now, mankind has been, in the course of its eventful history, from time to time convinced that many things do matter and that many do not, and opinions have varied and shall vary thereanent. But nobody has had any real success in convincing mankind that it does not matter whether it is happy or not—in the long-run. Mankind is obstinately of the contrary opinion.

At the church door Dennehy was waiting for her and Alice—his mass heard and ten good miles of country road behind him—spiritually and physically fortified. He was not handsome, but middle-age on its approach found him clean in wind and limb—temperate, kindly (outside politics), and really intensely happy.

"It's a concession for me to come as far as the door of this place," he said, smiling. Winnie glanced warningly at Alice. "You needn't mind her—the poor child hears everything! But it's my belief that Heaven has made her a fine old Tory, and they can't hurt her."

"You approving of Tories! Mr. Dennehy!" She turned to the child. "You liked it, Alice?"

"Didn't you hear me singing?" It seemed a good retort. Alice had sung lustily. She did not seem inclined to talk. She walked beside them in a demure and absent gravity. Over her head they looked at each other; the child was thinking of the story of the Child, and finding it not strange, but natural and beautiful, the greatest of all her beloved fairy stories—and yet true.

Dennehy gently patted Alice's shoulder. "In God's good time!" he murmured.

"What do you mean?" Winnie asked, in a low voice.

"True people will find truth, and sweet people do sweet things," he answered. Then he laughed and snapped his fingers. "And the divvle take the rest of humanity!"

"Everybody except the Irish, you mean?"

"I mustn't be supposed to let in Ulster," he warned her with a twinkle. "But there's an English soul or two I'd save, Mrs. Ledstone."

"I don't like your being false to your convictions. I've one name that I've not denied and that nobody denies me. It's Winnie."

"Winnie it shall be on my lips, too, henceforth," he answered. "And I thank you."

Respect for his convictions? Yes. But there was more behind her permission, her request. There was a great friendliness, and, with it, a new sense that "Mrs. Winifred

Ledstone" might prove to be a transitory being, that the title was held precariously. Why need her chosen friends be bound to the use of it?

Richard Dennehy was by now one of that small band. He was so loyal and sympathetic, though he was also very cocksure in his condemnations, and terribly certain that he and his organization alone had got hold of the right end of the stick. Yet the cocksureness was really for the organization only; it left him in himself a humble man, not thinking himself so clever as the emancipated persons among whom he moved, rather regretting that such able minds should be so led astray. One habit indeed he had, of which Stephen Aikenhead would humorously complain—he used emotion as an argumentative weapon. There are words and phrases which carry an appeal independent of the validity of the idea they express, a strength born of memory and association. They can make a man feel like a child again, or make him feel a traitor, and either against his reason.

"Spells and incantations I call them," said Stephen, "and I formally protest against their use in serious discussion."

"And why do you call them that?"

"Because they depend for their effect on a particular form of words—either a particularly familiar or a particularly beautiful formula. If you expressed the same idea in different language, its power would be gone; at least, it would seem just as legitimately open to question as any profane statement that I may happen to make. Now to depend for its efficacy on the exact formula and not on the force of the idea is, to my mind, the precise characteristic of a spell, charm, or incantation, Dick."

"I dare say the holy words make you uncomfortable, my boy!"

"Exactly! And is it fair? Why am I, a candid inquirer, to be made uncomfortable? Prove me wrong, convince me if you can, but why make me uncomfortable?"

Winnie, an auditor of the conversation, laughed gently. "I think that's what you tried to do to me, coming back from church—when you talked about 'God's good time,' I mean."

Dennehy scratched his head. "I don't do it on purpose. They just come to my lips. And who knows? It might be good for you!"

Alice ran in, announcing that it was time for the Christmas-tree. Even at Shaylor's Patch discussion languished for the rest of the day, and Winnie had her hours of respite.

Indeed, it was a matter of hours only; peace was not to endure for her even over the Sunday. Early in the morning the maid brought her a telegram from Godfrey Ledstone: "Caught slight chill. Think better not travel. Don't interrupt visit. Shall stay Woburn Square.—GODFREY."

It was significant of how far her mind had forecast probabilities that she brushed aside the excuse without a moment's hesitation. Does an hour's journey on a mild morning frighten a strong man if he really wants to go? At any rate, Winnie was not inclined to give Godfrey the benefit of that doubt. He did want to stay in Woburn Square, or he did not want to come to Shaylor's Patch. Whichever way it was put, it came to much the same thing. It was another defeat for her, another victory for the family. And for Mabel Thurseley? That, too, seemed very likely. Her heart quailed in grief and apprehension, as it looked into a future forlorn and desolate; but not for a moment did she think of giving up the struggle. Instead of that, she would fight more resolutely, more fiercely. This was not the common case of a variable man's affections straying from one woman to another. She knew that it was his courage which had failed first, and by its failure undermined the bastion of his love. He had been ashamed of her first; if he had now ceased—or begun to cease—to love her, it was because she made him ashamed before his family and friends, because she put him "in a false position" and made things awkward and uncomfortable. That he felt like that was in part—nay, largely—her own fault. Either from mistaken confidence or chivalry or scruple, or a mixture of the three, she had exposed him, unsupported, to the fullest assault of Woburn Square and of all it represented. She had been wrong; she should have stood on her rights and forbidden him to go there unless she were received also. At the beginning she could have done it; she ought to have done it. Was it too late to do it now?

She formed a plan of campaign. She would take him away, put the sea between him and his people, the sea between him and Mabel Thurseley. There was money in the till sufficient for a holiday. His very weakness, his responsiveness to his surroundings, favored success. He would recover his courage, and henceforward a ban should rest on his family till his family removed its ban from her.

There was no church for her that morning; she was not in the mood. Stephen had to go, since Tora sophistically maintained that she had attended by proxy the day before. Winnie strolled with Dick Dennehy, when he came back from his early expedition.

"It's funny we're such friends, when you think me so wicked," she said.

"You're not wicked, though you may do a wicked thing—through wrongheadedness."

"You can't understand that I look on myself as Godfrey's wife for all my life or his."

"Didn't you once think the same about Mr. Maxon?"

"Oh, you really are—!" Winnie laughed irritably.

"And you ran away from him. What happens if Master Godfrey runs away from you?"

Winnie glanced at him sharply. Rather odd that he should put that question! Was there any suspicion among her friends, any at Shaylor's Patch?

"Because," Dennehy continued, "you wouldn't go on from man to man, being married to each of 'em for life temporarily, would you?"

Winnie laughed, if reluctantly. But there is hardly anything that a ready disputant cannot turn to ridicule.

"How you try to pin people down!" she complained. "You and your principles! I know what I should like to see happen, Mr. Dennehy."

"Ah, now — 'Dick' — as a mere matter of fairness, Winnie!"

"Well, Dick, what I should just love to see is you in love with somebody who was married, or had been divorced, or something of that sort, and see how you'd like your principles yourself." She looked mischievous and very pretty.

Dennehy shook his head. "We're all miserable sinners. But I don't believe I'd do it."

"What, fall in love, or give way to it?"

"The latter. The former's out of any man's power, I think."

"What would you do?"

"Emigrate to America."

"Out of the frying-pan into the fire! It's full of divorced people, isn't it?"

"Not the best Irish society." He laughed. "Well, you're chaffing me."

"Oh no, I'm not. I'm serious. I should like to see the experiment. Dick, if Godfrey does run away, as you kindly suggest, give me a wide berth! Oh, is it quite impossible that, if I tried, I might—make you miserable ?"

"If you'll flirt with me after this fashion every time we meet, I'll not be miserable—I'll be very happy."

"Ah, but that's only the beginning! The beginning's always happy."

The sadness in her voice struck him. "You poor dear! You've had bad luck, and you've fallen among evil counsellors, in which term, Heaven forgive me, I include my dear friends here at Shaylor's Patch."

"I'll try your principles another way. If you were Godfrey, would you leave me—now ?"

He twisted his mustache and hesitated. "Well, there you have me," he admitted at last. "If a man does what he did, as a gentleman he must stand to be damned for it."

"Godfrey's free to go, of course—that's our bargain. But you wouldn't have made a bargain like that ?"

"I would not, Winnie. To do me justice, I believe I'd think it enough to be ruining one woman, without providing for my liberty to ruin another as soon as I wanted to."

Winnie laid her hand on his arm for a moment. "How pleasantly we quarrel!" she said.

"And why wouldn't we ?" he asked, with native surprise that a quarrel should be considered a thing inherently unpleasant. "Ah, here come Stephen and Alice, back from church! I'll go and run races with her, and get an appetite for lunch."

Stephen lounged up, his pipe in full blast.

"Stephen, how is it that this old world gets on at all, with everybody at loggerheads with everybody else ?"

"I've often considered that. The solution is economic—purely economic, Winnie. You see, people must eat."

"So far the Court is with you, Stephen."

"And in anything except a rudimentary state of society they must feed one another. Because no man has the genius to make for himself all the things he wants to eat. Consequently—I put the argument summarily—you will find that, broadly speaking, all the burning and bludgeoning and fighting, all the killing, in short, and equally all the refraining from killing, are in the end determined by the consideration whether your action one way or the other will seriously affect your supply of food—to which, in civilized society, you may add clothes, and so on."

"Does that apply to the persecution of opinions ?"

"Certainly it does—usually by way of limitation of killing, though an exception must be made for human sacrifice. There have been temporary aberrations of judgment, but, generally speaking, they never killed more than a decent minimum of any useful heretics—not, anyhow, where secular statesmen had the last word. They had to make some kind of a show, of course, to satisfy, as they supposed, their superior officers. Still — they left a good many Jews, Winnie!"

"Wasn't that the spread of toleration ?"

"Certainly — toleration based on food originally, and afterward perhaps reinforced by doubt." He broke into a laugh. "But even to-day I'm hanged if I'd trust to the doubt without the food!" He beamed on her. "I'll tell you a secret—religion's all food, Winnie."

Winnie had asked for the exposition—but she had had

enough of it. Even Stephen's last—and rather startling—thesis failed to draw further inquiries.

"It seems to follow that we oughtn't to keep lunch waiting," she said, laughing, as she put her arm through his. "I do love Shaylor's Patch," she went on, gently patting his arm. "You can always forget yourself and your troubles by talking nonsense—or sense—about something or other. If I come to grief again"—her voice shook for an instant—"you'll give me a shed to lie in here, won't you, Stephen?"

"My poor house is thine, and all that is in it," he answered, Orientally.

"Yes, in a way I know it is—and so I needn't quite starve," said Winnie.

XIV

TO Winnie's few but devoted adherents Cyril Maxon was not a man, but a monster, a type of tyranny, the embodied symbol of an intolerable servitude; even Dick Dennehy, stanch champion of the institution, had no charity for the individual. Needless to say that this was not at all the view Mr. Maxon took of himself, and not entirely the judgment which an impartial observer would form of him. There were many women with whom he might have got on very well, women of a submissive temper, meek women, limited women, sly women who hoodwinked under a show of perfect obedience. He would not have been hard to hoodwink, had Winnie been content to attack her problem in that old-fashioned way. Or, again, an extremely clever and diplomatic woman—but she can make a good husband out of the rawest of raw material, mere flesh and bone with (as Stephen Aikenhead would certainly have added) the economic prerequisite.

From the moment that his wife had identified herself with the Ledstone family—his memory of Mr. Ledstone was vivid and horrible—he had set aside the idea that she would soon "have had enough of it." It was no longer in his power to hold to that conclusion. Now it was he himself who had had more than enough of it. She was done with.

149

He took up his life alone. At first he sought to mitigate
solitude by constant work. It was not a complete success.
Then he installed an unmarried sister in his house. She was
his senior; her temper was akin to his; the experiment lasted
just a month, after which Miss Maxon returned to Broad-
stairs. Then gradually he began to seek society again, to
show his face at his old resorts, to meet the women who admired him, who gushed over him as interesting, clever, and
rising. They gushed still more now, hinting, each with what
degree of delicacy nature had given her, their sympathy with
him and their unlimited astonishment at the folly and perverseness of Mrs. Maxon. He found this the most effective
specific that he had tried.

It would be unpardonably rash to generalize, but it may
be hazarded that in some cases the man who treats his wife
worst misses her most. A comrade can perhaps be replaced,
a new slave is hard to come by. Besides, Cyril Maxon's
principles forbade the search for one, and now he had to
apply his principles to his own case. A year ago nothing in
the whole world would have seemed so unlikely—Fate at its
pranks again! It makes us pay for sins and principles alike
—perhaps the best way (with deference to the *à priori* philosophers) of learning to appraise either.

Cyril Maxon was very rising by now; people called him a
certainty for a judgeship in some ten years' time (he was
only thirty-eight); and the ladies were very sympathetic.
Several of them were members of Mr. Attlebury's congregation and the personal friends of that genial but exacting
apostle. Some of the ladies wondered how Mr. Attlebury
could be so responsive and yet so definitely restricted in his
responsiveness; they thought of his demeanor as of an occult
art, and might have been right had they stopped at calling

it esoteric. Attlebury himself felt no difficulty, not even a consciousness of effort. He met them in absolute intimacy of soul to soul. Happily in all creeds—and discreeds—there are men and women who can do it.

At first Cyril Maxon had refused to talk about his misfortune, which, of course, soon became public property, and the hints about it had to be almost impossibly delicate. But, as time went on, he found two or three friends to whom he could, more or less, open his heart. There was Mrs. Ladd, an elderly woman with hearty, kindly ways and a mind shrewdly matter of fact. There was Miss Fortescue, one of Attlebury's best "workers," a benevolent, sensible spinster of five-and-forty. There was also Lady Rosaline Deering, daughter of a Scotch peer, widow of a Colonial Administrator. She was a woman of three-and-thirty, or thereabouts, tall and of graceful carriage; her nose was too long, and so was her chin, but she had pretty hair and fine eyes. She was a bit of a blue-stocking and dabbled in theology and philosophy. "Not afraid to think for myself," was the way in which she defined her attitude, in contradistinction (as she implied) from the attitude of most of the women who sat at Mr. Attlebury's feet. She admired Attlebury, but she thought for herself.

"One can't quite give up one's reason," she would say with a winning smile. "Besides, I was brought up in the Church of Scotland, you know." This ecclesiastical origin seemed to give her independence; she paid only so much voluntary allegiance as she chose to Attlebury and his Church; she could, in case of need, fall back on her Church of origin, as though on a domicile never finally forfeited. Also in her husband's lifetime she had seen the cities of men and known their minds. In fact, she might be considered emancipated, and her adherence to Mr. Attlebury's school was rather æsthetic than dogmatic; she thought that religion should be invested with beauty, but she was not afraid to talk of some of its doctrines as possibly "symbolic."

All the three ladies took a great interest in Maxon, but by common consent the first place was yielded to Lady Rosaline. Mrs. Ladd could fortify him, Miss Fortescue could cheer him up; they both recognized that Lady Rosaline could do something else, a subtle thing into which femininity entered more specifically; one of the things which Mrs. Maxon ought to have given him, but obviously had not; perhaps something like what Lady Rosaline herself derived from Attlebury's church services, a blend of intellectual and æsthetic satisfaction. Mrs. Ladd and Miss Fortescue were weak in the æsthetic element. Moreover, there was a special bond of sympathy between Lady Rosaline and Maxon. The late Colonial Administrator had been by no means all that he should have been as a husband, and when death severed the union it was but a very slender string that its shears cut.

Mrs. Ladd and Miss Fortescue had hinted at this sad story; Lady Rosaline herself told it, though in reticent outline only, to Cyril one evening in November when he happened to have leisure to go to tea with her at her flat in Hans Place.

"It's a terrible thing to have to say, but really his death —poor fellow!—ended a situation which had become almost unendurable to any woman of fine feelings. He was never rude or unkind to me, but one's pride! And the solitude of the soul, Mr. Maxon!"

"Still you endured it bravely." His tone subtly asked sympathy, while his words gave it.

A COUNSEL OF PERFECTION

"I wonder if I could have gone on! I should shock Mr. Attlebury, I suppose, but I thought more than once of divorce. Our home—when we were at home—had always been in Scotland. That would have made it easier, and it needn't have hurt his career anything like so much. He could just have left me and stayed away the necessary time, you see. After the last—the last trouble—he offered me that, if I wished it."

"You must have been under a considerable temptation."

"Yes. But then his health began to fail, and—and things were different. I had to stay and look after him; and so we became better friends at the end. I really don't bear malice now."

"I think with Attlebury on that question, you know."

"Yes, I suppose you do. But, then, isn't there—room for doubt?"

"I scarcely think so, Lady Rosaline."

"Oh, but it is hard sometimes, then!" she murmured, looking into the fire. "Do you think there's nothing in the view that the offence itself is a dissolution? . . . That it's the offender himself—or herself—who puts asunder, not the judge, who merely deals with the legal consequences?"

"No, I can't see that." He paused, frowning, then went on, "I can understand a man maintaining that it's given as a counsel of perfection, rather than an absolutely binding rule—I mean, that a man should try, but, if it proves beyond his strength, he might not be absolutely condemned."

"Does it hurt you to talk about it?"

"Not to people who understand."

"How strange she didn't understand you better! Do you mind my saying that?"

"If I'd ever had any doubts about the substantial rights

of the matter, her subsequent proceedings would have dispelled them completely."

"Yes, they throw a light back, don't they?"

Cyril Maxon threw more light, setting forth the preposterous charges which his wife had levelled against him before she went away. He put them as honestly as he could; they were to him so unreasonable that he was not in the least afraid to submit them to an impartial judge. They seemed just as unreasonable to Lady Rosaline. She was as secure of herself as was Mrs. Lenoir; she was not afraid of being "crushed." (Perhaps being "Lady Rosaline" helped her a little there.) And Winnie's alleged grievances fell so short of her own tale of wrongs as to seem a ridiculously inadequate excuse.

"I can't understand her any more than you can," she said.

"There's really no use in saying any more about her, Lady Rosaline. It's a matter of character."

"And she's actually with this man Ledstone now?"

He spread out his hands and bowed his head. It was both answer and comment enough.

"They'd marry, I suppose, if they could?"

Cyril Maxon was not quick at marking the delicate shades of a woman's mood; there at least Winnie was right. He did not now detect the underlying note of pity in Lady Rosaline's voice. It was, indeed, no more than hinted. He made another gesture—this time of pronounced impatience and distaste. Lady Rosaline smiled faintly and changed the subject.

When he had left her, she sat on by the fire, musing. She was a widow with few happy memories and no fond regrets; she was childless; in spite of her high connections she was by no means rich; she could not afford to travel much in the style she desired, or to entertain much. And she was thirty-three. Surveying her position as a whole, she did not take a roseate view of it. "I'm bound to drop out in a few years" —that was how she summed up her prospects, not a cheerful summary, it must be admitted. She had not the contentment of a Mrs. Ladd nor the philanthropic zeal of a Miss Fortescue. She had a good deal of ambition, a love of luxury, and (as has been said) a commendable self-confidence. Masterful herself under all her graceful gentleness, she liked rather than feared masterful men; Cyril Maxon attracted her none the less because he had "crushed" Winnie. "A poor little thing like that!" So ran her verdict on Winnie, whom she had met half a dozen times. And he was very rising. She found herself recalling the precise words that he had used about "a counsel of perfection."

It needs little acuteness to detect a congruity between the interpretation of a rule as a counsel of perfection and the doctrine of the limits of human endurance. In fact, they come to very much the same thing, and are invoked, rightly or wrongly, plausibly or unplausibly, on much the same occasions and under very similar circumstances. If a man strikes you lightly on one cheek, you turn the other. But if he strikes the first cheek very hard? If he forces you to go a mile with him, will you go with him twain? Does the amenity of the road make no difference? If he takes your coat, shall he take your cloak also? Something might turn on the relative value of the two garments. In such cases the human race makes accommodations; and accommodations are not confined to any one class of thinkers.

Cyril Maxon had afforded scant countenance to Lady Rosaline's suggestion that the offender himself severed the tie. She had picked it up from an article of Catholic complexion, which set out the authorities for it only to confute them. His logical mind saw that the position implied rather startling consequences; for if an act can sever, an act can bind. But he did not so easily or readily reject his own idea of the counsel of perfection. Arguing before a court, he could have made a good case for it. Argued in the forum of his own conscience, it found pleas and precedents. Yet it was slowly that it gained even a hearing from the judge, and only by much dexterous pleading; for at first sight the authorities to which he bowed were all against it. They had seemed absolutely and immediately conclusive on the morning when Mr. Ledstone called in the Temple. "No proceedings!" Save as a record of his own attitude, Maxon attached no importance to the utterance so charged with relief to its auditor. It was in no sense a pledge; it was merely an expression of present intention. On what conceivable theory had that Ledstone family any right to pledges from him? If a pledge at all, it was one to himself and to the school of thought to which he belonged. To the Ledstones? Never!

So the slow, hidden current of his feelings began to bore for itself a new channel—away round the rock of principle that barred direct advance. Another change there was in him. A woman—his wife—had gibbeted him as a man impossible to live with. He was secretly, almost unconsciously, afraid of the world's agreeing with her. Seeking sympathy, he tried to manifest it; afraid of being misunderstood, he embarked on an effort to be understanding. He made a fair success of it. People said that he was human, after all, and that Mrs. Maxon ought to have seen it. The work which Winnie had done redounded to her discredit; it is not an uncommon case. The rebels are shot, flogged, or have to fly the kingdom. But reforms are introduced into the administration, and these make the rebels seem more guilty still—because, of course, the reforms were just going to be introduced, anyhow, if only the rebels would have had a little faith, a little patience. Who has not read it a score of times in the newspapers?

"That little wife of his can't have known how to manage a man," said old Mrs. Ladd, who had owned two husbands, the first an overfestive soul, the second a hypochondriac.

"The Vicar has the highest opinion of him," remarked Miss Fortescue.

Mrs. Ladd smiled. "He won't have such a high opinion of him if he goes gadding after Rosaline Deering."

Miss Fortescue was shocked and interested. "My dear, is there any chance of that?"

Mrs. Ladd pursed up her lips. "I don't see much harm in it myself," she said.

"Oh, Mrs. Ladd! If the Vicar heard you!"

"If you may marry again when your husband's dead—"

"It's allowed, but it's—it's not exactly recommended, is it?"

"Well, on the Vicar's theory, I don't see in the end any difference between the two cases—or, at any rate, not much." Mrs. Ladd destroyed her logic by a concession to her friend's pained surprise. She ought to have stuck to there being no difference at all. Then, on Attlebury's theory, she had an argument; "not much" came perilously near to cutting the roots of it.

Speculation as to Mr. Attlebury's attitude was not confined to these good members of his flock. It had a place in Cyril Maxon's own mind, so soon as he began to consider the idea of freeing himself from the legal bond of marriage

157

—and of reviewing his situation after that was done. But here the idiosyncrasy of the man came in, and cut across the loyalty of the churchman. He had given to Attlebury a voluntary allegiance. But if Attlebury tried to extort a forced obedience? Cyril's face set at the thought. Winnie's great offence had been that she would not "adapt herself." In his heart he demanded that the priest and the Church should adapt themselves also, should recognize his services and his value, and find a way out for him, if necessary. The "counsel of perfection" theory seemed more and more, on consideration, to be a possible way out, and already he began to feel, in anticipation, a resentment against the man or the institution that should say the contrary. He chafed beforehand at such dictation, such interference with a view conscientiously held by a man whom all must admit to be sincere and devout—and, moreover, an adherent very much worth having.

Among the various influences which caused the project of freeing himself to take definite shape in his mind, Rosaline Deering had to be reckoned first, no doubt, but she was not the only woman who counted. Done with as she was, out of his life, yet Winnie Maxon also had her share in the work. He felt a primitive desire to "show her," as children say—to show her that she had not the power to destroy his life, that there were women wiser than she, women who did not think him impossible to live with, but would hold it high fortune to become his wife. As soon as he began to think of Rosaline Deering, he thought oftener of his wife, setting the two women in opposition, as it were, and endowing Rosaline with all the virtues which Winnie had so conspicuously lacked. Even such an adventitious thing as Rosaline's courtesy title counted in this connection; it would help to convince Winnie of her own insignificance, of what a much greater career than her own she had tried—vainly tried—to spoil. When she was little better than a vagabond—he did not put things mercifully—Mr. Justice and Lady Rosaline Maxon might be entertaining in Devonshire Street—or perhaps Berkeley Square.

When the Law Courts rose for the Christmas vacation he went to Paris, and Lady Rosaline was gracious enough to make no secret of the fact that his presence there had a share in determining her also on a short visit. They did some of the sights together, they had many talks over the fire, and it was there—on the same Christmas Eve whereon Winnie had gone to Shaylor's Patch and Godfrey Ledstone to Woburn Square—that he told her that he had made up his mind to seek legal dissolution of his ill-starred marriage.

"I have looked at the question from all sides, and I have satisfied my conscience," he said. "Now I must act on my own responsibility."

In the last words there sounded anticipatory defiance of Mr. Attlebury—a defiance which indicated that the satisfaction of his conscience was not quite complete. The case rather was that his conscience had come to terms with the other influences, and under their pressure had accepted the way out.

"I think I may justly plead that the circumstances are exceptional." He leaned forward toward her and asked, "You don't condemn me?"

"What's my opinion worth? You know much more about it; you're much more able to form a judgment."

"But I want to know that I haven't forfeited your good opinion, your regard, if I may hope that I have ever gained it."

"No, I don't condemn you, if your own conscience doesn't, Mr. Maxon." She rose and stood—leaning her elbow on the mantelpiece, her back half turned toward him. The pose displayed well the grace of her tall figure; his eyes rested on her in satisfaction.

"Thank you," he said. "That—that means a great deal to me, Lady Rosaline."

Her elbow rested on the mantelpiece, her face on her hand; her mouth was hidden. But unseen by him a smile bent her lips. His words were entirely decorous—from a man still married—but they were explicit enough. "I can have him if I want him," probably sums up pretty accurately the lady's comfortable conclusion.

XV

MRS. NOBODY

IN spite of the untoward telegram, her visit to Shaylor's Patch heartened up Winnie in two ways. It checked the searching of conscience which is the natural and frequent result of threatened failure; by the evidence it afforded her of Stephen's affection and Dick Dennehy's loyal admiration, it strengthened her woman's confidence in her power to hold her man. After all, Mabel Thurseley was not very pretty; with the sea between Godfrey and Woburn Square, there would be full cause for hope. She dreamed of Italian skies. Though she had recalled and recognized his liberty, under their bargain, to leave her, it was not prominent in her mind. The natural woman was fighting—and fights, it may be supposed, much the same, whatever her status by law or her rights by agreement.

She had telegraphed to Godfrey the proposed time of her arrival at the studio, and expected to find him there; for surely the slight chill would be better by now? He was not there; yet apparently the chill was better, for he had been there earlier in the day. The old Irish servant gave her this news, looking at her in what Winnie felt to be rather an odd way. The woman lingered by the door for a minute, glancing round the room, seeming half in a mind to say something more and half in a mind not to. In the end she said nothing, and went out in silence—as a rule she was loquacious—when her mistress told her that she would give any necessary orders after she had unpacked. Winnie's mind was on the idea of carrying Godfrey off that very night.

Short as her absence had been, the studio looked somehow unfamiliar; it had less of the "lived in" look which she associated with it as a pleasant feature. She scanned it with awakening curiosity. The board on which he stretched his drawing-paper—what had become of that? His to-bacco-jar was not in its usual place; technical books of his were missing from their appointed shelf. He must have felt inclined for work in spite of the chill, and come to fetch them; at least, that would account for the board and books, if not as well for the tobacco-jar. She moved toward the kitchen, to inquire of the servant, but suddenly came to a full stop in the middle of the room. She stood there for a moment, then turned sharp round and went up the stairs that led to the bedrooms—not to unpack, for she left her own trunk and dressing-bag on the floor of the studio.

She went up-stairs slowly, determinedly calm, but with beating heart and a touch of vivid color on her cheeks. The door of his bedroom stood wide open. The furniture was all in its place; the toilet-table was no barer than his visit to Woburn Square accounted for; the little clock she had given him ticked away on the mantelpiece. But Winnie made straight for the chest of drawers, and quickly opened and shut one after another. They were all empty. The wardrobe yielded the same result. All his clothes had gone, and his boots—all of them. She went back to the landing and opened the door of a cupboard where his portmanteau was usually stowed away; it was gone. Preparation for a long stay—somewhere! Yet the chill was so much better that he had been able to visit the studio that morning, when, no doubt, he had carried off all these things—all of them, not merely drawing-board, books, and tobacco-jar.

She moved quickly into her own room. There all was as usual; but she had thought that perhaps there would be a letter. None was visible. A curious quiet, almost a desolation, seemed to brood over the little room; it, too, took on, suddenly, an uninhabited air. She sank into a wicker armchair and sat there quite still for some minutes. Then she sprang briskly to her feet again, exclaiming, "Oh, but nonsense!"

She was seeking indignantly to repel the conviction which was mastering her mind. Surely he would not, could not, do it like this? In her rare contemplation of their possible parting, as bargained for, there had always been, not indeed argument, much less recrimination, but much friendly discussion, a calm survey of the situation, probably an agreement to "try it again" for a longer or shorter time, till a mature and wise decision, satisfactory to the reason, if not to the feelings, of both should be arrived at. But this would be sheer running away—literal running away from her, from the problem, from the situation. It could not be. There must be some explanation.

Sounds were easily audible in the small, flimsy dwelling. She heard the front-door bell ring—and sat listening for his voice calling her, his step across the studio floor, and then coming up the stairs. Neither voice came nor step; besides—odd she had not remembered it before—of course he would have used his latch-key. She got up, took off her jacket, unpinned her hat, laid it on the bed, looked to her hair, and then went slowly down-stairs again.

Amy Ledstone was standing in the middle of the studio;

the knock had been hers. Then in an instant Winnie knew, and in an instant she put on her armor. Her tone was cool and her manner self-possessed; they need not both be cowards—she and Godfrey!

"How do you do, Miss Ledstone? You've come to tell me something?"

Yes." Amy Ledstone was neither cool nor self-possessed. Her voice trembled violently; it was an evident effort for her not to break into sobbing. "He—he still loves you; he told me to tell you that."

'Told you to tell me! Isn't that rather odd? After all our—well, he's been able to tell me for himself before. Won't you sit down?" She sat herself as she spoke.

"No, thank you. But he can't bear to see you; he can't trust himself. He told me to say that. He said you'd understand—that you had a—an understanding. Only he couldn't bear to say good-bye."

"He's not coming back?"

"He was really rather seedy on Sunday—so he stayed. And—and on Sunday night mother had a bad attack; we were really alarmed."

Winnie nodded. Always, from the very beginning, a dangerous enemy—mother's weak heart!

"Mother had been with him all day—she wouldn't leave him. I suppose she got over-tired, and there was the strain of—of the situation; and daddy—my father—broke out on Godfrey the next morning; and I'd broken out on him Christmas night."

"You?" There was a touch of reproach in the question.

"Yes, I told him he must choose. He really made love to Mabel all the time. So I told him—"

164

"I see." She smiled faintly. "The poor boy can't have had a pleasant Christmas, Miss Ledstone!"

"We were all at him, all three of us!'" She stretched out her hands suddenly. "Do try to understand that he had something to bear, too. And that we had—thinking as we do about it. It was hard for other people besides you. Father's getting old, and Godfrey's all mother and I—"

Winnie nodded her understanding of the broken sentence.

"I haven't said a word against him or any of you. He had a right to do what he has done, though he's done it in a way I didn't think he'd choose."

"He doesn't trust himself, and mother—oh!" Her forlorn murmuring ended hopelessly in nothing.

"Mother! Yes! What a lot of things there are to think of! I had just made up my mind to take him right away from all of you, to take him abroad. I could have done it if I'd found him here. Perhaps I could do it still—I wonder?"

Amy shivered uncomfortably under the thoughtful gaze of her companion's eyes.

"I might write letters, too—as you used to—and contrive secret meetings. He's said nothing about Miss Thurseley to me—I don't suppose he'd say anything about me to Miss Thurseley. But he'd meet me all the same, I think. That seems to be his way; only before your last visit I didn't know it."

"Indeed, he won't think of Mabel—not for a long while. He's so—so broken up."

Winnie raised her brows slightly; she was beginning to form an opinion of her own about that—an opinion not likely to be too generous to Godfrey.

Amy spoke with obvious effort, with an air of shame.

"Mother begged and prayed me to—to try and persuade you—" She broke off again.

"To let him alone? I suppose she would. She thinks I've done all the harm? As far as he's concerned, I suppose I have. If we'd gone about it in the ordinary way, he really needn't have suffered at all."

Again came Amy's uncomfortable shiver; she was not at home with steady contemplation of the ways of the world; it had not come across her path any more than love-making had.

"You can tell your mother that I'll let him alone. Then, I hope, she'll get better."

"Oh, I don't understand you!"

"No? Well, I didn't understand Godfrey. But in your case it doesn't matter. Why should you want to? You can all put me out of your thoughts from to-day."

"I can't!" cried Amy; "I shall never be able to!" Suddenly she came over to Winnie, and, standing before her rather awkwardly, burst into tears. "How can you be so hard?" she moaned. "Don't you see that I'm terribly unhappy for you? But it's hopeless to try to tell you. You're so—so hard. And I've got to go back home, where they'll be—"

Winnie supplied the word—"Jubilant? Yes." She frowned. "You cry, and I don't—it is rather funny. I wonder if I shall cry when you've gone?"

"Oh, do you love him, or don't you?"

Winnie's brows were raised again. In view of what had occurred that day, of the sudden revelation of Godfrey, of the abrupt change his act had wrought in her relations to him, the question seemed to imply an unreal simplicity of the emotions, a falsely uncomplicated contrast between two

166

states of feeling, standing distantly over against each other. Such a conception in no way corresponded with her present feelings about Godfrey Ledstone. The man she loved had done the thing she could not forgive—did she love him? Yet if she did not love him, why could she not forgive him? Unless she loved him, it was small matter that he should be ashamed and run away. But if he were ashamed and ran away, how could she love? Love and contempt, tenderness and repulsion, seemed woven into one fabric of intricate, almost untraceable pattern. How could she describe that to Amy Ledstone?

"I suppose I love my Godfrey, but he seems not to be the same as yours. I can't put it better than that. And you love yours, and not mine. I think that's all we can say about it."

Amy had her complications of feeling, too. She dried her eyes, mournfully saying: "That's not true about me. I like yours best—if I know what you mean. He was a man, anyhow. But then I know it's wicked to feel like that."

Winnie looked up at her. "Of course you must think it wicked—I quite see that—but you do understand more than I thought," she said. "And you won't think I'm abusing him? It wouldn't seem wicked to me at all—if I'd happened on the right man. But I didn't. That's all. And this way of ending it seems somehow to—to defile it all. The end spoils it all. That seems to me shamefully unfair. He had a right to go, but he had no right to be ashamed. And he is ashamed, and almost makes me ashamed. I could almost hate him for it."

"We've made him ashamed. You must hate us."

"I like you. And—no—how could I hate your father

and mother? They made me no promise; I've given nothing to them on the strength of a promise. But to him I've given everything I had; not much, I know, but still—everything."

Amy twisted her gloved hands round each other. She was calmer now, but her face was drawn with pain. "Yes, that's true," she said. Then she came out abruptly with what had been behind her spoken words for the last ten minutes, with what she had to say before she could bring herself to leave Winnie. "At any rate, you've pluck. Godfrey's a coward."

Winnie's lips bent in a queer smile. "Don't! Where does it leave me? Oh yes, it's true about him, I suppose. That's my blunder."

Amy walked back to the mantelpiece; she had left her muff on it. She took it up and moved toward the door. "I'll go. You must have had enough of the lot of us!"

Winnie had an honest desire to be just—nay, to be kind, to reciprocate a friendliness obviously extended toward her, and extended in spite of a rooted disapproval. But those limits of endurance had been reached again. She had, indeed, had enough of the Ledstones; not even her husband could have suffered more strongly from the feeling. She made an effort.

"Oh, you and I part friends," she called after her visitor's retreating figure. Without turning round, Amy shook her head dolefully, and so passed out. Her mission was accomplished.

Almost directly after Amy left, the servant, Dennehy's old Irishwoman, came in with tea and buttered toast. She drew a chair up to the gas-stove, and a little table.

"Make yerself comfortable, me dear," she said.

MRS. NOBODY

"Did he say anything to you, Mrs. O'Leary?"

"Said he was going to visit his relations in the North for a bit." Then, after a pause, "Cheer up, mum. There's as good fish—!" And out the old woman shuffled.

Now that was a funny thing to say! "There's as good fish—!" But Winnie's numb brain was on another tack; she did not pursue the implications of Mrs. O'Leary's remark. Nor did the tender mood, on whose advent she had speculated when she said, "I wonder if I shall cry when you've gone," arrive. Nor was she girding against the Ledstones and Woburn Square any more. Her thoughts went back to her own parting from her husband. "Anyhow, I faced Cyril—we had it out," was the refrain of her thoughts, curiously persistent, as she sat before the stove, drinking her tea and munching her toast, enjoying the warmth, really (though it seemed strange) not so much miserable as intensely combative, with no leisure to indulge in misery, with her back to the wall, and the world—the Giant—advancing against her threateningly. Because her particular little rampart had collapsed entirely, the roof was blown off her shelter, her scheme of life in ruins—a situation cheerfully countered by Mrs. O'Leary's proverbial saying, but not in reality easy to deal with. Her boat was not out fishing; it was stranded, high and dry, on a barren beach. "I did face Cyril!" Again and again it came in pride and bitter resentment. Here she was faced with a *dénoûment* typical of a weak mind — at once sudden, violent, and cowardly.

She smoked two or three cigarettes—Ledstone had taught her the habit, undreamed of in her Maxon days—and the hands of the clock moved round. Half-past six struck. It acted as a practical reminder of immediate results. She

had no dinner ordered; if she had, there was nobody to eat
it with. There was nobody to spend the evening with. She
would have to sleep alone in the house; Mrs. O'Leary had
family cares, and got home to supper and bed at nine o'clock.
She need not dine, but she must spend the evening and
must sleep, with no company, no protective presence, in
all the house. That seemed really rather dreadful.

Her luggage lay on the floor of the studio, still unpacked.
She had not given another thought to it; she did now.
"Shall I go back to Shaylor's Patch to-night?" It was a
very tempting idea. She got up, almost determined; she
would find sympathy there; even the tears might come.
She was on the point of making for her bedroom, to put on
her hat and jacket again, when another ring came at the
bell. A moment later she heard a cheery voice asking,
"Mrs. Ledstone at home?"

"But I'm not Mrs. Ledstone any more. Nor Mrs.
Maxon! I don't see that I'm anybody."

The thought had just time to flash through her mind
before Bob Purnett was ushered in by Mrs. O'Leary.

"Mr. Purnett, mum. Ye'll find the whiskey in the usual
place, sor, and the soda." It was known that Bob did not
affect afternoon tea.

"I thought you'd be back, Mrs. Ledstone. Where's
Godfrey? I've a free night, and I want you and him to
come and dine and go to a Hall. Don't say no, now! I'm
so lonely! Don't mind this cigar, do you, Mrs. Ledstone?"

There seemed a lot of "Mrs. Ledstone" about it; but she
knew that was Bob's good manners. Besides, it was a
minor point. How much candor was at the moment
requisite? Even that was not the main point. The main

point was, "Here's a friendly human being; in what way am I required by the situation to treat him?"

It was a point admitting of difficult consideration in theory; in practice it needed none whatever. Winnie clutched at the plank in her sea of desolation.

"Godfrey's staying over the night with his people; he's got a chill. I didn't know it, so I came back all the same from the Aikenheads'."—How glib!—"And I'm rather lonely, too, Mr. Purnett."

He sat down near her by the stove. "Well—er—old Godfrey wouldn't object, would he?"

"You mean—that I should come alone? With you?"

"Hang it, if he will get chills and stay at Woburn Square! This doesn't strike one as very festive!" He looked round the studio and gave a burlesque shudder.

"It isn't!" said Winnie. "Shall I surprise you, Mr. Purnett, if I tell you that I have never in my life dined out or gone to the theatre alone with any man except Mr. Maxon and Godfrey?"

She puzzled Bob to distraction, or, rather, would have, if he had not given up the problem long ago. "I believe it if you say so, Mrs. Ledstone," he rejoined, submissively. "But Godfrey and I are such good pals. Why shouldn't you?"

"I'm going to," said Winnie.

He rose with cheerful alacrity. "All right. I'll meet you at the Café Royal—eight sharp. Jolly glad I looked in! I say, what price poor old Godfrey—with a chill at Woburn Square, while we're having an evening out?" He chuckled merrily.

"It serves Godfrey quite right," she said, with her faintly flickering smile.

12   171

MRS. MAXON PROTESTS

Mrs. O'Leary was delighted to be summoned to the task of lacing up one of Winnie's two evening frocks—the better of the two, it may be remarked in passing.

"Ye might have moped, me dear, here all by yourself!" she said, and it certainly seemed a possible conjecture.

There was only one fault to be found with Bob Purnett's demeanor during dinner at the Café Royal. It was quite friendly and cheerful; it was not distant; but it was rather overwhelmingly respectful. It recognized and emphasized the fact of Godfrey Ledstone's property in her (the thing can hardly be put differently), and of Bob's perfect acquiescence in it. It protested that not a trace of treason lurked in this little excursion. He even kept on expressing the wish that Godfrey were with them. And he called her "Mrs. Ledstone" every other sentence. There never was anybody who kept the straitest rule of the code more religiously than Bob Purnett.

But he was in face of a situation of which he was ignorant, and of a nature which (as he was only too well aware) he very little comprehended. Winnie looked very pretty, but she smiled inscrutably. At least, she smiled at first. Presently a touch of irritation crept into her manner. She gave him back copious "Mr. Purnett's" in return for his "Mrs. Ledstone's." The conversation became formal—indeed, to Bob, rather dull. He understood her less and less.

It was, on Winnie's extremely rough and not less irritated computation, at the one hundred and fourth "Mrs. Ledstone" of the evening—which found utterance as they were driving in a cab from the restaurant to the selected place of entertainment—that her patience gave as with a snap, and her bitter humor had its way.

MRS. NOBODY

"For Heaven's sake, don't call me 'Mrs. Ledstone' any more this evening!"

"Eh ?" said Bob, removing his cigar from his mouth. "What did you say, Mrs. Led— Oh, I beg pardon!"

"I said, 'Don't call me "Mrs. Ledstone"'—or I shall go mad."

"What am I to call you, then ?" He was trying not to stare at her, but was glancing keenly out of the corner of his eye.

"Let's be safe—call me Mrs. Smith," said Winnie.

On which words they arrived at the music-hall.

XVI

A WORD TAKEN AT PLEASURE

THE excellent entertainment provided for them acted as a palliative to Winnie's irritation and Bob Purnett's acute curiosity. There are no "intervals" at music-halls; they were switched too quickly from diversion to diversion for much opportunity of talk to present itself; and during the "orchestral interlude," half-way through the programme, Bob left his place in search of refreshment. When they came out, the subject of "Mrs. Smith" had not advanced further between them.

Winnie refused her escort's offer of supper. By now she was tired out, and she felt, though reluctant to own it, a childish instinct—since she had to sleep in that desert of a house—to hide her head between the sheets before midnight. This aim a swift motor-cab might just enable her to accomplish.

Nor did the subject advance rapidly when the cab had started. Winnie lay back against the cushions in a languid weariness, not equal to thinking any more about her affairs that night. Bob sat opposite, not beside her, for fear of his cigar-smoke troubling her. She often closed her eyes; then he would indulge himself in a cautious scrutiny of her face as the street-lamps lit it up in their rapid passage. She looked exceedingly pretty, and would look prettier still—

174

indeed, "ripping"—with just a little bit of make-up; for she was very pale, and life had already drawn three or four delicate but unmistakable lines about eyes and mouth. Bob allowed himself to consider her with more attention than he had ever accorded to her before, and with a new sort of attention—on his own account as a man, not merely as a respectful critic of Godfrey Ledstone's taste. Because that remark of hers about not being called "Mrs. Ledstone" —on pain of going mad—made a difference. Perhaps it meant only a tiff—or, as he called it, a "row." Perhaps it meant more—perhaps it was "all off" between her and Godfrey—a final separation.

Whatever the remark meant, the state of affairs it in-dicated brought Winnie more within her present com-panion's mental horizon. Tiffs and separations were phe-nomena quite familiar to his experience. The truth might be put higher—tiffs were the necessary concomitant, and separa-tions the inevitable end, of sentimental friendships. They came more or less frequently, sooner or later; but they came. Growing frequency of tiffs usually heralded separations. But sometimes the "big row" came all at once—a storm out of a blue sky, a sudden hurricane, in which the consort ships lost touch of each other — or one went under, while the other sailed away. All this was familiar ground to Bob Purnett; he had often seen it, he had experienced it, he had joked and, in his own vein, philosophized about it. The thing he had not understood—though he had punctiliously feigned to accept—was the sanctity and permanence of a tie which was, as everybody really must know, neither sacred nor likely to be permanent. There he was out of his depth; when tiffs and separations came on the scene, Bob felt his feet touch bottom. And he had always been of opinion, in his heart, that, whatever Winnie might believe, Godfrey Ledstone felt just as he did. Of course, Godfrey had had to pretend otherwise—well, the face opposite Bob in the cab was worth a bit of pretending.

Winnie spoke briefly, two or three times, of the performance they had seen, but said nothing more about herself. When they arrived at her door she told him to keep the cab.

"Because I've got nothing for you to eat, and I think you finished even the whiskey! Thanks for my evening, Mr. Purnett."

He walked through the little court up to the door with her. "And you look as tired as a dog," he remarked—with a successful suppression of "Mrs. Ledstone." "What you want is a good sleep, and—and it 'll all look brighter in the morning. May I come and see you soon?"

"If I'm here, of course you may. But I haven't made up my mind. I may go back to the country, to the Aikenheads, my cousins—where I met Godfrey, you know."

He could not resist a question. "I say, is there trouble? You know how I like you both. Has there been a row?"

She smiled at him. "Godfrey avoided any danger of that. I don't want to talk about it, but—you may as well know. Godfrey has gone away."

"Oh, but he'll come back, Mrs.— He'll come back, I mean, you know."

"Never. And I don't want him. Don't ask me any more—to-night, anyhow." She gave him her hand with a friendly pressure. "Good-night."

"Good Lord! Well, I'm sorry. I say, you won't cut me now, will you?"

"I haven't so many friends that I need cut a good one. Now, if you drive off at once, you'll be back in time to get

176

some supper somewhere else." She smiled again, and in a longing for comfort owned to him—and to herself—her childish fears. "And I want to be snug in bed before the spooks come out! I feel rather lonely. So, again, goodnight." He had a last vision of her small, pale face as she slowly, reluctantly it seemed to him, shut the door. A great rattle of bolts followed.

"Well, I'm left outside, anyhow," Bob reflected philosophically as he walked back to the cab. But his mind was occupied with the picture of the proud, forlorn woman, there alone in the empty house, very much alone in the world, too, and rather afraid of "spooks." All his natural kindliness of heart was aroused in pity and sympathy for her. "I should like to give her a really good time," he thought. In that aspect his impulse was honestly unselfish. But the image of the pale, delicate face abode with him also. The two aspects of his impulse mingled; he saw no reason why they should not, if it were really "all off" between her and Godfrey Ledstone. "I think she likes me well enough—I wonder if she does!" He did not, to do him justice, ask an extravagant degree of devotion in return for any "good times" which he might find himself able to offer. When it is so easy for two people with good tempers, sound digestions, and plenty of ready cash to enjoy themselves, why spoil it all by asking too much? Surely he and Winnie could enjoy themselves? The idea stuck in his mind. Again, why—to him—should it not? His scrupulous behavior hitherto had been based on loyalty to Godfrey Ledstone. It appeared that he was released from the obligation by his friend's own act. "He can't say I didn't play the game while the thing lasted," thought Bob, with justifiable self-satisfaction.

The morrow of a catastrophe is perhaps harder to bear than the hour in which it befalls us. The excitement of battling with fate is gone; but the wounds smart and the bruises ache. Physically refreshed by sleep — a sleep happily unbroken by assaults from without or ghostly visitants within the house—Winnie braced her courage to meet the call on it. Her task, not easy, yet was plain. She would not weep for her Godfrey Ledstone; she would try not to think of him, nor to let her thoughts stray back to the early days with him. She would and must think of the other Godfrey, the one in Woburn Square. What woman would weep for such a man as that—except his mother? On him she would fix her thoughts, until she need think no more of either of them. She had to think of herself—of what she had done and of what she was now to do. On the first head she admitted a blunder, but no disgrace—a mistake not of principle or theory, only a mistake in her man; with regard to the second, she must make a decision.

Just before she had fairly settled down to this task she had a visitor. At half-past eleven—early hours for her to be out and about—Mrs. Lenoir appeared.

"I was supping at the Carlton grill-room last night," she explained, "with a couple of girls whom I'd taken to the play, and Bob Purnett came in. He drove me back home, and—I don't know if he ought to have—but he told me about some trouble here. So, as I'm an interfering old woman, I came round to see if I could be of any use." Her manner to-day was less stately and more cordial. Also, she spoke with a certain frankness. "You see, I know something about this sort of thing, my dear."

Winnie, of course, distinguished her "sort of thing" very broadly from the "sort of thing" to which Mrs. Lenoir must be assumed to refer, but she made no secret of the state of the case or of her own attitude toward it. "I accept it absolutely, but I'm bitterly hurt by the way it was done."

"Oh, you can put it that way, my dear; but you're human like the rest of us, and, of course, you hate having him taken away from you. Now shall I try what I can do?"

"Not for the world! Not a word, nor a sign! It's my mistake, and I stand by it. If he came back, it would never be the same thing. It was beautiful; it would be shameful now."

Mrs. Lenoir smiled doubtfully; she had an imperfect understanding of the mode of thought.

"Very well, that's settled. And, for my part, I think you're well rid of him. A weak creature! Let him marry a Bloomsbury girl, and I hope she'll keep him in fine order. But what are you going to do?"

"I don't quite know. Stephen and Tora would let me go back to Shaylor's Patch for as long as I liked."

"Oh, Shaylor's Patch! To talk about it all, over and over again!"

A note of impatience in her friend's voice was amusingly evident to Winnie. "You mean the less I talk about it, the better?" she asked, smiling.

"Well, you haven't made exactly a success of it, have you?" The manner was kinder than the words.

"And I didn't make exactly a success of my marriage, either," Winnie reflected, in a puzzled dolefulness. Because, if both orthodoxy and unorthodoxy go wrong, what is a poor human woman to do? "Well, if I mayn't go to Shaylor's Patch—at present, anyhow—I must stay here, Mrs. Lenoir—that's all. The studio's in my name, because

179

I could give better security than Godfrey, and I can stay if I want to."

"Not very cheerful—and only that dirty old Irishwoman to do for you!"

"Oh, please don't abuse Mrs. O'Leary. She's my one consolation."

Mrs. Lenoir looked at her with something less than her usual self-confidence. It was in a decidedly doubtful and tentative tone that she put her question, "I couldn't persuade you to come and put up with me—in both senses—for a bit?"

Winnie was surprised and touched; to her despairing mood any kindness was a great kindness.

"That's really good of you," she said, pressing Mrs. Lenoir's hand for a moment. "It's—merciful."

"I'm an old woman now, my dear, and most of my cronies are getting old, too. Still, some young folks look in now and then. We aren't at all gay; but you'll be comfortable, and you can have a rest while you look about you." There was a trace of the explanatory, of the reassuring, about Mrs. Lenoir's sketch of her home life.

"What's good enough for you is good enough for me, you know," Winnie remarked, with a smile.

"Oh, I'm not so sure! Oh, I'm not speaking of creature comforts and so on. But you seem to me to expect so much of—of everybody."

Winnie took the hand she had pressed and held it. "And you?" she asked.

"Never mind me. You're young and attractive. Don't go on expecting too much. They take what they can."

"They? Who?"

"Men," said Mrs. Lenoir. Then out of those distant,

thoughtful, no longer very bright eyes flashed for an instant
the roguish twinkle for which she had once been famous.
"I've given them as good as I got, though," said she. "And
now—will you come?"

Winnie laughed. "Well, do you think I should prefer
this empty tomb?" she asked. Yes—empty and a tomb—
apt words for what the studio now was. "You weren't as
nice as this at Shaylor's Patch—though you always said
things that made me think."

"They've all got their heads in the air at Shaylor's Patch
—dear creatures!"

"I shall enjoy staying with you. Is it really convenient?"
Mrs. Lenoir smiled. "Oh, but that's a silly question, because I know you meant it. When may I come?"

"Not a moment later than this afternoon."

"Well, the truth is, I didn't fancy sleeping here again.
I expect I should have gone to Shaylor's Patch."

Again Mrs. Lenoir smiled. "You're full of pluck, but
you're scarcely hard enough, my dear. If I'm a failure,
Shaylor's Patch will do later, won't it?"

"I shall disgrace you. I've nothing to wear. We were
—I'm very poor, you know."

"I'd give every pound at my bank and every rag off my
back for one line of your figure," said Mrs. Lenoir. "I
was beautiful once, you know, my dear." Her voice took
on a note of generous recognition. "You're very well—in
the *petite* style, Winnie." But by this she evidently meant
something different from her "beautiful." Well, it was
matter of history.

That afternoon, then, witnessed a remarkable change in
Winnie's external conditions. Instead of the desolate, uncomfortable studio, charged with memories too happy or too

unhappy—there seemed nothing between the two, and the extremes met—peopled, also, with "spooks" potential if not visualized, there was Mrs. Lenoir's luxurious flat in Knightsbridge, replete, as the auctioneers say, with every modern convenience. The difference was more than external. She was no longer a derelict—left stranded at the studio or to drift back to Shaylor's Patch. No doubt it might be said that she was received out of charity. Amply acknowledging the boon, Winnie had yet the wit to perceive that the charity was discriminating. Not for her had she been plain, not for her had she been uninteresting! In a sense she had earned it. And in a sense, too, she felt that she was in process of being avenged on Godfrey Ledstone and on Woburn Square. A parallel might be traced here between her feelings and Cyril Maxon's. They had made her count for nothing; she felt that at Mrs. Lenoir's she might still count. The sorrow and the hurt remained, but at least this was not finality. She had suffered under a dread suspicion that in their different ways both Shaylor's Patch and the solitary studio were. Here she had a renewed sense of life, of a future possible. Yet here, too, for the first time since Godfrey left her, she lost her composure, and the tears came—quite soon, within ten minutes after Mrs. Lenoir's greeting.

Mrs. Lenoir understood. "There, you're not so angry any more," she said. "You're beginning to see that it must have happened—with that fellow! Now Emily will make you comfortable, and put you to bed till dinner-time. You needn't get up for that unless you like. There's only the General coming; it's one of his nights."

Oh, the comfort of a good Emily—a maid not too young and not too old, not too flighty and not too crabbed, light of

hand, sympathetic, entirely understanding that her lady has
a right to be much more comfortable than she has ever
thought of being herself! In Maxon days Winnie had
possessed a maid. They seemed far off, and never had
there been one as good as Mrs. Lenoir's Emily. She had
come into Mrs. Lenoir's life about the same time as Mr.
Lenoir had, but with an effect that an impartial observer
could not but recognize as not only more durable, but also
more essentially important—save that Lenoir had left the
money which made Emily possible. Mrs. Lenoir had paid
for the money—in five years' loyalty and service.

Winnie reposed between deliciously fine sheets—why, it
was like Devonshire Street, without Cyril Maxon!—and
watched Emily dexterously disposing her wardrobe. It was
not ample. Some of the effects of the Maxon days she had
left behind in her hurried flight; most of the rest had worn
out. But there were relics of her gilded slavery. These
Emily tactfully admired; the humbler purchases of "Mrs.
Ledstone" she stowed away without comment. Also without comment, but with extraordinary tact, she laid out the
inferior of Winnie's two evening dresses.

"There's nobody coming but the General, Miss," said she.
"Now why does she call me 'Miss'—and who's the
General?" These two problems rose in Winnie's mind,
but did not demand instant solution. They were not like
the questions of the last few days; they were more like
Shaylor's Patch conundrums—interesting, but not urgent,
willing to wait for an idle hour or a rainy day, yielding place
to a shining sun or a romp with Alice. They yielded place
now to Winnie's great physical comfort, to her sense of
rescue from the desolate studio, to her respite from the feeling of finality and of failure. With immense surprise she

realized, as she lay there—in a quiet hour between Emily's deft and charitable unpacking and Emily's return to get her into the inferior frock (good enough for that unexplained General)—that she was what any reasonably minded being would call happy. Though the great experiment had failed, though Godfrey was at this moment in Woburn Square, though Mabel Thurseley existed! "Oh, well, I was so tired," she apologized to herself shamefacedly.

She got down into the small but pretty drawing-room in good time. Yet Mrs. Lenoir was there before her, clad in a tea-gown, looking, as it occurred to Winnie, rather like Mrs. Siddons—a cheerful Mrs. Siddons, as, indeed, the great woman appears to have been in private life.

"I got my things off early, so as to leave you Emily," said the hostess. She obviously did not consider that she had been getting anything on.

"What a dear she is!" Winnie came to the fire and stood there, a slim-limbed creature, warming herself through garments easily penetrable by the welcome blaze.

"Quite a find! The General sent her to me. Her husband was a sergeant-major in his regiment—killed in South Africa."

The General again! But Winnie postponed that question. Her lips curved in amusement. "She calls me 'Miss.'"

"Better than that silly 'Mrs. Smith' you said to Bob Purnett. Only unhappy women try to make epigrams. And for a woman to be unhappy is to be a failure."

"Isn't that one—almost—Mrs. Lenoir?"

"Quite quick, my dear!" her hostess commented. "But if it is, it's old. I told Emily you were a second cousin. I never know exactly what it means, but in my experience it's quite useful. But please yourself, Winnie. Who will you be ?"

"Did Emily believe what you told her ?"

The twinkle came again. "She's much too good a servant ever to raise that question. What was your name ?"

"My maiden name ? Wilkins."

"I think names ending in 'kins' are very ugly," said Mrs. Lenoir. "But a modification ? What about Wilson ? 'Winnie Wilson' is quite pretty."

"'Miss Winnie Wilson'? Isn't it rather—well, rather late in the day for that ? But I don't want to be Ledstone —and it's rather unfair to call myself Maxon still."

"Names," observed Mrs. Lenoir, "are really not worth troubling about, so long as you don't hurt people's pride. I used to have a fetish-like feeling about them—as if, I mean, you couldn't get rid of the one you were born with, or, my dear, take one you had no particular right to. But one night, long ago, somebody—I really forget who—brought an Oxford don to supper. We got on the subject, and he told me that a great philosopher—named Dobbs, if I remember rightly — defined a name as 'a word taken at pleasure to serve for a mark.'" She looked across the hearth-rug, confidently expecting Winnie's approval. "I liked it, and it stuck in my memory."

"It does make things simpler, Mrs. Lenoir."

"Mind you, I wouldn't take a great name I hadn't a right to. Courtenays and Devereauxes in the chorus are very bad form. But I don't see why you shouldn't be Wilson. And the 'Miss' avoids a lot of questions."

"All right. Miss Winnie Wilson be it! It sounds like a new toy. And now, Mrs. Lenoir, for the other problem that Emily has raised. Who's the General ?"

Mrs. Lenoir liked her young friend, but possibly thought that she was becoming a trifle impertinent. Not that she minded that; in her heart she greeted it as a rebound from misery; in the young it often is.

"If you've any taste in men—which, up to now, you've given your friends no reason to think—you'll like the General very much."

"Will he like me?"

"The only advantage of age is that I sha'n't mind if he does, Winnie."

Winnie darted toward her. "What a dear you've been to me to-day!"

"Hush! I think I hear the General's step."

The parlor-maid—not Emily, but a young woman, smart and a trifle scornful — announced, "Sir Hugh Merriam, ma'am—and dinner's served."

XVII

THE TRACK OF THE RAIDER

THE General was old-fashioned; he liked to be left alone with the port—or let us say port-wine, as he always did—after dinner for a quarter of an hour; then he would rejoin the ladies for coffee and, by their never assumed but always solicited permission, a cigar in the drawing-room. Thus Winnie had a chance of gratifying her lively curiosity about the handsome old man with gentle manners, who had seen and done so much, who talked so much about his sons, and came to dine with Mrs. Lenoir twice a week.

"I've fallen in love with your General. Do tell me about him," she implored her hostess.

"Oh, he's very distinguished. He's done a lot of fighting—India, Egypt, South Africa. He first made his name in the Kala Kin Expedition, in command of the Flying Column. And he invented a great improvement in gun-carriages—he's a gunner, you know—and—"

"I think," interrupted Winnie, with a saucy air of doubt, "that I meant something about him—and you, Mrs. Lenoir."

"There's nothing to tell. We're just friends, and we've never been anything else."

Winnie was sitting on a stool in front of the fire, smoking

13   187

her Ledstone-learned cigarette (destined, apparently, to be the only visible legacy of that episode). She looked up at Mrs. Lenoir, still with that air of doubt.

"Well, why shouldn't I tell you ?" said the lady. "He wanted something else, and I wouldn't."

"Were you in love with somebody else ?"

"No, but he'd brought those boys—they were just school-boys then—to see me, and it—it seemed a shame. He knew it was a shame too, but—well, you know what happens sometimes. But, quite soon after, his wife fell ill, and died in four or five days—pneumonia. Then he was glad. But he went abroad directly — without seeing me — and was abroad many years. When he came home and retired, I met him by accident, and he asked leave to call. He's very lonely—so am I, rather—and he likes a change from the club. I don't wonder! And, as you'll have gathered, we've known all the same people in the old days, and always have lots to talk about. That's the story, Winnie."

"I like it. Do you ever see the sons ?"

"They all come to see me when they're home on leave; but that's not often."

"The Major's coming next month, though. The General said so. Let's see if I've got them right. There's the Major —he's the eldest—in Egypt. But the second one is cleverer, and has become a colonel first; he's in Malta now. And then the one in India has only just got his troop; he ought to have had it before, but they thought he gave too much time to polo and horse-racing and private theatricals."

"That's Georgie—my favorite," said Mrs. Lenoir.

"I'm for the Major—because I think it's a shame that his younger brother should be made a colonel before him.

I'm glad it's the Major that's coming home on leave next month."

Mrs. Lenoir looked at Winnie and patted herself on the back. All this was much better for Winnie than the empty studio. She knew that the animation was in part an effort, the gayety in some measure assumed—and bravely assumed. But every moment rescued from brooding was, to Mrs. Lenoir's mind, so much to the good. According to some other ways of thinking, of course, a little brooding might have done Winnie good, and would certainly have been no more than she deserved.

Coffee came in, and, quick on its heels, the General. He produced his cigar, and advanced his invariable and invariably apologetic request.

"Please do. We neither of us mind, do we, Winnie?" said Mrs. Lenoir. There was really more reason to ask the General if he minded Winnie's cigarette, which had come from the studio and was not of a very fine aroma.

Winnie stuck to her stool and listened, with her eyes set on the fire. At first the talk ran still on the three sons— evidently the old soldier's life was wrapped up in them— but presently the friends drifted back to old days, to the people they had both known. Winnie's ears caught names that were familiar to her, references to men and stories about men whom she had often heard Cyril Maxon and his legal guests mention. But to-night she obtained a new view of them. It was not their public achievements which occupied and amused the General and Mrs. Lenoir. They had known them as intimates, and delighted now to recall their ways, their foibles, how they had got into scrapes and got out of them in the merry, thoughtless days of youth. Between them they seemed to have known almost everybody who was "in the swim" from thirty years to a quarter of a century before; if the General happened to say, "So they told me, I never met him myself," Mrs. Lenoir always said, "Oh, I did"—and *vice versa*.

"It was just before my dear wife died," the General said once, in dating a reminiscence.

There was a moment's silence. Winnie did not look up. Then the General resumed his story. But he cut it rather short, and ended with, "I'm afraid our yarns must be boring this young lady, Clara."

Evidently he accepted Winnie entirely at her face value— as Miss Winnie Wilson. The anecdotes and reminiscences, though intimate, had been rigidly decorous, even improbably so in one or two cases; and now he was afraid that she was bored with what would certainly interest any intelligent woman of the world. Winnie was amused, yet vexed, and inclined to wish she had not become Miss Wilson. But she had made a good impression; that was clear from the General's words when he took his leave.

"Bertie will come and see you directly he gets home, Clara. It'll be in about six weeks, I expect." He turned to Winnie. "I hope you'll be kind to my boy. He doesn't know many ladies in London, and I want him to have a pleasant holiday."

"I will. And I wish they were all three coming, Sir Hugh."

"That might end in a family quarrel," he said, with a courtly little bow and a glance from his eyes, which had not lost their power of seconding a compliment.

"Well, I think you've made a favorable impression, though you didn't say much," Mrs. Lenoir remarked when he was gone.

THE ANECDOTES, THOUGH INTIMATE, HAD BEEN RIGIDLY
DECOROUS

Winnie was standing, with one foot on her stool, now. She frowned a little.

"I wish you'd tell him about me," she said.

There was a pause; Mrs. Lenoir was dispassionately considering the suggestion.

"I don't see much use in taking an assumed name, if you're going to tell everybody you meet."

"He's such a friend of yours."

"That's got nothing to do with it. Now if it were a man who wanted to marry you—well, he'd have to be told, I suppose, because you can't marry. But the General won't want to do that."

"It seems somehow squarer."

"Then am I to say Mrs. Maxon or Mrs. Ledstone?"

There it was! Winnie broke into a vexed laugh. "Oh, I suppose we'd better leave it."

Thus began Winnie's cure, from love and anger, and from Godfrey Ledstone. Change of surroundings, new interests, kindness, and, above all perhaps, appreciation—it was a good treatment. Something must also be credited to Mrs. Lenoir's attitude toward life. She had none of the snarl of the cynic; she thought great things of life. But she recognized frankly certain of its limitations—as that, if you do some things, there are other things that you must give up; that the majority must be expected to demand obedience to its views on pain of penalties; if you do not mind the penalties, you need not mind the views, either; above all, perhaps, that, if you have taken a certain line, it is useless folly to repine at its ordained consequences. She was nothing of a reformer—Winnie blamed that—but she was decidedly good at making the best of her world as she found it, or had made it for herself; and this was the gospel she offered for Winnie's acceptance. Devoid of any kind of penitential emotion, it might yet almost be described as a practical form of penitence.

Winnie heard nothing of or from Woburn Square; there was nobody likely to give her news from that quarter except, perhaps, Bob Purnett, and he was away, having accepted an invitation to a fortnight's hunting in Ireland. But an echo of the past came from elsewhere—in a letter addressed to her at Shaylor's Patch, forwarded thence to the studio (she had not yet told the Aikenheads of her move), and, after two or three days' delay, delivered at Knightsbridge by Mrs. O'Leary in person. It was from her husband's solicitors; they informed her of his intention to take proceedings, and suggested that they should be favored with the name of a firm who would act for her.

Winnie received the intimation with great relief, great surprise, some curiosity, and, it must be added, a touch of malicious amusement. The relief was not only for herself. It was honestly for Cyril Maxon also. Why must he with his own hands adjust a lifelong millstone round his own neck? Now, like a sensible man, he was going to take it off. But it was so unlike him to take off his millstones; he felt such a pride in the cumbrous ornaments. "What had made him do it?" asked the curiosity; and the malicious amusement suggested that, contrary to all preconceptions of hers, contrary to anything he had displayed to her, he, too, must have his weaknesses—in what direction it was still uncertain. The step he now took might be merely the result of accumulated rancor against her, or it might be essential to some design or desire of his own. Winnie may be excused for not harboring the idea that her husband was acting out of consideration for her; she had the best of excuses—that of being quite right.

For the rest—well, it was not exactly pleasant. But she seemed so completely to have ceased to be Mrs. Maxon that at heart it concerned her little what people said of Mrs. Maxon. They—her Maxon circle, the legal profession, the public—would not understand her provocations, her principles, or her motives; they would say hard and scornful things. She was in safe hiding; she would not hear the things. It would be like what they say of a man after he has gone out of the room and (as Sir Peter Teazle so kindly did in the play) left his character behind him. Of that, wise people take no notice.

But Godfrey? It must be owned that the thought of him came second; indeed, third—after the aspect which concerned her husband and that which touched herself. But when it came, it moved her to vexation, to regret, to a pity which had even an element of the old tenderness in it. Because this development was just what poor Godfrey had always been so afraid of, just what he hated, a thing analogous to the position which in the end he had not been able to bear. And poor Woburn Square! Oh, and poor Mabel Thurseley too, perhaps! What a lot of people were caught in the net! The news of her husband's action did much to soften her heart toward Godfrey and toward Woburn Square. "I really didn't want to make them unhappy or shamed any more," she sighed; for had not her action in the end produced Cyril's? But, as Mrs. Lenoir would, no doubt, point out, there was no help for it—short of Winnie's suicide, which seemed an extreme remedy, or would have, if it had ever occurred to her; it did not.

Her solicitude was not misplaced. The high moralists say

193

MRS. MAXON PROTESTS

Esse quam videri—what you are and do matters, not what
people think you are or what they may discover you doing.
A hard, high doctrine! "He that is able to receive it, let
him receive it." Mr. Cyril Maxon also had found occasion
to consider these words.

For Winnie had been right. Jubilation had reigned in
Woburn Square, provisionally when Godfrey fetched his
portmanteau away from the studio, finally and securely (as
it seemed) when Amy made known the result of her mission.
Father read his paper again in peace; mother's spasms
abated. There was joy over the sinner; and the sinner
himself was not half as unhappy as he had expected—may
it be said, hoped ?—to be. Mercilessness of comment is out
of place. He had been tried above that which he was able.
Yet, if sin it had been, it was not of the sin that he repented.
It had been, he thought, from the beginning really impossible on the basis she had defined—and extorted. In time
he had been bound to recognize that. But he wore a
chastened air, and had the grace to seek little of Miss
Thurseley's society. He took another studio, in a street
off Fitzroy Square, and ate his dinner and slept at his father's house.

Things, then, were settling down in Woburn Square. By
dint of being ignored, Winnie and her raid on the family
reputation might soon be forgotten. The affair had been
kept very quiet; that was the great thing. (Here Woburn
Square and the high moralists seem lamentably at odds, but
the high moralists also enjoin the speaking and writing of
the truth.) It was over. It ranked no more as a defiance;
it became merely an indiscretion—a thing young men will
do now and then, under the influence of designing women.
There was really jubilation—if only Amy would have looked

a little less gloomy and been rather more cordial toward her brother.

"I don't understand the girl," Mr. Ledstone complained. "Our line is to make things pleasant for him."

"It's that woman. She must have some extraordinary power," his wife pleaded. Winnie's extraordinary power made it all the easier to forgive her son Godfrey. Probably few young men would have resisted, and (this deep down in the mother's heart) not so very many had occasion to resist.

Then came the thunderbolt—from which jubilation fled shrieking. Who hurled it? Human nature, Winnie, Lady Rosaline Deering—little as she either had meant to do anything unkind to the household in Woburn Square? Surely even the high moralists—or shall we say the high gods, who certainly cannot make less, and may perhaps make more, allowances?—would have pitied Mr. Ledstone. Beyond all the disappointment and dismay, he felt himself the victim of a gross breach of trust. He fumed up and down the back room on the ground-floor which was called his study—the place he read the papers in and where he slept after lunch.

"But he said there were to be no proceedings. He said he didn't believe in it. He said it distinctly more than once."

Mrs. Ledstone had gone to her room. The sinner had fled to his studio, leaving Amy to break the news to Mr. Ledstone; Amy was growing accustomed to this office.

"I suppose he's changed his mind," said Amy, with a weary listlessness.

"But he said it. I remember quite well. 'I am not a believer in divorce.' And you remember I came home and told you there were to be no proceedings? Monstrous! In a man of his position! Well, one ought to be able to

depend on his word! Monstrous!" Exclamation followed
exclamation like shots from a revolver—but a revolver not
working very smoothly.

"It 'll have to go through, I suppose, daddy."

"How can you take it like that? What 'll your Uncle
Martin say? And Aunt Lena—and the Winfreys? It 'll
be a job to live this down! And my son—a man with my
record! He distinctly said there were to be no proceedings. I left him on that understanding. What 'll Mrs.
Thurseley think? I shall go and see this man Maxon
myself." Of all sinners, Mr. Maxon was ranking top in
Woburn Square to-day—easily above his wife, even.

"I don't expect that 'll do any good."

"Amy, you really are— Oh, well, child, I'm half off my
head. A man has no right to say a thing like that unless he
means it. 'No proceedings,' he said!"

"I expect he did mean it. Something's changed him, I
suppose."

Something had—and it never occurred to Cyril Maxon
that the Ledstone family had any right to a say in the
matter. He would have been astonished to hear the interpretation that Mr. Ledstone put on the interview which he
remembered only with vivid disgust, with the resentment
due to an intrusion entirely unwarrantable. So the poor old
gentleman must be left fuming up and down, quite vainly
and uselessly clamoring against the unavoidable, an object
for compassion, even though he was thinking more of the
Thurseleys, of Uncle Martin, Aunt Lena, and the Winfreys
than of how his son stood toward divine or social law on
the one side, and toward a deserted woman on the other?
Respectability is, on the whole, a good servant to morality,
but sometimes the servant sits in the master's seat.

The culprit's state was no more enviable than his father's; indeed, it appeared to himself so much worse that he was disposed to grudge his family the consternation which they displayed so prodigally and to find in it an unfair aggravation of a burden already far too heavy. Nothing, perhaps, makes a man feel so ill-used as to do a mean thing and then be balked of the object for whose sake he did it. A mean thing it undoubtedly was, even if it had been the right thing also in the eyes of many people—for to such unfortunate plights can we sometimes be reduced by our own actions that there really is not a thing both right and straight left to do; and it had been done in a mean and cowardly way. Yet it was now no good. Things had just seemed to be settling down quietly; he was being soothed by the consolatory petting of his mother and father. Now this happened—and all was lost. His decent veil of obscurity was rent in twain; he was exposed to the rude stare of the world, to the shocked eyes of Aunt Lena and the rest. He had probably lost the girl toward whom his thoughts had turned as a comfortable and satisfactory solution of all his difficulties; and he had the perception to know that, whether he had lost Mabel or not, he had finally and irretrievably lost Winnie. Everybody would be against him now, both the men of the law and the men of the code; he had been faithful to the standards of neither.

He had not the grace to hate himself; that would have been a promising state of mind. But, fuming up and down in his studio off Fitzroy Square (just like his father in the back room in Woburn Square) and lashing himself into impotent fury, he began to feel that he hated everybody else. They had all had a hand in his undoing—Bob Purnett and his lot, with their easy-going moralities; Shaylor's Patch and its lot, with their silly speculations and vaporings over things they knew nothing about; Cyril Maxon, who did not stand by what he said nor by what he believed; Winnie, with ridiculous, exacting theories; Mabel Thurseley (poor, blameless Mabel!), by attracting his errant eyes and leading him on to flirtation; his parents, by behaving as if the end of the world had come; his sister, because she despised him and had sympathy with the deserted woman. He was in a sad case. Nobody had behaved or was behaving decently toward him, nobody considered the enormous—the impossible—difficulties of his situation from beginning to end. Was there no justice in the world—nor even any charity? What an ending—what an ending—to those pleasant days of dalliance at Shaylor's Patch! What was deep down in his heart was, "And I could have managed it all right my way, if she'd only have let me!"

He did not go home to dinner that evening. He slunk back late at night, hoping that all his family would be in bed. Yet when he found that accusing sister sitting alone in the drawing-room, he grounded a grievance on her solitude. She was sewing—and she went on sewing in a determined manner and in unbroken silence.

"Well, where's everybody? Have you nothing to say? I'm sent to Coventry, I suppose?"

"Mother's in bed. Oh, she's pretty easy now; you needn't worry. Daddy's in his study; he was tired out, and I expect he's gone to sleep. I'm quite ready to talk to you, Godfrey."

Perhaps—but her tone did not forebode a cheerful conversation.

He got up from the chair into which he had plunged himself when he came in.

THE TRACK OF THE RAIDER

"Pretty gay here, isn't it? Oh, you do know how to rub it in, all of you! I should think living in this house would drive any man to drink and blue ruin in a fortnight."

Amy sewed on. She had offered to talk, but what he said seemed to call for no comment. He strode to the door and opened it violently. "I'm off to bed."

"Good-night, Godfrey," said Amy; her speech was smothered by the banging of the door.

Poor sinner! Poor creature! Winnie Maxon might indeed plead that her theory had not been fairly tried; she had chosen the wrong man for the experiment.

Here, then—save for the one formality on which Cyril Maxon now insisted—Winnie and the Ledstone family were at the parting of the ways. Their concurrence had been fortuitous—it was odd what people met one another at Shaylor's Patch, Stephen's appetite for humanity being so voracious—fortuitous and ill-starred for all parties. They would not let her into their life; they would not rest till they had ejected her from her tainted connection with it. Now they went out of hers. She remembered Godfrey as her great disappointment, her lost illusion, her blunder; Amy, as it were, with a friendly stretching-out of hands across a gulf impassable; the old folk with understanding and toleration—since they did no other than what they and she herself had been taught to regard as right. How could the old change their ideas of right?

Their memory of her was far harder—naturally, perhaps. She was a raider, a brigand, a sadly disturbing and destructive invader. At last she had been driven out, but a track of desolation spread behind her retreating steps. Indeed, there were spots where the herbage never grew again. The old folk forgave their son and lived to be proud of him once more.

199

But Amy Ledstone had gauged her brother with an accuracy destructive of love; and within twelve months Mabel Thurseley married a stockbroker, an excellent fellow with a growing business. She never knew it, but she, at least, had cause for gratitude to Winnie Maxon.

Godfrey returned to the obedience of the code. He was at home there. It was an air that he could breathe. The air of Shaylor's Patch was not—nor that of the Kensington studio.

XVIII

"B^Y the law came sin—" quoted Stephen Aikenhead. "He only meant the Jewish law. Man, ye're hopeless." Dennehy tousled his hair.

The February afternoon was mild; Stephen was a fanatic about open air, if about nothing else. The four sat on the lawn at Shaylor's Patch, well wrapped up—Stephen, Tora, and Dennehy in rough country wraps, Winnie in a stately sealskin coat, the gift of Mrs. Lenoir. She had taken to dressing Winnie, in spite of half-hearted remonstrances, and with notable results.

"But the deuce is," Stephen continued—this time on his own account and, therefore, less authoritatively—"that when you take away the law, the sin doesn't go too."

Winnie's story was by now known to these three good friends. Already it was being discussed more as a problem than as a tragedy. Some excuse might be found in Winnie's air and manner. She was in fine looks and good spirits, interested and alert, distinctly resilient against the blows of fortune and the miscarriage of theoretical experiments. So much time and change had done for her.

"And it seems just as true of any other laws, even if he did mean the Jewish, Dick," Stephen ended.

"Don't lots of husbands, tied up just as tight as anything

or anybody can tie them, cut loose and run away just the same?" asked Tora.

"And wives?" added Winnie—who had done it, and had a right to speak.

"It's like the old dispute about the franchise and the agricultural laborer. I remember my father telling me about it somewhere in the eighties—when I was quite a small boy. One side said the laborer oughtn't to have the vote till he was fit for it, the other said he'd never be fit for it till he had it."

"Oh, well, that's to some extent like the woman question," Tora remarked.

"Are we to change the law first or people first? Hope a better law will make better people, or tell the people they can't have a better law till they're better themselves?"

"Stephen, you've a glimmer of sense in you this afternoon."

"Well, Dick, we don't want to end by merely making things easier for brutes and curs—male or female."

"I think you're a little wanting in the broad view to-day, Stephen. You're too much affected by Winnie's particular case. Isn't it better to get rid of brutes and curs, anyhow? The quicker and easier, the better." Tora was, as usual, uncompromising.

"Everybody seems to put a good point. That's the puzzle," said Stephen, who was obviously enjoying the puzzle very much.

"Oh, ye're not even logical to-day, Tora," Dennehy complained, "which I will admit you sometimes are, according to your wrong-headed principles. Ye call the man a brute or a cur, and this and that—oh, ye meant Godfrey!

What's the man done that he hadn't a right to do on your own showing? His manners were bad, maybe."

"It's our own showing that we're now engaged in examining, if you'll permit us, Dick," Stephen rejoined, imperturbably. "When a man's considering whether he's been wrong, it's a pity to scold him; because the practice is both rare and laudable."

"Oh, you mustn't even consider whether I've been wrong, Stephen," Winnie cried. "Wrong in principle, I mean. As to the particular person—but I don't want to abuse him, poor fellow. His environment—"

"That's a damnable word, saving your presence," Dennehy interrupted. "Nowadays whenever a scoundrel does a dirty trick, he lays it to the account of his environment."

"But that's just what I meant, Dick."

"Say the devil, and ye're nearer the mark, Winnie."

"Environment's more hopeful," Stephen suggested. "You see, we may be able to change that. Over your protégé we have no jurisdiction."

"He may have over you, though, some day! Oh, I'll go for a walk and clear my head of all your nonsense."

"Don't forget you promised to take me to the station after tea," said Winnie.

"Forget it!" exclaimed Dick Dennehy, in scorn indescribable. "Now, will I forget it—is it likely, Winnie?" He swung off into the house to get his walking-stick.

Tora Aikenhead shook her head in patient reproof. No getting reason into Dick's, no hope of it at all! It was just Dick's opinion of her.

A short ˙silence followed Dennehy's departure. Then Stephen Aikenhead spoke again:

14   203

"You've had a rough time, Winnie. Are you sorry you ever went in for it?"

"No, it was the only thing to try; and it has resulted— or is just going to—in my being free. But I did fail in one thing. I was much more angry with Godfrey than I had any right to be. I was angry—yes, angry, not merely grieved—because he left me, as well as because he was afraid to do it in a straightforward way. I didn't live up to my theories there."

"I don't know that I think any theory easy to live up to," said Tora. "Is the ordinary theory of marriage easy to live up to, either?"

"It's always interesting to see how few people live up to their theories." Stephen smiled. "It seems to me your husband isn't living up to his."

"No, he isn't, and it's rather consoling. I don't fancy it ever entered his head that he would have to try it in practice himself. Rather your own case, isn't it, Stephen? You've never really found what any—any difficulty could mean to you."

"Oh, I know I'm accused of that. I can't help it; it's absolutely impossible to get up a row with Tora. And even I don't say that you ought to walk out of the house just for the fun of it!"

"We prove our theory best by the fact of the theory making no difference," said Tora.

"I suppose that in the end it's only the failures who want theories at all," Winnie mused.

"Probably—with the happy result of reducing, *pro tanto*, the practical importance of the subject, without depriving it of its speculative interest," laughed Stephen. "Love, union, parentage, partnership—it's good to have them all,

but, as life goes on, a lot of people manage with the last two
—or even with only the last. It grows into a pretty strong
tie. Well, Winnie, you seem to have come through fairly
well, and I hope you won't have much more trouble over
the business."

"I sha'n't have any, to speak of. I've put it all in Hobart
Gaynor's hands. I went to see him and told him all he
wanted to know. He's taken charge of the whole thing;
I really need hear no more about it. He was awfully kind
—just his dear old self." She smiled. "Well, short of
asking me to his house, you know."

"Oh, that's his wife," said Tora.

"Mrs. Gaynor seems to live up to her theories, at any
rate," chuckled Stephen.

"It's not so difficult to live up to your theories about other
people. It's about yourself," said Winnie.

"I think your going to Mrs. Lenoir's is such a perfect ar-
rangement." Tora characteristically ignored the large body
of opinion which would certainly be against her on the
question.

"I'm very happy there—she's so kind. And I seem quite
a fixture. I've been there nearly two months, and now
she says I'm to go abroad with her in the spring." She
paused for a moment. "The General's very kind, too. In
fact, I think he likes me very much."

"Who's the General? I don't know about him."

Winnie explained sufficiently, and added, "Of course, he
thinks I'm just Miss Wilson. Mrs. Lenoir says it's all
right, but I can't feel it's quite straight."

"As he appears to be nearly seventy, and Mrs. Lenoir's
friend, if anybody's—" Stephen suggested.

Winnie smiled and blushed a little. "Well, you see, the

truth is that it's not only the General. He's got a son. Well, he's got three, but one of them turned up about a fortnight ago."

"Oh, did he? Where from?"

"From abroad—on long leave. It's the eldest—the Major."

"Does he like you very much, too, Winnie?"

Winnie looked across the lawn. "It seems just conceivable that he might—complicate matters," she murmured. "I haven't spoken to Mrs. Lenoir about that—aspect of it."

Stephen was swift on the scent of another problem. "Oh, and you mean, if he did—well, show signs—how much ought he to be told about Miss Wilson?"

"Yes. And perhaps even before the signs were what you'd call very noticeable. Wouldn't it be fair? Because he doesn't seem to me at all a—a theoretical kind of person. I should think his ideas are what you might call—"

"Shall we say traditional—so as to be quite impartial toward the Major?"

"Yes. And especially about women, I should think."

Stephen looked across at his wife, smiling. "Well, Tora?"

Without hesitation Tora gave her verdict. "If you'd done things that you yourself knew or thought to be disgraceful, you ought to tell him before he grows fond of you. But you're not bound to tell him what you've done, on the chance of his thinking it disgraceful, when you don't."

"I expect it's more than a chance," Winnie murmured.

"I'm groping after Tora's point. I haven't quite got it. From the Major's point of view, in the hypothetical circumstances we're discussing, what's of importance is not what Winnie thinks, but what he does."

"What's important to the Major," Tora replied, "is that he should fall in love with a good woman. Good women may do what the Major thinks disgraceful, but they don't do what they themselves think disgraceful. Or, if they ever do, they repent and confess honestly."

"Oh, she's got an argument! She always has. Still, could a good woman let herself be fallen in love with under something like false pretences?"

"There will be no false pretences, Stephen. She will be—she practically is—an unmarried woman, and, if she married him, she'd marry him as such. The rest is all over."

"It may be atavistic—relics of my public school and so on—but it doesn't seem to me quite the fair thing," Stephen persisted; "to keep him in the dark about our young friend, Miss Wilson, I mean."

"I think I agree with you, Stephen." Winnie smiled. "If he does show signs, that's to say!"

"Oh, only if he shows signs, of course. Otherwise, it's in no way his business."

"Because, whatever his rights may be, why should I risk making him unhappy? Besides, in a certain event, he might find out when it was—from his point of view—too late."

Stephen laughed. "At least admit, Tora, that from a merely practical point of view there's something to be said for telling people things that they may find out for themselves at an uncomfortably late hour."

"Oh, I thought we were trying to get a true view of a man's—or a woman's—rights in such a case," said Tora, with lofty scorn. "But it seems I'm in a minority."

"You wouldn't be happy if you weren't, my dear. It's

getting dusk, and here comes Dick back. Let's go in to tea."

Dick Dennehy often grew hot in argument, but his vexation never lasted long. Over tea he was in great spirits, and talked eagerly about a new prospect which had opened before him. The post he held as correspondent was a poor affair, ill-paid and leading to nothing. He had the chance of being appointed a leader-writer on a London daily paper —a post offering a great advance both in pay and in position. The only possible difficulty arose from his religious convictions; they might, on occasion, clash with the policy of the paper—in matters concerning education, for instance.

"But they're good enough to say they think so well of me in every other way that the little matter may probably admit of adjustment."

"Now don't you go back on your theories—or, really where are we ?" said Stephen, chaffingly.

"I won't do that; I won't do that. I should be relieved of dealing with those questions. And, Stephen, my boy, I'd have a chance of a decent place to live in and of being able to put by my old-age pension."

They all entered eagerly into the discussion of these rosy dreams, and it was carried, *nem. con.*, that Dick must build himself a "week-end" cottage at Nether End, as near as might be to Shaylor's Patch. Perhaps Winnie could find one to suit her, too!

"And we'll all sit and jaw till the curtain falls," cried Stephen Aikenhead, expressing his idea of a happy life.

"Ye're good friends here, for all your nonsense," said Dennehy. "I'd ask no better."

"Moreover, Dick, you can marry. You can tie yourself up, as Tora puts it, just as tightly as you like. Choose a

208

woman, if possible, with some breadth of view. I want you to have your chance."

"Oh, I'm not likely to be marrying." A cloud seemed to pass over his cheery face. But it was gone in a moment. "Well, who'd look at me, anyhow?"

"I think you'd make an excellent husband, Dick," said Winnie. "I should marry you—yes, even tie you up—with the utmost confidence."

He gave her a queer look, half-humorous, half-resentful. "Don't be saying such things, Winnie, or ye'll turn my head and destroy my peace of mind."

"Oh, last time I flirted with you, you said you liked it!" she reminded him, laughing.

On the way to the station, Winnie walked with her arm through his, for the evening had fallen dark and the country road was rough. With a little pressure of her hand, she said, "I'm so glad—so glad—of the new prospects, Dick. I believe in you, you know, though we do differ so much."

He was silent for a moment, and then asked, abruptly, "And what prospects have you?"

"Oh, I suppose I'm rather like the politician who had his future behind him. But I haven't made up my mind what to do. I'm living rather from hand to mouth just now, and taking a holiday from thinking."

"Oh, I'll mind my own business, if that's what you mean."

"Dick, how can you? Of course it wasn't. Please don't be huffy about nothing."

"I'm worried about you. Don't let those people up at the Patch get at you again, Winnie—for pity's sake, don't! Take care of yourself, my dear. My heart bleeds to see you where you stand to-day, and if you got into any other trouble—you don't understand that you're a woman a man might do bad as well as good things for."

Emotion was strong in his voice; Winnie lightly attributed it to his nationality.

"Don't fret about me. I've got to pay for my blunders, and, if I've any sense at all, I shall be wiser in future."

"If ye're ever inclined to another man, for God's sake try him, test him, prove him. Ye can't afford another mistake, Winnie. It 'd kill you, wouldn't it?"

"I shouldn't—like it," she answered, slowly. "Yes, I shall be cautious, Dick. And it would take a good deal to make me what you call 'inclined to' any man just yet." She broke into a laugh. "But it's your domestic prospects that we were discussing this afternoon!"

"I have none," he answered shortly, almost sourly.

"Oh, you've only just begun to think of it," she laughed. "Don't despair of finding somebody worthy some day!"

They had just reached the station—nearly a quarter of an hour ahead of their time. Dennehy was going back to sleep at the Aikenheads', but he sat down with her in the waiting-room under a glaring gas-lamp, to wait for the train. Seen in the light, Dennehy's face looked sad and troubled. Winnie was struck by his expression.

"Dick," she said, gently, "I hope we haven't been chaffing you when—when there's something serious?"

He shrugged his shoulders. "No, no, ye couldn't call it serious."

"I believe it is, because you were in good spirits till we began about that. Then you looked funny and—well, you don't look at all funny now. If there is anything—oh, don't despair! And all good, good wishes, dear Dick! Oh, what a pity this should come, just when everything else is looking so bright for you!"

"I tell ye, Winnie, there's nothing serious."

Winnie nodded an entirely unreal acquiescence. "Very well, my friend," she said.

A long silence fell between them. In direct disobedience to a large notice, Dennehy lit a cigarette and smoked it quickly, still looking sad and moody. Winnie, troubled by his trouble and unconvinced by his denial, was wondering why in the world she had never thought of such a thing happening to Dick Dennehy. Why not? There was no reason; he was a man, like the rest. Only we are in the habit of taking partial and one-sided views of our friends and neighbors. The most salient aspect of them alone catches our eye. To cover the whole ground we have neither time nor, generally, opportunity. They come to stand, to us, for one quality or characteristic—just as the persons in a novel or a play often, perhaps generally, do, however much the writer may have endeavored to give the whole man on his canvas. Now the quality of lover—of even potential lover—had never seemed to associate itself at all necessarily or insistently with Dick Dennehy, as it did, at once and of necessity, with Godfrey Ledstone. So Winnie had just not thought of it. Yet she knew enough to understand how it is that this very kind of man takes love hard, when it does chance to find him out—takes it hard and keeps it long—long after the susceptible man has got over his latest attack of recurrent fever. Was poor Dick Dennehy really hard hit? "Who'd look at me, anyhow?" he had asked. Well, he certainly was not handsome. But Winnie remembered her two handsome men "I should like to have a word with that girl!" she thought. Her reference was to Dick's hard-hearted mistress.

But Winnie was not of the women—if indeed they exist—whose innocence merges in denseness and who can successfully maintain for a twelvemonth a total ignorance of the feelings of a man with whom they are thrown into familiar acquaintance. Suddenly, some two minutes before her train was due, her brain got to work—seized on the pieces of the puzzle with its quick perception. Here was a man, naturally ardent, essentially sanguine, in despair—surely about a woman? He did not deny the woman, though he protested that the matter was not "serious." Merely to look at him now proved it, for the moment at least, grievous. Well, for "serious" she read practicable; for "not serious" she substituted hopeless. Then he had looked at her in that queer way; the words had been all right, conceived in the appropriate vein of jocular flirtation; but the look was out of joint. And then his extreme and emotional concern for her welfare and prudent conduct! Would he, even though a Celt, have felt that anxiety quite so keenly if another and hopeless affection had been dominating his mind? "Who'd look at me, anyhow?" That protest his modesty made consistent with an aspiration for any lady; it need not be taken too seriously. But his abrupt, curt answer about his prospects—"I have none"—?

The pieces of the puzzle seemed to fit pretty well, yet the proof was not conclusive. Say that the evidence was consistent, rather than demonstrative. Somehow, intangibly and beyond definition, there was something in the man's bearing, in his attitude, in the totality of his words and demeanor, which enforced the conviction. There even seemed an atmosphere in the bare, dirty little waiting-room which contained and conveyed it—something coming unseen from him to her, in spite of all his dogged effort to resist the transference. He smoked a second cigarette fiercely. Why, when he had been serene and cheerful all the afternoon, should he be so suddenly overcome by the thought of an absent woman that he could not or would not speak to or look at a friend to whom he was certainly much attached?

The train rumbled into the station. "Here it is!" said Winnie, and rose to her feet.

Dick Dennehy started and jumped up. For a second his eyes met hers.

"Come along and put me into a carriage," she added, hastily, and made her way at a quick pace to the train. "Where are the thirds?"

They found the thirds, and she got in. He shut the door, and stood by it, waiting for the train to start.

"You've got a wrong idea. I tell ye it's not serious, Winnie."

He made his protest again, in a hard, desperate voice. Then, with an effort, he took a more ordinary tone.

"I'm full of business over this new idea—and with winding up the old connection, if I do it. I mayn't be seeing you for a few weeks. You will take care of yourself?"

"Surely if anybody's had a warning, I have! Good-bye, Dick."

She put her hand out through the window. He took it and pressed it, but he never lifted his eyes to hers. A lurch back, a plunge forward, and the train was started. "Good-bye, Dick!" she cried again. "Cheer up!"

Leaning out of the window, she saw him standing with his hands in his pockets, looking after her. He called out something, which she heard imperfectly, but it embraced

213

the word "fool," and also the word "serious." She could supply a connection for the latter, but travelled to town in doubt as to the application of the former. Was it to her or to himself that Dick Dennehy had applied the epithet? "Because it makes a little difference," thought Winnie, snuggling down into the big collar of her sealskin coat—quite out of place, by-the-way, in a third-class carriage.

XIX

A POINT OF HONOR

M RS. LENOIR'S boast was not without warrant; in
the course of her life she had held her own against
men in more than one hard fight. She admired another
woman who could do the same. In her refugee from the
West Kensington studio she rejoiced to find not a sentimental
penitent nor an emotional wreck, but a woman scarred indeed with wounds, but still full of fight, acknowledging a
blunder, but not crushed by it, both resolved and clearly
able to make a life for herself still and to enjoy it. She
hailed in Winnie, too, the quality which her own career had
taught her both to recognize and to value—that peculiarly
feminine attractiveness which was the best weapon in her
sex's battles; Winnie fought man with her native weapons,
not with an equipment borrowed from the male armory and
clumsily or feebly handled. Under the influence of this
sex-sympathy, pity had passed into admiration, and admiration into affection, during the weeks which had elapsed since
she brought Winnie to her roof.

Her ethical code was pagan, as perhaps is already evident.
When she hated, she hurt if she could; when she loved, she
helped—she would not have quarrelled with the remark
that she deserved no credit for it. She was by now intent
on helping Winnie, on giving her a fresh start, on obliterating

the traces of defeat, and of co-operating in fresh manœuvres which should result in victory. But to this end some strategy was needful. Not only other people, but Winnie herself, had to be managed, and there was need of tact in tiding over an awkward period of transition. As a subsidiary move toward the latter object, Mrs. Lenoir projected a sojourn abroad; in regard to the former she had to be on her guard against two sets of theories—the world's theories about Winnie, which might perhaps find disciples in her own particular friends (the General and his son, Major Merriam), and Winnie's theories about the world, which had before now led their adherent into a rashness that invited, and in the end had entailed, disaster.

She had pleasant memories of Madeira, which she had visited many years ago under romantic circumstances. She outlined a tour which should begin with that island, include a sea trip thence to Genoa, and end up with a stay at the Italian lakes. On the day that Winnie spent at Shaylor's Patch she sketched out this plan to her friend, the General.

"Upon my word, it sounds uncommonly pleasant. I should like to go with you, but I don't want to leave Bertie for so long, now he's at home for once."

"No, of course you don't." For reasons of her own, she preferred that any suggestion should come from him.

The General pondered, then smiled rather roguishly. "What would you say, Clara, if two handsome young officers turned up at Madeira, for a few days anyhow? Just to bask in the sun, you know?"

"I should say that two handsome young women wouldn't be much annoyed."

"By Jove, I'll suggest it to Bertie!" All right—so long as it was the General who suggested it!

Mrs. Lenoir smiled at him. "Of course, it would be very pleasant." A slight emphasis on the last word suggested that, if there were any reasons to weigh against the obvious pleasantness, they were matters for her friend's consideration, not for hers. If he chose to go out of his way to expose his eldest son to the fascination of a young woman about whom he knew nothing at all, it was his own lookout. By now there was no doubt that Bertie Merriam was quite conscious of the fascination, though by no means yet dominated by it.

"We should make a very harmonious quartette," the General declared. "I shall certainly suggest it to Bertie."

"Oh, well, you must see how it strikes him. Remember, he may prefer the gayeties of London. Don't press him on our account!" She would not in any way invite; she preserved the attitude of a kindly, but not an eager, acquiescence in any decision at which Bertie might arrive. But she was strongly of opinion that the handsome officers would turn up—on the island, and not improbably even at Southampton docks.

All this, then, was in Mrs. Lenoir's mind when Winnie came back from Shaylor's Patch, her thoughts still occupied with two questions. One related to Dick Dennehy; it was a private matter and did not concern her hostess. But the problem of conduct which she had submitted to the Aikenheads did. On that she was bound in loyalty to consult Mrs. Lenoir. That lady had indeed given an opinion once, but circumstances alter cases. As she ate her dinner, she described humorously the difference of opinion between husband and wife, putting the case in the abstract, of course, without explicit reference to the Major, and taking the liberty of implying that it was Stephen who had initiated

the debate. These concessions to modesty and discretion
scarcely deceived Mrs. Lenoir, though she accepted them
decorously. Both women knew that it was Bertie Merriam
who might make a settlement of the point necessary before
many days, or, at all events, many weeks, were out.

Worldly-wise Mrs. Lenoir took up a middle position.
She was not prepared for Tora's uncompromising doctrine;
yet she agreed with the view that there was much to be said
for telling people what they might probably find out—and
find out too late in their own opinion. All the same, she
dissented from Stephen's extreme application of the rule of
candor.

"You wouldn't accept a man without telling him, but
you needn't blurt it out to anybody who makes you a few
pretty speeches."

"Wouldn't it be fair to tell him before he got much in
love ?"

"If he wasn't much in love, he'd be rather inclined to
smile over your telling him, wouldn't he ?"

The suggestion went home to Winnie. "I shouldn't want
to risk that."

"Unless circumstances make it absolutely necessary, I
should let things stay as they are till your case is over, at all
events. It 'll be so much pleasanter for you to be incog.
till then."

There was something in that suggestion, too. Not great
on theory, Mrs. Lenoir took good, practical points.

"It's rather giving up my point of view," Winnie objected.

Mrs. Lenoir smiled in a slightly contemptuous kindness.
"Oh, my poor child, take a holiday from your point of view,
as well as from all the rest of it. And really it's quixotic of

you to be so much afraid of giving some man or other a little shock, after all they've made you suffer."

Winnie felt the appeal to the cause of the sex also. In short, all Mrs. Lenoir's points told; they seemed full of workaday wisdom and reasonable common-sense.

"Just don't think about it again till after the case. Promise me."

"That is best, I think, in the end. Yes, I promise, Mrs. Lenoir."

Mrs. Lenoir said nothing about the possibility of the two officers "turning up" at Madeira—or at Southampton docks. Diplomacy forbade; the connection would have been too rudely obvious; it might have led Winnie to reconsider her pledge. In fact, things were so managed—mainly by a policy of masterly inactivity, tempered by just one hint to the General—that the first Winnie heard of this idea came neither from Mrs. Lenoir nor from the General, but from Bertie Merriam himself. Emanating from that quarter, the suggestion could not be brusquely repelled; it was bound to meet with courteous consideration. Indeed, to refuse to accept it would be extremely difficult. To Mrs. Lenoir, Winnie might have avowed the only possible objection; she could not so much as hint at it to the Major. Mrs. Lenoir knew her way about, as the colloquial phrase has it.

Winnie's relations with Bertie Merriam had now reached the stage which a mature and retrospective judgment, though not, of course, the heat of youth, may perhaps declare to be the pleasantest that can exist between man and woman—a congenial friendship colored into a warmer tint by admiration on the one side and a flattered recognition of it on the other. Winnie' recent experience raised recogni-

15   219

tion to the height of gratification, almost to that of gratitude. Not only her theory had suffered at Godfrey Ledstone's hands; deny it though she might, her vanity also had been wounded. She welcomed balms, and smiled kindly on any who would administer them. After an unfortunate experience in love, people are said often to welcome attentions from a new-comer "out of pique"; it is likely that the motive is less often vexation with the offender than gratitude to the successor, who restores pride and gives back to life its potentiality of pleasure. This was Winnie's mood. She was willing to take Mrs. Lenoir's advice not merely on the specific point on which it was offered. She was willing to accept it all round—willing, so far as she could, to forget her theories and her point of view, as well as what they had entailed upon her. She wanted to enjoy the pleasant things of life for a while; one could not be playing apostle or martyr all the time! She was ready to see what this new episode, this journey and this holiday, had to offer; she was not unwilling to see how much she might be inclined to like Major Merriam. Yet all this is to analyze her far more than she analyzed herself. In her it was, in reality, the youthful blood moving again, the rebound from sorrow, the reassertion of the right of her charms and its unimpeded exercise. Such a mood is not one where the finer shades of scruple are likely to prevail; it is too purely a natural and primitive movement of mind and body. Besides, Winnie could always, as Mrs. Lenoir reminded her, soothe a qualm of conscience by a staggering *tu quoque* launched against the male sex in general.

Again, in an unconscious and blindly instinctive way, she was a student of human nature, and rather a headstrong one. She did not readily rest in ignorance about people, or even find repose in doubt. She liked to search, test, classify, and be guided by the result. Her history showed it. She had tested Cyril Maxon, classified him, and acted on her conclusion. She had experimented on Godfrey Ledstone, classified him, found that she had miscalculated, paid the expense of an unsuccessful experiment, and accepted the issue of it. Here, now, was new material—men of a kind to whom her experience had not previously introduced her in any considerable degree of intimacy. She might often have dined in the company of such; but under Maxon's roof real knowledge of other men was not easily come by.

Men of views and visions, men of affairs and ambitions, men of ease and pleasure—among these her lot had been cast since she left her father's house. The Merriams were pre-eminently men of duty. They had their opinions, and both took their recreations with a healthy zest; but the Service was as the breath of their nostrils. The General was the cleverer soldier of the two, as the Kala Kin Expedition bore witness. The son was not likely ever to command more than a regiment or, at most, a brigade; higher distinctions must be left to the second brother. Bertie's enthusiasm corresponded nicely with his gifts. He adored the regiment, and in due course a few months would see him Lieutenant-Colonel; if only the regiment could see service under his command, how joyously would he sing his *Nunc dimittis*, with duty done and his name on an honorable roll!

Winnie sat regarding his pleasant tanned face, his sincere, pale-blue eyes, and his very well-made clothes with a calm satisfaction. She had been hearing a good deal about the regiment, but the gossip amused her.

"And where do the officers' wives—I suppose some of you have wives?—come in?" she asked.

"Oh, they're awfully important, Miss Wilson. The social tone depends so much on them. You see, with a parcel of young chaps—the subalterns, you know—well, you do see, don't you?"

"Well, I think I can see that, Major Merriam. They mustn't flirt with the subalterns? At any rate, not too much?"

"That's rotten. But they ought to teach them their manners."

"Ought to be motherly? You don't look as if that sounded quite right! Elder-sisterly?"

"That's more like it, Miss Wilson."

He said "Miss Wilson" rather often, or so it struck Winnie—just as Bob Purnett used to say "Mrs. Ledstone" much too often. He gave her another little jar the next moment. He left the subject of officers' wives, and leaned forward to her with an ingratiating yet rather apologetic smile.

"I say, do you know what the General has had the cheek to suggest to your cousin?"

Winnie had forgotten her cue. "My cousin?" she exclaimed in surprise.

"Why, Mrs. Lenoir! She is your cousin, isn't she?"

The lie direct Winnie disliked. Yet could she betray her benefactress? "It's so awfully distant that I forget the cousin in the friend," she said, with an uneasy little laugh. "But what has the General had the cheek—your phrase, not mine—to suggest to Mrs. Lenoir?" She seemed to have forgotten the cousin again, for she said "Mrs. Lenoir," not "Cousin Clara." As, however, the Major had never heard her say anything else, the point did not attract his notice.

"Why, that we four might make a party of it as far as Madeira. Nice little place, though I suppose it won't be as lively now as it was when the war was going on."

"It sounds delightful."

"I've got a paper to read to the Naval and Military Institute in six weeks' time. I could just fit it in—and write the thing out there, you know."

"We'd all help you," said Winnie.

The Major detected raillery. "I should have a go at it before you were up in the morning."

"Oh, well, then I must be content with the humble function of helping to relax your mind afterward."

"But you wouldn't mind our coming?"

"You don't appreciate how fond I am of the General."

"Well, he half worships you, Miss Wilson. And you'll put up with my company for his sake?"

"He's too distinguished a man to carry the rugs and cushions."

"You can fag me as much as you like on board. The difficulty is to get enough moving about."

"On that distinct understanding, I won't veto the party, Major Merriam." She laughed. "But, of course, I've really got nothing to say to it. It's for Mrs. Lenoir to decide, isn't it?"

Bertie Merriam felt that he had obtained permission, but hardly encouragement—just as the General was convinced that he had made a suggestion and not received one. But permission was enough.

"I shall tell the General I've squared you," he said, beaming. "There are jolly excursions to be made, you know. You can either ride, or be carried in a hammock—"

"I wonder if Mrs. Lenoir will care for the excursions?"

"Well, if the seniors want to take it easy, we could do them together, couldn't we, Miss Wilson?"

"To be sure we could," smiled Winnie. "More rugs and cushions for you! Won't it be what you call fatigue duty?"

"I'll take it on," he declared. "I don't shirk work in a good cause, you know."

One thing about him surprised Winnie, while it also pleased her. Obviously he considered her witty. She had never been accustomed to take that view of herself. Cyril Maxon would have been amazed at it. Though Stephen Aikenhead now and then gave her credit for a hit, her general attitude toward him was that of an inquirer or a disciple, and disciples may not becomingly bandy witticisms with their masters. Because Bertie Merriam visibly enjoyed—without attempting to equal—her fencing, she began to enjoy it herself. Nay, more, she began to rely on it. No less than her staggering *tu quoque* to the male sex, it might serve, at a pinch, to quiet a qualm of conscience. "I can always keep him at his distance." That notion in her mind helped to minimize any scruples to which his admiration, the expedition, the excursions, the rugs and the cushions might give rise. For if fencing can accord permission, it can surely also refuse it? If the Merriams were anything in this world, they were gentlemen. In matters of the heart a gentleman need not be very clever to take a hint; he feels it.

But the most dexterous soother of qualms and scruples was Mrs. Lenoir. Her matter-of-fact treatment of the joint excursion shamed Winnie out of making too much of it.

A POINT OF HONOR

What reason was there to suppose that Bertie would fall in love? A pleasant passing flirtation perhaps—and why not? Moreover—here the subject was treated in a more general way, though the special application was not obscure—suppose he did! What did it matter? Men were always falling in love, and falling out of it again. A slight shrug of still shapely shoulders reduced these occurrences to their true proportions. Finally she took occasion to hint that Bertie Merriam was not what he himself would call "pious." He accepted the religion of his caste and country as he found it; he conformed to its observances and had an honest, uninquiring belief in its dogmas. It was to him a natural side of life and an integral part of regimental discipline—much, in fact, as church-going was to Alice Aikenhead at school. But there was no reason to suppose that he would carry it to extremes, or consider that it could ask more of him than the law asked. So far as the law went, all objections would vanish in a few months. Strong in her influence over the General, Mrs. Lenoir foresaw, in the event of the falling in love coming to pass, a brief trouble and a happy ending. The second was well worth the first. In fact, she was by now set on her project—on the fresh start and the good match for Winnie. She was ready to forward it in every way she could, by diplomacy, by hard fighting if need be, by cajolery, and, finally, by such an endowment for Winnie as would remove all hindrances of a financial order. Though most of her money was sunk in an annuity, she could well afford to make Winnie's income up to four hundred a year —not a despicable dower for the wife of a regimental officer. With three sons in the army, the General was not able to make very handsome allowances; the four hundred would be welcome with a bride.

225

She would have been interested to overhear a conversation which took place between the General and his son while they were dining together at Bertie's club two days before the expedition was to set out. The General filled his glass of port and opened the subject.

"Bertie, my boy, you ought to get married," he said. "A C. O., as you will be soon, ought to have a wife. It's good for the regiment, in my opinion—though some men think otherwise, as I'm aware—and it makes it much less likely that a man will get into any scrape on his own account —a thing a bachelor's always liable to do, and in these days a much more serious matter than it used to be."

The General, at least, did not sound unpracticably "pious." Mrs. Lenoir might take comfort.

Bertie Merriam blushed a little through his tan. "Well, to tell the truth, I have been just sort of thinking about it— in a kind of way, you know."

"Anybody special in your eye ?" asked the General.

"It's rather early days to give it away," Bertie pleaded.

"Yes, yes. I quite see, my boy. I beg your pardon. But I'm very glad to hear what you say. I know you'll choose a good girl—and a pretty one, too, I'll lay odds! I won't ask any more. A little bit of money wouldn't hurt, of course. Take your own time, Bertie, and I'll wait." Thus the General ostensibly passed from the subject. But after finishing his glass and allowing it to be refilled, he remarked: "I'm looking forward to our jaunt, Bertie. It was a happy idea of mine, wasn't it ? I shall enjoy talking to Clara—I always do—and you'll be happy with little Miss Wilson. I like her — I like her very much. Of course, twenty years ago it wouldn't have been wise for Clara to chaperon her, but at this time of day it's all forgotten. Only

old fogies like me remember anything about it. It oughtn't
to prejudice the girl in any sensible man's eyes."

He exchanged a glance with his son. Nothing explicit
was said. But a question had been answered which Bertie
had desired to put. It was now quite clear to him that, if
he were desirous of courting Miss Winnie Wilson, he need
expect no opposition from the General.

"I'm quite with you there, father. It would be very unfair to Miss Wilson."

With what mind would Mrs. Lenoir—and Miss Wilson
—have overheard the conversation? Might they have
recognized that they were not giving quite such fair treatment as was being accorded to them? Or would Winnie's
theories and her ability to launch a staggering *tu quoque*, and
Mrs. Lenoir's practical points of difficulty, still have carried
the day? It is probable that they would. Taken all together,
they were very powerful, and Stephen Aikenhead's atavistic
"public-school" idea of honor could hardly have prevailed.

Father and son walked home, arm in arm. The talk of
his son's marriage, the prospect of his son's commanding
his regiment, moved the old soldier to unwonted feeling.

"I shall be a proud man when I can boast of two Colonels
—and if that scamp George 'll stick to work, he ought to
give me a third before many years are over. There's no
finer billet in the world than the command of a regiment—
no position in which you can do more good, in my opinion,
or serve the king to better purpose. And a good wife can
help you, as I said—help you a lot."

He pressed his son's arm and added, "Only you mustn't
let her interfere with your work. The regiment must still
come first in everything, Bertie—ay, even before your wife!
That's the rule of the Service."

XX

BOB PURNETT spent nearly two months in Ireland; it was much longer than he had intended, but he liked the hunting there, and, when that was over, found excellent quarters and amusing society at the house of a squire whom his prowess in the field had won to friendship and who maintained the national tradition in the matter of good claret. Bob had no cause for hurry; his year's work was done. A holiday on the Riviera was the next item in his annual programme.

He arrived in London two days before the expedition to Madeira was to start. Of it he knew nothing. He had written a couple of friendly, breezy letters to Winnie (under the idea that she might be downhearted), and the answer to the first—she had not answered the second—told him where she was and conveyed the impression that she still found life bearable. Where she was possessed a certain significance in his eyes; he nodded his head over it. It was a factor—precisely how important he could not say— in answering the question he had been, not with oppressive frequency, yet from time to time, asking himself in the intervals of hunting and of drinking his host's good claret. "Why shouldn't she?" was the form the question assumed in his thoughts. If she had with Godfrey Ledstone—not

much of a chap, after all!—why shouldn't she with somebody else? True, Winnie had always puzzled him. But
there was the line of division—a fixed line surely, if anything
was fixed? She had crossed it once. He could not see why,
with the proper courtesies observed, she should not make
another transit. Yet, because she had always puzzled him,
he was, as he told himself, stupidly nervous about making
the proposition. People who do things, and yet do not
seem to be the sort of people who generally do them, occasion these doubts and hesitations, confusing psychology
and perplexing experience. Yet, finally, he was minded to
"chance it"—and, let it be said, not without such a sense
of responsibility as it lay in his nature to feel. She had
crossed the line, but he knew that she did not regard herself
as a denizen of the other side. He was ready to concede
that, to allow for it, to be very much on his good behavior.
Above all, no hint of the mercantile! He had the perception
to see not only how fatal, but how rude and unjustifiable
such a thing would be. He was (in a sentence) prepared to
combine a charming companionship with an elevating influence. Permanently? Ah, well! If bygones are to be
bygones, futurities may, by a parity of treatment, be left to
the future.

He called at the flat in Knightsbridge on Friday afternoon.
In the drawing-room neighborhood no signs of the im-
pending expedition were visible; invaluable Emily restricted
the ravages of packing to the bedrooms and their immediate
vicinity. Mrs. Lenoir and Winnie were together, drinking
tea. Winnie received him with glad cordiality; in the
hostess he felt vaguely a hint of reserve. Mrs. Lenoir, full
of her new project, did not see why Bob Purnett should
come. She had nothing against him, but he was irrelevant;

if her scheme succeeded, he would naturally drop out. She was distantly gracious—the "grand manner" made its appearance—and, after giving him a cup of tea, went back to her packing, concerning which neither she nor Winnie had said a word—Winnie waiting for a lead from her friend, and her friend not being minded to give it.

Winnie had not thought of Bob for weeks, but her heart warmed to him. "He saved my life that first night," was her inward utterance of gratitude. She lounged back on the sofa and let him talk. But he did not talk idly for long; Bob Purnett took his fences; after all, he had made a thorough inspection of this particular "teaser" before he mounted his horse.

"I've been thinking á lot about you since I've been away."

"Flattered, Mr. Purnett."

"Oh, rot. I mean, hoping you weren't unhappy, and so on, you know."

Winnie moved her small hands in a gesture expressive of a reasoned endurance.

"But, I say, pretty quiet here, isn't it?"

"Oh yes, but I don't mind that."

"Don't want to sit down here all your life, do you?"

"That is rather a large order, isn't it? Have you anything else to suggest?"

"You've begun to laugh at a fellow already!"

"Already? Good gracious, is there anything tremendous coming?"

Bob got up from his chair, moved across the hearth-rug, and stood by her. He cleared his throat and lit a cigarette. Winnie began to be curious; she smiled up at him. "I believe you've got something on your mind. Out with it."

A sudden idea flashed into her head. "You've not come from Godfrey? Because that's utterly impossible."

"What do you take me for? I haven't seen the fellow. I say, what made you think that?"

"Oh, I beg your pardon—I'm sorry. But you asked whether I wanted to stay here; that was like suggesting I should go somewhere else, wasn't it? So I thought you might mean that I should go—go back, you know. I'd sooner kill myself."

"Oh, please drop it. I wasn't talking about that. I'm off to Monte Carlo on Tuesday." He looked down at his well-polished, broad-welted brown boots; he was always admirably shod. Yet he seemed to find no inspiration, or not a very happy one. "Got over it, haven't you?"

Winnie shrank into her shell. "I think I prefer your dumb sympathy. How can you expect me to talk about it?"

"Put my foot in it?"

"Well, yes, rather." Her right hand beat a tattoo on the arm of her chair.

"Always do," remarked Bob, reflectively, his eyes still on his boots. He was not surprised that she thought his question badly phrased—necessary preliminary as it was in substance.

"Oh, nonsense! You're a dear. But have you really anything you're trying to say?"

He must jump now—or he must refuse. He saw it, and courage came with the need for it.

"I say, could you think of going with me to Monte?" He raised his eyes and looked her full in the face as he put the question. He had courage—but the puzzle was terribly persistent. "Will she go, or will she kick me out?" is a brief summary of his inward questioning; he thought it about equal betting.

"Go with you ?"

"Yes. Have a bit of fun, you know. We'd have a rare time." He was down at his boots again. "And everything just as you like, honor bright, Winnie, till—till you saw what you wanted, don't you know ?"

Winnie sat quite still for a few moments. She looked at Bob Purnett with an inquiring glance. He was a very good fellow. That she knew. Was he quite sane? He was certainly funny—so funny that indignation refused to adorn the situation. Slowly a smile bent the lines of her mouth. Here was a pretty contrast to Dick Dennehy's heartfelt appeal to her to "take care of herself," and not less to Bertie Merriam's respectfully cautious attentions. Ay, and to Mrs. Lenoir's schemes! She was aware that Bob had never grasped the true significance of her action in regard to Godfrey Ledstone. But to think that he had missed it so tremendously as this! And there were the trunks packed, not for Monte Carlo, but for Madeira— trunks redolent of respectability! She might be amused, but her amusement could not be devoid of malice; she might smile, but Bob must suffer—well, just a little, any- how. She looked up at him, smiling still in treacherous amiability.

"Is this a proposal of marriage, Bob ?" she asked.

He flushed. "Well — er — you can't marry, can you, Winnie ?"

"Not at the moment. But I can in a little more than six months. Would you and Monte Carlo wait for me ?"

"In a little more than—? What, is Maxon—?"

"Yes, he is—very soon now."

AN HEROIC OFFER

"You never told me!"

"Up to now I had no reason to suppose you were interested."

Bob Purnett was obviously upset, very much upset indeed. He stared at her for a moment, his eyes seeming prominent in their aghast surprise. "Good Lord!" he muttered, and started striding across the room, then back again—like Mr. Ledstone in the back room at Woburn Square or Godfrey in his new studio. He went on with this for three or four minutes. Winnie sat with her head resting on the high back of her arm-chair, her eyes following him in scornful amusement and gratified malice. Bob was suffering for his presumption, his inability to appreciate plain differences, his gross misjudgment of her. His wrigglings under the chastisement were entertaining to watch. In his unfortunate person she seemed to be punishing all the great world which had refused to understand her; she was getting a little bit of her own back at last.

Once, as he walked, he looked at her. His face was red, and he was frowning. Winnie's steady smile seemed to give him no comfort. With a queer jerk of his head he resumed his restless pacing.

Indeed, Bob felt himself fairly caught. What a fool he had been not to reconnoitre the ground before an advance which had proved so rash! But he was not a scoundrel; he prided himself on "playing the game." Some men he knew would lightly give a promise if it were likely to serve their purpose and make no bones about breaking it six months hence. That was not his way, even where it would serve his purpose. What he was asking, as he paced, was whether he were bound to make the promise; if he made it, it should be kept. Of course, it was the last thing he had ever meant; it was entirely outside his scheme of life, and his feeling for Winnie was not nearly strong enough to oust his scheme from the first place in his affections. But could he get out of the hole he was in without brutality, without insulting her? He did not see that he could. She had not married Godfrey Ledstone—it had been impossible. In his heart Bob had never believed in there being any other really operative reason. Her theories had been just a making the best of it. Now it would be possible, shortly, for her to marry him. It was, he conceded, entirely natural that she should jump at the chance. Could he decline, after his first proposal? That would be to put the case—both his and her cases, in fact—in disagreeably plain terms. But he felt that it was terribly bad luck, and he, too, had his resentment—an angry protest against inconsistency. Why did Maxon first refuse, and then take back his refusal? Why did Winnie cross the line, and then want to cross back again? They "let a man in" by behavior like that—let him in very badly.

Still, he was in his way very fond of her; and he was sorry for her. It did not lie in him to hurt her wilfully, even though not hurting her were to his own damage. And, then, it would be rather heroic—so very much the right thing to do. In common with most of mankind, he was susceptible to the attractions of the heroic; the glamour of it would—or, at all events, might—help him to bear the situation.

He came and stood in front of her, his hands in his pockets; he looked rather sheepish.

"All right, Winnie. Just as soon as it's possible. There's my word on it." He mustered a smile. "Don't be too down on me, though. I never pictured myself as a husband, you know."

234

AN HEROIC OFFER

"You certainly needn't picture yourself as mine," said Winnie.

"You mean—you won't do it?"

"Of course I won't—any more than I'll go with you to Monte Carlo." She broke into a laugh at the perplexity of his red face. "Oh, you old goose, to think that I should do either!"

Bob knew that his first proposal was irregular, and might have been taken as insulting—at least by a woman so inconsistent as Winnie; his second was undoubtedly handsome and heroic. He could not see that either was ridiculous. He flushed redder still under the friendly contempt of Winnie's words.

"I don't see anything so particularly absurd about it. When I thought you couldn't marry, I didn't ask you to. When you told me you could, I did. What's the matter with that?"

"Why, you are—and I am—very much the matter with it! But don't fly out at me, Bob. I might have flown out at you, but I didn't."

"Oh, you got home all right in your own way. You've made me look an ass." His tone expressed a grudging, resentful admiration; his glance was of the same order. He was furious, and Winnie, in her animation and triumph, was very pretty.

"I don't see that it's altogether my doing. I think you helped. Come, don't be cross. You know that you're most awfully relieved. Your face, as you considered the question, was a study in consternation."

He was certainly relieved about the marriage; but he was disappointed and hurt about the trip to Monte Carlo. If she had "flown out" at him in moral indignation, that would have been intelligible—though, again, in his opinion, hardly consistent—conduct on her part; as it was, she had called him, not a scoundrel, but a goose, and had played her trick on him with a smiling face, looking the while most attractive and hopelessly unapproachable.

"Well, I mean what I say. My offer stands. Perhaps you'll think better of your answer." His voice was doggedly angry now. He plainly suggested that she—in her position —might go farther and fare worse.

Winnie did not miss the hint, but let it pass with a gay contempt.

"I won't quarrel; I don't mean to. If I had, I should have quarrelled at the beginning." She jumped up from her chair and laid a hand on his arm. "Let's forgive each other, Bob!"

Under a sudden impulse he caught her round the waist. Winnie's figure stiffened into a sudden rigidity, but she made no other movement. Bob's arm fell away again; he walked off toward a chair behind the door, on which he had left his hat and gloves. "I expect I'd better go," he said, in an unsteady voice, without turning his head toward her.

"Please, Bob."

The situation was relieved, or, at least, ended, by the opening of the door. The parlor-maid announced, "Major Merriam, Miss!"

The Major came in briskly. A large funnel-shaped parcel of white paper proclaimed a bouquet of flowers. Bob, behind the door, was not within the Major's immediate range of vision.

"Well, Miss Wilson, are you all ready for the voyage? I've brought you a few flowers for your cabin."

"Oh, thank you so much. May I—er—introduce you to

236

my friend, Mr. Purnett? Mr. Purnett—Major Merriam."
The Major bowed politely; Bob rather stiffly.

"I was just off," he said, coming back toward Winnie,
with hat and gloves in his left hand. He was wondering
"who the devil is that chap?"—and "what was that about
a voyage and a cabin?"

"Yes, we're actually nearly ready, women though we are!
Emily's so splendid at it! Must you go, Bob? It'll be
some time before we meet again. We're off to Madeira
to-morrow morning, and then on to Italy—to the Lakes."
She smiled on Bob. "But I'm afraid we sha'n't get to
Monte Carlo!"

"I didn't know you were—were going away."

"I was just going to tell you when Major Merriam came
in. We're all looking forward to it; aren't we, Major?
Major Merriam and his father are going with us as far as
Madeira."

"The ladies are good enough to accept our escort and our
company for two or three weeks," said Bertie Merriam.
He thought the other fellow looked rather sulky.

"Going to be away long?" Bob jerked out the inquiry.

"Oh, about three months, I think. Well, if you must go,
good-bye, Bob. So good of you to come and see me."
She smelled the nosegay which she had taken from Bertie.
"Your flowers are delicious, Major Merriam!"

Bob Purnett had never dreamed of such a factor in the
situation as the Major now presented — this perfectly
equipped, much-at-ease Major, who had no doubt that his
flowers would be welcome, and whose company was accepted as far as Madeira—for two or three weeks, indeed, in
Madeira. The feelings which had prompted him to put
his hand round Winnie's waist transformed themselves into

237

a fierce jealousy. She had laughed at his proposal—his heroic offer. Would she laugh at the Major's, if he made one? In one way and another his feelings had by now carried him far from the mood in which he had originally braced himself up to the proposal. He had made it for honor's sake. He would have made it now to stop her from going to Madeira with the Major. His mind was not quick of movement, yet he suddenly realized that not improbably he would see no more of her. His world was not, save in the casual intercourse of the hunting-field, the world of men like the Major.

"Well, good-bye; I wish you a pleasant voyage," he managed to say, under the eyes of the Major.

"Good-bye—and *au revoir*—when I come back!"

How he hated the eyes of the Major! He did not dare even to press her hand; the Major would detect it and laugh at him! A limp shake was all he could give. Then he had to go away and leave her with the Major—leave her to make ready, not for Monte Carlo with him, but for Madeira with the Major. That was a fine reward for an heroic offer! Certainly, in her duel against the male sex, Winnie had scored some hits that afternoon.

Listlessly and disconsolately he strolled toward Piccadilly. He was at odds with the world. He had nobody to go to Monte Carlo with—nobody he cared a straw about. Indeed, whom did he care about really, or who really cared about him? He had a lot of friends of a sort; but how much did he care for them, or they for him? Precious little—that was the truth, seen in the unusual clarity of this afternoon's atmosphere. Other men had wives or children or devoted friends. He seemed to have nobody. Disgusting world it was! And he liked Winnie—nay, he more than liked her. He had learned that also this afternoon. And he had, in the end, proposed the handsome thing. For nobody else in the world would he have done that. His reward had been ridicule from her—and the appearance of the Major. "It's all a bit too thick," reflected poor Bob Purnett, thus suddenly brought up against the sort of thing that is prone occasionally to happen to people who lead the sort of life he led. But he did not explicitly connect the sort of life and the sort of thing. He had no more than a general, but desperate, sense of desolation. The times were out of joint.

When a man is miserable he is under sore temptation to hurt somebody—even some blameless individual, whose only crime is that he forms a minute (and involuntary) part of the world which is behaving so badly. Should a particularly vulnerable person chance to pass by, let him look out for himself! One connected, however remotely, with the cause of the misery, for instance. Misery is apt to see a foe everywhere—and to seek a companion.

Just as Bob was passing Hyde Park Corner he ran plump into Godfrey Ledstone, who came out from the Park at a quick walk. The street-lamp revealed them to each other. Godfrey would have passed by with a nod and a "How are you?" That was not at all Bob's idea. He was resolute in buttonholing his friend, in saying how long it was since they had met, in telling him about his doings in the mean time. He enjoyed Godfrey's uneasiness; for Godfrey set him down as a sympathizer with Winnie and was in fear of reference to the topic. Bob made the reference in his own good time.

"Funny I should meet you!" he observed, with a strong draw at his cigar.

"Is it? I don't know. I often take this walk."

"Because I've just come from calling on Winnie." He eyed his prospective victim gloatingly. He was like a savage who thinks that he can unload some of his misfortune onto his neighbor by employing the appropriate ceremonies.

"Oh, I—I hope she's all right?"

"Seems blooming. I didn't have much talk with her, though. There was a chap dancing attendance—a Major somebody or other. Oh yes, Merriam—Major Merriam. He came in pretty soon with a bouquet of flowers as big as your head. Seems that she and Mrs. Lenoir are off abroad to-morrow, and our friend the Major goes too. I don't think you need make yourself unhappy about Winnie, old chap."

"Who is he? I never heard of him."

"Well, I didn't suppose you and she were keeping up a correspondence! If you come to that, I should rather doubt if he ever heard of you." Bob smiled in a fashion less amiable than was his wont.

"Well, I'm in a hurry. Good-bye, old man.'"

"Walking my way?" He indicated Piccadilly and eastward.

It had been Godfrey's way home. "I've got to go to a shop in Sloane Street," said Godfrey.

"Ta-ta then! It'll be a relief to you if she settles down all right, won't it?"

Godfrey said nothing more than "Good-bye." But his face, as he said it, was very expressive; it quite satisfied Bob Purnett's impulse to hurt somebody. Godfrey Ledstone did not like Major Merriam any more than he himself did! The magical ceremony had worked; some of his misfortune was unloaded.

AN HEROIC OFFER

Well, the two were in the end much in the same case.
Winnie had led Godfrey into the great experiment, and
through it into the great failure. She had, this afternoon,
made Bob Purnett, in his turn, false to his settled plan of
life, had sent him away sore and savage because he could
not do the one thing which he had always scornfully declared that he would never do. She had left them both—
left Godfrey to those proceedings, to the family woe, to
Miss Thurseley's immediate repudiation; left Bob to contemplate a lost pleasure, a fruitless heroism, and the Major
in Madeira. The two ought to have sympathized with
each other. Yet their thoughts about each other were not
friendly. "If I'd known the sort of chap he was I'd have
had a shot at it sooner," thought Bob. Godfrey's protest
went deeper. "Of course, it'll happen, but why in Heaven's
name need he tell me about it?" For Bob had suppressed
all that part of the story which accounted for his telling.

They went their separate ways—artificially separate on
this occasion, since there was no shop in Sloane Street at
which Godfrey Ledstone desired to call. They went their
ways with their thoughts, in whose mirror each saw Winnie
smiling on the Major. Precisely what Miss Wilson was
doing at the moment! Jealous men see more than happens,
but what happens they generally see.

XXI

IS HE A BULLY?

CYRIL MAXON'S strong-willed and domineering nature registered its own decrees as having the force of law, and regarded its own resolutions as accomplished facts. When he had once achieved the requisite modification of his opinions, and had decided that he wanted to marry Lady Rosaline in due time, he thought of her in his secret soul as already his—at any rate, as set apart for him— and he found no difficulty in declaring that she had given a tacit consent in their interview in Paris and in the relations of friendship which now existed between her and himself.

But, naturally, the lady did not adopt the same view, either of his rights or of her own actions. The "very most" she had given him was leave to try his fortune, to recommend himself to her during the interval of time which was unavoidable. She was really rather glad of the interval, and observed one day to Mrs. Ladd that it would be no bad thing if everybody were forced to wait either eight or nine months before they married. "Especially if we are to be bound by Mr. Attlebury's opinion!" she added, laughing.

She liked the idea of the marriage; it was suitable, and she was lonely and not rich. She was not yet sure how much she liked the man as she came to know him more intimately; now and then she saw signs of something which helped her to a better understanding of Mrs. Maxon's attitude. "Oh, I'm not afraid of fighting," she would then say to herself; "but I don't want to have to fight all the time. It's fatiguing, and rather vulgar." So she temporized, as the situation enabled her to do; for Maxon was still a tied man, however technical the tie had become; he was not in a position to force the pace. This accidental fact helped her to hold her own against his strong will and domineering instincts; for his conscience had granted him relief only on one point (if really on that), and it did not allow him to forget that he was still a married man.

Lady Rosaline's attitude excited, of course, the liveliest curiosity and an abundance of gossip on the part of her friends, Mrs. Ladd and Miss Fortescue. What did Rosaline mean to do? "Oh, she means to have him," exclaimed Miss Fortescue, "in the end, you know!"

"I think she will, but I believe that quite a little thing might turn her," was Mrs. Ladd's more cautious verdict. Cyril Maxon would not have received it pleasantly.

The good ladies' great disappointment was that they could not induce their revered pastor to say a word on the subject, accessible and, indeed, chatty as he generally was with his flock. When Maxon had taken the first step in those proceedings which had so maddened poor old Mr. Ledstone, he had written to his friend a long and highly argumentative letter, justifying his course. Attlebury had replied in kind, and suggested an interview. This Maxon declined as painful to him, and ended with an asseveration that his conscience approved the course he was taking.

"If it does, there's not much use in my saying any more; but make sure it does," was Attlebury's answer. Maxon took some offence at it, as though it impugned his sincerity.

MRS. MAXON PROTESTS

There was no open rupture, but the men did not meet any more in intimate friendship; there was a reserve between them. Yet Attlebury had said no more, or very little more, than Lady Rosaline herself; she also had asked that his own conscience should approve. But Attlebury could not, or, at all events, did not, keep the note of authority out of his counsel. Maxon stiffened his neck instinctively. Before the necessary interval had run half its course, this instinct was powerfully seconded by another.

He had gone to tea with Mrs. Ladd one Sunday. They were old acquaintances, and for several years back he had been accustomed to pay her five or six calls in the course of a twelvemonth; on which occasions, since his marriage, Mrs. Ladd had discreetly condoled with him over Winnie's shortcomings. But Winnie had disappeared for good; there was now a topic even more attractive.

"Rosaline and I talk of a little trip abroad together in a month's time." She smiled at him. "Will you forgive me if I take her away for three or four weeks?"

"I shall miss you both very much. I wish I could go too, but it's quite impossible."

"I think she wants a change." What Mrs. Ladd wished to convey was that the necessary interval might be tiresome to Lady Rosaline, but she did not quite see how to put it delicately. "It's a long drag from Christmas to Easter, isn't it? Have you seen her lately?"

"I paid her a late call one day last week—that's all. I'm very busy."

"Of course you are—with your practice! Have you met a Sir Axel Thrapston at Rosaline's?"

"Axel Thrapston? No, I don't think so. No, I'm sure not." He very seldom met anybody at Lady Rosaline's, as his visits were timed so as to avoid, as far as possible, such a contingency. "Who is he?"

"I don't know much about him myself. He comes from Northumberland, I think, and lives there generally. I believe his wife was an old friend of Rosaline's; she died about two years ago. I've met him there twice—a middle-aged man, rather bald, but quite good-looking."

"No, I haven't met him, Mrs. Ladd."

"He seems just to have made his appearance, but I think he's rather assiduous." She laughed again. "And two years is just about the dangerous time, isn't it?"

Thus Mrs. Ladd, hinting to Cyril Maxon, in all friendship, that he was not the only man in the world and had better not forget the fact. Friend as she was, she knew enough of her man to feel a certain pleasure in administering the wholesome warning.

It needed more to drive Cyril Maxon from his confident appropriation of Lady Rosaline, but that something more was not long in coming. He, too, met Sir Axel at her flat—once or twice in the hours which he had grown into the habit of considering as reserved for himself; he tried very hard to show neither surprise nor annoyance, but he felt an immediate grievance. Here was he, the busiest of men, painfully contriving a spare hour; was he to spend it in three-cornered, trivial talk? Thrapston had all the long, idle day to call. Lady Rosaline really might give him a hint! But it appeared not to strike her that she might. And she seemed to like Sir Axel's company—as, indeed, most people would. He was a simple country-gentleman, no fool at all at his own business, but without much pretension to intellectual or artistic culture. This, however, he could recognize and respect; he recognized and respected it in Lady

245

Rosaline, was anxious to learn from her, and deferred to her authority. "When people wish to attach, they should always be ignorant. To come with a well-informed mind is to come with an inability of administering to the vanity of others which a sensible person would always wish to avoid." Jane Austen perhaps allows herself a little malice in this remark, but we cannot deny that she speaks with authority on human nature.

On one occasion, when he did find his friend alone, Maxon complained of the times when he had not.

"I've nothing against him, of course, but it's you I come to talk to. Why, I scandalize my clerk, and sometimes my clients, for the sake of coming!" He managed to keep voice and manner playful.

She was gracious, admitting the force of his plea. "It was stupid of me not to think! Of course Sir Axel can come at any time. I'll give him a hint to call earlier. Is that satisfactory, my lord?" She sometimes called him by that title—partly in anticipation of the judgeship, but also with a hint of raillery at the domineering nature.

"It's very kind—and don't you like it better like this yourself?"

"Perhaps I do. And clearly you do. And"—she smiled —"very likely Sir Axel does. We shall all three be pleased! Delightful!"

"I wasn't thinking of his point of view, I confess." He was rather too scornful.

"No, but he may think of it, I suppose? And I suppose I may, if I like, Mr. Maxon?"

He looked at her sourly for just a moment, then recovered himself and, without replying, passed on to the subject of a book which he had brought her. But he was annoyed that

246

she should resist him, stand up to him, and claim her liberty
—especially her liberty to receive Sir Axel alone. However, it was not good fighting-ground; he had brought her
rebuke upon himself.

Lady Rosaline was quite alive to the fact that Sir Axel's
appearance and Sir Axel's attentiveness were a valuable
asset to her, but she did not think of her old friend's husband in any other light. To begin with, he himself, though
assiduous, had shown no sign of sentiment. If he were
moving in that direction at all, he was moving slowly and
secretly. And then she was still inclined to Maxon. She
had a great opinion of his ability—she was more sure about
that than about how much she liked him—and the chances
of a high career for him allured her. But Sir Axel and his
assiduity enhanced her value and buttressed her independence. They helped her to establish her position; she had
an idea that the more firmly she established it now, the
better it would resist any attacks on it if and when she
became Lady Rosaline Maxon. Here she was probably
right. But she had another idea too. She was not going
to be dictated to; she would not be browbeaten into becoming Lady Rosaline Maxon.

In this state of external affairs and internal disposi-
tions, the "proceedings" came and went—really meaning
no more than a transitory quarter of an hour's annoyance to
the rising Cyril Maxon, for whom everything was made as
easy and sympathetic as possible. Other effects in Woburn
Square, no doubt—possibly others in Madeira! Yet transitory and formal as they were, the proceedings left behind
them a state of affairs more essentially transitory and formal
still. The tie was now a mere technicality, and when conscience took the position that Cyril Maxon was still a mar-

ried man for all purposes, conscience began to seem to put the matter too high. For present conduct, yes—and he had no wish to run counter to the injunction, for reasons both moral and prudential; but for laying down the future on definite lines? That seemed a different point. He reconsidered his attitude—not without being influenced, more or less consciously, by Lady Rosaline's independence and by the assiduity of Sir Axel Thrapston. The hint that she still considered herself free, the notion of a rival, turned the necessary interval from a mere nuisance into a possible danger. Moreover, she was going abroad with Mrs. Ladd, and he could not follow. Mrs. Ladd was a friendly influence, but he would like to define the situation before Lady Rosaline went. Not desiring to risk a peculiarly annoying collision with Sir Axel, he wrote and asked her for an appointment.

She neither desired to refuse the interview, nor well could. But she scented an attack, and stood instinctively on the defensive. She wanted just the opposite of what Cyril Maxon did; the trip first and the decision afterward was her order of events. She relied on the necessary interval, while he was now out of patience with it. "I won't be rushed!" she said to herself. She gave him the appointment he asked on a Saturday afternoon (he had suggested that comparatively free day) at half-past four, but she let drop to Sir Axel that she would be at home at half-past five on the same afternoon. Her motive in doing this was rather vague—just a notion that some discussions can go on too long, or that she might like to relax an agitated mind in talk with a friend, or, possibly, that she might like to be told that she had done right. Her reasons for the intimation to Sir Axel defy conclusive analysis.

"Lady Rosaline," said Cyril Maxon, as he put down his

empty tea-cup, "last week saw the end of an episode in my life." (Mr. Attlebury would hardly have referred to it as an episode.) "The future is my concern now. I took the action I did take on the fullest consideration, and I'm glad to think, from what you said in Paris, that it had your approval." He paused a moment. "I hope I'm not wrong in thinking that you understood why I took it, when once I had made up my mind that it was permissible?"

"Oh, you mustn't make too much of what I said in Paris. I'm no authority. I left it to you."

He smiled. "The question of permissibility—naturally. But the other altogether? Well, never mind that." He rose from his chair and stood by her. "You must know that it was for your sake that I took the step I did?"

She moved restlessly, neither affirming nor denying. She knew it very well.

"Before the world we must remain as we are for the present. But it would make a vast difference to me, during this time of waiting, to know that I—that I could rely on you, Rosaline. You can have no doubt of my feelings, though I have exercised self-restraint. I love you, and I want you to be my wife as soon as possible."

"Well, it's not possible at present, is it?"

"No. But there's no reason why we shouldn't have a perfect understanding between ourselves."

"Wouldn't it make gossip, and perhaps raise awkward questions, if we—well, if we arranged anything definitely now—before the time's up?"

"It would be quite between ourselves. There could be no questions. There would be no difference in our present relations—we should neither of us wish that. But the future would be secure."

"I can't see the good of being engaged now, if it's to make no difference," she murmured, fretfully.

"It'll make an enormous difference in my feelings. I think you know that."

"It seems to me to set up rather a—rather a difficult state of things. You know how much I like you—but why shouldn't we both be free till the time comes?" She took courage to raise her eyes to his on this suggestion.

"I have no desire to be free." His voice grew rather harsh. "I didn't know that you had. In Paris—"

She flared out suddenly; for her conscience was, in fact, not quite easy. "Well, what did I say in Paris after all? You never said in Paris what you're saying now! If you had—well, I should have told you that I wasn't at all ready to give a decision. And I'm not ready now. I want this time of waiting to make up my mind. You're trying to drive me into saying 'Yes' before I'm ready. What's the good of that, even to you? Because what prevents me from changing my mind in the next six months—even if you make me say 'Yes' to you now?"

"I took an important—and to me a difficult—step in reliance on your feelings toward me. I seem to have been mistaken about them." His voice was sombre, even rather rancorous.

"Don't say that, Cyril. But why must I give up my liberty long before—well, long before I can get anything instead of it?" She smiled again, propitiating him. "Let me go abroad, anyhow. I'll try to tell you when I come back. There!"

"I confess to thinking that you had practically told me long ago. On the faith of that I acted."

"You've not the smallest right to say that. I liked you and let you see it. I never pledged myself."

"Not in words, I allow."

"Cyril, your insinuation isn't justifiable. I resent it. Whatever I may have felt, I have said and done nothing that I mightn't have with anybody."

He had held his temper hard; it gave a kick now. "With Thrapston, for instance?" he sneered.

"Oh, how absurd! I've never so much as thought of Sir Axel in that way!" As she spoke she glanced at the clock. No, there was plenty of time. She did not desire an encounter between the two this afternoon. She rose and stood by Maxon. "You're being rather exacting and—and tyrannical, my lord," she said. "I don't think I like you so much to-day. You almost bully me—indeed you do!"

He bent his eyes on hers, frowning heavily. "I did it for you."

"Oh, it's not fair to put that on me! Indeed, it isn't. But, please, don't let's quarrel. It's really such a little thing I ask—not much more than a month to think it over—when nothing can happen for more than six! Indeed, I think a year would—well, would look better for both of us."

"Oh, make it two years—make it five!" he growled.

"Cyril, if you go on like this, I'll make it never—here, now, and for good!"

Even he saw that he had gone too far. He contrived to smooth brow and voice, and put in the man's usual plea to excuse his rough impatience. "It's only because I love you."

"Yes, but you needn't be like a bear making love," she retorted, pettishly. Yet, to a certain extent, she was appeased by the apology; and she by no means wanted to

17   251

"make it never" then and there. His rudeness and his apology together gave her a tactical advantage which she was not slow to use. "But if you do love me as you say, you won't refuse what I ask of you," she went on. Then she indulged him with a touch of sentiment. "If I say 'Yes,' I want to say it without any doubt—with my whole heart, Cyril. 'Yes' now wouldn't be what it ought to be between you and me."

She maintained her advantage to the end of the interview. She won her respite; nothing more was to be said till after her return from abroad. Meanwhile they would correspond as friends—"As great friends as you like!" she threw in, smiling. As friends, too, they parted on this occasion; for when he offered to embrace her she held out her hand gracefully, saying, "That 'll do for to-day, I think, Cyril." His frown came again, but he submitted.

In fact, in the first encounter between them, Cyril Maxon was beaten. She stood up against him, and had won her way. True, she was almost bound to; her position was so much the more favorable. Yet, however defeat came, Maxon was not accustomed to it, and did not like it. And he liked her the less for inflicting it—he used one or two hard words about her as he drove home from Hans Place —but he did not the less want to marry her. The masterful element in him became the more urgent to achieve that victory, to make up all the ground that he had lost to-day— and more. But, if he contrasted to-day's interview with his previous assumptions, it was plain that he had lost a lot of ground. What had seemed the practically certain became merely the reasonably probable. Instead of being to all intents and purposes accepted, he was told that he was only a suitor, though, no doubt, a suitor who was entitled to

entertain good hopes of success. Yes, very good hopes, if
nothing intervened. But he hated the trip abroad, and he
hated Sir Axel Thrapston—in spite of Lady Rosaline's disclaimer of any sentimental interest in that gentleman. The
mere fact of her asking for a delay made every delay dangerous, and, while she doubted at all, any man much about
her might make her more doubtful. "If she throws me
over now—" he muttered angrily to himself; for always in
his mind, as now and then on his lips, was that "I did it for
you." She had accepted the sacrifice of his conscience;
was she now to refuse to answer his prayer? In the new
light of her possibly refusing, he almost admitted the sacrifice. At any rate, he asserted, he had acted on a conclusion
full of difficulty and not quite free from doubt. It was beyond question that the case of conscience might vary in aspect, according as Lady Rosaline Deering did or did not say
"Yes."

If the vanquished combatant was decidedly savage, the
victorious was rather exhausted. Lady Rosaline lay prone
in a luxurious arm-chair before the fire, doing nothing, feeling very tired. She had won, but a succession of such
victories—a perpetual need of such victories—would be
Pyrrhic in its effect on her nerves. The room seemed suddenly filled with an atmosphere of peace. She gave a little
stretch, a little yawn, and nestled down farther into her big
chair.

Thus Sir Axel Thrapston, punctual to his half-past five,
and missing Cyril Maxon by some ten minutes, found her.
His arrival did not disturb her sense of repose, but, perhaps,
rather accentuated it; for with him she had no quarrel, and
about him no complication of feelings difficult to unravel.
Moreover, he was an essentially peaceful person, a live-and-

let-live man. She received him graciously, but without rising from the big chair.

"Forgive my not getting up; I'm rather tired. You take the little chair, and draw it up."

He did as he was bid. "Been doing too much?" he asked.

"Oh, not particularly, but I am tired. But you'll rest me, if you'll sit there, and not mind if I don't talk much." However, she went on talking. "There are some people whom one likes and admires tremendously, and yet who are rather—well, exacting—aren't there?"

Sir Axel would have been dull not to surmise that his friend had had recent experience of some such person as she described.

"No, exacting isn't quite the word I want. I mean, they take their own point of view so strongly that it's really a struggle—a downright struggle—to make them see that there may be another."

"I know the sort of fellow. My Scotch gardener's one of 'em."

"Well, I don't know your Scotch gardener, but I do know one or two men of the sort."

"I should think you could stand up for yourself!"

His glance was one of friendly appreciation of her—and of her appearance. She certainly looked well in the firelight.

"Oh, I think I can, but one doesn't want always to be having to do it."

"Not good enough to live with people like that, Lady Rosaline!"

He meant no personal reference, but his companion had little difficulty in finding a personal application. Her eyes

wandered from the fire and settled on his face in a medita-
tive gaze.

"Unless, I mean, you were quite sure of coming out on
top. And even then—well, I hate rows, anyhow."

"So do I—even when I win, Sir Axel! I do so agree with
you." The eyes took on a grateful look. Sir Axel was
making a more favorable impression than the good man had
any idea of. Cyril Maxon was responsible for Sir Axel's
success this afternoon; it was a true instinct that had led
Lady Rosaline to make a second appointment! Her nerves
were soothed; her weariness passed into a pleasant languor.
She smiled at him indolently, in peaceful contentment.

"When did you say you were off?" she inquired. In asking when he might come to see her, he had founded his plea
on the ground of an early departure from London.

"Next Tuesday. I'm looking forward to it. I've never
seen Venice. I shall be at Danieli's."

"Now, did I ask your address, Sir Axel?"

He laughed. "Oh, I was playing my own hand. I
thought perhaps, if I couldn't stand my own society all the
time, you'd let me pay a call on you at the Lakes on my
way back."

Lady Rosaline and Mrs. Ladd had planned an absolutely
quiet time at the Italian Lakes. But, then, Sir Axel was
absolutely quiet—after Cyril Maxon.

"Well, I might go so far as to send you an address.
Don't consider it a command—or even an invitation!"

"You see, I don't know a soul out there, and can't speak
a word of the language."

"Well, if absolute desperation drives you to our door,
perhaps we'll let you stay a little."

"Oh, I say, I didn't quite mean that!"

" The fact is, you're not very good at pretty speeches, are you ? But I don't mind that—and you know I should always be glad to see you."

Sir Axel departed well pleased, not knowing to whom or to what the better part of his pleasure might justly be attributed. So may we profit by our neighbors' blunders, and find therein some consolation for our sufferings from their superior brilliancy.

XXII

CERTAINLY the quartette made a very agreeable party in Madeira. It proved to be as happily composed as the Major had anticipated. The two elders enjoyed the sunshine, the fine nights, the casino, much gossip with each other and with casual coevals who had anything to add. The young couple made their excursions, had their bath and a little lawn-tennis (Winnie could not be roused to enthusiasm over this), gambled mildly, and danced enthusiastically. Not all these things with each other exclusively. There were other young women there, and other young men. The Major was in request among the former; Winnie among the latter. There was no overdoing of the *tête-à-tête*. Among the colors, the flowers, and the fun, life ran very pleasantly.

But Mrs. Lenoir was a little impatient. Her pet scheme seemed to hang fire. She could not quite make out why. It was not, she thought, the other young men and women; there was no sign of any foreign attraction such as might induce either of her predestined lovers to wander from the appointed path. Yet the Major's advances were, in her judgment, painfully deliberate, and Winnie's good-fellowship with him was almost demonstratively unsentimental. Mrs. Lenoir felt her experience at fault; she had expected that, in such a favorable climate, the affair would ripen more quickly. But there are ways of forcing plants, and she was a skilful gardener.

One day, a week after the party had arrived on the island, she came out into the hotel garden after lunch and settled herself, with the General's gallant assistance, in a long chair; the spot commanded a view over the harbor. The General, his offices performed, sat in a shorter chair and smoked his cigar. Far below them the ramshackle, pretty town seemed to blink in the sunshine; a rather sleepy blinking is the attitude it takes toward existence, except when a tourist ship comes in, or a squadron of men-of-war. Then it sits up and eats, and anon sleeps again.

"I suppose, when they come down from the Mount, they'll go straight to the casino," said the General.

"Yes, I told them we'd meet them there. Hugh!"

She did not very often call him Hugh. In the use of his name he was in the habit of recognizing some rather special call on his services or his attention.

"Yes, my dear Clara? Now you're not going to worry about your share of the wine again?"

"No," said she, smiling, "I'm not. I've a little confession to make to you. I told you a fib about Winnie. I told you the fib I told everybody—that she was a distant cousin. She isn't. I met her at some friends'—very nice people. She was quite adrift. I asked her to come to me for a bit, and we got on so well that she's stayed. She's an orphan, I know—her father was a parson—and I think she's quite alone in the world, though she has a small income." She laughed. "You see what a long story it is. With most people it's so much easier to tell the little fib. But I've told you the truth about her now." Yet not all the truth. Mrs. Lenoir's conscience seemed sometimes to work on easy springs.

"Thank you for telling me, Clara. I suppose I know why you told me. But I think my boy knows already that, if he has any designs about Miss Winnie, he'll not find me an obstacle. Only she doesn't seem to me to be anything more than friendly toward him."

"Well, she'd naturally wait for a lead, wouldn't she?"

"You think it's that?" Mrs. Lenoir's slight wave of her fan was non-committal. "He's a very conscientious fellow. He looks at a thing all round. I'm sure he'd consider not only whether he liked her, but whether he could satisfy her —whether the life he could offer her would be to her liking. Being a soldier's wife isn't all beer and skittles. And getting on with all the regiment!"

"Dear me, is there all that to consider?" Her tone was playful, yet rather contemptuous. "It doesn't look as if he was desperately in love."

"Men differ," mused the General. "Look at my three sons. Bertie's as I tell you—slow and solid—make an excellent husband to a woman of sense. The Colonel never looks at a woman, so far as I know. George runs after every petticoat he meets, and hangs the consequences—confound him!"

"And which," asked Mrs. Lenoir, "is most like father, Hugh?"

"Ancient history, ancient history!" he murmured, half in pleasure, half in contrition, yet with a glance at his companion. "Shall I tell him what you've told me about Miss Winnie?"

"Just as you like." She laughed. "I don't think he's gone far enough to have any rights yet, you know."

"I don't think he has," agreed the General, laughing too —and not aware of the bearings of his admission.

Mrs. Lenoir, however, treasured it in her armory; she might have need of it. Plainly the General might consider that, confession once begun, confession ought to have gone further. She had the same plausible answers she had given to Winnie herself. She had another; she acknowledged her own fib, but she would plead that she had no right to betray her friend. In the end she had not much doubt that she could manage the General. She had managed him before—in a much more difficult case; and he was very fond of Winnie. Something of partisanship influenced her mood; the free lance renewed memories of old raids in this little skirmish against convention; she was minded to fight at the best advantage she could—with the father "contained" and the son as deeply committed to his position as she could get him before the blow was struck.

As a result of this conversation the General carried away an uneasy idea—born of the confidence so pointedly re-posed in him, enforced by the slight touch of contempt in Mrs. Lenoir's voice—that one of the ladies, even possibly both, considered his son, if not a laggard, yet at least some-what prosaically circumspect in his love-making. Such a view, if really entertained, did some injustice to Bertie Merriam. He was not impulsive; he was not passionate. He took time to make up his mind. It would be almost true to say that, before falling in love, he made up his mind that he would—not the commonest order of events. But he had pretty well made up his mind by now. Only, he received very little encouragement. Winnie was always "jolly" to him; but she asked nothing of him, made no special claims on him—and took the same liberty as she accorded. In the pleasant round of their life he was one comrade among many; more intimate than the rest, no doubt, by reason of his habitual escort, the excursions, and the messing together at table, but not different in kind. Vaguely the Major felt that there was some barrier, real but imperceptible, which he could not pass—a thing made up out of a thousand unobtrusive trifles, yet composing in the mass a defence that he could not see how to penetrate.

There was a curious little man in the hotel—a man of about forty-five, short, bald, shabby, yet clean, though he did not bathe. In fact, he did nothing—no excursions, no sports, no dancing, no flirtation. He did not even read; he sat about—meditating, it must be presumed. Something in him made the girls giggle and the men wink as he passed by; the men said "Dotty!" and the girls sniggered at the witticism. His name, sought out in the hotel register, proved to be Adolphus Wigram. The wit who had made the search called him "Dolly"—and the name became his at once, varied back to "Dotty" sometimes by an ultra-witticism.

When Winnie came home from the casino this evening, having some minutes to spare before dressing for dinner, she went onto the hotel balcony, which overlooks the town from a loftier and, so to say, a more condescending altitude than the garden. She rested her elbows on the railing and surveyed the beauty of the scene, so artfully composed of hill and slope and sea that one can hardly conceive it the outcome of nature's mere—and probably violent—caprice. She was lost in thought, and was startled to find elbows on a level with hers and a head in close neighborhood, though rather lower. She recognized "Dolly," in the shabbiest of all suits, looking meditatively down on the lights of the town and harbor of Funchal.

"Quite a small place, Miss Wilson," said "Dolly." "Full of people!"

"I suppose it is," Winnie agreed, politely. She had come out on the balcony occupied with another question than the population of Madeira.

"I tried to understand things once—to grasp them in the large, you know. Seems easy to some people, but I couldn't do it. I teach history. I was a bit overworked; some of my friends subscribed to send me out here for just a fortnight. Doing me good."

Winnie turned her face toward the funny, jerky little man. "Are you going to grasp things in the large when you get back?" she asked.

"No, no; I'm afraid not. Thirty thousand or so of them down there, I suppose! All thinking they're very important. All being born or dying or love - making or starving or filling their bellies, and so on. Quite a small place!"

Winnie smiled. "Yes, I dare say. It sounds true but rather trite. I have problems of my own, Mr. Wigram."

"So have I—income and taxation and necessary expenditure. Still, these thirty thousand are interesting."

"They're awfully lucky to want very few clothes and hardly any fires, and to live in such a beautiful place. What do you mean by things in the large, Mr. Wigram?"

"Well, I mean truth," said the absurd little man, clutching the balcony railings, just as if he were going to vault over them and crack his skull on the nut-shaped stones which served for a path thirty or forty feet beneath. "Truth is things in the large, you know."

"I don't think I know that, but I know a friend in England who talks rather like you."

"Poor devil! How much money does he make?"

"He's got independent means, Mr. Wigram."

"Then he can afford to talk a great deal better."

"You really make me rather uncomfortable. Surely everybody can say what they like nowadays?"

The little man gave an abrupt, hoarse laugh. "I teach history in a school, and get a hundred and fifty pounds a year for it. Can I say what I like? Do I tell the truth about the history? Oh, dear, no!"

"I've got just a hundred and fifty pounds a year. Can I do what I like?" asked Winnie.

"Dolly" turned to her with a queer, ridiculous solemnity. "It seems to me," he observed, "a competency for an able-bodied young woman. I don't know what you can do, but I think you're quite in a position to tell the truth—if you happen to know it. Anybody dependent on you?"

"Not a soul," smiled Winnie.

"I've a mother and an unmarried sister. You see the difference? I think I heard the gong. Good-evening."

"Good-evening, Mr. Wigram." Winnie rushed in to dress for dinner, pitiful, smiling, and thoughtful.

The quartette was not as merry as usual that evening. Bertie Merriam was rather glum, and when Winnie perceived it she grew remorseful. Up at the Mount he had, at last, shown signs of making a definite advance; if she had not snubbed him, she had at least fought him off by affected unconsciousness of his meaning, by persistent unsentimentality. It was almost against her own will; she could not help it; the instinct in her was irresistible. She might have been equal to standing by Tora Aikenhead's

view—"As long as my own conscience is clear, it's no affair
of yours what I did before I knew you, and I sha'n't say a
word about it." She could certainly have followed Stephen's
atavistic "public-school" idea of honor with perfect readi-
ness. These were both, in their different ways, forms of
defiance. But Mrs. Lenoir's compromise—"I'll wait till
the truth can't hurt me, though it may hurt you"—was not
defiance; it was deceit. Under the influence of gratitude to
the friend to whom she owed so much kindness, and of the
deference which she honestly accorded to her adviser's experience and wisdom, she had accepted it. All very well
to accept it in words! She found that she could not act
upon it. Instead of making Bertie Merriam like her so
well that the truth could be told to him without risk—or, at
any rate, with the minimum of risk—she was spending her
time in trying to prevent him from liking her in that way at
all. If she went on, she would succeed; he was sensitive,
proud, easy to discourage. Yet, as things stood, she knew
that she would not be able to resist going on. Then it came
to this—Mrs. Lenoir's compromise would not work. It
might or might not be justifiable, but it simply would not
work in Winnie's hands. She could not carry it out, because it meant in the end that she was to behave just as
Godfrey Ledstone had. The *gravamen* of his offence was
that he had been ashamed of her; now she was being
ashamed of herself. He had conceded to his family the
right to think her shameful; she was allowing the same
right to the Major, and merely trying to curry favor enough
to override his judgment. Such a course was not only
flat against her theories; it was flat against the nature which
had produced the theories. And, in practice, it resulted in
a deadlock; it kept the Major at a standstill. He did

not retreat, because his feelings dictated an advance. He could not advance, because she would not let him. There he stuck—up against that impalpable, impenetrable barrier.

"I've been talking—out on the balcony—with that funny little man they call 'Dolly,'" she remarked. "He told me that, if you had nobody dependent on you, and had a hundred and fifty pounds a year, you were in a position to tell the truth."

"Is it exactly a question of what money you've got, Miss Winnie?" asked the General.

She let the question pass. "Anyhow, that happens to be exactly my income. Rather funny!" She looked across the small table at Mrs. Lenoir—and was not surprised to find that Mrs. Lenoir was looking at her already.

"I suppose he meant that if you weren't absolutely obliged to get or keep some job—" the Major began.

"That's what he meant; and there's a lot in it, isn't there, Major Merriam?"

"Well, it's not what we're taught at school, but perhaps there is."

"More luxuries for the rich," smiled Mrs. Lenoir.

"The Radicals can make a new grievance out of it at the next election," said the General.

Of course, the two men did not know what underlay Winnie's talk. Equally, of course, Mrs. Lenoir did; she saw it in a minute, and her reading hardly needed the confirmation of Bertie's glum demeanor. Winnie was in rebellion—probably in irreconcilable rebellion. Mrs. Lenoir glanced across at her with a satirically protesting smile. Winnie smiled back, but her eyes were resolute—rather merrily resolute, as though she liked this new taste of her favorite cup of defiance.

"There are times and seasons," said Mrs. Lenoir. "Isn't there even a thing called the economy of truth? I don't thing I know the exact doctrine."

"You wouldn't tell a child everything—or a fool, either," observed the General.

"Would you choose the wrong time to tell the truth to anybody?" Mrs. Lenoir asked.

"Are you entitled to settle what's the right time—all by yourself?" Winnie retorted, gayly. Her spirits had begun to rise. This was almost like a discussion at Shaylor's Patch. There was a deeper reason. With her determination had come a sense of recovered honesty, and, more, of liberty regained. Whatever the Merriams might think, she would be herself again—herself and no longer Miss Winnie Wilson, a young person whom, in the last week or so, she had begun to hate cordially.

Winnie did not go to the casino that evening; she left the General and his son to walk there together. She followed Mrs. Lenoir into the drawing-room, and sat down by her.

"So you've made up your mind, Winnie?" Mrs. Lenoir did not seem angry or hurt. She merely recognized Winnie's resolution.

"Yes. I can't go on with it. And it's a good moment. The newspapers come to-morrow, and, if what Hobart Gaynor told me was right, there 'll be something about me in them."

"Yes, I remember. Well, if you're set on doing it, that doesn't make such a bad—occasion." Mrs. Lenoir was considering how the "occasion" could best be twisted into a justification of previous silence. With the Major that would not be so much a pressing question—other factors

266

would probably decide his action—but it was a point that
her friend the General might raise. She looked thoughtfully at Winnie. "How much do you like him?" she asked.
"I like him as much as I know him, but I don't know
him very much. I shall know a little more to-morrow."
She paused. "I should like the life, the whole thing, very
much, I think."

"She's not in love, but she'd take him," Mrs. Lenoir inwardly interpreted.

"I'm sorry to act against your advice, after all you've done
for me. It does look ungrateful."

"Oh, I don't expect people to give up their liberty just
because I'm fond of them." She rose. "I'm off to my
room, my dear. Good-night—and good-luck."

Winnie went out on the balcony to seek for Mr. Adolphus
Wigram and some more talk about truth. But he was not
there; he had gone down to the casino, where he lost exactly
half a dollar with unbroken bad-luck every night—probably
one of the things which the claims of his family and the
figure of his salary would cause him to suppress the truth
about when he got back to his school. So she remembered
that there was an impromptu dance going on down-stairs,
and went and danced and flirted furiously till midnight.
The girls said that they had never seen Miss Wilson look so
well, and never had the young men crowded round Miss
Wilson so eagerly. In fact, Miss Wilson had her fling.
Small blame to her. It was the last night of her life—at
least, so far as that life had any real significance. Though
Winnie did not propose to change her name in the hotel
book or on the lips of casual companions during her stay in
Madeira, yet for essential purposes that night saw an end of
Miss Winnie Wilson.

MRS. MAXON PROTESTS

Since English newspapers arrive in the island only once a week, the competition for them on the mail-day is formidable. Persons who combine agility and selfishness with a healthy interest in public affairs may be observed sitting on five copies of their favorite journal, reading a sixth, and anon glaring angrily round at potential applicants for one of the spare copies. Winnie took no part in the scramble, and attacked nobody's reserve pile of intelligence. She knew that her paper would come in a separate wrapper, addressed to her personally by Hobart Gaynor; she wanted only one day's paper.

She found it laid by her plate at lunch—a meal which passed in the discussion of the news of the world; the Major had been a successful competitor in the struggle, and was well-primed. Winnie rose when coffee appeared, her paper in her hand. She addressed Bertie Merriam rather pointedly.

"I'm going into the garden—that seat under the trees. You know?"

"I'll come, too. Directly I've drunk my coffee." As Winnie walked off he exchanged a glance with his father. They had had a confidential little talk at the casino the evening before, in which Winnie's behavior was the subject of some puzzled comment. This invitation to the garden looked more promising. Mrs. Lenoir was busy reading a letter. Winnie had read one letter, too—from Hobart Gaynor, telling her all she needed to know, and referring her to a certain page of her paper.

Yes, there it was—very short, matter of fact, and hard. Well, what else should it be? Only it seemed oddly to reproduce Cyril Maxon himself. The report sounded as if his exact words, nay, his very tones, had been caught; they

"I WAS MRS. MAXON, THAT'S ALL," SAID WINNIE

seemed to echo in her ears; she almost heard him saying it all. And what more appropriate, what so inevitable an ending could there be to Cyril's utterances than the words which closed this brief record—"Judgment accordingly"? Those words might always have been written at the end of Cyril's remarks. "Judgment accordingly." It seemed to sum up, as well as to close, the story of her relations with him. From the beginning right through to this, the end, on her and her works—on all she did and was—there had been "Judgment accordingly."

She let the copy of the *Times* fall on her lap, and sat idle—waiting for Bertie Merriam, yet not thinking much of him. The figure of "Dolly" shuffled into view. The odd little man was smoking a cigarette, and, in the intervals of puffing, was apparently talking to himself in a cheerful and animated way—no sounds, but the lips moved quickly. As he passed, Winnie hailed him. "Had your mail, Mr. Wigram?"

He stopped. "I've had good news, Miss Wilson—good news from home. They've raised my salary."

"Oh, I am glad, Mr. Wigram."

"A twenty-pound rise, Miss Wilson. Well, I've done fifteen years. But still it's liberal." He seemed to swell a little. "And it's a recognition. I value it as a recognition." The transient swelling subsided. "And it 'll help," he ended, soberly.

"Shall you be able to tell the truth to any greater extent, Mr. Wigram?"

"Oh, I think not, I think not. I—I hadn't thought of it from that point of view, Miss Wilson."

"I've had no rise in my income, but I'm going to do it."

He was not really listening. He gave a feeble cackle of a

laugh. "I'm just making a few calculations, Miss Wilson." On he went, apportioning every penny of that hard-earned increase of twenty pounds per annum. Valuable—but not enough to enable him to teach true history.

Major Merriam sauntered toward her with his cigar. He was really rather eager, but he did not look it. The invitation might be merely a tardy apology for the snubs of yesterday.

"May I sit down by you?"

"Please do. Have you seen the *Times*?"

"I looked through the lot of them."

"Have you seen this one—the 26th?" She held up her copy.

"I suppose I have. I had a run through them all."

"Read that." Her finger indicated the report.

He read it; the process did not take long. He took his cigar out of his mouth. "Well, Miss Wilson?"

"I was Mrs. Maxon; that's all," said Winnie.

XXIII

THE REGIMENT

HAD Bertie Merriam displayed righteous indignation or uncontrollable grief, Winnie would have left him to digest his emotion in solitary leisure. Since, however, he merely looked extremely thoughtful, as he let the *Times* flutter to the ground and took a long pull at his cigar, it seemed natural to tell him the story. This she proceeded to do, neither boastfully nor apologetically, but with sober veracity, tempered by a humorous appreciation of how the various parties to it, herself included, came out of their various ordeals. Now and then her auditor nodded his understanding of the points—of the impossibility of life with Cyril Maxon; of how Shaylor's Patch enlarged the horizon; of the experiment with Godfrey Ledstone and its comico-tragic failure; of how Maxon, for reasons unascertained, had found open to him a course which he had always declared to be lawfully open to no man; finally, of the considerations, sufficient or insufficient, which had led to the incarnation of Miss Winnie Wilson. In fact, so far as it lies within a human being's power to tell the truth about himself or herself, Winnie told it; she had no dependents and she had a hundred and fifty pounds a year.

As has been said, the Major was not an especially religious man. He had himself lived an unusually steady and regular life, keeping himself in strict training for the work to which his whole heart was devoted, but his moral ideas were those of his class and generation. He was not straitlaced. Moreover, he was heavily biassed in favor of the lady who now took him into her confidence, and not only had the advantage of telling her side of the story without anybody to criticise or contradict, but succeeded in telling it so as to carry conviction of her sincerity, if not of her wisdom. He was ready to see with her eyes, at least to the point of admitting excuse where she pleaded justification. Though he imputed to her a great want of worldly wisdom in her dealings with Godfrey Ledstone, her moral character did not suffer in his estimation, nor (what was perhaps more remarkable) were his feelings toward her perceptibly chilled. Neither did he cherish any personal grievance. She was entitled to protect herself from the idle curiosity of casual acquaintances. So soon as she had definite ground for according to him a special treatment, she had dealt openly with him and made a clean breast of it.

"Thank you," he said at the end. "I shall respect your confidence."

"What I've told you is meant for the General, too, please."

"Thank you again. It's very straight of you. You must be glad to have it all over at last?"

Winnie made the slightest grimace. "Isn't that rather a sanguine view?" Her own views about things being "all over" had become less sanguine than of yore.

"Well, yes, I suppose it is." Even while he had been speaking the same idea was at the back of his own mind. Things have a way of never getting "all over," of possessing no absolute ends, of continuing, for good and evil, to affect life till life itself ends—and even, after that, of affecting other lives sometimes. Bertie Merriam himself, thoughtfully considering, saw that the thing was by no means "all over" with the coming of the news contained in the *Times* of the 26th.

"And now," said Winnie, rising from her chair, "I'm going to talk nonsense with the Layton girl and the Anstruther boys, and forget all about it for a bit." She stood looking at him for a moment in a very friendly, rather puzzled, way. She wanted to convey to him that she would consider it very natural for her disclosure to make all the difference, but the assurance was not easy to frame without assuming more than she was, by the forms of the game, entitled to assume. She got as near to it as she could. "I've been prepared to accept the consequences all through. If I claim liberty of opinion myself, I allow it to others, Major Merriam."

"Yes, yes, I quite understand. You surely don't fear a harsh judgment from me?" He added, after the briefest pause, "Or from my father?"

"I don't think I need. You've both been such kind, good friends to me." She broke into a smile. "And, of course, on my theory I don't admit that I'm properly a subject of judgment at all."

"But you admit that I may think differently if I like?"

"Yes, I admit that. We may all think what we like, and do as we like, so long as we do it sincerely."

"Wouldn't things get rather—well, chaotic—under that system?" he asked, smiling in his turn.

"I knew I shouldn't convert you—you stickler for discipline!"

He heard the description with a laugh, but without protest or disclaimer. To his ears it was a compliment. Nor did he think Winnie, so far as he claimed to understand her, quite so scornful of all discipline as her playful taunt implied, nor in practice so thoroughgoing an anarchist as her theory of the unbridled liberty of private judgment required in logic that she should be. She did not appear to him a naturally lawless woman, nor even unusually volatile. She had had "hard luck" and had fought against it blindly and recklessly. But, given good conditions, she would readily conform to the standards, since she would not want to do anything else. Taking this view, he saw little reason to revise his judgment or to alter his intentions, so far as the judgment and intentions depended on his estimate of the woman herself. Her candor was even a new point in her favor.

So far, then, neither Winnie nor even Mrs. Lenoir need regret the disclosure. The case, when fully explained, seemed to the Major eminently pardonable—at worst, a piece of visionary folly in which an ignorant young woman had rashly matched herself against the world. But there was another aspect of the case. *Tout comprendre c'est tout pardonner.* Perhaps. But some people shrink from understanding things for that very reason; the consequences seem too alarming and even revolutionary. And the great bulk of people, even if they were willing to understand every case, have really no time to do it; it cannot be expected of them in this busy life. They find themselves obliged to work by generalizations and categories, to bind by rules and prohibitions admitting of no exception. It is the only way by which people in a society can tackle the job of estimating the conduct of other people, or, indeed, of regulating their own. The world labels in rows and pronounces judgment on squads, an inevitably rough-and-ready method, but—

the world pleads—the only practical alternative to a moral anarchy against which it must protect itself, even though at the cost of constantly passing the same sentence on offenders of widely different degrees of criminality.

Now the world, or society, or public opinion, or whatever collective term may be used for that force to which all gregarious animals, whether they like it or not, are of necessity amenable, possessed for Major Merriam a meaning which was to him all-important, but to which Winnie and Mrs. Lenoir had accorded only the faintest—if. indeed, any—consideration; it meant something not vague and distant, but near, potent, with close and imperative claims on him. This thing it was which occupied his mind as he walked through the garden to the annex in which his father and he were lodged, and where he would find the General reading on the veranda until it should be time to go to the casino. For society at large, for the moralists or gossips of London, he had not much regard. He was not a prominent man; few people would know, of those few half would not care, and the thing would soon blow over. But neither his life nor his heart was in London, and it was not about the feelings or views of the great city that he went, with Winnie's copy of the *Times* in his hand, to consult his father.

The General had been reading, and was now dozing, on the veranda. He woke up at the sound of his son's step. "Ready for the casino, my boy?" he asked, briskly.

"Well, I've something I want to talk about first, if you don't mind." He laid the *Times* on the table.

When the General heard the story, told more briefly than Winnie had related it, but with no loss to its essential features, he conceived a grudge against Mrs. Lenoir—Clara's silence, rendered more deceitful by that delusive half-confi-

275

dence of hers, seemed to him unkind—but, as regards the prisoner at the bar herself, his judgment was even more lenient than his son's, as perhaps might be expected from his more various experience. The thing was annoying, distinctly annoying, but he liked Winnie none the less. The poor girl had been in a fix!

"However, it's really not our business to judge her," he concluded, looking across at his son. "We've got nothing to do with that. That's for her and her own conscience."

"She's had devilish hard luck," said Bertie.

"Yes, she has. Heavens, my boy! who am I to be hard on her?"

The Major gazed out over the garden. "As far as I'm concerned myself, I'd take the chances and go on with it." He knew that his father would understand what he meant by "it."

"Well, well, there are things to consider—"

Bertie turned sharply round again. Conviction rang in his voice as he interrupted: "By Jove, there are! There's the regiment!"

The General pursed up his lips and gave two quick little nods of his head. "Yes. In a few months you'll be in command."

"It might not get out, of course. There's always that chance."

"Next year you go to India. Everything gets out in India."

"Of course, if people could be got to understand the case as we do—"

"Don't you build on that, Bertie. The mere fact of this"—he tapped the *Times*—"will be all they want; take my word for it. They wouldn't make things comfortable for her."

For the moment, at least, Bertie's mind was not on that point; it was directed toward the subject on which he had once discoursed to Winnie herself—the influence which the wife of a commanding officer does and ought to exercise on the tone of the small society over which she is naturally called upon to exercise a sort of presidency. "Would it be good for the regiment?"

The General wore a mournful air as he took out and lighted a long, lean cheroot. He did not look at Bertie as he murmured, "Must consider that, in your position."

Certainly that had to be considered; for here the two men touched what was their real effective religion—the thing which in truth shaped their lives, to which they were both loyal and uncompromising adherents, in regard to which the son was almost a fanatic. What was important to the regiment was of vital importance to Bertie Merriam and to his life's work. One of the things important to the regiment was the wives of its officers; most important was their influence on the "young chaps"—as he had said to Winnie. It ought to be, if not motherly, at least "elder-sisterly." Viewed in this connection, there was evidently matter for consideration, assuming that everything got out in India, as according to the General it did. To present to the "young chaps" such an "elder sister" as Winnie—certainly consideration was needed.

Later in the afternoon Mrs. Lenoir sat in a wicker chair on the casino terrace which overlooks, from a respectable and precipitous height, the roadstead and the sea. She had spent a lonely afternoon; she had seen none of her three friends, and by herself had drifted down to a solitary cup of tea at this resort, which she was at the moment feeling to be insecurely entitled to be called one of pleasure. She had an instinct that something was happening, that things were being settled behind her back. The feeling made her fretful; when she was fretful the lines on her face showed a deeper chiselling. And by a very human instinct, because she thought that her friend the General was going to be angry with her, she began to get angry with him—so as not to start the quarrel at a disadvantage. They were making a fuss; now what in Heaven's name was there to make a fuss about? Hugh to make a fuss! A smile more acrid, less kind than usual bent Mrs. Lenoir's lips; it made her look older.

Suddenly, without seeing where he came from, she found the General beside her—rather a stiff General, raising his hat very ceremoniously. "You've had your tea, Clara? May I sit down by you?"

"Yes, I've had my tea, thank you. And you?"

"No, thank you. I—in fact, I've had a whiskey-and-soda."

The indulgence was unusual. It confirmed Mrs. Lenoir's instinct.

"Where's Bertie?"

"He's gone for a walk to Camara de Lobos."

The instinct was proved infallibly correct. A stride along the one level road—clearly a case of mental disturbance needing physical treatment!

The General sat down. He was not even smoking; he rested the big silver knob of his stick against his lips. She looked at him out of the corner of her eye. Oh yes, certainly yes!

When he spoke, it was abruptly. "I don't know exactly how long you mean to stay here, Clara, but I'm afraid Bertie and I must take the next boat home. We must get back to London."

278

"Who's inconsolable in London ?"

"I've had a letter which makes it advisable—"

"Oh, nonsense!" She did not disguise her impatience. "She's told him, has she ?"

"I don't think you've treated me quite fairly."

The sun began to sink below the promontory which bounded the view on the right. The growing sombreness of the atmosphere seemed to spread over Mrs. Lenoir's face. Her voice was hard, too, when she spoke.

"I've treated you absolutely fairly. You men always want to play with your cards held up and ours down on the table. That's the masculine idea of an even game! Oh, I know it! For my part I think she's silly to have told him so soon. I wouldn't have. And so she's not good enough for him, isn't she ?"

Mrs. Lenoir had certainly done well to whip up her anger. It enabled her to deliver the assault and forestall the General's more deliberate offensive movement. Also by her plainness she exposed ruthlessly her friend's tactful invention of a letter from London making it advisable for him and his son to take the next boat back to England.

"It's not quite a question of that," said the General, his pale-brown old cheek flushing under the roughness of her scornful words. "You know how much I like her, and how much Bertie likes her, too. But we must look facts in the face—take things as they are, Clara. It's not so much a matter of his own feelings. There's the regiment."

Mrs. Lenoir grew more annoyed—because she perceived in a flash that, old student of men as she was, she had neglected an important factor in the case. Being annoyed, and being a woman, she hit out at the other women who, as she supposed, stood in her way.

"A parcel of nobodies, in a garrison or cantonment some-where!" Whatever the judgment on her life, she was always conscious that she herself had been famous.

"I suppose you're referring to the women? I wasn't thinking so much of them. It 'd be sure to get out, and it wouldn't do with the youngsters."

She turned to him almost fiercely, but his next words struck a new note.

"And it 'd prejudice my boy's career, Clara."

The sun had set. There was an interval of cold light before the glories of the afterglow. Mrs. Lenoir's face looked wan and hard. "Yes, it would follow them all over the world," she said. "Now a mail ahead of them, now a mail behind—always very close. Yes, the women would chatter and lift their skirts; the old men would snigger and the youngsters make jokes. Is there anything at all to choose between us, Hugh—between you men and us women? Anything at all?"

He would not enter on that. "You don't quite under-stand. I may think about his interest—well, I'm his father, and he's my eldest. He sees it in the light of his duty to the Service."

"My poor little Winnie!" Gradually the afterglow was coming and seemed to soften the hard lines of her face.

"You know I—why, I fairly love her myself!" His voice trembled for a moment. "Pretty nearly as much, I believe, in the end, as the boy does. But—could I tell him any-thing different? I'd give a year's pay not to hurt her feelings."

"A year's pay! You old goose, Hugh! You'd give your life—but you wouldn't give one button off the tunic of one of the soldiers in your blessed regiment." She held out her hand to him, smiling under misty eyes. "You men are queer," she ended.

After a stealthy look round, the General raised her hand to his lips. They were friends again, and he was glad. Yet she would not forego her privilege of ridicule and irony —the last and only weapon of the conquered.

"I don't know that anything need be said—"

"So you two valiant soldiers have decided that I had better say it?" she interrupted.

"How could either of us so much as hint that she—that she was the least interested in our movements?"

"Not even in your retreats? Oh, I'll tell her you're going by the next boat. Nearly a week off, though, isn't it?" She hinted maliciously that the week might be difficult— even dangerous. Whether it would be depended on how Winnie took their decision. Mrs. Lenoir's unregenerate impulse would have been to make that week rather trying to the Major, had she been in Winnie's place. By being disagreeable to him? No, she would have found a better way than that.

A merry laugh sounded from the door of the casino. Winnie was there, in animated conversation with the Anstruther boys. A great event had happened, calculated to amuse the whole hotel. "Dolly" had come down with his usual half-dollar—and had lost it as usual. He walked round the room, then up and down the concert-room adjoining. He went to the other table; he came back to the one at which he had played. He fidgeted about, behind the second Anstruther boy, for some minutes. Then he fished out another half-dollar, and put it on a single number—twenty! Could Winnie, his confidant, doubt what was in his mind? The number twenty was the gage of Dame Fortune; he would wear it on his sleeve! Number twenty came up; the little man, with a quick gasp for breath, pounced on his handful of money.

"Well, any of us may win after that!" said the elder Anstruther boy, who had been strongly for the view that Mr. Wigram was a "hoodoo" to the whole hotel.

With rapid yet gracious dexterity Winnie got rid of her companions. She had caught sight of the General's tall figure as he left Mrs. Lenoir's side. She came down to her friend's chair and laid a hand on her shoulder.

"Not cold?" Mrs. Lenoir shook her head. "Well, let's go home, anyhow, shall we? I've had a long afternoon with those boys—I'm tired."

"Sit down for a minute, child. So you let the cat out of the bag?"

"I told you I had to. Has he been here? I haven't seen him."

"Bertie? No—only the General. Bertie's gone for a walk by himself. But, before he went, he told the General."

"Well?" Winnie was drawing on the gloves she had taken off to count out her money in the room.

"They're going home by the next boat." Winnie gave no sign, made no movement. "A letter from London—if you want to observe the usual fiction." Her malice, her desire that her sex should fight for itself and avenge its injuries, twinkled in her eyes again. "But they can't go till Tuesday!"

Winnie's eyes turned out to sea. "Tuesday, or Tuesday twelvemonth—what difference does it make?" She gave a little sigh; she had liked the idea of it—of the life it meant, of seeing the world, of a fresh start, of his great courtesy and kindness. "I don't think that we need consider ourselves responsible for a broken heart," she added, suddenly.

"No, but he'd have gone on, even after you told him." Her voice took on its ironical inflexion. "He'd have gone on but for the regiment."

Winnie had been leaning back in her chair. She sat up straight, almost with a jerk. "Gone on but for what?" she asked, in a tone of genuine amazement.

Mrs. Lenoir's acrid smile penetrated the twilight. After a moment's blank staring, Winnie's parted lips met in a smile too. To both of them, in the end, it seemed funny—rather unaccountable.

"The regiment, Winnie!" Mrs. Lenoir repeated, as she rose from her seat.

"It really never entered my head," said Winnie.

19

XXIV

AN ENLIGHTENMENT

I T might well seem that by now Winnie would have become accustomed to the discovery that things which had never entered her head might none the less occupy a large and unassailable position in the heads of other people —nay, that she might, for safety's sake, allow for the likelihood of such a revelation when she laid plans or embarked on a course of conduct. But, in fact, this would be asking her to have learned very early a very hard lesson. It was not as if there were only one or two of these entrenched convictions; fresh ones leaped, as it were, from ambush at every step of her advance, at every stage of her pilgrimage, and manifested a strength on which she had not calculated, for which the airy and untrammelled flight of Shaylor's Patch speculation had not prepared her. It was all very well for her to declare that she accorded to others the freedom of thought and opinion which she claimed for herself. Of course she did; but the others made such odd uses of their liberty! Maxon's point of view, Dick Dennehy's point of view, Woburn Square's point of view, Bob Purnett's point of view (his—and Godfrey Ledstone's!)—let these be taken as mastered and appreciated. Between them they had seemed to cover the ground pretty completely, to comprehend all the objections which could be raised by standards religious, social, or merely habitual. But no. Here was a man who was willing, for himself, to waive all the usual objections, but suddenly produced a new cult, an esoteric worship, a tribal fetish of his own, evidently a very powerful fetish, to be propitiated by costly sacrifices, which he regarded himself as obviously necessary, and had no doubt would be easily understood by other people.

"How could I be expected to think of the regiment?" asked Winnie, pathetically. "I declare I thought of everything else—that's why I told him. He doesn't mind all the great world, but he does mind half a dozen women and a dozen boys somewhere in India! People are queer, aren't they, Mrs. Lenoir?"

But by now Mrs. Lenoir had been schooled; talks with both father and son had made her understand better, and, since the thing had to be thus, it was desirable that Winnie should understand also.

"Well, Winnie, that may be all his regiment is to you—a pack of women and boys in India; indeed that's pretty much what I called it myself. But, in justice to Bertie, we must remember that to him it's a great—a great—"

"A great what?" Winnie was looking malicious over her friend's hesitation.

"Well, a great institution," Mrs. Lenoir ended, rather lamely.

"An institution! Yes!" Winnie nodded her head. "That's it—and I'm absolutely fated to run up against institutions. They wait for me, they lie in hiding, they lurk round corners. And what a lot of them there are, to break one's shins over!"

"They all come back to one in the end, I think," said Mrs. Lenoir, smiling. She was glad to hear Winnie's philosophizing. It was a fair proof that neither here was there a broken heart, though there might be some disappointment and vexation. "I was very hurt at first," she went on, "and it made me rude to the General. It's no use being hurt or angry, Winnie. We bring it on ourselves, if we choose to go our own way. Whether it's worth taking the consequences—that's for each of us to decide."

"Worth it a thousand times in my case," said Winnie. "All the same I didn't in the least understand what it would be like. Only—now I do understand—I'm going to face it. Fancy if I'd had fewer scruples, and effected a furtive entrance into the regiment! What mightn't have happened?"

Three days had elapsed from the date of Winnie's confession to the Major; they had changed the relative attitudes of the two women. Mrs. Lenoir had got over her disappointment and returned to her usual philosophy, her habitual recognition of things as they were, her understanding that with men their profession and their affairs must come first. Winnie had hardened toward her late suitor. Ready to be rejected on her own account, she could not bring herself to accept rejection on account of the regiment with meekness. After the great things she had defied, the regiment seemed a puny antagonist. All the same, little thing as it was, a mere dwarf of an institution compared with her other giant antagonists, it, not they, now vanquished her; it, not they, now held Bertie Merriam back.

It must be confessed that she behaved rather maliciously during the days when the two officers were waiting for their ship. An exaggerated interest in the affairs of the regiment, an apparently ingenuous admiration of the wonderful *esprit de corps* of the British service, earnest inquiries as to the means by which the newly promoted Commanding Officer hoped to maintain a high moral tone among his subalterns —these were the topics with which she beguiled the hours of lunch and dinner. The Major wriggled, the General looked grave and pained; Mrs. Lenoir affected to notice nothing, for she saw that her young friend was for the moment out of hand and only too ready to quarrel with them all. For the rest, Miss Wilson—whose artificial existence was to end when she got on the steamer for Genoa—flirted with the Anstruther boys and lost her money gambling.

So time went on till the eve of the departure of father and son. At dinner that night Winnie was still waywardly gay and gayly malicious; when the meal was over she ran off into the garden and hid herself in a secret nook. The Anstruther boys sought her in vain, and discontentedly repaired to the casino. But there was a more persistent seeker.

She was roused from some not very happy meditations by finding Bertie Merriam standing opposite to her. He did not apologize for his intrusion nor, on the other hand, ask leave to sit by her; he stood there, looking gravely at her.

"Why do you take a pleasure in making me unhappy?" he asked. "Why do you try to make me look ridiculous, and feel as if I'd done something ungentlemanly? I'm not ridiculous, and I'm not aware of having done anything ungentlemanly. The subject is a very difficult one for me even to touch on with you; but I'm acting from honest motives and on an honest conviction."

Winnie looked up in a moody hostility. "Whenever I've acted from honest motives and on honest convictions, people have all combined to make me unhappy, Major Merriam."

"I'm sincerely, deeply sorry for that, and I don't defend it. Still, the cases are not the same."

"Why aren't they?"

"Because you wanted to do what you did. No doubt you were convinced you had the right, but you wanted to, besides. Now I don't want to do what I'm doing. That's the difference. I want it less and less every hour I spend with you—in spite of your being so disagreeable." He smiled a little over the last words.

Winnie looked at him in curiosity. What was he going to say?

"You're not consistent. You say you like people to act up to their convictions; you feel wronged when people blame you for acting up to your convictions. Yet you punish me for acting up to mine. Will you let me put the thing before you frankly—since we're to part, probably for good, to-morrow?"

"Yes, you can say what you like—since we're to part to-morrow."

"Mine isn't the absurd idea you think it is, and I'm not the grandmother you try to make me out. I'm going to be called on to serve the King in a position of great responsibility, where my example and my standards will affect many lives. I must be true to my responsibilities as I see them. If I did what my feelings incline me to do—pray believe that I assume nothing as to yours—I shouldn't be true to them. Because in the regiment you wouldn't be understood—neither your position nor your convictions. What do most officers' wives, and what do most young men in the army, know about the sort of society or the sort of speculations which produce convictions like yours? They would neither understand nor appreciate them. And if they didn't—well, what opinion must they hold about you? And what effect would that opinion have? I don't

288

speak of your position—that would be for you to consider
—but what effect would it have on my position and my
influence ?"

" They'd just put me down as an ordinary—an ordinary
bad woman ?"

"Let's say the ordinary case of a woman who has made
a scandal. Because I agree with you in thinking that such
a woman needn't be a bad woman. But even when she's
not bad she may in certain positions be injurious to the
commonwealth—and a regiment's a commonwealth. I'm
not clever, as my brother is. I'm not likely ever to get a
bigger job than this. It'll be the most important trust I
shall get, I expect. I want to be loyal to it. I'm being
loyal to it at a great cost to me—yes, a great cost now. And
you try to make me look ridiculous! Well, let that pass.
Only, feeling as I do, I want to put myself right in your eyes,
before we say good-bye."

"I'm sorry I tried to make you look ridiculous. Is that
enough, Major Merriam ?"

"It's something," he smiled. "But couldn't you go so
far as not to think me ridiculous ?"

"Have I got to think the officers' wives and the subalterns
not ridiculous, too ?"

"I can leave that to your later reflections. They're not
going to part from you to-morrow, and they don't care so
much about your good opinion."

"No, I don't think you ridiculous any more." She
spoke now slowly and thoughtfully. "I didn't understand.
I see better what you mean and feel now. Only understanding other people doesn't make the world seem any
easier! But I think I do understand. The King pays you
for your life, and you're bound to give it, not only in war,

if that's required of you, but in peace, too—is it something like that?"

"Yes, that's the sort of thing it is. Thank you."

"And you mustn't do anything that makes the life he's bought less valuable to him either in war or peace?"

"Yes, that's it, too." He smiled at her more happily now, and in a great kindness.

"In fact, you've sold yourself right out and quite irrevocably?"

"Ah, well, that's not quite the way I should put it. We Merriams have always done it."

"Hereditary slaves!" smiled Winnie. "It's really rather like marriage, as Cyril conceived it. You mustn't have another wife. The regiment's yours. It would be bigamy!"

"Charming people can talk great nonsense," the Major made bold to observe. He was rather chilled again.

"We're veering round in this discussion. Now you're making out that I'm ridiculous!"

He made a gesture of protest. Winnie laughed. "Six days ago I didn't care particularly about you, but I should have married you if you'd asked me."

"So you told me why I'd better not ask you? Yes?"

"Now I like you very particularly, but nothing on earth would induce me to marry you," said Winnie. She shot a quick glance of raillery at him. "So, if you're struggling, you needn't struggle."

"I am struggling, rather, Winnie."

"To-morrow ends it."

"Yes, but what's going to happen to you?"

"That's become rather more difficult to answer than it used to be." She rose from her chair. "But now I'm going in, to beg the General's pardon for having been so naughty."

AN ENLIGHTENMENT

She stood there before him, slim, almost vague in the soft darkness. Her black gown was a darker spot on the gloom; her face and shoulders gleamed white, her brows and the line of her red lips seemed black, and black, too, the eyes with which she regarded him, half-loving, still half-ridiculing, from across the gulf that parted them. He made a quick, impulsive step toward her, putting out his arms. It seemed to him that hers came out to meet them; at least, she did not retreat. With a sigh and a shiver she yielded herself to his embrace. "I'm half sorry it's so utterly impossible all round," she whispered.

After his passionate kiss the man let her go and drew back. "Now I'm thoroughly ashamed of myself," he said.

"Oh, my dear, you needn't be. Here we are, two small, puzzled things, together on this beautiful night for just a little while, and then a long way from each other forever! And we've done nothing very dreadful. Just what you like in me has kissed me, and just what I like in you has kissed you, and wished you godspeed, and been sorry for the trouble I've made, and told you how much I hope for you and your dear regiment. I'm glad you did it, and I'm glad I did it. Surely it makes us friends for always that our lips have met like that?"

"I'll give it all up if you ask me, Winnie."

"No, no. I've been learning to think how one will feel about things to-morrow. Forget you said that. You don't really mean it."

He stood silent for a moment. "No, I didn't really mean it. I beg your pardon."

"I bear you no malice. I liked you to think it for just a minute. It's all over." She smiled reassuringly. "But I shall remember—and like to remember. Everything of

291

me won't leave you, nor everything of you leave me now,
to-morrow—not absolutely everything. Well, it never does,
with people you've met intimately, I think. But what you
leave to me is all good. I was getting hard. This glimpse
of you as you really are has stopped it. Dear friend, kiss
me once again, and so good-bye."

Very gently now he kissed her lips again—for it was her
lips she gave him in a perfect confidence.

"Let's go in now," said Winnie, putting her arm through
his.

They sauntered slowly through the fragrant garden. The
night was still; no envious wind disturbed the island's rest.
Merriam, deeply moved, but now master of himself, did not
speak, but once or twice gently pressed the hand that lay
on his arm. With Winnie there was a sense of sadness,
yet also of peace. She had made a friend, and now was
to lose him—yet not wholly. And, in winning him, she
had won back herself also, and had done with the Miss
Wilson who had been flouting and flirting these last few
days, with intentions none too kind and manners none too
good; she was again trying to understand to be fair, to strike
a true balance between herself and other people.

"You're very different from the others," she said, suddenly; "but, somehow, you're helping me to be more just
to them, too." She gave a little sigh. "But justice is most
awfully difficult. It's really much more comfortable to believe that there's absolutely nothing to be said for people.
You believe that about a lot of people, don't you? You'd
believe it about my friend Dick Dennehy, I expect, who
wants to have Ireland independent, and to destroy the
monarchy, and put down the army and navy, and all that
sort of thing. Yet he's one of the greatest gentlemen."

AN ENLIGHTENMENT

"Then I'd hang him, but I'd shake hands with him first," said the Major.

"Rather like what he's done to me!" thought Winnie to herself; but Merriam did not read the meaning of the glance, the smile, and the gentle pressure on his arm.

"But he's got his regiment, too!" she went on. Then, glancing up at her companion, she saw that he was not heeding her words, and the rest of her meditation over the parallel was conducted in silence.

The General was not to be found that night—he had retreated to his own quarters in the annex. Winnie said her farewell to him on the balcony after breakfast the next morning, as they stood and looked at the big hull of the liner in the roadstead; she was to start in a couple of hours' time.

"Have you forgiven me, General? Will you say goodbye to me? I said good-bye to your son last night."

"He'll be gone before you get back to England. He told me something about last night. You're friends, he and you, now? And, of course, my dear, you and I. And we shall meet."

The ship sent out a warning hoot. "Come on, if you're coming," she seemed to say.

"But he and I sha'n't meet. I'm so glad we have met—just for an hour once."

The funny little man, "Dolly," fussed onto the balcony, monstrously encumbered with impedimenta — a rug, a "nest" of wicker baskets, a cap, and a pair of shoes of the country, a huge bunch of bananas, and a specimen of sugar-cane. The ship hooted again, and he made a hurried rush up to Winnie.

"Good-bye, Miss Wilson, good-bye," he said, dropping

293

half a dozen things on the floor in order to give her a hand-shake. "I've got something for everybody, I think. I won—yes, I won—last night, and I went down to the town early and bought these presents."

"How fine! Good-bye, Mr. Wigram. Tell all the truth you can, won't you?"

He put his head on one side, in a comical seriousness. "I've been thinking—since I talked to you, Miss Wilson— that my senior class could stand a little." Another hoot! "Oh, good-bye!" he exclaimed, in an extraordinary fluster, as he picked up the things he had dropped and made a bolt for the stairs. Winnie watched him running down the steps that led through the garden to the landing-stage.

"I think the senior class can stand a little, don't you, General?"

"You're over-young to be in it, my dear."

She turned to him. "I'm not unhappy, and I don't reckon myself unfortunate, because I think that, to some extent at least, I can learn. The only really unhappy people are people who can't learn at all, I think. Fancy going through it all and learning absolutely nothing!"

A longer, more insistent hoot! Bertie Merriam sauntered onto the balcony. No observer would have guessed that the hoot meant anything to him or that he had any farewell to make. The General held out his hand to Winnie. "I'll take the steps gently—Bertie can overtake me. *Au revoir*, Miss Winnie, in London!"

Bertie Merriam came to her. "You slept well?" he asked.

"Oh yes. Why not? I was so at peace. Say nothing this morning. We said good-bye last night."

"Yes, I know, but—" He was obviously embarrassed.

"But I want to ask you one thing. It 'll seem jolly absurd, I know, and rather conceited."

"Will it ?" asked Winnie, with bright eyes glistening.

"Well, if there should be any little row in India—I know people at home don't take much notice of them—any little expedition or anything of that kind, could you keep your eye on it ? Because we might have the luck to be in it, and I should like you to know how the regiment shows up."

"If you've the luck to be getting killed, I'll read about it," said Winnie. She smiled with trembling lips. "It's really the least I can do for a friend, Major Merriam."

"Killed ? Oh, rot! Just see first how near to full strength we turn out—that's my great test—and then, if you read of any other fellows showing us the way, you might let me know, and I'll inquire about it—because we don't reckon to let it happen very often. Hullo, that whistle really sounds as if she meant business!" He gripped her hand tightly and looked into her eyes. "Here's the end, Winnie!"

"I wouldn't have had it not happen; would you ?"

"I shall often wonder if I did right."

She smiled. "You needn't. What you did would have made no difference—only you'd have been a little less loyal to your duty."

"I wish I knew what was going to become of you."

"I'm not afraid any more. God bless you, dear."

He waited one moment longer. "You've no grudge against me ?"

Winnie turned sharply away and leaned over the balcony. "Oh, please, please!" she stammered.

When she saw him again he was half-way down to the landing-stage. He turned, waved his hand, and so passed out of sight—and out of life for Winnie Maxon.

XXV

"PERHAPS!"

"GOOD gracious!" exclaimed Mrs. Ladd, laying down her knife and fork.

From her table in the dining-room of the Hôtel de la Grande Bretagne at Bellaggio she commanded a view of the door, and could scrutinize her fellow-guests as they entered. The hotel was full of fresh birds of passage every evening, for the end of the season was approaching, and all the world was travelling through on its way northward. A lady of lively curiosity, possessed, moreover, by that sense of superiority over the casual visitor which a long stay in a hotel always gives, Mrs. Ladd allowed few of the newcomers to escape without comment or criticism. Lady Rosaline, whose back was toward the door, often felt compelled to twist her head round in order to estimate for herself the justice of her companion's remarks; but on this occasion she merely asked, "What's the matter, dear?"

"Why, that woman who's just come in!" Her voice was full of pleasurable excitement. "It's Cyril Maxon's wife. Who is it with her, I wonder!" Mrs. Ladd was not acquainted personally, or even by hearsay, with Mrs. Lenoir.

Lady Rosaline's head went round, not quickly or eagerly, but with a well-bred show of indifference. She watched

Winnie walking down the room. "Did she see us?" she asked of Mrs. Ladd.

"No, she didn't look this way. What shall we do, Rosaline? It's very awkward." Awkward as it was, Mrs. Ladd sounded more puzzled than pained.

"I only knew her very slightly—three or four quite formal calls—in the old days."

"Oh, I used to see her now and then, though it was her husband who was my friend, of course."

"Well, then, I think we can do as we like."

"I don't know. As friends of his—well, what's the right thing toward him?"

"I don't mind what's the right thing—toward Mr. Maxon," said Lady Rosaline, pettishly. "It won't hurt him if we're civil to her. I shall please myself. I sha'n't go out of my way to look for her, but if we meet I shall bow."

"Oh, well, I must do the same as you, of course. Only I must say I hope Cyril won't hear about it and be hurt. He always expects his friends to make his quarrels theirs, you know!"

Lady Rosaline allowed herself a shrug of the shoulders; she was not bound to please Cyril Maxon—not yet. The friendly correspondence was still going on, but things looked as if it would either cease or assume a different complexion before long. She had a letter up-stairs in her writing-case at this moment—an unanswered letter—in which he informed her that the last tie between Winnie and himself would be severed in a few weeks, and asked leave to join her at Bellaggio, or wherever else she was going to be, for two or three days during the Whitsuntide vacation.

"Then there will be nothing to prevent our arriving at a complete understanding," he added.

Lady Rosaline knew what that meant. She must make up her mind. Unless she could make it up in the manner desired by Mr. Maxon, she did not think that they had better meet in the Whitsuntide vacation; he would not be an agreeable companion if his wishes were thwarted. Even now, while he was still in hope and had every motive to be as pleasant as he could, there ran through the friendly letter a strain of resentment imperfectly repressed.

Under these circumstances, with this decision of hers to make, it was not strange that Lady Rosaline should be interested by the chance which threw across her path the woman who had been—and technically still was, for a little while longer—Cyril Maxon's wife. Mrs. Ladd, who guessed her friend's situation pretty shrewdly, was hardly less curious, though more restrained by her loyalty to Cyril. Still, she was glad that Lady Rosaline had determined that they need not cut Mrs. Maxon. That she was "Mrs. Maxon"—"Mrs. Winifred Maxon"—became apparent from an examination of the visitors' book, which Mrs. Ladd initiated directly after dinner. Winnie was sailing under her own flag again, and proposed to continue to fly it unless Cyril Maxon objected. If he heard of it he probably would object; then she could find another sobriquet if Mrs. Lenoir was still obdurate as regards the "kins" which disfigured her own maiden name of "Wilkins."

"And the woman with her seems to be a Mrs. Lenoir. At least, their names are next each other, and so are their rooms. Did you ever hear of her?"

"Never," answered Lady Rosaline. It was just as well; they had plenty of material for gossip already.

They were sitting in the hall of the hotel, where wicker chairs and little tables were set out, and where it was customary to take coffee after dinner. Mrs. Ladd had made her inspection and rejoined her friend.

"Have they come out from dinner yet ?" she asked.

"No. They were late in beginning, you see. Where we're sitting, they needn't pass us when they do come out. Well, we don't want to make a rush for them, do we, Mrs. Ladd ?"

"Indeed, no. I shall only speak if it's forced on me— just not to be unkind, Rosaline. But I do wish they'd come out!"

At last the new-comers entered the hall, Mrs. Lenoir leading the way. She looked handsome still, but rather old and haggard. By bad-luck the voyage had been stormy the last two days, and the railway journey had wearied a body not very robust. But Winnie looked well, bright, and alert. They did not pass Mrs. Ladd and Lady Rosaline, but sat down at a table near the dining-room door. As they sat, their profiles were presented to the gaze of the two ladies who were observing them so closely.

"The other woman must have been very handsome once," Mrs. Ladd pronounced. "I wonder who she was !" Mrs. Lenoir's air of past greatness often caused people to speak of her in a corresponding tense.

"Winnie Maxon's looking well, too. I think she's somehow changed; don't you, Mrs. Ladd ? There's a new air about her, it seems to me—a sort of assured air she hadn't before."

"My dear, she must carry it off ! That's the meaning of it."

"I wonder !" Lady Rosaline was not satisfied. Her memory of Winnie, slight as it was, reminded her quite definitely that Cyril Maxon's wife possessed a rather timid air, a deprecatory manner. The woman over there was in no way self-assertive or "loud," but she seemed entirely self-possessed and self-reliant, and was talking in an animated fashion. Mrs. Ladd looked again.

"Cyril said she accused him of tyrannizing over her. I'm sure she doesn't look as if she'd been tyrannized over," she remarked. "All nonsense, I've no doubt."

Lady Rosaline made no answer; she merely went on looking. But she could not forget that many months had passed since Winnie ended her married life with Cyril Maxon.

No encounter between the two couples occurred that night; indeed, Mrs. Lenoir and Winnie remained unconscious of the scrutiny to which they were subjected, and of the presence of the ladies who were conducting it. Wearied by travel, they went early to bed, and Mrs. Ladd, feeling immediately very dull, went and hunted out an elderly novel from the drawing-room shelves. Lady Rosaline did not read; she sat on idly in the hall—thinking still of Winnie and of Mrs. Ladd's remark which she herself had not answered. Should she—could she—question the one person who might give it a pertinent answer? Could even she answer to any purpose? That is, would Winnie's experience and opinion be any guide to Lady Rosaline in settling her own problem? Perhaps it would be strange to question, and perhaps no answer, useless or useful, would be forthcoming. Yet, on the other hand, it might be possible to get some light. These thoughts engrossed her mind till she went discontentedly to bed, and, even after she had got into bed, remained to vex and puzzle her still. But there was really no doubt what, in the end, she would do. She was bound to try. Both curiosity and personal interest drove her on. They were too strong to be suppressed, either by the fear of a snub or by the doubt of useful results.

The next morning, directly after breakfast, she went out onto the broad terrace in front of the hotel, and sat down on a bench close by the main doorway. No one could leave the house without her seeing. She reckoned on the newcomers being early afoot to explore their surroundings; she even surmised that the young woman would very likely be out before her elderly companion—and that (said Lady Rosaline's secret thoughts) would afford the best chance of all. She put up her parasol and waited. She was safe from Mrs. Ladd, whom she did not want at that moment, for Mrs. Ladd was up-stairs, repairing some ravages suffered by one of her gowns.

"It's a funny situation!" So Lady Rosaline reflected, and she wondered, in a whimsical mood of speculation, what Cyril Maxon himself would think of it. "What I really want to do is to ask for his character from his last place!" Yes, that was what it came to; and the parallel held good still further, in that it was quite likely that the character would not tell her very much, would not show whether the applicant were likely to suit her, however well or ill he had suited in his previous situation. Still, it must surely reveal something about him or about his wife herself; even knowledge about the wife who had left Maxon would be, in a way, knowledge about Maxon himself. But it was an odd situation. What would Cyril think of it?

A surprising number of people came out of that doorway before Winnie; but in the end Lady Rosaline's forecast was justified. Winnie did come out, and she came out alone. She wore her hat, carried a parasol, and walked with a quick step, as though she were bound on an expedition. Lady Rosaline rose from her chair and intercepted her.

"I thought it was you last night at table d'hôte, and now I'm sure! How do you do, Mrs. Maxon? You remember me—Rosaline Deering?" She held out her hand. "I'm so glad to see you."

Winnie shook hands. "Yes, I remember you, Lady Rosaline, and I'm glad to see you—if you're glad to see me, I mean, you know." She smiled. "Well, you needn't have shaken hands with me if you hadn't wanted to, need you? Isn't it lovely here?"

"It is, indeed. Mrs. Ladd—you remember her, too, of course?—and I have been here together for nearly a month, and hope to be here another fortnight. Are you staying long?"

"We hoped to, but my friend isn't very well—she's staying in bed this morning—and I'm afraid she's set her mind on getting home. So we might be off, really, at any moment."

Clearly Lady Rosaline had no time to lose. "Are you going for a walk?" she said.

"Oh, I'm just going to saunter through the town and look about me."

"May I go with you?"

"Of course! It 'll be very kind." There was just the faintest note of surprise in Winnie's voice. Her acquaintance with her husband's friend Rosaline Deering had been very slight; it had never reached the pitch of cordiality on which it seemed now, rather paradoxically, to be establishing itself.

Off they went together—certainly a strange sight for Cyril Maxon, had his eyes beheld it! But even eager Lady Rosaline could not plunge into her questions at once, and Winnie,

full of the new delight of Italy, was intent on the sights of
the little town and on the beauty of the lake and the hills.
It was not till they had come back and sat down on a seat
facing the water that the talk came anywhere near the point.
Yet the walk had not been wasted; they had got on well
together, the cordiality was firmly established—and Lady
Rosaline had enjoyed an opportunity of observing more
closely what manner of woman Cyril Maxon's wife was.
The old impression of the timid air and deprecatory manner
needed drastic revision to bring it up to date; these were not
words that anybody would use to describe the present Winnie
Maxon.

Still, Lady Rosaline found it hard to begin, hard to make
any reference, however guarded, to the past. In fact, it was
Winnie herself who in the end gave the lead. Lady Rosaline
was thankful; she had begun to be afraid that a nervous
desperation would drive her into some impossibly crude
question, such as "Do you think I should be a fool if I
married your husband ?"

"I suppose you see Cyril sometimes, Lady Rosaline ? Is
he all right ?"

"Oh yes, he's very much all right, I think, and I see him
pretty often, for so busy and sought-after a man." She
decided that she must risk something if she were to gain
anything. "Isn't it rather a strange feeling, after having
been so very much to each other, to be so absolutely apart
now ? I hope you'll tell me if you'd rather not talk ?"

"I don't mind," smiled Winnie. "It's a great change, of
course, but really I don't often think of him—nor he of me,
I expect." She added, with a little laugh: "At least I hope
he doesn't, because he wouldn't think anything compli-
mentary. Of course I was surprised about the divorce."

"We were all rather surprised at that," Lady Rosaline murmured, discreetly; her object was to obtain, not to give, information.

"It's the one inconsistent thing I've ever known him do." She laughed. "I wonder if it's possible that he's fallen in love with somebody else!"

Lady Rosaline threw no light. "Oh, well, he wouldn't have to ask in vain, I should think."

Winnie said nothing. She looked at the sea with a smile which her companion felt justified in calling inscrutable. Lady Rosaline took another risk.

"So much the worse for the woman, you'd say, I suppose?"

"I don't want to say anything. What I felt seems pretty well indicated by what I did, doesn't it, Lady Rosaline? Because I wasn't in love with anybody else then, you know."

No, what she felt was not sufficiently indicated for Lady Rosaline's purposes. What Winnie had done showed that, to her, life with Cyril was impossible; but it did not show why. Just the point essential to Lady Rosaline was omitted.

"I should think some women might get on very well with him, though?" she hazarded.

Winnie gazed over the lake; she appeared to ruminate. Then she turned to her companion, smiling.

"Perhaps!" she said. "And now I really must go and see how Mrs. Lenoir—my friend—is. I hope we shall have another talk before we go—I don't mean about Cyril!"

Lady Rosaline watched her erect figure and her buoyant step as she walked back to the hotel, recalled her gayety and the merriment of her smile as she enjoyed lake, mountains, and the little town, caught again the elusive twinkle of her eyes as she referred to the one inconsistent thing that Cyril Maxon had ever done. And that "Perhaps!"—that most unsatisfactory, tantalizing "Perhaps!" Was it a genuine assent, or merely a civil dismissal of the question, as one of no moment to the person interrogated? Or was it in effect a dissent—a reception of the suggestion profoundly sceptical, almost scornful? Probably a different woman could—possibly some woman might—no woman conceivably could—that "Perhaps" seemed susceptible of any of the three interpretations. Lady Rosaline made impotent clutches at the slippery word; it gave her no hand-hold; it was not to be tackled.

It was no use consulting Mrs. Ladd; she had not heard the elusive answer. Could Lady Rosaline unbosom herself plainly to Mrs. Maxon? That was her secret and urgent instinct, but, somehow, it did not seem an admissible thing to do; it was bizarre, and distasteful to her feelings. Yet before long she must answer Cyril's letter. To allow him to come and meet her would be tantamount to an acceptance. To refuse to allow him would be, at least, such a postponement as he would bitterly resent and probably decline to agree to; he would either take it as a definite rejection, or he would come without leave—and "bully" her again? She could hide herself—but could she? Mrs. Ladd would want to know why, and laugh at her—and not improbably put Cyril on the track. Lady Rosaline felt herself wrapped in perplexity as in a garment.

"Bother the man!" she suddenly said to herself aloud. Then she started violently. A tall, handsome, elderly lady, carrying a parasol, a large cushion, and a book, was absolutely at her elbow. She recognized Winnie's companion, Mrs. Lenoir.

"I'm afraid I startled you? May I sit down here? Winnie Maxon told me who you were, and you've been talking to her, haven't you?" Mrs. Lenoir's amused expression left no doubt that she was aware of the subject of the conversation. "Oh, she only just mentioned that you were a friend of Mr. Maxon's," she added. "She didn't betray your confidences."

"I really don't think I made any," smiled Lady Rosaline. "But Mr. Maxon is a friend of mine. Oh, do let me settle that cushion comfortably for you. You're not feeling very well this morning, Mrs. Maxon told me."

"I feel better now," said Mrs. Lenoir, graciously accepting the proffered service. "And the day's so beautiful that I thought I'd come out. But I didn't mean to make you jump, Lady Rosaline."

She gave a sigh of contentment as she achieved a satisfactory position in regard to the cushion. "I don't know Mr. Maxon myself," she remarked.

"I like him very much."

"Yes?" She was just as non-committal as Winnie had been with her "Perhaps."

"Of course, you've heard her side of the story."

"I have," said Mrs. Lenoir. "Or as much of it as she'd tell me."

Lady Rosaline determined to try what a little provocation would do.

"Of course, we who are his friends think that all might have gone well with a little more wisdom on her part."

Mrs. Lenoir raised her brows ever so slightly. "Oh, perhaps!" she murmured, gently.

It was really exasperating! To be baffled at every turn by that wretched word, with its pretence of conceding that

306

was no real concession, with its feigned assent which might so likely cloak an obstinate dissent! It was like listening for an expected sound from another room—the noise of voices or of movements—and finding, instead, absolute silence and stillness; there was something of the same un-canny effect. Lady Rosaline passed from mere perplexity into a vague discomfort—an apprehension of possibilities which she was refused the means of gauging, however vitally they might affect her. Dare she walk into that strangely silent room—and let them bolt and bar the door on her ?

"After all, it's not our business," Mrs. Lenoir remarked, with a smile. "Winnie couldn't stand it, but, as you say, perhaps a wiser woman—"

"Couldn't stand what ?" Lady Rosaline broke in im-patiently.

"Oh, Cyril Maxon, you know."

Not a step in advance! Silence still! Lady Rosaline, frowning fretfully, rose to her feet. Mrs. Lenoir looked up, smiling again. She was not sure of the case, but she was putting two and two together, helped by the exclamation which she had involuntarily overheard. In any case, she had no mind to interfere. This woman was Cyril Maxon's friend, not Winnie's. Mrs. Lenoir instinctively associated the husband's women friends with the wife's hardships. Let this friend of Maxon's fend for herself!

"But, of course, one woman's poison may be another woman's meat. Are you going in ?"

"Yes, I think so. The sun's rather hot."

"Oh, I'm a salamander! Good-bye, then, for the present, Lady Rosaline."

Lady Rosaline had come from abroad for a breathing-space, to take stock of the situation, to make up her mind about Cyril Maxon. It had not proved easy, and her encounter with these two women made it harder still. The perplexity irked her sorely. She bore a grudge against the two for their baffling reticence; insensibly the grudge extended itself to the man who was the ultimate cause of her disquiet. He was spoiling her holiday for her. "I shall fret myself into a fever!" she declared, as she wandered disconsolately up to her bedroom, to make herself tidy for *déjeuner.*

On her dressing-table lay a letter—from Venice. She had not forgotten her promise to send an address to the Hôtel Danieli. Now Sir Axel Thrapston informed her that he was starting for home in a couple of days' time, and would make it convenient—and consider it delightful—to pass through Bellaggio on his way; would she still be there, and put up with his company for a day or two? "Pictures and churches and gondolas are all very well; but I shall like a gossip with a friend better still," wrote Sir Axel.

As she read, Lady Rosaline was conscious of a relief as vague as her discomfort had been, and yet as great. The atmosphere about her seemed suddenly changed and lightened. Almost with a start she recalled how she had experienced a similar feeling when Cyril Maxon had gone and Sir Axel had come that afternoon in Hans Place. The feeling was not of excitement, nor even primarily of pleasure; it was of rest, instead of struggle—of security, as against some unascertained but possibly enormous liability. And it was present in her in even stronger force than it had been before, because of those two women and their baffling, slippery "Perhaps!" As she took off her hat and arranged her hair before going down-stairs, the import of this vague

change of feeling began to take shape in her mind. Slowly
it grew to definiteness. Lady Rosaline was making up her
mind at last! The possibilities lurking in the darkness of
that "Perhaps" were too much for her. "If I feel like this
about it, how can I dare to do it?" was the shape her
thoughts took. Yet, even if she dared not do it, there was
trouble before her. Cyril Maxon would not sit down
tamely under that decision. He would protest, he would
persist, he might "bully" her again; he might seek her even
though she forbade him, and, if he found her, she was not
quite confident of her power to resist.

A smile came slowly to her lips as she looked at herself
in the pier-glass and put the finishing touches to her array.
It would be pleasant to have Sir Axel's company; it might
even be agreeable to travel home under Sir Axel's escort, if
that gentleman's leisure allowed. Lady Rosaline's thoughts
embraced the idea of Sir Axel as an ally, perhaps envisaged
him as a shield. Possibly they went so far as to hazard the
suggestion that a man who will not bow before a decision
may be confronted with a situation which he cannot but
accept. At any rate, when she went down-stairs to the
dining-room, Lady Rosaline's fretful frown had disappeared;
passing Mrs. Lenoir and Winnie in the doorway, she smiled
at them with no trace of grudge. "I'm glad I met them
now," was her reflection. She forgave "Perhaps!"

XXVI

A FRIEND DEPARTS

MRS. LENOIR and Winnie stayed at Bellaggio four or five days, during which time their acquaintance with the other two ladies blossomed into a more intimate cordiality. Yet neither of the two who knew the position, nor yet the one who confidently suspected it, thought it well to suggest to Winnie the existence of any special situation or any urgent question in which Lady Rosaline and Cyril Maxon were concerned. Such a disclosure would, it was felt by all three, lead to awkwardness. But when once the two parties had said farewell, and Winnie and she were on their way home, Mrs. Lenoir saw no reason against mentioning the conclusion at which she had arrived, or against conjecturing what, if any, bearing on the state of affairs the arrival of Sir Axel Thrapston might have; he had reached Bellaggio the day before their own departure, and had been received by Lady Rosaline with much graciousness.

Winnie had not stumbled on the truth for herself; indeed, her mind had been occupied with the thought of another man than Cyril Maxon. She heard it from her friend without surprise, and was not unable to appreciate Mrs. Lenoir's grimly humorous embroidering of the situation. Yet her native and intimate feeling was one of protest against that way of the world which, under the pressure of her various experiences, she was beginning to recognize and to learn that she would have to accept. On the day she left Cyril Maxon's house for good and all, she had conceived herself to be leaving Cyril Maxon also for good and all, to be putting him out of her life, away from and behind her, without the right or power to demand one backward glance from her as she trod a path conditioned, indeed, in one respect by his existence, but, for the future, essentially independent of him. The course of events had hardly justified this forecast. Freedom from the thought of him had not proved possible; he did more than impose conditions; he still figured as rather a determining factor in life and her outlook on it. She seemed to take him with her where she went, so to say, and thus to bring him into contact with all those with whom she had relations herself. Both in small things and in great it happened—as, for example, in this queer encounter with Rosaline Deering, and in the moving episode of her acquaintance with Bertie Merriam, no less than in the earlier history of the West Kensington studio. She had not succeeded in disassociating her destiny from his, in severing to the last link the tie which had once so closely bound her to him. Complete freedom, and the full sense of it, might come in the future; for the moment her feeling was one of scorn for the ignorant young woman who had thought that a big thing could so easily be undone—robbed of effect and made as if it had never been. And suppose that complete freedom, now possible in action to her, should really come, and with it a corresponding inward emancipation; yet there stood and would stand the effect on those other lives—effects great or small, transitory or permanent, but in the mass amounting to a considerable sum of human experience, owing its shape and color in the end to her own action.

Though she had not loved Bertie Merriam, their intercourse, his revelation of himself, and the manner of their parting had deeply affected her. For the first time she had seen the enemy, convention—the established order, the proper thing—in a form which she could not only understand, but with which she was obliged to sympathize. What had seemed to her hard dogmatism in her husband and Attlebury, and a mere caste-respectability, external, narrow, and cowardly, in the denizens of Woburn Square, took on a new shape when it was embodied in the loyalty of a soldier and found its expression, not in demands upon another, but in the sacrifice of self to an obligation and an ideal. Liberty had been her god, and she would not desert the shrine at which Shaylor's Patch had taught her to worship; but Merriam had shown her, had brought home to her through the penetrating appeal of vivid emotion, that there were other deities worthy of offerings and noble worshippers who made them. It was a great revulsion of feeling which drove her to declare that Merriam could do no other than sacrifice his hope of her to his sworn service and to the regiment.

In justifying, or more than justifying, himself, in some sort Merriam pleaded for Cyril Maxon. Winnie held herself to a stricter account of her dealings with her husband. When she understood why he had deviated from his strict conviction, and how it was likely that the deviation would be in vain, she was anxious to rid her soul of any sense of responsibility. She recalled just what she had said, as near as she could ; she listened carefully to Mrs. Lenoir's account of her own conversation with Lady Rosaline.

"Do you think that we influenced her—that we stopped

her ?" she asked. "Because I wouldn't have done that on purpose."

"I certainly wouldn't have encouraged her on purpose. And, if you ask me, I think that our attitude of—well, of reserve (Mrs. Lenoir was smiling), will have its weight—combined, perhaps, with Sir Axel's attractions."

"I'm sorry. If Cyril does want her, and it doesn't come off, he'll hate me worse than ever."

"He won't guess you've had anything to do with it—supposing you have."

"No, but he'll trace the whole thing back to me, of course. He'll blame me for having forced him into acting against his conscience."

"Tut, tut, he shouldn't have such a silly conscience," said Mrs. Lenoir easily. To her, consciences were not things to be treated with an exaggerated punctilio. "After all, if she'd asked you right out, what would you have said ?"

"I should have refused to say anything, of course."

"She probably thought as much, so she tried to pump you indirectly. I think you seem to have been very moderate—and I'm sure I was. And, as one woman toward another, you ought to be glad if Lady Rosaline does prove quick at taking a hint. I shall be glad too, incidentally, because I like her, and hope to see something of her in town —which I certainly shouldn't do if she became Lady Rosaline Maxon."

"Well, I had no idea how matters stood, and I said as little as I could," Winnie ended, protesting against any new entry on the debit side of her account with Cyril—a column about which she had not been wont greatly to concern herself.

Winnie soon found distraction from curious probings of

her conscience in the care and tendance of her friend, in which she assisted the invaluable Emily. As they travelled gradually homeward, Mrs. Lenoir developed a severe and distressing cough, which made sleep very difficult and reduced her none too great strength to dangerous weakness. Yet home she would go, rejecting almost curtly any suggestion of a return to a milder climate. She faced her position with a fatalistic courage, and her attitude toward it was marked by her habitual clearness of vision.

"If I'm going to die—and I rather think I am—I'd sooner die at home than in a hotel."

"Oh, don't talk about dying!" Winnie implored. "What am I to do?" Indeed she was now bound to her friend by a strong affection.

"Well, there's just you—and the General. But the General will die too quite soon, and you'll go away anyhow. Oh yes, you'll have to, somehow; it 'll happen like that. There's nobody else who cares. And I don't know that women like me do themselves any good by living to be old. I'm not complaining; I chose my life and I've enjoyed it. Let me go home, Winnie!"

The appeal could not be resisted, and the beginning of May found them at home. A late cold spring filled Winnie with fears for her friend. Yet Mrs. Lenoir neither would nor, as it now seemed, could make another move. She lay on her sofa, her beautiful eyes steadily in front of her. She moved and spoke little. She seemed just to be waiting. Often Winnie wondered through what scenes of recollection, through what strains of meditation, her mind was passing. But she preserved all that defensiveness which her life had taught her—the power of saying nothing about herself, of giving no opening either to praise or to blame, of asking no outside support. Perhaps she talked to the General. He came every day, and Winnie was at pains to leave them alone together. Toward the rest of the world, including even Winnie, she was evidently minded to maintain to the end her consistent reticence. Sickness puts a house out of the traffic of the world; day followed day in a quiet isolation and a sad tranquillity.

What had passed left its mark on Winnie's relations with the General. He was, of course, courteous and more than that. He was uniformly kind, even affectionate, and constituted himself her partner in all that could be done or attempted for the patient whom they both loved. That link between them held, and would hold till another power than theirs severed it. But it was all that now kept them together; when it was gone he would be in effect a stranger to her. If she said to herself, with a touch of bitterness, "He has lost all his interest in me," there was a sense in which she spoke the truth. He had pictured her as coming into the inner circle of his life, and had urgently desired the realization of the picture. Now she was definitely relegated to the outskirts; she was again just Mrs. Lenoir's young friend—with this change—that he cherished a pathetically amiable grudge against her for the loss of the picture. How much he knew of what had passed between herself and his son on that last evening, she was not aware; but he knew the essence of it. Though in charity he might refrain from censure, she had been an occasion of sore distress to his best-beloved son. To her sensitive mind, in spite of his kindness, there was a reserve in his bearing; he now held their friendship to its limits. The love he had borne her was wounded to death by the pain she had given him. She could imagine his thoughts made articulate in

21   315

the words, "You sha'n't have it in your power to hurt mine and me again." She opened her eyes to the fact that she had lost a good friend, in these days which menaced her, only too surely, with the loss of a dear one. This chapter of her life seemed like to come to its end—as other chapters had before. . . . One visitant from the outside world—the General seemed a part of the household—made an appearance in the person of Mrs. Ladd. She came to call on Mrs. Lenoir, unaware of her illness; it was one of the patient's days of exhaustion, and Winnie had to entertain the good lady, and, after listening to her appropriate sympathy, to hear her news. She had come back to England alone. Rosaline had gone to stay with friends at Biarritz.

"I think she didn't want to come home just now," said Mrs. Ladd, with a glance at Winnie which plainly fished for information.

"Mrs. Lenoir has told me a certain impression of hers, which I didn't form for myself at Bellaggio," Winnie remarked. "Are you referring to that, Mrs. Ladd?"

"Yes. Rosaline told me that you suspected nothing. But since it's all settled, there's no harm in speaking of it now. Sir Axel is at Biarritz too. I think they'll probably be married as they pass through Paris on their way home."

"Oh, it's as settled as that, is it?" Winnie's speculations revived. How much had she and Mrs. Lenoir between them contributed to the settlement?

"I think she's right to bring it to a point. It avoids all question." Mrs. Ladd put her head on one side. "I've seen Mr. Maxon. Of course he doesn't know that you've ever seen Rosaline since—since the old days—much less that you had anything to do with it?"

"Had I? I never meant to have."

SHE SUDDENLY LEANED FORWARD AND PATTED WINNIE'S
HAND

A FRIEND DEPARTS

"Oh, I think so. Rosaline spoke vaguely, but I think something in your manner—of course you couldn't help it, and you didn't know. And, as I say, he has no notion of it."

"I'm glad. He'd be so angry with me, and I don't want him to be more angry than he must."

"I don't think he's got any anger to spare for you. He never referred to you. But her! Oh, my dear!" Mrs. Ladd's kindly old face assumed an almost frightened expression. "Well, I just had to stop him. I told him Rosaline was my friend, and that I wouldn't listen to it. He declared that he had a promise from her, and that on the faith of it, and of it alone, he—well, you know, don't you? Of course I said that there must have been a complete misunderstanding, but he wouldn't have it. Really, we all but quarrelled, if not quite."

How well Winnie knew! The domineering man, so sure both of his desires and of his claims, so confident in his version of the facts, so impervious to any other impression of them—from out the past the picture of him rose complete.

"I knew, of course, that he liked his own way," said Mrs. Ladd. "But, really, I was rather startled." She suddenly leaned forward and patted Winnie's hand. No words passed, but Winnie understood that Mrs. Ladd had been, to some extent at least, revising a judgment, and wished her to know it.

"He'll marry, though—mark my words! I know him, and I know something about that sort of man. He'll marry in a twelvemonth, if it's only to show Rosaline he can, and to hold up his end against Mr. Attlebury. I told Mr. Attlebury so. 'He's taken his line, and he'll go through with it,' I said, 'as soon as he finds a woman to help him.'"

"What did Mr. Attlebury say?"

317

"Nothing! He wouldn't talk about it. He just waved his hands in that way he has. But you may take it from me that that's what will happen."

The prophecy, born of the old woman's amiable worldly wisdom, seemed likely of fulfilment. There was nothing Cyril Maxon hated so much as failure or the imputation of it, nothing he prized so dearly as proving himself right, to which end it was ever necessary to refuse to admit that he had been wrong. Winnie seemed to hear him grimly declaring that, since he had taken his course, not Lady Rosaline, not a dozen Attleburys, should turn him from it. He would follow it to the end, even though he had little desire for it; antagonism was often to him stimulus enough. Thus it was that he became an implacable enemy to the liberty of those about him, warring with them if they asserted any independence, tyrannizing if they submitted. Such people create resistance, as it were out of a vacuum—even a wild and desperate resistance, which takes little heed of what it may hurt or overthrow in its struggle against domination. Venerable institutions, high ideals, personal loyalty may have to pay the price. All go by the board when the limits of human endurance are reached.

Had Winnie Maxon received a classical education—the absence of which had not in her case proved a panacea against all forms of failure—she might have found in wise old Mrs. Ladd a good embodiment of the Greek Chorus—usually people with little business of their own (as would appear for all that appears to the contrary) and bent on settling other people's on lines safely traditional; yet with a salt of shrewdness, not revolutionaries, but brave enough to be critics, admitting that acceptance and submission present their difficulties—but you may go further, and fare worse by a great deal! Those limits of endurance must be stretched as far as possible.

On the next day but one, the expected blow fell. Pneumonia declared itself; the patient took the doctor's diagnosis as a death sentence—final, hardly unwelcome. Her nights were pain; day brought relief, yet increasing weakness. Now the General could not endure much of the sick-room; he came, but his visits were briefer. Besides his grief for his friend, some distress was upon him—distress still for her sake, perhaps also for the sake of others who had gone before, even for himself, it may be. He knew so much more than Winnie did. Infinitely tender to his dying friend, he said but one word to Winnie. "When I suggest that she might see somebody she only smiles."

Winnie understood the suggestion. "We must all of us settle that for ourselves in the end, mustn't we? I think she seems happy—at least, quite at peace."

He made a fretful gesture of protest. She had no right to be quite at peace. He lived in the ideas in which he had been bred. If he had offended a gentleman, let him apologize before it was too late. Insensibly he applied the parallel from the seen world to the unseen—as, indeed, he had been taught. His mind stuck in particular categories of conduct; for some credit was to be given, for some penalties had to be paid; it was a system of marks good and bad. Even in the education of the young this is now held to be a disputable theory.

He thought that he had known very intimately his dear old friend who now lay dying. He found that he knew her very little; he could not get close to her mind at the end. For Winnie Maxon she had one more revelation. Mrs. Lenoir would not "see anybody"—she also detected the

319

special meaning, and, with a tired smile, repelled the suggestion—but in hints and fragments she displayed to Winnie
in what mood she was facing death. Courageously—
almost indifferently; the sun was set, and at night people go
to bed—tired people they are generally. She had not
thought much of responsibility, of a reckoning; she suffered
or achieved none of the resulting impulse to penitence; she
even smiled again at the virtue of a repentance become compulsory, because it was possible to sin no more. "Some
women I've known became terribly penitent at forty," she
said to Winnie. "I never knew one do it at twenty-five."
Her attitude seemed to say that she had been born such and
such a creature, and, accordingly, had done such and such
things—and thus had lived till it became time for the conditioned, hardly voluntary, life of the creature to end. On
the religious side it was pure negation, but on the worldly
there was something positive. As verily as the General, as
Bertie Merriam himself, she had "played the game." Her
code was intact; her honor, as judged by it, unsmirched.
"I've been straight, Winnie," she said, in almost the last
conscious minute.

Then came oblivion; the soul was rid of its burden many
hours before the body was. She passed from the life in
which she had been so great an offender against the rules,
had played so interesting a part, had done so many kind
things, had been such a good friend, even on occasion so
resolute a resister of temptation—and a woman not to be
mentioned. As Winnie wept over her and paid her the last
offices of love—for she, at least, had received the purest gold
of unseeking love—her heart suffered a mighty searching
pang of tenderness. Old words, of old time familiar, came
back. "I was an hungered and ye gave me meat; I was

thirsty and ye gave me drink; I was a stranger and ye took me in." Such things had her dead friend done for her.

An exaltation and a confidence took hold on her after she had kissed the cold brow. But outside the room stood the old General, sad, gray, heavy of face. His voice was broken, his hands tremulous.

"I wish—I wish she'd have seen somebody, Winnie!"

Winnie threw herself into his arms, and looked up at him, her eyes streaming with tears. "Dear General, she sees nothing or she sees God. Why are we to be afraid ?"

XXVII

MRS. LENOIR did not, as the phrase runs, "do as much for" Winnie Maxon as she had been prepared to do for the prospective Mrs. Bertie Merriam. Perhaps because, though she had accepted the decision, her disappointment over the issue persisted. Perhaps merely because, as matters now stood, her bounty would not go in the end to benefit her old friend's stock. After providing an annuity for her precious Emily, and bequeathing a few personal relics to the General, she left to Winnie the furniture of her flat and fifteen hundred pounds. The residue which was at her disposition she gave — it may be with a parting kick at respectability, it may be because she thought he would enjoy it most—to her favorite, and the least meritorious, of the General's sons—the one who went in for too much polo and private theatricals in India.

"There's no immediate need for you to hurry out of here," the General added; he was the executor. "The rent must be paid till the summer anyhow, and Clara told me that she wished you to stay till then if you liked. I've no doubt Emily will stay with you."

"It was very kind of her, but I can't afford to live here long."

"Oh, well, just while you look about you, anyhow. And

322

if there's anything I can do for you, you won't hesitate to let me know, will you ?"

Winnie promised to call upon his services if she required them, but again the feeling came over her that, however kind and obliging he might be, the General did in his heart —even if unwillingly—regard their connection with each other as over. The bond which Mrs. Lenoir had made was broken; that other and closer bond had never come into existence. It would have been unjust to say that the General was washing his hands of her. It was merely a recognition of facts to admit that fate—the course of events —was performing the operation for him. They had no longer any purchase on each other's lives, any common interest to unite them. His only surviving concern now was in his three sons, and it had been irrevocably decided that there Winnie was not to count.

The consciousness of this involuntary drifting apart from the old man whom she liked and admired for his gentleness and his loyalty intensified the loneliness with which Mrs. Lenoir's death afflicted Winnie. She was in no better case now than when her friend had rescued her from the empty studio and thereby seemed to open to her a new life. The new life, too, was gone with the friend who had given it. Looking back on her career since she had left Cyril Maxon's roof, she saw the same thing happening again and again. She had made friends and lost them; she had picked them up, walked with them to the next fork in the road, and there parted company. "Is it mere chance, or something in me, or something in my position ?" she asked herself. A candid survey could not refuse the conclusion that the position had contributed largely to the result. The case of Godfrey Ledstone, the more trivial instance of Bob Purnett, was there to prove it. The position had been a vital and practically exclusive factor in bringing about her parting from Bertie Merriam; she had an idea that its action was to be traced in the continued absence and silence of Dick Dennehy. The same thing which had parted her from her men friends had forbidden her friendships with women. She could, she felt, have made a friend of Amy Ledstone. To-day she would have liked to make a friend of kindly, shrewd old Mrs. Ladd; but though Mrs. Ladd came to see her at the flat which had been Mrs. Lenoir's, she received no invitation to Mrs. Ladd's house. The pressure of public opinion, the feelings of Mr. Attlebury's congregation, the "awkwardness" which would arise with Mrs. Ladd's old, if too exacting, friend Cyril Maxon, forbade. The one friendship which had proved able to resist the disintegrating influence was ended now by death.

Well, great benefits cannot reasonably be expected for nothing. If she was alone, she was also free—wonderfully free. And, of a certainty, complete freedom can seldom be achieved save at the cost of a voluntary or involuntary severing of ties. Must every one then be either a slave or a solitary? She was not so soured as to accept that conclusion. She knew that there was a way out—only she had not found it. The Aikenheads had, down at Shaylor's Patch! Thither—to her old haven—her thoughts turned longingly. While it stood, she did it injustice in calling herself friendless. Yet to retire to that pleasant seclusion went against pride; it seemed like a retreat, a confession that the world had been too much for her, that she was beaten. She was not prepared to acknowledge herself beaten—at least, not by the enemy in a fair, square fight. Her disasters were due to the defection of her allies. So she insisted, as she sat long hours alone in the flat—ah, now so quiet indeed!

Shaylor's Patch had not forgotten her. The Aikenheads did not attend their friend Mrs. Lenoir's funeral—they had a theory antagonistic to graveside gatherings, which was not totally lacking in plausibility—but Stephen had written to her, promising to come and see her as soon as he could get to town. He came there very seldom—Winnie, indeed, had never met him in London—and it was above a fortnight before he made his appearance at the flat. Delighted as Winnie was by his visit, her glad welcome was almost smothered in amazement at his appearance. He wore the full uniform of a man about town, all in the latest fashion, from the curl of the brim of his silk hat to the exact cut of his coat-tails. Save that his hair was a trifle long and full, he was a typical Londoner, dressed for a ceremonial occasion. As it was, he would pass well for a poet with social ambitions.

"Good gracious!" said Winnie, holding up her hands. "You got up like that, Stephen!"

"Yes, I think I can hold my own in Piccadilly," said Stephen, complacently regarding himself in the long gilt mirror. "I believe I once told you I had atavistic streaks? This is one of them. I can mention my opinions if I want to—and I generally do; but there's no need for my coat and hat to go yelling them out in the street. That's my view; of course it isn't in the least Tora's. She thinks me an awful fool for doing it."

Winnie did not feel it necessary to settle this difficult point in the philosophy of clothes—on which eminent men hold widely varying opinions, as anybody who takes his walks abroad and keeps his eyes open for the celebrities of the day will have no difficulty in observing.

"Well, at any rate, I think you look awfully nice—quite handsome! I expect Tora's just afraid of your being too fascinating in your best clothes."

He sat down with a laugh and looked across at her inquiringly. "Pretty cheerful, Winnie?"

"Not so very particularly. I do feel her loss awfully, you know. I was very fond of her, and it seems to leave me so adrift. I had an anchorage here, but the anchor won't hold any more."

"Come and anchor at Shaylor's Patch. The anchor always holds there for you."

Winnie both made her confession and produced her objections "I can't deny I've been thinking of you rather wistfully in these melancholy days, but it seems like—like giving up."

"Not a bit of it. You can be absolutely in the thick of the fight there if you like." He looked across at her with his whimsical smile. "I'm actually going to do something at last, Winnie. I'm about to start on my life's work. I'm going to do a *Synopsis of Social Philosophy.*"

"It sounds like a life's work," Winnie remarked. His society always cheered her, and already her manner showed something of its normal gayety.

"Yes, it's a big job, but I'm a healthy man. You see, I shall take all the great fellows from the earliest time down to to-day, and collect from them everything that bears on the questions that we of to-day have to face—not worrying about their metaphysics and that sort of stuff, but taking what bears on the things we've really got to settle—the live things, you know. See the idea? There'll be a section on Education, for instance, one on Private Property, one on Marriage, one on Women and Labor. I want it to reach

the masses, so all the excerpts will be in English. Then
each section will have an appendix, in which I shall collate
the excerpts, and point out the main lines of agreement and
difference. Perhaps I shall add a few suggestions of my
own."

"I think you very likely will, Stephen."

"Now don't you think it's a ripping idea? Of course
I shall take in poetry and novels and plays, as well as
philosophers and historians. A comparison between Lecky
and Ibsen, for instance! Bound to be fruitful! Oh, it 'll
be a big job, but I mean to put it through." He leaned
forward to her. "That's not giving up, is it? That's
fighting! And the point is—you can help me. You see
there'll be no end of books to read, just to see if there's anything of possible use in them. You can do lots of spade
work for me. Besides, you've got very good judgment."

"Wouldn't Tora help you better than I could?"

His eyes twinkled. "I wouldn't trust Tora, and I've
told her so plainly. She's so convinced of what she thinks
herself that she considers the other view all nonsense—or
if she did hit on a particularly clever fellow who put the case
too well against her, it's my firm belief that she'd have no
scruple about suppressing him. Yours is much more the
mind for me. We're inquirers, not dogmatists, you and I.
With you, and a secretary learned in tongues, and a couple
of typewriters, we shall make a hole in the work in no time."

Winnie could not be sure that he was not building a
golden bridge for her retreat. Perhaps she did not wish to
risk being made quite sure. The plan sounded so attractive.
What things she would read and learn! And it was certainly possible to argue that she would still be fighting
the battle of liberty and progress. After all, is it not the

students who really set the line of advance ? They originate the ideas, which some day or other the practical men carry out. It was Moltke who won the campaign, not the generals in the field. Such was the plea which inclination offered to persuade pride.

"But, Stephen, apart from anything else, it would mean quartering myself on you practically forever!"

"What if it did ? But, as a matter of fact, Tora thought you'd like to have your own place. You remember that cottage Godfrey had ? He took it furnished; but it's to be let on lease unfurnished now, and if you liked it—"

"Oh, I shouldn't mind it. And Mrs. Lenoir has left me her furniture."

"The whole thing works out beautifully," Stephen declared. He grew a little graver. "Come and try it, anyhow. Look here—I'll take the cottage, and sublet it to you. Then you can give it up at any moment, if you get sick of it. We shall be a jolly little colony. Old Dick Dennehy's house—you remember how we put him up to it ?—is almost finished, and he'll be in it in six months. Of course he'll hate the *Synopsis*, and we shall have lots of fun with him."

"Oh, my dear, you're good!" sighed Winnie—and a smile followed the sigh. For suddenly life and activity, comradeship and gayety, crossed her path again. The thing was not over. It had almost seemed over—there in the lonely flat. "How is dear old Dick Dennehy ?" she asked.

"We've hardly seen him—he's only been down once. He's left me to build his house for him, and says encouragingly that he doesn't care a hang what it's like. He's been settling into his new job, I suppose. After a bit, perhaps, he'll be more amiable and accessible. You'll come and give it a trial, Winnie ?" He got up and came over to her.

"You've done enough off your own bat," he said. "I don't quite know how to put it to you, but what I think I mean is that no single person does any good by more than one protest. Intelligent people recognize that; but if you go on, you get put down not as a Protestant, but just as an anarchist—like our poor dear old friend here, you know."

He touched, with a true and discerning hand, on one of the great difficulties. If you were burned at the stake for conscience sake, it was hard to question your sincerity—though it appears that an uncalled-for and wanton quest of even the martyr's crown was not always approved by the soberer heads of and in the Churches. It was far harder to make people believe or understand that what you wanted to do might seem also what it was your duty to do—that the want made the duty. Only because the want was great—a thing which must be satisfied if a human life were not to be fruitlessly wasted—did the duty become imperative. A doctrine true, perhaps, but perilous! Its professors should be above suspicion.

"It's awfully difficult," Stephen went on, stroking his forehead the while. "It's war, you see, and in any war worth arguing about both sides have a lot to say for themselves. We shall bring that out in the *Synopsis*."

"Don't be too impartial, Stephen!"

"No, I've got my side — but the other fellows shall have a fair show." His smile grew affectionate. "But I think you're entitled to come out of the fighting line and go into the organizing department—whatever it's called technically."

"I'll tell you all about it some day. I'll wait a little. I seem only just to be getting a view of it."

"You're very young. You may have a bit more practical

work to deal with still. At any rate, I shall be very glad to hear all about it." He rose and took his resplendent silk hat—that symbol of a sentimental attachment to the old order, from which he sprang, to which his sceptical mind had so many questions to put. "Look here, Winnie, I believe you've been thinking life was finished—at any rate, not seeing any new start in it. Here's one—take it. It'll develop. The only way to put a stopper on life is to refuse to go along the open lines. Don't do that." He smiled. "I rather think we started you from Shaylor's Patch once. We may do it again."

The plain truth came suddenly in a burst from her. "I'm so tired, Stephen!"

He laid down the hat again and took her two hands in his. "The *Synopsis* will be infinitely restful, Winnie. I'm going straight back to take the cottage, and begin to whitewash it. Send me word when you're ready to come. I'll tell you the truth before I go—or sha'n't I? Yes, I will, because, as I've told you before now, you've got pluck. You tell yourself you're facing things by staying here. You're not. You're hiding from things—and people. There are people you fear to meet, from one reason or another, in London, aren't there? Leave all that then. Come and live and work with us—and get your nerve back."

She looked at him in a long silence, then drew her breath. "Yes, I think you're right. I've turned afraid." She threw out her arms in a spreading gesture. "Here it is so big—and it takes no notice of me! On it goes—on—on!"

"You didn't expect to stop it, all on your own, did you?" asked Stephen, smiling.

"Or if it does take notice for a minute, half of it shudders, and the other half sniggers! Is there nothing in between?"

"Oh, well, those are the two attitudes of conservatism. Always have been—and, I suppose, always with a good deal of excuse. We do blunder, and we have a knack of attracting ridiculous people. It sets us back, but it can't be helped. We win in the end." He took up his hat again. "And the *Synopsis* is going to leaven the lump. Send me a wire to-morrow, Winnie, and the whitewashing shall begin!"

Faith, patience, candor—these were the three great qualities; these composed the temper needed for the work. Stephen Aikenhead had them, and, even though he never put himself to the ordeal of experience, nay, even though he never finished the *Synopsis* (a contingency likely enough), encouragement radiated from him, and thus his existence was justified and valuable. There were bigots on both sides, and every cause counted some fools among its adherents. Probably, indeed, every individual in the world, however wise and open-minded in the sum, had his spot of bigotry and his strain of folly. After Stephen's departure Winnie did much moralizing along these and similar lines, but her moralizing was at once more cheerful and more tolerant than it had been before he came. She had a greater charity toward her enemy, the world—even toward the shudders and the sniggers. Why, the regiment would have been divided between shudders and sniggers—exactly the attitudes which Bertie Merriam had sketched—and yet she had felt, under his inspiration, both liking and respect for the regiment. Why not then for that greater regiment, the world? Liking and respect, yes—but not, therefore, assent or even acquiescence. And on her own proceedings, too, Stephen enabled her to cast new eyes—eyes more open to the humorous aspect, taking a juster view of how much she might have expected to do and could reasonably consider herself to have done. Both seemed to come to very little compared with the wear and tear of the effort. But, then, if everybody did even a very little—why, the lump would be leavened, as Stephen said.

Three days later—just after she had made up her mind for Shaylor's Patch and the *Synopsis*, and had given notice to the General—and to Emily—of her approaching departure, there came a short note from the obstinately absent and invisible Dick Dennehy. It was on the official notepaper of the great journal:

"I hear from Tora that you're going back to Shaylor's Patch, to settle down there quietly. Thank God for it! Perhaps I shall see you there before very long, but I'm still very busy.—Yours, R. D."

She read with a mixture of affection and resentment. She had been arriving at her own verdict on her efforts and adventures. Here was Dick Dennehy's! He thanked God that efforts and adventures were at an end, and that she was going to settle down quietly—in fact, to take care of herself, as he had put it that evening when he walked with her to the railway station. A very unjust verdict, thought Winnie, but then—she added, smiling—"It's only old Dick Dennehy's!" What else was to be expected from him—from him who liked her so much and disapproved of her "goings-on" so strenuously? What about his own? How was he settling that question of his? Or how had he settled it? That problem which was "not serious"! "Perhaps I shall see you"! Only "perhaps"? Yet she was going to settle down at Nether End, and he was building his house there. The probabilities of an encounter between them seemed to warrant more than "perhaps." The atmosphere of the railway waiting-room, the look on his face, that shout, muffled by engine-snorts, about somebody being a fool—they all came back to her. "But I'm very busy"—meaning thereby—Winnie took leave to add the innuendo—"I sha'n't be able to see you often!" Irresistibly her lips curved into a smile. It looked as if the problem weren't quite settled yet! If it were finally settled either way, why should Dick be so busy, so entirely unable to give reasonable attention to his house, or—as Stephen had told her—to care a hang about it?

"Oh, nonsense!" Winnie contrived to say to herself, though not with absolute conviction. "If it ever was that, he must have got over it by now, and I shall bury myself in the *Synopsis*."

It was really rather soon to find herself pitted against another institution!

XXVIII

WINNIE shut Doctor Westermarck on *The Origin and Development of the Moral Ideas* with a bang. "I'm not going to do any more at the *Synopsis* to-day," she announced. "It's much too fine. And what are you chuckling at, Stephen?"

With the help of Liddell and Scott and a crib Stephen was digesting Aristophanes' skit on Socrates. "An awful old Tory, but it's dashed good stuff. On no account work if you don't want to, Winnie. This job's not to be done in a day, you know."

It certainly was not—and least of all in one of his working days, in which the labor of research was constantly checked by the incursion of distantly related argument. Winnie could not make out how far he was in earnest about the *Synopsis*. Sometimes he would talk about its completion— and the consequent amelioration of society—in sanguine words, yet with a twinkle in his eye; at other moments he would declare in an apparent despair that it was properly the work of fifty men, and forthwith abandon for the day a labor impossibly Herculean. Tora maintained toward the great undertaking an attitude of serene scorn; she did not see the use of delving into dark ages in search of the light which only now, at last, was glimmering on the horizon

334

WINNIE SHUT DOCTOR WESTERMARCK ON "THE ORIGIN
AND DEVELOPMENT OF THE MORAL IDEAS" WITH A BANG

of the future. Alice, however, was all for the *Synopsis*, it was to make her father famous, and itself became famous among her schoolmates these many years before there was the least chance of its coming to birth. "To find out all that any one ever said since the world began, and tell us whether it's true or not," was Alice's handsome description of the proposed work; no wonder the schoolmates were impressed.

Though the "awful old Tory" might well have seen in Shaylor's Patch a lesser Phrontisterion, to Winnie Maxon the passage of the summer months there proved a rest-cure. The tissues of brain and heart recovered. She was neither oppressed as in the days of her marriage, nor hurried from emotion to emotion as in the period of struggle which had followed her escape. Her memories—of exultation, of pain, of poignant feeling—softened in outline; becoming in some degree external to all that she had done and suffered, she was the better able to assess it and to estimate where it left her. A great gulf separated her from the woman who had fled from Cyril Maxon; yet the essential woman had passed through the flood of the gulf undrowned—with all her potentialities of life, with her spirit schooled, but not broken. This is, perhaps, to say that she had fought a drawn battle with the world; if it really came to that, it was no mean achievement.

Dick Dennehy's new house was finished—at least it wanted only its last coat of paint and, if the weather held fine, would soon be dry enough to receive it profitably. By fits and starts consignments of its necessary gear—conceived on extremely Spartan lines—arrived from London. But the master of it had himself made no appearance. Every invitation from Shaylor's Patch—and now and then the invitation amounted to an entreaty, since Tora could not for

the life of her make out what he wanted done at the house
—was met by protestations of absorbing work. The problem which Winnie's imagination had forecasted did not
arise—or at least it exhibited no development. Dick's obstinate absence did not disprove its existence, but might be
said to suspend its animation. Winnie, dwelling in the
cottage where Godfrey Ledstone once abode, had a rest
from the other sex; here, too, a truce was called, after her
brisk series of engagements. She welcomed it; it would
have seemed shallow to pass too quickly from the thought
of Bertie Merriam. She neither rejected nor winced at the
idea that the truce might be perpetual. With Dennehy still
away, the thought of the problem died down, leaving traces
only in the compassionate amusement with which she again,
from time to time, reflected that he had "got over it." She
acquiesced very willingly in the conclusion. As matters
stood, life was full, pleasant, peaceful, and fruitful in the
growth of her mind.

"I don't know whether you'll ever transform the world,
but at least you're educating one ignorant woman, Stephen,"
she said.

Doctor Westermarck being finished, Stephen had, with a
sudden jump, transferred her to the study of Utopias, old
and new; for these, of course, must figure in the *Synopsis*.

"Ah, you bring some knowledge of life with you now.
That makes learning ever so much easier." He smiled at
her. "I really ought to go and get into some scrapes too.
But there—I couldn't put my heart into the job, so it
wouldn't be much use."

"Wouldn't Tora object ?"

"I'm the one exception which mars the otherwise perfect harmony of Tora's conception of the male sex. She

336

would be bound to greet any lapse on my part with scientific exultation. But, I say, I'm not going to have you burying yourself in the *Synopsis*."

"That's just what I came here to do—exactly as I put it to myself!"

"You sha'n't do it. You're much too young and pretty. I shall get some young men down, to tempt you."

Two or three young men came, but they did not tempt Winnie. She found herself possessed by a great caution. Her old confidence in her own impulses was replaced by a deep distrust of any impulse. She stood on the defensive against the approach of even a liking; she constituted herself *advocatus diaboli* whenever Stephen ventured to praise any of his young friends. She found one shallow and conceited, another learned, but a bore, a third—well, there were limits to the allowable degree of ugliness, now weren't there? Stephen laughed; his poor friends were contributing to the payment of a score run up by other men.

At last in very decency Dick Dennehy had to come; Stephen sent him word that, as he had built the house, so he would pull it down, if its owner continued to show such a want of appreciation of his friendly labors. He arrived early one afternoon in mid-September. He was perceptibly changed; being broken into London harness had set its mark on him in manner and in appearance. He was better groomed, his hair had been persuaded to lie down, he had cut off the upturned bristly ends of his mustache. His brogue had lost in richness; he said "ye" much seldomer when he meant "you." His ways were quieter, his arguments less tempestuous, and his contradictions not so passionate. Though thus a little outwardly and possibly inwardly conventionalized, he displayed all his old friendly

337

heartiness in his greeting of Tora and Stephen—Alice had just gone back to school. Only when he turned to Winnie, who was in the garden with them, did a shade of constraint appear in his demeanor. She put it down to the memory of the note he had sent her; she had not replied, and probably he thought that she had resented it.

The constraint was due to a deeper cause. He had determined not to make love to Winnie Maxon, and now, at the sight of her, he found that he wanted to do it, and that the assurances which he had managed to make to himself that he would not want to do it—at least would not be seriously tempted to do it—were all in vain. In loyalty to his convictions, and in accordance with a personal obstinacy which buttressed the convictions, all these months he had fought his fight. Winnie was forbidden to him; he had taken no pains to conceal his views from his and her friends; he had taken great pains to conceal his feelings from her, and conceived that he had, in the main at least, succeeded. But for that house of his—but for wounding the Aikenheads' feelings—he would have given himself a little longer period of quarantine. Yet he had felt pretty safe until he saw Winnie. And he had brought his bag; he was booked for a three days' stay—there in the very zone of danger.

"I was a fool to come," he kept saying to himself, while he was being politely, and now and then urgently, requested to take note of and to admire this and that feature of his new house. In truth he could take very little interest in the house, for it had come over him, with sudden but irresistible certainty, that he would never be able to live in it. He could not say so, of course—not just now, and not without a much better parade of reasons than he could manage to put into line impromptu. But there the cer-

tainty was—full-blown in his mind. Unless he could away
with his convictions and his obstinacy, unless he could undertake and succeed in his quest, it would be impossible for
him to live in the house here on the hill, with Winnie hardly
a stone's-throw away at the cottage on the road to Nether
End. The idea was preposterous. Yet he had to go on
looking at the house and admiring it. The Aikenheads demanded nothing short of enthusiasm. About a house he
could never live in! Poor Dick Dennehy did his best to
pump it up, but the trials inherent in his position were terribly aggravated by this incidental addition of the house.
Cyril Maxon and Bertie Merriam, in their kindred struggles
with loyalties and convictions, had at least been spared this
irritating feature. Why, there, actually visible from his
study windows, were the chimneys of Winnie's cottage.
Tora triumphantly pointed them out to him.

Dick Dennehy had the gift—the genius—of his race; he
saw the fun of his own sufferings. As he surveyed the tops
of Winnie's chimneys—with Winnie at his elbow, discreetly awaiting his opinion as to whether their presence
enhanced the beauty of the landscape—his face wore a look
of rueful amusement, instead of the simple admiration which
the outlook from his study ought to have inspired in him.
At the moment Tora and Stephen were having an animated
wrangle in the passage outside, relative to the merits of a
dustbin, sent on approval.

"I hope I don't intrude?" said Winnie, waving her hand
toward her chimney-pots.

"I'll be reminded of you, if I'm ever in danger of forgetting."

"We could almost start a system of communication—
flag-wagging, or even wireless. Anything except thought-

transference! I couldn't risk that with you—though you could with me quite safely."

"Ah, you're always teasing me, Winnie."

"You've not been nearly enthusiastic enough about the house, you know. Make an effort."

"I'll be trying to say a few words on it after dinner. Will you be at dinner?"

"I shall. Tora has asked me to entertain you."

"You can do that—and more when you've the mind to it."

"I must warn you at once that I take most of my meals, except breakfast, at the Patch—in brief intervals of relaxation from the *Synopsis*."

Dick had heard of the *Synopsis*. "You'll be learning a lot of nonsense," he remarked.

"Oh, I don't need the *Synopsis* to learn that. Just talking to people is quite enough."

"We won't have a telegraph; we'll have a telephone, Winnie. Then I'll hear your voice and admire your conversation." "And not see your face," he had very nearly added.

Winnie demurely surveyed the landscape again. "My chimneys are a pity, aren't they? They spoil the impression of solitude—of being alone with nature—don't they? But judging from Tora's voice—it sounds really aggrieved —I think it's time we went and umpired about the dustbin. When those two do quarrel, the contempt they express for each other's opinions is awful."

If the situation had its pathetic side for poor Dick Dennehy, there was more than one aspect on which a sense of humor could lay hold. Besides Dick, impelled by love yet racked by conscience, and, in consequence, by chimney-pots in the middle distance, there were the Aikenheads. En-

340

grossed in each other, in their studies and theories, they saw nothing of what was going on under—and seemed now to Winnie as plain to see as—their noses. They had bestowed immense pains on the house, and had counted on giving Dick a triumphant surprise. His behavior—for even after dinner he achieved but a very halting enthusiasm—was a sore disappointment. They understood neither why he was not delighted, nor why, failing that, in common decency and gratitude, he could not make a better show of being delighted. Good-tempered as they were, they could not help betraying their feelings—Tora by a sudden and stony silence touching the house of whose beauties she had been so full; Stephen by satirical remarks about the heights of splendor on which Dick now required to be seated in his daily life and surroundings. Dick marked their vexation and understood it, but could not so transform his demeanor as to remove it, and, being unable to do that, began by a natural movement of the mind to resent it. "They really might see that there's something else the matter," he argued within himself in plaintive vexation. Within twenty-four hours of his arrival the three were manifestly at odds on this false issue, and the tension threatened to become greater and greater. It was all ridiculous, a comedy of mistakes, but it might end in a sad straining of an old and dear friendship.

To avert this catastrophe Winnie determined to give the go-by to coy modesty. Dick Dennehy had not told her that he loved her, but she determined to acquaint the Aikenheads with the interesting fact. What would happen after that she did not know, but it seemed the only thing to do at the moment.

After lunch on the second day of the visit Dick Dennehy,

in a desperate effort to be more gracious, said that he would go across and have another look at the house. Nobody offered to accompany him. Tora seemed not to hear his remark; Stephen observed sarcastically that Dick might consider the desirability of adding a ball-room and a theatre, and with that returned to his labors on the *Synopsis*. Winnie sat smiling while Dick departed and left her alone with Tora.

"You think he's not appreciative enough about the house, don't you, Tora?" she asked.

"I think he just hates it, but I really don't know why."

"It's not his own house that he hates; it's my chimneys."

"Your chimneys? What in the world do you mean?"

"He can see them from his study window—just where he wants to be undisturbed."

Tora might be a profound speculative thinker, but, no, she was not quick in the little matters of the world. "Do you mean to say that the man objects to seeing any single house from his windows? Really Dick is putting on airs!"

"It depends on who lives in the single house."

"But you live there." Tora stared at her. "Have you quarrelled with him? Do you mean to say he dislikes you?"

Winnie broke into a laugh. "On the contrary, Tora."

At last light dawned. A long-drawn "Oh!" proclaimed its coming. "I see. I never do notice things like that. Then you've refused him, have you?"

"Oh no, he's never asked me. He never told me anything about it—not directly, or meaning to, at least." This qualification in view of the talk at the railway station. "But I'm sure of it."

"Then why doesn't he tell you? Or have you snubbed him hopelessly?"

"I haven't done much either way, but it's not that. You see, he thinks that he's not free to marry me, and that I'm not free to marry anybody."

"Then he'd better stop thinking such nonsense," said Tora, with her habitual and most unphilosophical contempt for other people's opinions.

"I don't know about that." Winnie shook her head doubtfully. "But I think that it would ease the situation if you gave Stephen just a hint."

"I'll go and tell him at once." Hints were not in Tora's line.

The first result of her friend's mission which reached Winnie's ears was a ringing peal of laughter from the sanctum where the *Synopsis* was in course of preparation. It was Wednesday — a half-holiday for the assistants — and Stephen was alone. When once the situation was elucidated, he enjoyed the humor of it immensely.

"Well, we have been a pair of dolts, you and I, Tora. Poor old Dick! He must have been wishing us, and the house too, at the bottom of the sea. But what's to be done?"

"Why, you must tell him not to be so silly, of course; I don't know what she'll say, but let him take his chance."

"I'm getting a bit shy of taking a hand in these complications. We didn't make much of a success out of the Ledstone affair, among us! I think I shall let it alone and leave them to settle it for themselves."

"You never have the courage of your convictions. It's one of your worst faults, Stephen." With this condemnation on her lips, Tora departed into the garden.

When Winnie went in to resume her labors, Stephen looked up from his books with a twinkle in his eye.

"Trouble again, Winnie ?"

"I really thought you'd better know about it, or you'd burn Dick's house down."

"You seem to have a knack of setting fires ablaze too."

"You might just let it appear that you've come to the conclusion that it's not the house which makes Dick so grumpy. Don't say a word about me, of course."

"He'll think me much cleverer than I have been."

"Well, I should think you'd like that, Stephen. I should, in your place."

He laughed good-humoredly. "Oh, well, I deserve that dig."

"It's rather funny how this sort of thing pursues me, isn't it? But it's quite half your fault. If you will collect a menagerie of opinions, and throw me into the middle of it—"

"It's not strange that the animals like the dainty morsel, even though the keepers don't approve of the diet? But I didn't collect all the animals."

"No," said Winnie, smiling reflectively. "I did pick up one or two for myself in the course of my journeyings through the world. I'm not quite sure I want any others."

"He's an awfully good fellow, old Dick."

"Yes. And now I'm going back to Utopia—where animals like only their proper diet."

Meanwhile Dick Dennehy was not taking another look at his house, nor endeavoring to form a more favorable estimate of it. He was walking up and down in the field behind it, which under Tora Aikenhead's skilled care had already assumed something of the semblance of a garden. He had to settle his question one way or the other. If one way, then good-bye, for a long while at least, to the new house and to Shaylor's Patch; if the other, he would try his

344

fortune with a good courage. Although his case had points of similarity enough to justify Winnie in linking it with those others which had presented themselves in her experience, it was not identical with any one of them, but had its own complexion. He was not called upon to defy public opinion and to confuse the lines of social demarcation, as Godfrey Ledstone had been. Nor to revolutionize his ideas and mode of life, like Bob Purnett. Nor to be what he must deem disloyal to his profession and false to his work in the world, like Bertie Merriam. Cyril Maxon's case was closer; yet Cyril had only to pass, by an ingeniously constructed bridge, from the more extreme to the less extreme of two theories, and in so doing found abundance of approval and countenance among men of his own persuasion. Dick was confronted with a straight, rigid, unbending prohibition from an authority which he had always respected as final and infallible.

Yet he seemed asked to give up the whole of his real life, to empty life of what made it worth living. Save for one or two boyish episodes of sentiment, he had kept clear of love-affairs. He brought to Winnie's service both the fresh ardor of a young man and the settled conviction of maturity. He had never a doubt in his mind that for him it was this woman or no woman; his knowledge of himself and his past record made the certainty more trustworthy than it generally is. Given then that he had a chance of winning her, it was a mighty sacrifice which was demanded of him —even to the spoiling and maiming of his life, and the starvation of his spirit.

His was a perfectly straight case; there was no confusing it, there could be no golden bridge; a supreme authority on the one side, on the other the natural man, fortified by

345

every secular justification—for he would be breaking no
law of the land, infringing no code of honor, injuring no
man whose rights or feelings he was under an obligation to
respect. And he would be affording to the creature he
loved best in the world happiness, as he believed, and, of a
certain, peace, protection, and loving care—things of which
she stood in need; to Dick Dennehy's notions, notwithstand-
ing his love and admiration, her record showed that she
stood sorely in need of them. Here, on one side of his
mind, he found himself in a paradoxical agreement with the
authority which the other side wanted to defy. It and he
agreed about her past doings, but drew from them a different conclusion. He adored her, but he did not think that
she could take care of herself. He believed that he could
take care of her—at the cost of defying his supreme authority; or he would not use the word defying—he would
throw himself on its mercy in a very difficult case. The
creature he loved best of all things in life would do, he
feared, more unpardonable things, unless he himself did a
thing which he had been taught to think unpardonable in
itself. He invited her to nothing that she was obliged to
hold as wrongdoing; he did not ask her to sin against the
light she possessed. That sin would be his. His chivalry
joined forces with his love; to refrain seemed cowardice as
well as almost impossibility. There was the dogma—but
should there be no dispensation? Not when every fibre of
a man's heart, every impulse of a man's courage, cried out
for it?

The sun sank to its setting. He stood in the garden and
watched how its decline made more beautiful the gracious
prospect. A little trail of smoke rose in leisurely fashion
from the chimneys of Winnie's cottage. The air was very

still. He turned and looked at the new house with a new interest. "Would it be good enough for her, now?" asked Dick Dennehy. The sudden vision of her in the house —of her dainty ways and gracious presence, her chaff and her sincerity—swept over his mind. She had been wrong—but she had been brave. Braver than he was himself?.

To the horizon sank the sun. Dick Dennehy turned to look at it again. As the glow faded, peace and quiet reigned. Very gradually evening fell. He lifted his hat from his head and stood watching the last rays, the breeze stirring his hair and freshening his brow. He stood for a long time very still, as he was wont to stand, quiet, attentive, obedient, at the solemn offices of his Church—the Church that was to him creed, conscience, and half motherland. Suddenly his soul was at peace, and he spoke aloud with his lips, even as though in response to the voice of One walking in the garden in the cool of the day. "I must do what I must do, and leave it to the mercy of God."

23

XXIX

"ON further inspection it turns out to be a perfectly corking house—a jewel of a house, Stephen!"

Winnie had gone home, and Stephen was working alone at the *Synopsis* when Dick Dennehy walked into the room with these words on his lips. Stephen looked up and saw that something had happened to his friend. The embarrassed hang-dog air had left his face. He looked a trifle obstinate about the mouth, but his eyes were peaceful and met Stephen's straightforwardly.

"In fact, there's only one fault at all to be found with it."

"Give it a name, and Tora will put it right," said Stephen, in genial response to his friend's altered mood.

Dick smiled. "I'm afraid Tora can't, but I know of another lady who can—if she will. It's a bit big for a bachelor; I'll be feeling lonely there."

"Oh, that's it, is it?" Stephen laughed. "Now I rather thought it was all along." At some cost to truth, he was carrying out Winnie's injunction. "You were so—well—restless."

"I was. And Tora was cross with me, and you laughed at me, and then I got savage. But it's all over now—so far as I'm concerned, at least. You know who it is?"

"Well, I almost think I can guess, old fellow. We're not blind. Winnie?"

348

Dick Dennehy nodded his head. "I'll have it settled before I'm many days older."

His mouth was now very firm, and his eyes almost challenging. It was evident even to the lover of discussion that here was a decision which was not to be discussed, one which only the man who came to it himself could judge. Stephen felt the implication in Dick's manner so strongly that he even retrenched his faint smile of amusement, as he held out his hand, and said, "Good luck!"

Dick nodded again, gave a tight grip, and marched out of the room.

Leaving the patient *Synopsis* and lighting a pipe, Stephen indemnified himself for the self-restraint he had exercised in not talking the case over with Dick by indulging in a survey of a wider order—one which embraced all Winnie's career from the time of her rebellion; there were few features with which confidential talks, interspersed between their labors, had not familiarized him. His mind was not now on Winnie's share in the matter—neither on how she had conducted herself nor on how she had been affected by her experiment and experience. It fastened, with its usual speculative zest, on the conflict and clash of theory and practice, opinion and conduct, which the story revealed throughout its course and exemplified in instance after instance. When put to a searching personal test, everybody, or almost everybody, had in some way or another broken down; if they were to be judged by the strict standards which they professed, or by the canons which habitually governed their lives, they had been failures. Here was Dick Dennehy ending the series with a striking example. But Godfrey Ledstone had begun it. His was a twofold failure; he was false to his own theories—to that code of his—when he

349

adopted Winnie's; he was false in turn to Winnie's when he
was ashamed of her and fled back to respectability tempered
by elasticities. Cyril Maxon followed suit, bartering his
high doctrine, wriggling out of its exacting claims, for the
chance of Rosaline Deering. Even that fellow Purnett, to
whom regularity and domesticity were anathema, had offered to become regular and domestic. The only exception
seemed to be the soldier Merriam; even here Stephen
doubted the existence of a sure exception. Winnie had left
the details of that talk in the garden at Madeira in obscurity,
yet it was clear enough that she had not put out her power.
Supposing she had ? Yet, granting the exception, he proved
it to his own satisfaction to be more apparent than real.
Merriam's case was not a conflict of opinion and conduct;
it was more properly a clash between two allegiances both
in essence personal in their nature; between inclination and
a conception of duty, no doubt, but of a duty so specialized
and (if the word might be used) so incarnated as to lose its
abstract quality and, by virtue of concreteness, to acquire a
power of appeal really as emotional in character as the
emotion with which it came into collision. It seemed to
him that here was a case of an apparent exception test-
ing the rule, not disproving it. The rule emerged triumphant from the test—so declared Stephen Aikenhead, very
anxious to find a clue to the labyrinth and fast colors in the
shifting web of human nature. When it came to a pitched
battle, the views and theories were worsted; the man himself won the day, calling to his aid reserves ordinarily hidden
in the depths of his nature. By a pardonable instinct they
all made the best case they could for their failures and deviations—explanations, excuses, bridges; they saved the
show of consistency as far as they could. But however

great or small the success of this special pleading, it did not alter the truth. The natural, essential—to use a new word, the subliminal—man himself in the end decided the issue.

Small wonder! thought Stephen; for these opinions were a motley host—enemies among themselves. If one of them were putting up a good fight, another was already ready to fall on its flank. If one were making a strong case, there was another to whisper its weak point in the adversary's ear, or to suggest insinuatingly—"Well, if he can't allow you what you want, try me! I'm much more accommodating. I recognize exceptions. I know the meaning of counsels of perfection. I understand the limits of human nature." Or conversely—"You'll get no real comfort from that shifty fellow. He'll betray you in this world, to say nothing of the next. Rest on me. I'm a rock. Rocks make hard beds, you say? A little, perhaps, now and then, but think how safe they are! And how they appeal to your imagination, rising foursquare to heaven, unshakable, eternal!" And then there was that plausible little rogue of an opinion which protests always that it is not an opinion at all— nothing so troublesome—"Don't bother your head with any of those fellows. Please yourself! What does it matter? Anyhow, what do any of them really know about it? You might just as well toss up as try to decide between them. I'm an opinion myself, you say—just as bad as they are? Not at all! How dare you?" So they went on, betraying, competing, outbidding one another—like a row of men selling penny toys in the street, each trying to shout louder and to get more custom than the other. In such an irreverent image did Stephen Aikenhead envisage the Quest after Truth, whereof he was himself so ardent a devotee.

He had got back to his old formula. Things were in so-

351

lution. It was a very welter of opinions. Was that state of things to last forever? "Or"—he mused—"shall we to some future age seem, oh, ridiculously mixed? Will they have settled things? Will they have straightened out the moral and social world as the scientific fellows are straightening out the physical universe? If they have, they'll never understand how we doubted and squabbled. Only some great historian will be able to make that intelligible to them. Or will men go on forever swirling round and round in a whirlpool and never sail on a clear, strong stream to the ocean of truth?"

So the muser mused in his quiet study, with the roar of the water in his ears. Had he chanced to think of it, he would have found that he was himself an example of the conclusion to which his survey of Winnie Maxon's experiences had led him. His speculations might ask, with "jesting Pilate," "What is truth?" and stay not for an answer that could never come. The natural man, Stephen Aikenhead, was irresistibly bent on finding out. He returned briskly to the *Synopsis*—to his own little task of blasting away, if by chance he could, one fragment of the rocks that dammed the current.

He worked on, reading and making notes. The clock struck six, and seven, and half-past. He did not notice. Five minutes later the door opened, and Winnie came in.

"What's come over the house?" she asked. "You invited me to dinner at half-past seven! Here you are, not only not dressed, but with your hair obviously unbrushed! And Tora and Dick went off to the new house, Ellen tells me, at half-past five, with a lantern, and haven't come back yet!"

"Oh, did they? Then Dick's evidently made it all right

with Tora too." He rose and stretched himself. "I think you'll have to look out for something to-night or to-morrow, Winnie. Dick has made up his mind; he's decided that the house is otherwise delightful, but has just one fault. He'd be lonely in it as a bachelor."

Winnie sat down and looked at him thoughtfully. "I wish it hadn't come so soon. I'm not ready. And I do have such bad luck!"

"He'll wait as long as you like. And how does the bad luck come in here?"

"I'm always forced into seeming to exact a sacrifice of some sort."

"Well, from some points of view that was likely to follow from the line you took. From your own side of the matter, is it altogether a bad thing that a man should have to search his heart—to ask what you're really worth to him?"

"Suppose he should bear me a grudge afterward?"

"Dick's too square with his conscience to do that. He knows it's his own act and his own responsibility."

"At any rate I won't have any more vows, Stephen, no more on either side. I don't like them. I broke mine once. I thought I had a right to, but I didn't like doing it. Cyril had broken most of his, in my view, but people seem so often to forget that there's more than one." She gave an abrupt little laugh. "Cyril vowed to 'comfort' me! Imagine Cyril being obliged to vow to comfort anybody, poor man! He couldn't possibly do it."

"In the matter of vows they let you down easy at the registry office."

"In his heart Dick won't think that a marriage at all."

"You put that just wrong. In his opinions he mayn't, in

353

his heart he will. I know Dick Dennehy pretty well, and you may be sure of that."

"I never wanted to be a lawless woman. But it was coming, or had come, to hatred; and it's such awful ruin to live with a person you hate—much worse, I think, than the things they do set you free for."

Stephen smiled. "I can find you some very respectable authority for that—a good passage in Döllinger—but, I think, don't you, to-morrow? After all, there's such a thing as dinner!"

"There is, and it'll be disgracefully overcooked." She rose and came across to him. "Give me your blessing and a kiss, Cousin Stephen. I think I see happiness glimmering a long way off."

"I don't think it's ever very far off, if you can see it," said Stephen, and kissed her.

Winnie shook her head doubtfully. She had suffered such a tossing and buffeting; the quiet of harbor seemed a distant goal, even if she could now steer a straight course toward it. Her feelings were still on edge; she shrank instinctively from any immediate call to strong emotion. There was another trouble in her mind, secret, hardly explicit, but real; if, because of what she had done, Dick Dennehy, still dominated by the convictions which he meant to disobey, should show that he thought she was to be had for the asking, she would resent it bitterly—even to a curt and final refusal. That would be almost as great a failure as Godfrey Ledstone's, and such a rock might still lie in the way of her ship to its harbor. Much turned on Dick Dennehy's bearing toward her.

But the days that ensued at Shaylor's Patch were full of healing grace. There was the cordiality of friendship again

354

unclouded, Tora's serenity, Stephen's alert and understanding comradeship. Dick came when his work allowed—it may be surmised that he stretched its allowance to the full —and there were now infinite interest and unbounded fun over furnishing his house. In this work a formula was hit upon, suitable to the state of suspense in which the master's affairs stood. "Eventualities must be borne in view," said Stephen, with treacherous gravity. Dick bore them in view to the full limit of his purse—and how could Winnie refuse a friendly opinion on questions of taste? Nobody mentioned Mrs. Lenoir's furniture, now at the cottage. It was not really very suitable for a country-house, and in any case it would be pleasanter to make the fresh start in wholly fresh surroundings. Winnie mentally transmuted it into new frocks, in which shape it would serve a purpose, temporary indeed, but less charged with associations.

In no set confession, but in various intimate talks, the whole of her story, and the whole of her own attitude toward it, came to Dick's knowledge. She attempted to conceal neither her passion for Godfrey Ledstone nor the attraction with which at the last Merriam had drawn her. The latter case she was especially anxious that he should understand.

"I was angry at first at being thought impossible, but he made me see his point of view, and then I almost fell in love with him," she said, smiling. "Only almost!"

It was not the old Dick Dennehy who listened; he would have had a ready explanation of how all the troubles had come about, and a vehement, though good-humored, denunciation for the origin of them. Not only his feeling for Winnie, but his own struggle, with its revelation and its compromise, changed him. He listened with a grave at-

355

tention or, sometimes, with a readily humorous sympathy. If he was rightly or wrongly—probably he himself would have used neither word, but would have said "perforce"—disobeying his supreme authority, yet, as a man here in this world, he found some compensation in an increased humanity, a widened charity, an intensified sense of human brotherhood. He deliberately abandoned the effort to strike a balance between loss and gain, but the gain he accepted gladly, with a sense, as it were, of discovery, of opened eyes, of a vision more penetrating. He got rid of the idea that it was easy for everybody to believe what he believed, if only they would be at the pains, or that it was mere perverseness of spirit which prevented them from acting in exact accord with his standards—or even with their own. Thus, as the days passed, his aim was no more to forgive and forget, but to appreciate and to understand. With Winnie this was an essential, if their harmony were to be complete. So much of the spirit—or the pride—of the theorist survived in her. She would not take even a great love if it came accompanied by utter condemnation; perhaps she could not have believed in it, or, believing in it for the time, would have seen no basis of permanence.

In the early days the ardor of love was all on his side; her heart was not so easily kindled again into flame. Only gradually did the woman's absolute faith and grateful affection for the man blossom into their natural fruit—even as by degrees Winnie's joy in life and delight in her own powers emerged from their eclipse. Again, now, her eyes sparkled and her laugh rang out exultantly.

"She sounds in a good humor," said Stephen Aikenhead. "If one did happen to want anything of her, it might be rather a good moment to ask it, I should think."

IS THE RESULT?

Dick looked up from the evening paper. "Is she ready, Stephen ?"

"I think so, Dick."

With a buoyant step Dick Dennehy walked out into the garden, whence the laugh had come. Winnie was alone; her laugh had been only for a hen ludicrously scuttling back to her proper territory in fear of the menace of clapped hands. She wore a black lace scarf twisted about her head; from under its folds her eyes gleamed merrily.

"Would you be walking with me in the meadow a bit, by chance ?" he asked.

Something in his gaze caught her attention. She blushed a little. "Yes, Dick."

But they walked in silence for a long while. Then she felt her eyes irresistibly drawn to him. As she turned her head he held out his hands. Slowly hers came forward to meet them.

"You couldn't send me away now, could you, Winnie ?"

"Oh, Dick, have you thought it all over, looked at every side of it—twenty times, a hundred times, five hundred times ?"

"Not I! I looked at it all round once for all, and I've never doubted of it since. I've been waiting for you to do all that." His smile was happy and now confident.

"Well, in the end, I like it better like that. I like you to think so, anyhow, even if you're deceiving yourself. Because it shows—" She broke off mischievously. "What does it show, Dick ?"

"Why, that you're the jewel of the world! What else would it be showing ?"

"But what about the lady you were unhappy over, that evening at the station ?"

357

"You knew it was yourself all the time!"

"Then how did you dare to say it wasn't serious? And to call yourself—or me—a fool?"

"You're teasing me to the end, Winnie."

She grew grave and slipped her arm through his. "I knew really why it wasn't and couldn't be serious to you—and why just in that way it became terribly serious. Time was when I should have thought you silly to think it so serious, and when you would have kept it 'not serious' right to the end. We've changed each other, Dick. I you, you me—and life both of us! And so we can make terms with each other."

"Terms of perfect peace," he answered. He knew what was in her mind. "I give you my honor—in my soul I'm at peace."

"Then so be it, dear old Dick. For neither am I ashamed." She turned round to face him, and, putting her hands on his shoulders, kissed his lips. "Now let's go over to your house, and see that this eventuality really has been properly borne in view. Dear Stephen! He'll philosophize over us, Dick!"

That was, of course, only to be expected. Yet it did not happen when Stephen and his wife were told the great news after dinner. On the contrary, after brief but hearty congratulations, the host and hostess disappeared. Winnie thought that she had detected a glance passing between them.

"They needn't be so very tactful!" she said, laughing.

They were very tactful; for even to lovers the time they stayed away was undeniably long. There could be no illusion about the progress of the hands of the clock. Yet when Tora and Stephen came in and were accused of an excessive display of the useful social quality in question, Tora blushed, denied the charge rather angrily, and bade them all a brief good-night. Stephen glared through his spectacles in mock fury.

"You two think yourselves everybody! As a matter of fact, for the last hour or so—how late is it? Eleven! Oh, I say! Yes, of course! Well, for the last two hours or so, Tora and I have forgotten your very existence; and, if I may use the candor of an old friend, it's rather a jar to find you here. You'd better escort your friend home, Mr. Dennehy."

"Well, what have you been doing then?" laughed Winnie.

"It's one of Tora's theories that I should propose to her all over again about once a year—and somehow to-night seemed rather a suitable opportunity," Stephen explained. "She's at perfect liberty to refuse me, and, as a matter of fact, she's generally rather difficult about it. That's why it's so late." His eyes twinkled again. "She imposes all sorts of conditions as to my future conduct. I argue a bit, or she wouldn't respect me. Then I give in—but, of course, I don't observe them all, or what fun would it be next year? She's accepted me this time, but she says it's the last time unless I mend my ways considerably.'"

A spark of Dick Dennehy's old scorn blazed out. "So that's the way she gets round her precious theory, is it? And the woman a respectable wife and mother all the time!"

Winnie laid her hand on his arm. "There is one thing that can get round everything, Dick."

"A fact which, in all its bearings for good and evil, must be carefully brought out in the *Synopsis*," said Stephen Aikenhead.

359

They left him twinkling luminously at them through clouds of tobacco-smoke.

"Hang the man, is he in earnest about his old *Synopsis*, as he calls the thing?" asked Dick Dennehy, as they started for the cottage.

Winnie considered. "I don't quite know. That's the fun of Stephen! But, anyhow,"—she pressed his arm—"if this thing—our thing—doesn't end before the *Synopsis* does, we're all right! It'll last our lives, I think, and be still unfinished." Her laugh ended in a sigh, her sigh again in a smile. "Oh, I'm talking as if it were a fairy-tale ending, out of one of Alice's stories. Well, just for to-night! But it isn't really—it can't be, Dick. It's not an ending at all. It's a beginning, and a beginning of something difficult. Look what you're giving up for me—the great thing I'm accepting from you! And it's not a thing to be done once and for all. It'll be a continuing thing, always cropping up over other things great and small. Oh, it's not an ending; it's only a start. Is it even a fair start, Dick?"

"It's matter of faith, like everything else in the world that's worth a rap," said Dick Dennehy. "At all events, we know this about each other—that we're equal to putting up a fight for what we believe in and love. And odds against don't frighten us! I call that a fair start. What do you make of life, anyhow, unless it's a fight? We'll fight our fight to a finish!"

His voice rang bravely confident; his sanguine spirit soared high in hope. When she opened the cottage door and the light from a hanging-lamp in the narrow passage fell on him, his face was happy and serene. With a smile he coaxed her apprehensions. "Ah, now, you're not the girl you were if ye're afraid of an experiment!"

IS THE RESULT?

She put her hands in his. "Not the girl I was, indeed! How could I be, after it all? But here's my life—am I to be afraid of it? Any use I am, any joy I have—am I to turn tail? I won't, Dick!"

"Always plucky! As plucky as wrong-headed, Winnie!"

"Wrong-headed still?" she laughed, now gayly. "That question, like everything else, is, as Stephen says, 'in solution.' It's not my fate to settle questions, but it seems as if I couldn't help raising them!"

To those who would see design in such matters—in the interaction of lives and minds—it might well seem that here she put her finger on a function to which she had never aspired, but for which she had been effectually used in several cases. She had raised questions in unquestioning people. Her management of her life put them on inquiry as to the foundations and the canons of their own. For Dick Dennehy even her chimney-pots had streaked the sky with notes of interrogation! She had been, as it were, a touchstone, proving true metal, detecting the base, revealing alloy; a test of quality, of courage, of faith; an explorer's shaft sunk deep in the ore of the human heart. She had struck strata scantily auriferous, she had come upon some sheer dross, yet the search left her not merely hopeful, but already enriched. Twice she had found gold—in the soldier who would not desert his flag even for her sake, in the believer who, for her soul's sake and his love of her, flung himself on the mercy of an affronted Heaven. Both could dare, sacrifice, and dedicate. They obeyed the call their ears heard, though it were to their own hurt—in this world or, mayhap, in another. There was the point of union between the man who forswore her for his loyalty's sake and the man who sheltered her against his creed.

361

MRS. MAXON PROTESTS

In the small circle of those with whom she had shared the issues of destiny she had unsettled much; of a certainty she had settled nothing. Things were just as much in solution as ever; the welter was not abated. Man being imperfect, laws must be made. Man being imperfect, laws must be broken or ever new laws will be made. Winnie Maxon had broken a law and asked a question. When thousands do the like, the Giant, after giving the first-comers a box on the ear, may at last put his hand to his own and ponderously consider.

THE END